Forbidden *in*
Regency
Society

MARGUERITE
KAYE

MILLS
BOON

Published in Great Britain 2014
by Mills & Boon, an imprint of Harlequin (UK) Limited,
Eton House, 18-24 Paradise Road, Richmond, Surrey, TW9 1SR

FORBIDDEN IN REGENCY SOCIETY
© 2014 Harlequin Books S.A.

The Governess and the Sheikh © 2011 Marguerite Kaye
Rake with a Frozen Heart © 2012 Marguerite Kaye

ISBN: 978-0-263-25014-5

052-0515

Harlequin (UK) policy is to use papers that are natural, renewable and recyclable products and made from wood grown in sustainable forests. The logging and manufacturing processes conform to the legal environmental regulations of the country of origin.

Printed and bound
by CPI Group (UK) Ltd, Croydon, CR0 4YY

Born and educated in Scotland, **Marguerite Kaye** originally qualified as a lawyer, but chose not to practise. Instead, she carved out a career in IT and studied history part-time, gaining a first-class honours and a master's degree. A few decades after winning a children's national poetry competition, she decided to pursue her lifelong ambition to write and submitted her first historical romance to Mills & Boon. They accepted it and she's been writing ever since.

You can contact Marguerite through her website at: www.margueritekaye.com.

The Governess and the Sheikh

MARGUERITE KAYE

In loving memory of W,
who helped make me the person I am
and whose spirit, hopefully, lives on in me

Chapter One

Daar-el-Abbah, Arabia—1820

Sheikh Jamil al-Nazarri, Prince of Daar-el-Abbah, scrutinised the terms of the complex and detailed proposal laid out before him. A frown of concentration drew his dark brows together, but could not disguise the fact that his face, framed by the formal head dress of finest silk, was an extraordinarily handsome one. The soft golden folds of the cloth perfectly complemented the honeyed tones of his skin. His mouth was set in a firm, determined line, but there was just a hint of a curve at the corners, enough to indicate a sense of humour, even if it was seldom utilised. The sheikh's nose and jaw were well defined, his flawlessly autocratic profile seemingly perfectly designed for use on the insignia of his kingdom—though Jamil had, in fact, refused to consent to his Council's request to do so. But it was his eyes that were his most striking feature, for they were the strangest colour, burnished like autumn, with fiery glints and darker depths which seemed to reflect his changing mood. Those eyes transformed Jamil from a striking-looking man into an unforgettable one.

Not that the Prince of Daar-el-Abbah was easily overlooked at the best of times. His position as the most powerful sheikh in the eastern reaches of Arabia saw to that. Jamil had been born to reign and raised to rule. For the last eight years, since he had inherited the throne at the age of twenty-one following the death of his father, he had kept Daar-el-Abbah free from incursion, both maintaining its independence and enhancing its supremacy without the need for any significant bloodshed.

Jamil was a skilled diplomat. He was also a formidable enemy, a fact that significantly enhanced his negotiating position. Though he had not used it in anger for some time, the wicked scimitar with its diamond-and-emerald-encrusted golden hilt that hung at his waist was no mere ceremonial toy.

Still perusing the document in his hand, Jamil got to his feet. Pacing up and down the dais upon which the royal throne sat, his golden cloak, lined with satin and trimmed with *passementerie* twisted with gold thread and embedded with semi-precious stones, swung out behind him. The contrasting simple white silk of the long tunic he wore underneath revealed a slim figure, athletic and lithe, at the same time both graceful and subtly powerful, reminiscent of the panther, which was his emblem.

'Is there something wrong, your Highness?'

Halim, Jamil's trusted aide, spoke tentatively, rousing the prince from his reverie. Alone of the members of the Council of Elders, Halim dared to address Jamil without first asking permission, but he was still wary of doing so, conscious of that fact that, although he had the prince's confidence, there was no real closeness between them, nor any genuine bond of friendship.

'No,' Jamil replied curtly. 'The betrothal contract seems reasonable enough.'

'As you can see, all your terms and conditions have been met in full,' Halim continued carefully. 'The Princess Adira's family have been most generous.'

'With good reason,' Jamil said pointedly. 'The advantages this alliance will give them over their neighbours are worth far more than the rights to the few diamond mines I will receive in return.'

'Indeed, Highness.' Halim bowed. 'So, if you are satisfied, perhaps I may suggest we proceed with the signing?'

Jamil threw himself back down on to the throne, in essence a low stool with a scrolled velvet-padded seat. It was made of solid gold, the base perched upon two lions, while the back was in the shape of a sunburst. It was a venerable and venerated relic, proof of the kingdom's long and illustrious history. More than three hundred years old, it was said that any man who sat upon it who was not a true and destined ruler would fall victim to a curse and die within a year and a day. Jamil's father had cherished the throne and all it stood for, but Jamil loathed it as ostentatious and impractical—though, as with most things ceremonial, he continued to tolerate it.

He lolled on the unforgiving seat, resting his chin upon his hand, the long index finger of his other hand tapping the document that lay on the low table before him. The various members of his Council of Elders, seated in order of precedence on low stools facing the dais, gazed up at him anxiously.

Jamil sighed inwardly. Sometimes the burden of royalty was wearisome. Though the betrothal contract was important, it was not really uppermost in his mind right now. He recognised that the marriage his Council had for so long entreated him to enter into was a strategic and dynastic necessity, but it was of little personal interest to him. He would marry, and the union would seal the numerous political and commercial agreements that were the foundation of the contract. Daar-el-Abbah would gain a powerful ally and—once Jamil had done his duty—an heir. He personally would gain…

Nothing.

Absolutely nothing.

He had no wish to be married. Not again. Especially not again for the sake of Daar-el-Abbah, this kingdom of his, which owned him body and soul. He didn't want another wife, and he certainly didn't want another wife selected by his Council—though, truth be told, one royal princess was bound to be very much like another. He hadn't disliked his first wife, but poor Karida, who had died in childbirth not long after Jamil came to power, had seemed to prefer the comfits of the liquorice and crystallised ginger she ate with such relish over almost anyone or anything else.

Jamil could happily do without another such, as this Princess Whatever-her-name-was, to whom Halim and his Council were so keen to shackle him, would no doubt turn out to be. He was perfectly content with his single state, but his country needed an heir, therefore he must take a wife, and tradition decreed that the wife should be the choice of the Council. Though he railed against it, it didn't occur to Jamil to question the process. It was the way of things. Anyway, in principle he was as keen to beget a son as his people were for him to provide them with a crown prince. The problem he was having was in reconciling principle with practice. The fact was, Jamil was not at all sure he was ready for another child. At least not until he had the one he already had under some semblance of control. Which brought him back to the matter uppermost in his mind: his eight-year-old daughter, Linah.

Jamil sighed again, this time out loud. A rustle of unease spread through the assembled Elders in response. Twenty-four of them, excluding Halim, each man wearing the distinctive Council insignia, an al-Nazarri green checked head dress with a golden tie, or *igal*, to hold it in place, the sign of the panther embroidered on his tunic. Behind the Elders, the throne room stretched for almost a hundred feet, the floor made of polished white marble edged with green-and-gold tiles. Light flooded the chamber from the line of round windows set high into the walls, reflecting through the gold-plated iron grilles, bouncing off the teardrop crystals of the five enormous chandeliers.

Most of the men arrayed before Jamil had served on his father's Council, too. The majority were traditionalists, resistant to every attempt at change, with whom Jamil found himself becoming increasingly irked. If he could, he would retire the lot of them, but though he was coming to the end of his patience, the prince was not a foolish man. There were many ways to skin a goat. He would take Daar-el-Abbah into the modern world, and he would take his people with him whether they wanted to join him on the journey or not—though he preferred that they came of their own accord, just as he favoured diplomacy over warfare. This marriage now being proposed was his gesture towards appeasement, for the hand that gives is the hand that receives.

He should sign the contract. He had every reason to sign. It made no sense to postpone the inevitable.

So he would sign. Of course he would. Just not yet.

Jamil threw the papers at Halim. 'It won't do any harm to make them wait a little longer,' he said, getting so swiftly to his feet that the Elders were forced to throw themselves hurriedly on to their knees. 'We don't want them thinking they are getting too much of a bargain.' He growled impatiently at his Council. 'Get up! Get up!' No matter how many times he said he no longer wished them to show their obeisance in private meetings, they continued to do so. Only Halim stood his ground, following in his wake as Jamil took the two steps down from the dais in one and strode quickly up the long length of the throne room towards the huge double doors at the end.

'Highness, if I may suggest…?'

'Not now.' Jamil threw open the doors, taking the guards on the other side by surprise.

'But I don't understand, Highness. I thought we had agreed that—'

'I *said* not now!' Jamil exclaimed. 'I have another

matter I wish to discuss. I've had a most interesting letter from Lady Celia.'

Halim hurried to keep pace as they headed along the wide corridor towards the private apartments. 'Prince Ramiz of A'Qadiz's English wife? What possible reason can she have for writing to you?'

'Her letter concerns Linah,' Jamil replied as they entered the courtyard around which his quarters were built.

'Indeed? And what precisely does she have to say on the matter?'

'She writes that she has heard I'm having some difficulty finding a female mentor up to the challenge of responding to my daughter's quite particular needs. Lady Celia's father is Lord Armstrong, a senior British diplomat, and she has clearly inherited his subtle way with words. What she really means is that she's heard Linah is out of control and has run rings around every single woman in whose charge I've placed her.'

Halim bristled. 'I hardly think that your daughter's behaviour is any business of Lady Celia's. Nor is it, if I may be so bold, the business of A'Qadiz, or its sheikh.'

'Prince Ramiz is an upstanding man and an excellent ruler who has forward-thinking views similar to my own. I would suggest, Halim, that any opportunity to bring our two kingdoms closer together is something to be encouraged rather than resented.'

Halim bowed. 'As ever, you make an excellent point, Highness. That is why you are a royal prince and I a mere servant.'

'Spare me the false modesty, Halim, we both know you are no mere servant.'

Jamil entered the first of the series of rooms that ran in a square round the courtyard, unfastened his formal cloak and threw it carelessly down on a divan. His head dress and scimitar followed. 'That's better,' he said, running his fingers through his short crop of hair. It was auburn, inherited from his Egyptian mother. Reaching into a drawer of the large ornate desk that dominated the room, he found the letter and scanned it again.

'May I ask, does Lady Celia offer a solution to our supposed problem?' Halim asked.

Jamil looked up from the elegantly worded missive and smiled one of his rare smiles, knowing full well that Lady Celia's proposal would shock his Council and drive a pack of camels through the dictates of convention relating to the upbringing of Arabian princesses. Today's Council meeting had bored him to tears, and he was sick of tradition. 'What Lady Celia offers,' he said, 'is her sister.'

'Her sister!'

'Lady Cassandra Armstrong.'

'To what purpose, precisely?'

'To act as Linah's governess. It is the perfect solution.'

'Perfect!' Halim looked appalled. 'Perfect how? She has no knowledge of our ways—how can you possibly think an English woman capable of training the Princess Linah for her future role?'

'It is precisely because she will be incapable of such a thing that she is perfect,' Jamil replied, his smile fading. 'A dose of English discipline and manners is exactly what Linah needs. Do not forget, the British are one of the world's great powers, renowned for their capacity for hard work and initiative. Exposure to their culture will challenge my daughter's cosy view of the world and her place in it. I don't want her to become some simpering miss who passes the time while I'm finding her a husband by lolling about on divans drinking sherbet and throwing tantrums every time she doesn't get her own way.' *Like her mother did.* He did not say it, but he did not have to. Princess Karida's tantrums were legendary. 'I want my daughter to be able to think for herself.'

'Highness!' Shock made Halim's soft brown eyes open wide, giving him the appearance of a startled hare. 'Princess Linah is Daar-el-Abbah's biggest asset; why, only the other day the Prince of—'

'I won't have my daughter labelled an asset,' Jamil interrupted fiercely. 'In the name of the gods, she's not even nine years old.'

Slightly taken aback at the force of his prince's response, for though Jamil was a dutiful parent, he was not prone to displays of parental affection, Halim continued with a little more caution. 'A good marriage takes time to plan, Highness, as you know yourself.'

'You can forget marrying Linah off, for the present. Until she learns some manners, no sane man would take her on.' Jamil threw himself on to the tooled leather chair that sat behind the desk. 'Come on, Halim, you know how appallingly she can behave. I'm at my wits' end with her. It is partly my own fault, I know, I've allowed her to become spoilt since she was deprived of her mother.'

'But now you are to be married, the Princess Adira will fill that role, surely.'

'I doubt it. In any case, you're missing the point. I don't want Linah to be raised in the traditional ways of an Arabian princess.' Any more than he would wish his son to be raised in the traditions of an Arabian prince. As he had been. A shadow flitted over Jamil's countenance as he recalled his father's harsh methods when it came to child-rearing. No, of a certainty he would not inflict those traditions on his son.

'You want her to behave like an English lady instead?' Halim's anxious face brought him back to the present.

'Yes. If Lady Celia is an example of an English lady, that is exactly what I want. If this Lady Cassandra is anything like her sister, then she will be perfect.' Jamil consulted the letter in his hand again. 'It says here that she's one-and-twenty. There are three other sisters, much younger, and Lady Cassandra has shared responsibility for their education. Three! If she can manage three girls, then one will be—what is it the English say?—a piece of cake.'

Halim's face remained resolutely sombre. Jamil laughed. 'You don't agree, I take it? You disappoint me. I knew the Council would not immediately perceive the merits in such a proposition, but I thought better of you. Think about it, Halim—the Armstrongs are a family with an excellent pedigree, and, more importantly, impeccable connections. The father is a diplomat with influence in Egypt and India, and the uncle is a member of the English government. It would do

us no harm at all to have one of the daughters in our
household, and in addition they would be in our debt.
According to Lady Celia, we would be doing them a
favour.'

'How so?'

'Lady Cassandra is already in A'Qadiz and wishes
to extend her stay, to see more of our lands, our culture.
She is obviously the scholarly type.'

'One-and-twenty, you say?' Halim frowned. 'That is
rather old for a female to be unwed, even in England.'

'Quite. Reading between the lines, I suspect her to
be the spinsterish type. You know, the kind of women
the English seem to specialise in—plain, more at home
with their books than the opposite sex.' Jamil grinned.
'Once again, exactly what Linah needs. A dull female
with a good education and a strict sense of discipline.'

'But Highness, you cannot be sure that—'

'Enough. I will brook no more argument. I've tried
doing things the traditional way with Linah, and tradition has singularly failed. Now we'll do it my way, the
modern way, and perhaps in doing so my people will
see the merits in reaching out beyond the confines of
our own culture.' Jamil got to his feet. 'I've already
written to Lady Celia accepting her kind offer. I did
not bring you here to discuss the merits of the proposal, merely to implement my decision. We meet at the
border of A'Qadiz in three days. Lady Celia will bring
her sister, and she will be accompanied by her husband,
Prince Ramiz. We will cement our relationship with his
kingdom and take delivery of Linah's new governess at
the same time. I'm sure you understand the importance

of my caravan being suitably impressive, so please see to it. Now you may go.'

Recognising the note of finality in his master's voice, Halim had no option but to obey. As the guards closed the doors to the courtyard behind him, he made for his own quarters with a sinking heart. He did not like the sound of this. There was going to be trouble ahead or his name wasn't Halim Mohammed Zarahh Akbar el-Akkrah.

At that moment in the kingdom of A'Qadiz, in another sunny courtyard in another royal palace, Ladies Celia and Cassandra were taking tea, sitting on mountainous heaps of cushions under the shade of a lemon tree. Beside them, lying contentedly in a basket, Celia's baby daughter made a snuffling noise, which had the sisters laughing with delight, for surely little Bashirah was the cleverest and most charming child in all of Arabia.

Cassie put her tea glass back on the heavy silver tray beside the samovar. 'May I hold her?'

'Of course you may.' Celia lifted the precious bundle out of the basket and handed her to Cassie, who balanced her niece confidently on her lap, smiling down at her besottedly.

'Bashirah,' Cassie said, stroking the baby's downy cheek with her finger, 'Such a lovely name. What does it mean?'

'Bringer of joy.'

Cassie smiled. 'How apt.'

'She likes you,' Celia replied with a tender smile, quite taken by the charming image her sister and her daughter presented. In the weeks since Cassie had arrived in A'Qadiz she seemed to have recovered some of her former sunny disposition, but it saddened Celia to see the stricken look that still made a regular appearance in her sister's big cornflower-blue eyes on occasions when she thought herself unobserved. The shadows that were testimony to the many sleepless nights since *that thing* had happened had faded now, and her skin had lost its unnatural pallor. In fact, to everyone else, Cassandra was the radiant beauty she had always been, with her dark golden crown of hair, and her lush curves, so different from Celia's own slim figure.

But Celia was not everyone else, she was Cassie's oldest sister, and she loved her dearly. It was a bond forged in adversity, for they had lost their mother when young, and though the gap between Cassie and their next sister, Cressida, was just a little more than three years, it was sufficient to split the family into two distinct camps, the two older ones who struggled to take Mama's place, and the three younger ones, who needed to be cared for.

'Poor Cassie,' Celia said now, leaning over to give her sister a quick hug, 'you've had such a hard time of it these last three months—are you sure you're ready for this challenge?'

'Don't pity me, Celia,' Cassie replied with a frown. 'Most of what I've been forced to endure has been of my own doing.'

'How can you say that! He as good as left you at the altar.'

Cassie bit her lip hard. 'You exaggerate a little. The wedding was still two weeks away.'

'The betrothal had been formally announced, people were sending gifts—we sent one ourselves—and the guests had been invited to the breakfast. I know you think you loved him, Cassie, but how you can defend him after that…'

'I'm not defending him.' Cassie opened her eyes wide to stop the tears from falling. 'I'm just saying that I'm as much to blame as Augustus.'

'How so?' Until now, Cassie had refused to discuss her broken betrothal, for she wanted only to forget it had ever happened, and Celia, who could see that the wound to her sister's pride was as deep as that to her heart, had tactfully refrained from questioning her. Now, it seemed, her patience was about to pay off, and she could not help but be curious. She leaned over to lift Bashirah from Cassie, for she was making that little impatient noise that preceded an aggressive demand for sustenance. Celia thought of Ramiz and smiled as she settled the baby at her breast. The child had clearly inherited her demanding temperament from her father. 'Won't you tell me, Cassie?' she said gently. 'Sometimes talking about things, however painful, helps, and I've been so worried about you.'

'I'm perfectly all right,' Cassie replied with a sniff.

She looked so patently not 'all right' that Celia laughed. 'Liar.'

Cassie managed a weak smile in return. 'Well, I may not be all right at the moment, but I will be, I promise. I just need to prove myself, make a success of something for a change, give everyone, myself included, something to be proud of.'

'Cassie, we all love you, no matter what. You know that.'

'Yes. But there's no getting away from it, Celia, I've behaved very foolishly indeed, and Papa is still furious with me. I can't go back to England, not until I've proved I'm not a complete nincompoop.'

'Cassie, Augustus failed you, not the other way round.'

'He was my choice.'

'You can't choose who you fall in love with, Cass.'

'I'll tell you something, Celia, I'm going to make very sure I choose not to fall in love ever again.'

'Oh, Cassie, you say the silliest things.' Celia patted her sister's knee. 'Of course you will fall in love again. The surprising thing is that you have not fallen in love before, for you are such a romantic.'

'Which is precisely the problem. So I'm not going to be, not anymore. I've learned a hard lesson, and I'm determined not to have to learn it again. If I tell you how it was, maybe then you'll understand.'

'Only if you're sure you want to.'

'Why not? You can't think worse of me than I already do. No, don't look like that, Celia, I don't deserve your pity.' Cassie toyed with the cerulean-blue ribbons that were laced up the full sleeves of her delicate-figured muslin dress. 'Augustus said these ribbons were the same colour as my eyes,' she said with a wistful smile. 'Then again, he also told me that my eyes were the colour of the sky at midnight, and that they put a field of lavender to shame. He brought me a posy of violets

in a silver filigree holder and told me they were a hymn
to my eyes, too, now I come to think about it. I didn't
even question the veracity of it, though I know perfectly
well what colour of blue my own eyes are. That should
give you an idea of how deeply in love I thought I was.'

A pink flush stole up the elegant line of Cassie's
throat. Even now, three months after it had all come to
such a horrible end, the shame could still overwhelm
her. Hindsight, as Aunt Sophia said, was a wonderful
thing, but every time Cassie examined the course of
events—and she examined them in minute detail most
frequently—it was not Augustus's shockingly caddish
behaviour, but her own singular lack of judgement that
mortified her most.

'Augustus St John Marne.' The name, once so precious, felt bitter on her tongue. Cassie made a moue of
distaste. 'I first met him at Almack's, where I was fresh
from another run-in with Bella.'

'Bella Frobisher!' Celia exclaimed. 'Who would have
believed Papa could stoop so low? I still can't believe
she's taken Mama's place. I doubt I will ever be able
to bring myself to address her as Lady Armstrong.'

'No, even Aunt Sophia stops short of that, and she
has been pretty much won over since James was born.
I have to say though, Celia, our half-brother is quite
adorable.'

'A son and heir for Papa. So the auspicious event has
mollified even our terrifying aunt?'

Cassie giggled. *'Bella Frobisher may be a witless
flibberty-gibbet,'* she said in a fair imitation of their
formidable Aunt Sophia's austere tone, *'but her breed-
ing is sound, and she's come up trumps with young*

James. A fine lusty boy to secure the title and the line, just what the family needs. And honestly, Celia, you should see Papa. He actually visits James in the nursery, which is far more than he did with any of us, I'm sure. He has him signed up for Harrow already. Bella thinks I'm jealous, of course.' Cassie frowned. 'I don't know, maybe I am, a little. Papa has only ever been interested in us girls as pawns in his diplomatic games—he and Bella had drawn up a short list of suitors for me, you know. I mean, I ask you, a short list! How unromantic can one get. It was what I was arguing with Bella about the night I met Augustus.'

'Ah,' Celia said.

'What does that mean?'

'Nothing. Only you must admit that when someone tells you to do something you are very much inclined to do the exact opposite.'

'That's not true!' Cassie's bosom heaved indignantly. 'I fell in love with Augustus because he was a poet, with a poet's soul. And because I thought he liked all the things I did. And because he is so very good-looking and most understanding and—'

'And exactly the sort of romantic hero you have always dreamed of falling in love with.' Celia kissed the now-sated and sleeping Bashirah and placed her carefully back into her basket. 'And partly, Cassie, you must admit, because you knew Bella and Papa would not approve.'

'I concede, that might have been a tiny part of the attraction.' Cassie frowned. Celia had merely articulated what she herself had long suspected. When Bella had handed her the list of suitors her father had compiled, Cassie had promptly torn it in two. The confrontation had ended, as most of her confrontations with Bella ended, in an impasse, but over dinner, and during the coach ride to King Street, Cassie had found her resentment growing. It was while in this rebellious mood that she had encountered Augustus, a singularly beautiful young man who was most gratifyingly disparaging of her stepmother's treatment of her.

'We danced a quadrille that night at Almack's,' she told Celia, forcing herself to continue with her confession, 'and during supper Augustus composed a quatrain comparing me to Aphrodite. He dashed it off right there on the table linen. I thought it was just the most romantic thing ever. Imagine, being a poet's muse. When he told me about his impoverished state, I positively encouraged myself to fall in love, and the more Papa and Bella protested against my betrothal, the more determined I was to go through with it.' Cassie brushed a stray tear away angrily. 'The terrible thing is, in a way I knew it wasn't real. I mean, there was a part of me that looked at Augustus sometimes and thought, *Are you seriously intending to marry this man, Cassandra*? Then I'd think about how much he loved me, and I'd feel guilty, and I'd think about how smug Bella would be if I changed my mind, for it would prove her right, and—and so I didn't do anything. And the funny thing is that, though there were times when I questioned my own heart, I never once doubted Augustus. He was so impassioned and so eloquent in his declarations. When he—when he jilted me it was such a shock. He did it in a letter, you know; he didn't even have the decency to tell me to my face.'

'What a coward!' Celia's elegant fingers curled into two small fists. 'Who was she, this heiress of his, whom he abandoned you for? Do I know her?'

'I don't think so. Millicent Redwood, the daughter of one of those coal magnates from somewhere up north. They say she has fifty thousand. I suppose it could have been worse,' Cassie replied, her voice wobbling, 'if it had been a mere twenty…'

'Oh, Cassie.' Celia enfolded her sister in a warm embrace and held her close as she wept, stroking her golden hair away from her cheeks, just as she had done when they were girls, mourning their poor departed mama.

For a few moments Cassie surrendered to the temptation to cry, allowing herself the comfort of thinking that Celia would make everything better, just as she always had. But only for a few moments, for she had resolved not to spill any more tears. Augustus did not deserve them. She had to stop wallowing in self-pity, and anyway, what good did tears do? She sat up, fumbling for her handkerchief, and hastily rubbed her cheeks dry, taking a big gulp of air, then another. 'So you see, Bella and Papa were right all along. I'm selfish, headstrong and foolish, and far too full of romantic notions that have no place in the real world. *"A heart that can be given so easily cannot be relied upon, and must never again be given free rein."* That's what Aunt Sophia said, and I have to say I agree with her. I have tasted love,' Cassie declared dramatically, temporarily forgetting that she had abandoned her romantic streak, 'and though the first sip was sweet, the aftertaste was bitter. I will not drink from that poisoned chalice again.'

Celia bit her lip in an effort not to smile, for Cassie in full unabridged Cassandra mode had always amused her terribly. It was reassuring that her sister wasn't so completely given over to the blue melancholy as to have lost her endearing qualities, and it gave her the tiniest bit of hope that perhaps her very tender heart would recover from the almost-fatal wound dealt it by Augustus St John Marne. Ramiz would have dispensed swift retribution if he ever got his hands on him. Celia toyed momentarily with the satisfying vision of the feckless poet staked out, his pale foppish skin blistering and desiccating under the fierce desert sun, a legendary punishment meted out to transgressors in bygone days in A'Qadiz. And then, as was her wont, she turned her mind to practicalities.

'You are expected at the border of Daar-el-Abbah in three days. Ramiz will escort you there, but Bashirah is too young to travel and I'm afraid I can't bear to leave her so I won't be coming with you. It's not too late to change your mind about all this though, Cassie. The city of Daar is five days' travel from here and you are likely to be the only European there. You will also have sole responsibility for the princess. She has a dreadful reputation, poor little mite, for she has been left to the care of a whole series of chaperons since her mother died in the process of giving birth to her. The prince will expect a lot from you.'

'And I won't let him down,' Cassie said, clasping her hands together. 'Who better than I to empathise with little Linah's plight—did I not lose my own mother? Have I not helped you to raise our three sisters?'

'Well, I suppose in a way, but...'

'I am sure all she needs is a little gentle leading in the right direction and a lot of understanding.'

'Perhaps, but…'

'And a lot of love. I have plenty of *that* to give, having no other outlet for it.'

'Cassie, you cannot be thinking to sacrifice your life to a little girl like Linah. This position cannot be of a permanent nature, you must think of it as an interlude only. It is an opportunity to allow yourself to recover, and to do some good along the way, nothing more. Then you must return to England, resume your life.'

'Why? You are content to stay here.'

'Because I fell in love with Ramiz. You, too, will fall in love one day, properly in love, with the right man. No matter what you think now, there will come a time when looking after someone else's child will not be enough.'

'Perhaps Prince Jamil will marry again, and have other children. Then he will need me to stay on as governess.'

'I don't think you understand how unusual it is, his taking you into the royal household in the first place. Daar-el-Abbah is a much more traditional kingdom than A'Qadiz. Should he take another wife—which he must, eventually, for he needs a son and heir—then he will resort to the tradition of the harem, I think. There will be no need for governesses then.'

'What is Prince Jamil like?'

Celia furrowed her brow. 'I don't know him very well. Ramiz has a huge respect for him so he must be an excellent ruler, but I've only met him briefly. In many ways he's a typical Arabian prince—haughty, distant, used to being revered.'

'You make him sound like a tyrant.'

'Oh, no, not at all. If I thought that, I'd hardly allow you to go and live in his household. His situation makes it difficult for him to be anything other than a bit remote, for his people idolise him, but Ramiz says he is one of the most honourable men of his acquaintance. He is anxious to forge an alliance with him.'

'Yes, yes, I'm sure he is, but what does Prince Jamil actually look like?'

'He's very good looking. There's something about him that draws attention. His eyes, I think—they are the most striking colour. And he's quite young, you know, he can't be any more than twenty-nine or thirty.'

'I didn't realise. I had assumed he would be older.'

'Though he has not married again, it is not for lack of opportunity. I don't know him well enough to like him—I doubt any woman does—but what's important is, I trust him. The thing is though…' Celia hesitated, and took Cassie's hand in her own '…he's not a man who will readily tolerate failure, and he's not a man to cross either. You must curb your tongue in his presence, Cassie, and try to think before you speak. Not that I expect you'll see very much of him—from what I've heard, one of the contributing factors to his daughter's bad behaviour is his complete lack of interest in her.'

'Oh, how awful. Why, no wonder she is a bit of a rebel.'

Celia laughed. 'There, you see, that is exactly what I have just cautioned you about. You must not allow your heart to rule your head, and you must wait until you understand the whole situation before leaping in with opinions and judgements. Prince Jamil is not a man to get on the wrong side of, and I am absolutely certain that should you do so he would have no hesitation in trampling you underfoot. The point of this exercise is to restore your confidence, not have it for ever shattered.'

'You need have no fear, I will be a model governess,' Cassie declared, her flagging spirits fortified by the touching nature of the challenge that lay ahead of her. She, who had resolved never to love again, would reunite this little family by showing Linah and her father how to love each other. It would be her sacred mission, her vocation. 'I promise you,' Cassandra said with a fervour that lit her eyes and flushed her cheeks and made Celia question her judgement in having ever suggested her sister as a sober, level-headed governess, 'I promise you, Celia, that Prince Jamil will be so delighted with my efforts that it will reflect well on both you and Ramiz.'

'I take it, then,' Celia said wryly, 'that you are not having second thoughts or falling prey to doubts?'

Cassie got to her feet, shook out her dress and tossed back her head. Her eyes shone with excitement. She looked, Celia could not help thinking, magnificent and quite beautiful, all the more so for being completely unaware of her appearance. Cassie had many faults, but vanity was not one of them. Celia felt a momentary pang of doubt. How much did she really know of Jamil al-Nazarri the man, as opposed to the prince? Cassie was so very lovely, and she would be very much alone and therefore potentially vulnerable. She stood up, placing a restraining hand on her sister's arm. 'Maybe it is best that you should take a little more time, stay here for a few more days before committing yourself.'

'I have decided. And in any case, it is all arranged. You are worried that Prince Jamil may have designs on me, I can see it in your face, but you need not, I assure you. Even if he did—which seems to me most unlikely, for though in England I pass for a beauty, here in Arabia they admire a very different kind of woman—it would come to nothing. I told you, I am done with men, and I am done for ever with love.'

'Then I must be done with trying to persuade you to reconsider,' Celia said lightly, realising that further protestations on her part would only unsettle Cassie further. 'Come then, let me help you pack, for the caravan must leave at first light.'

Chapter Two

At dawn the next day, Cassie bade Celia a rather tearful goodbye and set off, following closely behind Prince Ramiz, who led the caravan through the dark and empty streets of Balyrma and out into the desert. She wore the royal blue linen riding habit she'd had Papa's tailor make up especially for this trip, which she fervently hoped would not prove too stifling in the arid heat of the desert. The skirt was wide enough to ensure she could sit astride a camel with perfect modesty. The little jacket was cut in military style, with a high collar and a double row of buttons, but was otherwise quite plain, relying on the severity of the masculine cut to emphasise the femininity of the form beneath it. By the time the caravan began to make its way through the first mountain pass, however, the sun was rising and Cassie was wishing that a less clinging style was currently more fashionable. Though she wore only a thin chemise under her corset, and no other petticoats, she was already frightfully hot.

The first two days' travel took a toll on both her appearance and spirits. The heat seared her face through her veil so that her skin felt as if it were being baked in a bread oven. Her throat ached from the dust and constant thirst, and the unfamiliar sheen of perspiration made her chemise cling like an unpleasant second skin that had her longing to cast both stays and stockings to the winds.

The excitement of the journey was at first more than compensation for these discomforts. The dramatically shifting scenery of ochre-red mountains and undulating golden dunes, the small grey-green patches that marked the location of oases, the ever-changing blue of the sky and the complete otherness of the landscape all fascinated Cassie, appealing at an elemental level to her romantic heart.

Until, that is, she started to lose sensation in the lower half of her body. The camel's saddle, a high-backed wooden affair with a padded velvet seat that gave it a quite misleading air of comfort, began, on the second day, to feel like an instrument of torture. Renowned horsewoman that she was, Cassie was used to the relative comfort of a leather saddle with the security of a pommel, ridden for pleasure rather than used as a mode of long-distance transport. Six hours was the longest she'd ever spent on horseback. Counting up the time since she'd left Celia at the royal palace, she reckoned she'd been aboard the plodding camel for all but eight hours out of the last thirty-six. What had

begun as a pleasant swaying motion when they had first
started out, now felt more like a side-to-side lurching.
Her bottom was numb and her legs ached. What's more,
she was covered from head to toe in dust and sand, her
lashes gritty with it, her mouth and nose equally so, for
she had been forced to put up her veil in order to see
her way as dusk fell and Ramiz urged his entourage
on, anxious to make the pre-arranged meeting point by
nightfall.

*Sway left, sway right, sway forward. Sway left, sway
right, sway forward,* Cassie said over to herself, her
exhausted and battered body automatically moving in
the tortuous wooden saddle as she bid it. *Sway left,
sway right, sway—'Oh!'*

The lights that she'd vaguely noticed twinkling in
the distance now coalesced into a recognisable form.
A camp had been set up around a large oasis. A line of
flaming torches snaked out towards them, forming a
pathway at the start of which Ramiz bid his own entourage to halt. Her aches and pains temporarily forgotten, Cassie dismounted stiffly from her camel, horribly
conscious of her bedraggled state, even more conscious
of her mounting excitement as she caught a glimpse of
the regal-looking figure who awaited them at the end
of the line of braziers. Prince Jamil al-Nazarri. It could
only be him. Her heart began to pound as she made a
futile attempt to shake the dust from her riding habit
and, at Ramiz's bidding, communicated by a stern look
and a flash of those intense eyes that had so beguiled
her sister, put her veil firmly back in place.

Following a few paces behind her brother-in-law,
Cassie saw Prince Jamil's camp take shape before

her, making her desperate to lift her veil for just a few moments in order to admire it properly. She had never seen anything so magical—it looked exactly like a scene from *One Thousand and One Nights*.

The oasis itself was large, almost the size of a small lake, bordered by clumps of palm trees and the usual low shrubs. The water glittered, dark blue and utterly tempting. She longed to immerse her aching body in it. On the further reaches of the shore was a collection of small tents, typical of the ones she had slept in on her overland journey from the Red Sea to Balyrma. They were simple structures made of wool and goatskin blankets held up with two wooden poles and a series of guy ropes. The bleating of camels and the braying of mules carried on the soft night air. The scent of cooking also, the mouth-watering smell of meat roasting on an open spit, of fresh-baked flat bread and a delicious mixture of spices she couldn't begin to name. Two much larger tents stood slightly apart from the others, their perimeter lit by oil lamps. Their walls were constructed from what looked to Cassie like woven tapestries or carpets, topped by a pleated green-damask roof bordered with scalloped edges trimmed with gold and silver.

'Like little tent palaces,' she said to Ramiz, momentarily forgetting all he had told her about protocol and tugging on his sleeve to get his attention. She received what she called his sheikh look in return, and hastily fell back into place, chiding herself and praying that her lapse had not been noted.

Another few paces and Ramiz halted. Cassie dropped to her knees as she had been instructed, her view of the prince obscured by Ramiz's tall frame. She could see the open tent in front of which the prince stood. Four carved wooden poles supporting another scallop-edged green roof, the floating organdie curtains that would form the walls tied back to reveal a royal reception room with rich carpets, a myriad of oil lamps, two gold-painted divans and a plethora of silk and satin cushions scattered around.

Cassie craned her head, but Ramiz's cloak fluttered in the breeze and frustrated her attempts to see beyond him. He was bowing now, making formal greetings. She could hear Prince Jamil respond, his voice no more than a deep sonorous murmur. Then Ramiz stepped to one side and nodded. She got to her feet without her usual grace, made clumsy by her aching limbs, and made her curtsy. Low, as if to the Regent at her presentation, just as Celia had shown her, keeping her eyes lowered behind her veil.

He was tall, this prince, was her first impression. A perfectly plain white silk tunic beneath an unusual cloak, a vivid green that was almost emerald, bordered with gold and weighted with jewels. A wicked-looking scimitar hung at his waist. He certainly wasn't fat, which she'd been expecting simply because Celia told her that it was a sign of affluence, and she knew Prince Jamil to be exceedingly rich. But the thin tunic was unforgiving. Prince Jamil's body showed no sign of excess. He was more—lithe.

The word surprised Cassie. Apt as it was, she hadn't ever thought of a man in such a way before. It was his stance, maybe; the way he looked as if he was ready to pounce. A line of goose bumps formed themselves like sentries along Cassie's spine. Celia was right. Prince

Jamil was not a man to cross. As he put his hands together in the traditional welcome, Cassie tried to sneak a quick look at his face, to no avail.

'Lady Cassandra. *As-salamu alaykum*,' Prince Jamil said. 'Peace be with you.'

'*Wa-alaykum as-salam*, Your Highness,' Cassie replied from behind her veil, her voice raspy with thirst, 'and with you also.' She caught a glimpse of white teeth as he smiled in response to her carefully rehearsed Arabic. Or to be more accurate, he made something approximating a smile, which lasted for about two seconds before he held out his hand in greeting to Ramiz, and then ushered him into the throne room, where a servant pulled the organdie curtains into place, thus effectively obscuring them from view. Cassie was left to follow another man who emerged from the shadows to lead her towards the smaller of the two large tents.

'I am Halim, Prince Jamil's man of business. The prince asks me to ensure you have all you require. Refreshments will be served to you in your tent.'

'But—I assumed I would dine with Prince Jamil and Ramiz—I mean Prince Ramiz.'

'What can you be thinking of to suggest such a thing?' Halim looked at the dusty-veiled female who was to be the Princess Linah's governess with horror, thinking that already his worst fears were being confirmed. She had no idea of the ways and customs of the East. 'You are not in London now, Lady Cassandra. We do things very differently here—Prince Jamil would be shocked to the core.' The latter statement was a lie, for Prince Jamil was forever lamenting the outmoded segregation of the sexes at meal times, but this upstart governess was not to know that, and the sooner she was put firmly in her place the better.

'Please, don't mention it to him,' Cassie said contritely. 'I did not mean to offend. I beg your pardon.'

'It shall be so, but you would do well to heed my warning, Lady Cassandra. Daar-el-Abbah is a very traditional kingdom. You must tread extremely carefully.' Halim bowed and held back the heavy tapestry that formed the door of the tent. Cassie stepped across the threshold and turned to thank him, but he was already gone. She stared in wide-eyed amazement at the carpets, the wall hangings, the divans and cushions, the carved chests and inlaid tables. Another heavy tapestry, depicting an exotic garden in which nymphs sported, split the tent into two. In the smaller of the compartments she found, to her astonishment, a bath of beaten copper filled with warm water and strewn with petals. It had a delightful fragrance, orange blossom, she thought. A selection of oils in pretty glass decanters stood beside it on a little table, along with a tablet of soap and the biggest sponge Cassie had ever seen.

She needed no further encouragement, stripping herself of her travel-worn clothes and sinking with a contented sigh into the bath. She lay luxuriating in it for a long time, allowing the waters to ease her aching muscles. Eventually she sat up and washed her hair, then chose a jasmine oil with which to anoint herself before donning one of her own nightgowns and a loose wrapper in her favourite shade of cerulean blue. Her hair she brushed out and left loose to dry in its natural curl.

'Since I'm obviously surplus to requirements while

the men discuss weighty matters of state, I may as well be comfortable,' she muttered to herself. Part of her resented being so completely excluded, despite the fact that she was perfectly well aware her presence would be unprecedented in this deeply patriarchal society. As Papa's daughter, playing a role, albeit a small one, in the world of politicking and diplomatic shenanigans was second nature to Cassie. Though she was not the trusted confidante that Celia had been, she was used to pouring oil on troubled waters and providing a sympathetic ear. It irked her, though she knew it should not, that both Ramiz and her new employer should so casually dismiss her.

But as she emerged into the main room of the tent and found a silver tray covered in a huge selection of dainty dishes had been provided for her, along with a jug of sherbet, Cassie's mood brightened significantly and common sense reasserted itself. She was expecting too much—and she would do well to remember that she was here to govern a small girl, not a country! The princes were welcome to their weighty affairs of state.

Stacking up a heap of cushions on the floor beside the tray, she set about making an excellent meal. Far better to enjoy her own company than to have to make polite conversation with the prince tonight, all the time on tenterhooks lest she overstep some invisible mark. Far better to have a good night's sleep, to be introduced to him formally in the morning when she was refreshed and able to make a better impression.

She washed her fingers in the bowl and lolled back on the cushions in a most satisfyingly un-ladylike manner, which would have immediately prompted

Aunt Sophia into one of her lectures about posture and politesse. The thought made Cassie giggle. Despite the fact that Celia was inordinately happy in her marriage, and despite the fact that, having met Ramiz, her initial reservations were quickly assuaged by his charm and patent integrity, Aunt Sophia thought Arabia a decadent place. *For once a female has abandoned her corsets, there is no saying what else she will abandon*, had been her parting words to Cassie. *Firmly laced stays signify firmly laced morals. Remember that, and you will be safe.*

Safe from what? Cassie wondered idly now, yawning. She should go to bed, but instead settled back more comfortably on the mound of cushions and examined her surroundings. The ceiling of the tent was constructed from pleated silk, decorated with gold-and-silver tassels. It reminded her a little of one of the rooms at the Brighton Pavilion, to which she, in the company of Papa, had been invited to take tea with the Prince Regent. Which room was it? Her eyes drooped closed as she tried to remember. Tea had been delayed for over an hour because Prinny was being bled. Papa was most upset, considering it very poor form. But at least she had been allowed to socialise with the prince, unlike here. Strange to think that Prinny was king now. Which room had it been?

Cassie fell fast asleep.

An hour later the princes, having concluded discussions to their mutual satisfaction, parted company. Ramiz, who had never before left Celia alone for more than one night since they were married, was anxious to return to Balyrma, and could not be persuaded to stay on, despite Jamil's entreaties.

'I won't disturb Cassandra,' Ramiz said to Prince Jamil, 'you will pass on my goodbyes, my friend, if you would be so kind.' Ramiz headed back to his own waiting caravan, glancing up at the night sky, reassured that the moon was full enough for him to be able to travel for a few hours before having to stop for the night.

Jamil waited until his new ally was beyond the torch-lit path, and turned to Halim. 'That went well, I think.'

'Indeed, Highness. Extremely well.'

'I'll see the Lady Cassandra now.'

'But, Highness, it's very late.'

'Nonsense. She'll be expecting me to welcome her formally into my household, as is the custom. You know that until I do, she will not be considered under my protection. I hope you told her, as I instructed you, that I would call on her when my business with Prince Ramiz was concluded?'

Halim swallowed. 'Not in so many words, Highness. My English is not the best, perhaps something was lost in translation.'

'That is news to me. You speak, to my knowledge, seven languages fluently.' Jamil looked sharply at his aide. 'I hope, Halim, I can be assured that your enthusiasm for this endeavour matches my own? I would not like to contemplate the consequences, were it otherwise.'

'Highness! I promise you that—'

'I do not want promises, Halim, I want your unequivocal support. And now, whether she is expecting me or not, I intend to see Lady Cassandra. We start for home at first light. Make sure all is ready.'

Jamil nodded his dismissal and turned towards Lady Cassandra's tent. Over the last few days, he had constructed his own mental image of his daughter's new governess. His fleeting glimpse of her had done little to confirm or deny the figure that existed in his mind's eye, that of a rather frumpy, slightly forbidding bluestocking, austere and businesslike. He hoped he would not be disappointed.

He pulled back the door curtain of the tent and stepped through into the main room. The vision that greeted him was so far from the one he had imagined that Jamil stopped in his tracks. Was the sleeping beauty who lay before him some sort of offering or gift that Lady Cassandra had brought with her? It was a ridiculous notion, he realised almost immediately, but how else to explain the presence of this alluring female?

Her long hair, a dark golden colour with fiery tints, rippled over the cushions. Her face had all the classical proportions of beauty, but it was not that which made her beautiful. It was the way her mouth curved naturally upwards. It was the colour of her lips, like Red Sea coral. It was the hint of upturn on her nose, which made it not quite perfect. And it was her curves. There was something so pleasing, so tactile about a curve, which was why it was such a prominent feature of the Eastern architecture. Curves were sensual, and this female had them in plentiful supply, from the roundness of her full breasts, to the dip and swell from her waist to her hips.

She was wearing some sort of loose gown with long

sleeves trimmed with lace, an absurdly feminine piece of clothing, obviously designed for the boudoir. The sash had come undone to reveal a thin garment that left little to the imagination. He could see the rise and fall of her breasts at the neckline. He could see the dark aureole of her nipples through the gauzy material. He could see all too clearly that underneath it she was completely naked. She gave off an aura of extreme femininity, the type of yielding softness that begged for a corresponding male hardness. A sharp pang of desire jagged through him. This woman had the type of beauty that turned heads. The type of beauty that inevitably spelled trouble.

'Lady Cassandra?'

The temptress opened her eyes. They were the blue of a turquoise gemstone, under heavy lids that gave her a slumberous appearance. A woman waiting to be woken, stirred into life.

'Yes?' Cassie gazed sleepily up at the man standing over her and rubbed her eyelids. Her surroundings came into focus. And then so did the man. The first thing she noticed was his eyes, which were the strangest colour she had ever seen, burnished like an English autumn, though his gaze was wintery. His mouth was set in a straight line, his brows in a frown. His skin, framed by the traditional white silk head dress, was the colour of honey.

A man of loneliness and mystery, scarce seen to smile, and seldom heard to sigh. Lord Byron's words popped into her head, as if they had been waiting for just this opportunity to be heard, so pertinent were they. Like the Corsair, this man was both intriguing and inscrutable. He had an imperious air about him, as if he surveyed the world from some higher, more exclusive plane. Intimidating, was the word which sprang to mind. *Who was he? And what was he doing in her tent in the middle of the night?*

Clutching at the neck of her nightgown, the sash of her robe, her unbound hair, Cassie tried to get up off the cluster of cushions upon which she had been lying and succeeded only in catching her bare foot on a particularly slippery satin one, which pitched her forwards. 'Oh!'

His reactions were lightning quick. Instead of falling on to the carpet, Cassie found herself held in a hard embrace. She had never, even dancing a waltz, been held this close to a man—not even by Augustus, that soul of propriety. She hadn't realised how very different was the male body. A sinewy arm, lightly tanned under the loose sleeve of his tunic, held her against his unyielding chest. Were all men this solid? She hadn't really realised either, until now, that she was so very pliant. Her waist seemed designed for his embrace. She felt helpless. The feeling was strange, because it should have made her feel scared, but she wasn't. Not completely.

'Unhand me at once, you fiend!'

The fiend, who was actually remarkably un-fiend-like, retained his vice-like hold. 'You are Lady Cassandra?' he said, gazing at her in something akin to dismay. 'Sister to Lady Celia, daughter of Lord Henry Armstrong?'

'Of course I am.' Cassie clutched her robe more firmly together. 'More to the point, who are you, and what, pray, are you doing in my tent in the middle of the night? I must warn you,' she declared dramatically, throwing herself with gusto into the role of innocent maiden, safe now in the knowledge that the stranger meant her no harm, 'I will fight to the death to protect my honour.'

To her intense irritation the man smiled, or made as if to smile, a slight curl of the mouth that she'd seen somewhere before. 'That will not be necessary, I assure you,' he said. He had a voice like treacle, rich and mellow, his English softly accented.

'I am here as Prince Jamil's guest, you know,' Cassie said warily. 'If any harm were to come to me and he were to hear of it, he would—he would…'

'What would he do, this Prince Jamil, who you seem to know so well?'

'He would have you beheaded and dragged through the desert by a team of wild horses,' Cassie said defiantly. She was sure she had read about that somewhere.

'Before or after the beheading?'

Cassie narrowed her eyes and set her jaw determinedly. 'You are clearly not taking me seriously. Perhaps I should scream.'

'I would prefer it if you did not. My apologies, Lady Cassandra, allow me to introduce myself. I am Sheikh Jamil al-Nazarri, Prince of Daar-el-Abbah. I did not intend to alarm you, I merely wished to formally welcome you into my protection. Protection,' he added sardonically, 'that you obviously feel in urgent need of.'

Prince Jamil! Dear heavens, this was Prince Jamil! Cassie stared aghast at his countenance, forgetting all about the heinous crime of meeting a prince's eyes, which Celia had warned her about. 'Prince Jamil! I'm sorry, I didn't realise, I thought…'

'You thought I was about to rip your nightclothes unceremoniously from you and ravish you,' Jamil finished for her, eyeing the luscious curves, barely concealed by her flimsy garment.

Cassie clutched her nightdress even tighter to her and tried, not entirely successfully, to banish this shockingly exciting idea from her mind. 'I wasn't aware that you were going to call on me,' she said in what she hoped was an unflustered tone.

'Halim did not mention that I intended to visit you?'

'No.' She saw a fierce frown form on the prince's countenance. She would not like to be in Halim's shoes. Cassie bit her lip. 'I'm sure it was an oversight. He may even have mentioned it, but I didn't hear him. I was very tired.'

'Your generosity does you credit. Don't worry, I won't have him beheaded and dragged through the desert by wild horses.'

His words were accompanied by a half-smile that Cassie could not help but return. 'I'm afraid I let my imagination run away with me a bit.'

She was not the only one. Reality crashed down on Jamil's head with a vengeance, forcing him to bid a metaphorical goodbye to his cherished vision of a dowdy, sober, English aristocrat. He looked at the dishevelled female standing before him who apparently was Lady Cassandra Armstrong, Linah's new governess. This ravishing, curvaceous, luscious creature with lips that were made to cushion kisses was to stay at the royal palace and teach Linah manners. Respect. Discipline.

Jamil clutched at the golden band of his headdress and pulled it from his head along with the *gutrah* itself and threw both onto a nearby divan. He ran his hands through his short hair, which was already standing up in startled spikes, and tried to imagine the reception his Council would give her. Almost, it would be worth bringing her back to Daar just to see their stunned expressions. Then he imagined Linah's reaction and his mouth straightened into its familiar determined line. 'No,' he said decisively.

'No? No—what, may I ask?'

'I cannot permit you to be my daughter's governess.'

Cassie's face fell. 'But why not? What have I done?'

Jamil made a sweeping gesture. 'For a start you look like you belong in a harem, not a schoolroom.'

Dismay made Cassie forget all about the need for deference and the necessity of not speaking without thinking. 'That's not fair! You caught me unawares. I was prepared to go to my bed, not to receive a formal state visit. You talk as if I lie around half-naked on a divan all day, buffing my nails and eating sweetmeats.'

Jamil swallowed hard. The idea of her lying around half-naked was most distracting. To be fair, she was actually showing less flesh than if she had been clad in an evening gown. Except that he knew her to be naked underneath. And the folds of her robe clung so lovingly to her, he could not help but notice her contours. And there was something about her, the slumberous eyes, the full bottom lip, the fragrance of her skin, jasmine and something else, sensuous and utterly female.

'What I meant is, you don't look—strict enough to be a governess,' he said.

Despite the very awkward situation, Cassie's sense of the ridiculous was tickled. She bit hard on her lower lip, but her smile quivered rebelliously.

'I don't know what you find in the situation to amuse you,' Jamil snapped.

'I beg your pardon,' Cassie said, trying very hard to sound contrite. 'If you would perhaps tell me how you expect me to look, I will endeavour to change my appearance accordingly. I have lots of perfectly demure dresses, I assure you.'

'It's not a matter of clothing. Or lack of it. It's—it's you. Look!' He took her by surprise, taking her by the arm and turning her towards the full-length mirror that stood in a corner of the tent.

Cassie looked at her reflection in the soft glow of the lamp that hung from the canopied ceiling. Her hair was burnished, more auburn than gold, curling wildly about her face, tangling with the lace at the neckline of her negligee. Her skin was flushed. Her eyes had a sparkle to them that had of late been missing. She had an air of disarray that made her look a little—wanton—there was no denying it. *How could that be?*

Behind her, Prince Jamil moved closer. She could feel the hardness of his body just barely touching her back. She could sense him, warm and male, hovering only inches away from her. He reached over her shoulder to brush her hair back from her face and his touch, for some reason, made her shiver, though she wasn't cold in the slightest.

'Look,' he said, gazing at her intently, straightening

the lace at her neck, running a hand down her arm to twitch the lace straight there, too, to tighten the sash of her robe which kept coming undone despite her best efforts to knot it securely. 'Look,' he said, his hand brushing her waist. Their eyes met in the mirror, autumn gold and summer blue, and she looked—not at herself but at them, the two of them, close enough to almost merge into one—as he did, too, at precisely the same moment.

And at that precise moment something happened. The air seemed to crackle. Their gazes locked. Cassie's breath caught in her throat. Prince Jamil bent his head. She watched in the mirror as he lifted the fall of her hair from her shoulders, as if she were watching a play, as if it was happening to someone else, as if the sensual creature before her was not her.

But if it was not her, why was it that she could feel his lips on the bare skin of her neck? The tiniest touch, but it was searing. Her skin contracted and burned. Now her breath came, rapid and shallow, too fast, like her heart, suddenly galloping. She realised only a fraction of a second before he did so that he was going to kiss her.

Kiss her properly.

Kiss her on the mouth.

He turned her around and tilted her chin up. His eyes met hers again, darker gold now, intensely gold, irresistibly gold. He made the tiniest movement towards her, so subtle as to be almost undetectable, except she detected it and responded, stepping into his arms and lifting her face and slanting her lips. And he kissed her.

Cassie had been kissed before. Truth be told, men

had a habit of trying to kiss her, though she gave them no encouragement as far as she was aware, and had never had any problem in actively discouraging them when necessary. But strangely, discouraging Prince Jamil simply did not occur to her.

Augustus's kisses had been worshipful and chaste rather than intimate. To be honest, Augustus's kisses had failed singularly to arouse *the rapture which dwells on the first kiss of love*, which Lord Byron had so beautifully evoked and which Cassie had been led to expect. It had been one of the things that had made her question the depth of her feelings for Augustus, for neither the *first kiss of love* nor the twentieth had roused in her anything but mild indifference. But as Prince Jamil's mouth met hers, indifference was the furthest thing from her mind, and she knew that when he finished kissing her, she would be in no doubt whatsoever that she had been kissed.

His hand cupped her head, urging her to close the space, the tiny space, between them. She did, relishing the way her curves seemed to meld into the hard planes of his muscular frame. Her breasts brushed tantalisingly against his chest and her nipples puckered in response, as they did when she was cold, except she wasn't cold, and it was quite a different sensation. His other arm curved round her waist, nestling her closer. She licked her lips, because they felt dry. His eyes widened as she did so. He made a guttural noise like a moan that made her stomach knot. Then his lips touched hers, and she knew instantly that Lord Byron had been right after all.

Rapture. A soaring, giddy feeling surged through

her as Prince Jamil's mouth moulded itself to hers. He kissed as if he were tasting her, his touch plucking tingling strings of sensation buried deep in her belly. He pulled her closer, settling her against him, his fingers sinking into her hair, into the soft, yielding flesh of her waist. His mouth coaxed hers open, his lips settled on hers, harder now, making her sigh at the taste of him. She felt herself unfurling like a flower as his tongue touched hers, a shockingly sensual and intimate act. If he had not held her, if she had not clutched, with both hands, at his tunic, his arms, his shoulders, his back, she felt as if she would have fallen into an abyss. She felt wanton. She felt wild abandon. She wanted the kiss to go on for ever. She pressed herself against him, and encountered something solid and heavy pressing against her thigh.

Jamil leapt back at once. He stared at her as if she was a stranger. Cassie stared, too, her hand to her lips, which were burning, seared, marked. Shame and embarrassment washed over her. *What must he think of her?*

Jamil looked at her in horror. *What was he doing? And by the gods, why was he still thinking of doing more!* 'You see what I mean now,' he said, taking his frustration out on the cause of it, 'you are clearly not governess material.'

Cassie was too bewildered to do anything other than stare at him. She felt a strange, needy ache, as if she had been starving, had been shown a banquet and allowed just one bite before the feast was withdrawn. Her body hummed and protested and begged for more. She was mortified and confused. *Had she encouraged him? Was it her fault?*

'Well? Have you nothing to say for yourself?'

She licked her lips. They felt swollen. 'I…'

Jamil gave an exclamation of disgust, as much at his own actions as anything else. It was not like him to behave with such a lack of control. A prince must be above such emotions. 'This arrangement is clearly not going to work. It is best we acknowledge that now. I will have you returned to your sister in the morning.'

The heavy edge of his cloak brushed against her ankle as he made for the door, rousing Cassie from her stupor. 'Returned!' she gasped, as the consequences of her entirely inappropriate behaviour began to dawn on her. She was to be sent back, like an unwanted present or a misdirected missive! Why could she not just for once think before she spoke or acted? 'Please. I beg of you, Prince Jamil, to reconsider.' Cassie tugged on his cloak in an effort to halt his retreat, and succeeded in earning herself an extremely haughty stare, but desperation made her ignore it. If he left now, he would not change his mind. He would send her back, she would be disgraced for the second time, only this time it was even worse because she would be letting not only herself but Celia down, and Ramiz, too, and she could not bear that. 'Oh, please,' she said again, 'I implore you, your Highness, don't be so hasty. Just listen to me, give me a chance to prove myself, I beg of you.'

Jamil hesitated momentarily and Cassie threw herself into the breach. 'Prince Jamil. Your Highness. Sheikh al-Nazarri.' She made a low and extremely elegant curtsy, completely unaware that she was granting

Jamil a tantalising glimpse of cleavage. 'You would concede that your daughter is in urgent need of a governess and I—well, to be frank, I am in urgent need of an opportunity to prove myself, so you see, we both stand to profit from making this arrangement work. I know I'm not what you were expecting, though indeed I'm still not sure what exactly you *were* expecting, but I assure you I am extremely capable of looking after a little girl like Linah. I myself lost my mother at an early age, and I have three younger sisters whose education and upbringing I've been closely involved in. I'm sure she and I will get on. I know I can get through to her, make a difference to her. Please. Don't send me back. Give me a chance. You won't regret it.'

She clasped her hands in supplication and only just resisted the urge to throw herself on her knees. Prince Jamil gave no indication of wavering, his face set in an implacable expression. Only his eyes betrayed a flicker of something else. What, she couldn't discern.

Why on earth had he kissed her like that? To teach her a lesson? And why had she let him? She wasn't attracted to him, she couldn't be, she wasn't going to allow herself to be attracted to anyone. Not ever. She'd never allowed a man such liberties before. No man had ever attempted to take such liberties before, but Prince Jamil did not seem to think his behaviour questionable. Only her own.

And he was right about that. She had behaved like a very wanton. No wonder he thought—*oh, God, she didn't want to even think about what he thought.* Cassie clasped her hands together tighter and swallowed her pride. What use was pride, after all? She had no right to it, and no use for it either, if it prevented her from using all her powers to persuade the prince that she was worthy of his trust. 'I don't know what came over me—when you—when you—when I allowed you to kiss me, I mean,' she said, blushing madly but forcing herself to continue to meet those strange golden brown eyes. 'I can only assure you that I am not in the habit of allowing—of indulging—in kissing.'

'I know,' Jamil said, surprised out of his rigid hold on his control by this naïve admission.

'You do?'

'Your kisses were hardly expert.'

Cassie wasn't sure if this was an insult or a compliment. Though she was much inclined to pursue this very interesting question, for once sense prevailed and she held her tongue. 'Anyway, whatever they were or were not, I assure you I won't subject you to them again.'

Despite his determination not to be persuaded, Jamil was intrigued. And amused. It had been so long since he had found anyone so entertaining as Lady Cassandra. Or so—confounding. Unexpected. *Interesting.* He would be quite happy to be subjected again to her kisses. More than happy. The question was, was this a good thing or a bad? 'My daughter…'

'Linah.'

'She is…'

'Unhappy.'

He raised a supercilious brow. 'I was going to say difficult.'

'Yes, but that's because she's unhappy.'

'Nonsense. She has no reason to be so. She has everything any little girl could wish for.'

'Children are not born difficult, they are difficult for a reason,' Cassie persisted, feeling herself on surer ground. 'The trick is to work out what that reason is. Linah is only eight years old, she has not the language to express her feelings properly. So instead she expresses them by…'

'Being difficult.' Jamil pondered this. All his experience told him that leniency was the root cause of Linah's tantrums. It had not occurred to him until now that Linah could actually be unhappy; he had assumed that withholding the harsh physical discipline which had been meted out to him would be enough. Could he be wrong? The thought was discomfiting.

'You see, I do understand little girls,' Cassie continued, sensing from the look on the prince's face that she had struck a chord. 'I want nothing more than to help Linah. If we could forget about what happened tonight—make a fresh start in the morning…'

Jamil raised an imperious hand. 'Enough. I admit, you've given me food for thought, but it's late. I will sleep on it and inform you of my decision in the morning.'

'Sleep is the wisest counsel. That's what my sister Celia always says.'

Jamil smiled properly this time, showing a fleeting hint of a single dimple. 'My father used to say something similar. I will bid you goodnight, Lady Cassandra.'

Dazzled by the way his face changed, from intimidating sheikh to an extraordinarily attractive and somehow more youthful man, Cassie gazed up at him. Only his turning to go brought her to her senses. 'Goodnight, Highness,' she said, dropping another curtsy. By the time she emerged from it, he was gone.

Chapter Three

The next morning found Jamil, most unusually for him, still in two minds. It did not help that Lady Cassandra had haunted his dreams. It did not help that the memory of her lips, her skin, her nubile body, had awakened his own slumbering desires, conjuring endless teasing fantasies that made sleep impossible. He had finally quit his divan in desperation, plunging into the refreshing water of the pool before dawn had even risen, in an effort to cool his body and order his mind. He was quite unused to such carnal thoughts getting in the way of his decision-making process. The base needs of his body had never before intruded on the logical processes of his brain. Lady Cassandra confused him by blurring the neatly ordered boundaries of his mind. She was made for pleasure. She was here for a much more pragmatic purpose.

Returning to his tent to don his travelling clothes, Jamil resorted to drawing up a mental list of the advantages and disadvantages of employing Lady Cassandra as Linah's governess, and in doing so uncovered one of the questions that had been niggling away in the back of his mind. Lady Cassandra had said she urgently needed an opportunity to prove herself. Why? he wondered. Prove herself after what?

It was the first question he put to her when she appeared before him in the makeshift throne room. She wore her travelling outfit, the blue riding habit and veil in which she had arrived yesterday, and was at pains to keep her head correctly bowed, but Jamil was in no mood to allow her to hide behind the trappings of propriety. He bade the servants draw forwards the light curtains and instructed her to put back her veil. He did not, however, bid her sit, choosing to keep her standing before him, like a supplicant. 'Explain to me, if you please, what you meant by needing an opportunity to prove yourself,' he said in clipped tones.

Cassie stared at the prince in consternation. All through the long night she had rehearsed her arguments and mustered her reasons, drilling them into a tight formation, readying them to be paraded, impeccable and indisputable, before the prince. She was ready to recite lesson plans in everything from watercolour painting to deportment, map reading to account keeping, playing upon the pianoforte—though she wasn't particularly sure that such an instrument would be available—French conversation—though she didn't know, when it came down to it, if Linah even spoke English—botany—though she had no idea what flowers—if any—grew in the desert—and horse riding, the one subject on which Cassie knew herself to be expert. All of this she had ready at her fingertips, along with her ideas for instilling strict but fair discipline, and most of all her ardent desire to give Linah some much-needed affection.

But it seemed Prince Jamil was not interested in any of this. Instead he wanted to know about her motives, a subject Cassie herself was a little hazy on, just at the moment. 'I suppose I meant that it would be good to be of use,' she fumbled.

Prince Jamil's mouth tightened. 'Of all things, I abhor prevarication. It leads, more often than not, to deceit. If you are to be my daughter's governess, I must be able to trust you implicitly. To deceive me as to your motives...'

'Oh, no, I would never do that.'

'Then I ask you again, what precipitated this burning desire to prove yourself?'

Blushing, Cassie shuffled from one foot to the other, trying desperately to find a way of satisfying the prince's curiosity without putting herself in too unflattering a light, but a glance up at his stern countenance told her she would do far better to give him the unvarnished truth. He would not tolerate anything else, and she most assuredly did not want to risk being discovered in what he would then assume to be a lie. She clasped her hands together and began the sorry tale of her ill-fated betrothal to Augustus, though telling it rather to her riding boot than to Prince Jamil, not daring to look up for fear that his countenance would betray his disapproval.

'I made a mistake, a terrible lack of judgement,' she

concluded. 'Had I not been so headstrong, so indulgent of my sentimental inclinations, I and my family would have perhaps been spared the humiliation of my being so publicly jilted.'

'But surely it is this man Augustus—if you can call such a desert scorpion a man—surely it is he who should feel shame?' Jamil said contemptuously. 'You are the innocent party. He, on the other hand, has behaved in a manner that shows a complete lack of honour and integrity. He deserves to be the outcast, not you.'

Cassie shook her head. 'It is not how the world sees it, nor indeed how my—my papa sees it.'

'In my world we would see such a thing quite differently.'

Cassie jutted her chin forwards determinedly, a gesture Jamil found strangely endearing. 'Well, however anybody else chooses to see it,' she said, 'I assure you, no one could be more ashamed than I, nor more determined to change. I do not intend ever to give my heart rein again.'

'A wise decision. The heart is not, in my opinion, a logical organ.'

'No. Nor a reliable one. I have my faults, but I do not need to be taught something twice.'

'He who is burned must always beware the fire, hmm?'

'Exactly.'

'So, not to put too fine a point on it, Lady Cassandra, you're telling me that you were sent out here in disgrace?'

Cassie wove and unwove her long fingers. 'No, not

precisely. Papa wished me to retire to the countryside until the scandal had blown over. It was Celia's suggestion that I come out here—she knows, you see, how very taken I was with Arabia when Aunt Sophia and I came to rescue—' Jamil raised his eyebrows quizzically. 'That is to say, came to visit Celia before she was married. And I was also most eager to…to put some distance between myself and Papa's new wife, who seemed to relish adding fuel to the fire with regards to my predicament.' Cassie's breast heaved at the thought of her stepmother. 'Bella Frobisher is a grasping, selfish cuckoo in the nest and now, of course, that she's produced an heir—well! You can imagine how she crows.'

She broke off with an exclamation of dismay. 'I beg your pardon, we seem to have strayed rather from the point. The thing is, your Highness, that I'm afraid my betrothal rather confirmed Papa's opinion of me as—as a little lacking in judgement and not very dependable,' she said, blushing deeper than ever, 'and I would very much wish to prove him wrong.'

'It seems to me that your father is at fault in allowing you far too much latitude. Here in Arabia, we recognise that women are the weaker sex, and do not permit them to make life-changing decisions, such as a choice of husband, for themselves.'

Cassie's immediate reaction was to inform Prince Jamil that here in Arabia, in her opinion, women were not so much protected as subjected, but even as the words formed she realised that they undermined her cause no end. 'My papa would heartily agree with you on that topic,' she said instead.

'Meaning?'

'Meaning, if Papa had his way, he would marry all of us off to his advantage, regardless of our wishes.'

'That is not what I meant at all. It is not my intention that Linah become a state asset, not that that is any of your business. All I want is for her to learn respect for authority, to understand that there are boundaries she must not cross.'

'Children who are unhappy are wont to misbehave in order to gain attention,' Cassie said carefully.

'Yes, so you said last night. What do you mean by that?'

'Well, Linah has been without a mother since she was a baby, hasn't she?'

'She has had any number of females to look after her and pander to her every whim. In fact, she has been over-indulged. I concede that's partly my fault. I have allowed her to be spoiled in order to compensate for the loss of her mother and as a consequence have been reluctant to discipline her.'

'It's not spoiling or discipline she really needs. Tell me, Prince Jamil, are you close to your daughter?'

'What do you mean?'

'Do you see her every day? Play with her? Talk to her? Show any sort of interest at all?'

Jamil stiffened perceptively. 'Of course I take an interest, she is my daughter.'

'How?'

'I beg your pardon?'

'How do you show an interest?'

'I am given a weekly report of her behaviour and her progress with her lessons—at least I was, until the last female I hired departed. Linah is brought to me at the end of each week to discuss this.'

Cassie bit her lip. It was exactly as she had suspected. Poor little Linah was desperate for affection, and her cold-hearted father did nothing but mete out criticism. 'So, the only time you see her is to chastise her?'

Jamil stiffened. 'I have *never* laid a hand in anger upon my daughter.'

'Good heavens, I should hope not,' Cassie said, startled by the sudden harshness in his face. His eyes glittered fiercely, and she remembered Celia's caution again. Prince Jamil was not a man to cross. 'I'm sorry, I didn't mean to suggest such a thing for a minute.

'I do not want my daughter beaten.'

'Of course not! When I said chastise, I meant tell her off.'

'Oh. I see. I misunderstood. Yes. If that is what you meant, then I do. When Linah behaves so badly, she can hardly expect—'

'She behaves badly to get your attention!' Cassie interrupted. 'For goodness' sake, can't you see that? You said last night that Linah had everything a child could wish for.'

'She does, she wants for nothing.'

'Except for the most important thing of all.'

'And what would that be?'

'Love. A father's love, your love.'

'My feelings for my daughter are—'

'Unspoken!' Cassie declared roundly. She glared at the prince, all deference forgotten in the heat of the moment. 'Well, are they not?'

Jamil got swiftly to his feet and descended the step upon which the throne stood. 'As I was saying, Lady Cassandra,' he said through gritted teeth, 'what Linah needs is discipline.'

'And as I was saying,' Cassie riposted, 'what she needs is affection.'

'Respect is what she should have for me. I see no evidence of it, and showing her affection is hardly likely to induce it. As well expose an open wound and suggest she strike there.'

Cassie stared at him, appalled. How could he talk so coldly of his own daughter? Even her own father was not so—so clinical. 'She needs love,' she said obstinately, forcing herself to continue to look straight into the prince's stormy eyes, 'I can provide that. I can teach you how to do the same.'

'How dare you! How dare you presume that you can teach me anything?' Jamil replied angrily. 'I am a royal prince, a direct descendent of generations of wise and powerful potentates, a leader of thousands. And you, a mere woman, dare to tell me how to treat my own daughter.'

'The poor girl is obviously starved of love. For goodness' sake, you're all she has. How would you have felt if your mother had died when you were a baby? Wouldn't you have made every effort to make sure you didn't lose your father's love, too? I know when my own mother…'

The rest of what she was about to say died on Cassie's lips as she took in the prince's stark white countenance. With horror, she realised just how presumptuous her hasty words must have sounded. She had no idea, after all, about the prince's own experience. 'I'm so sorry,' she whispered, 'I didn't think—did your mother die young?'

'No, but she may as well have.' He had been five when he had been forcibly removed to the east wing. She might as well have been dead for all the contact he was allowed with her. Jamil's knuckles whitened. Realising by the way the English woman was looking at him, that his anguish was plain to see, he made a huge effort, forced the past back into its box and turned the key. 'You are impertinent, and you raise issues that are entirely irrelevant. We are talking about Linah, not me.'

Too relieved at being spared any more serious rebuke to even consider pursuing the interesting question of Prince Jamil's as-good-as-dead mother, Cassie could only nod her agreement. It was time, most definitely time, to take another tack. Time enough, when she had Linah's confidence, to return to the subject. 'Please. I didn't mean to offend you. Let me talk to you instead of what I mean to teach Linah.' Giving him no chance to interrupt, haltingly at first, then with growing confidence and enthusiasm, Cassie put forward the plans she had made for her charge. As she talked, gesticulated and talked more, Jamil watched her closely, listening even more closely, trying to focus only on what she said about Linah, not to be distracted by the way enthusiasm lent a glow to her beautiful countenance, the way her body rippled under her ridiculously inappropriate travelling dress when she made her point with extravagant hand gestures. He tried to see her as a governess. To imagine her as Linah's governess. To picture her there, in the schoolroom of the palace, and not, definitely not, as he had seen her last night, strewn invitingly over a divan, reflected lusciously in a mirror.

Her forthright attack on him rankled, and it was ridiculous nonsense, of course, but Jamil was a ruthlessly fair man. Loath though he was to admit it, Lady Cassandra talked at least some sense. And there was the point, the worrying point, she had made about Linah being unhappy. *Did all this add up to enough for him to take a chance on her?* If he did not, what were the alternatives? None, and Prince Ramiz would be offended into the bargain.

'And as to geography,' Cassie was saying, 'I have sent to England for a dissected map just exactly like the one the royal princes had. It is in French, too, which will help Linah with the language. Which puts me in mind—I assumed she spoke English, but of course that is rather arrogant of me and—'

'She is badly behaved, not stupid,' Jamil said haughtily. 'As she is a daughter of the House of al-Nazarri I would expect nothing less. She already speaks good English and a little French. I would wish her to have also Italian, the rudiments of Latin and Greek, and perhaps some German.'

'Oh. Right. Capital. I'm afraid I don't have any German, though,' Cassie admitted, looking somewhat downcast. 'But in my humble opinion that's no great loss. I've met the Prussian ambassador and frankly he was as tedious and long-winded as the language. Oh, I hope you don't have any German friends, I meant no offence.'

Jamil smiled inwardly. Despite this female's

appalling lack of deference and her seeming oblivi-
ousness to all the rules of protocol, he found her amusing. On the whole—yes, on the whole, the positives of
taking her on outweighed the negatives. Though of a
surety both Halim and his Council would be ready to
pounce on any gaffes.

'You understand,' he said, 'that your appointment
would be most unusual. My country is a very traditional
one—in fact, you may as well know that the majority
of my Council and trusted aides will oppose your role.'

Cassie's face fell. 'You mean I will have to win their
approval?'

Jamil pursed his lips. 'They may voice their opinions, but they may not dictate to me. I mean merely that
it will be better not to offend them.'

Her brow furrowed. 'How might I offend them?'

'As I have already informed you, Lady Cassandra,
you look as if you belong not in the schoolroom, but
the boudoir.'

'Harem, actually, is what you said. I can't help how
I look, your Highness. And I assure you, that I will
not—last night—it was…'

'Nothing of that sort will pass between us again,'
Jamil said firmly, speaking as much to himself as to
Lady Cassandra. 'As Linah's governess you must be
beyond reproach—is that understood?' As Linah's governess, she must now be strictly out of bounds. *Why
did he feel instinctively that this would prove so difficult?* It should have been a warning, but Jamil, whose
own self-discipline was so ingrained as to have become
instinctive, did not heed it.

'I understand perfectly, your Highness,' Cassie said,

trying hard not to feel indignant. The prince had every reason to doubt her ability to conduct herself properly after all, given what she had just told him and how she had behaved last night. There was no point in telling him it was out of character; she must let her future conduct demonstrate that.

'You will most effectively contradict any criticism by obtaining results,' Jamil said brusquely, unwittingly echoing Cassie's own thoughts.

'Can I assume then that you will visit Linah regularly to check her progress?' Cassie asked sweetly.

'I am an extremely busy man. Affairs of state keep me occupied.'

Cassie took a deep breath. 'Forgive me, your Highness, but Linah will fare much better if I can reward her behaviour with the promise of a visit from you,' she said in a rush.

'She can be equally rewarded by the knowledge that her good behaviour pleases rather than angers me,' Jamil replied implacably.

'With respect, it's not quite the same.'

'Your persistence in this matter is becoming tedious, Lady Cassandra. If you are so sure my daughter is in need of affection, then supply it yourself. Consider it part of your duties of employment.'

Cassie's eyes widened. 'Does this mean you'll give me a chance, then? Am I indeed to be Linah's governess?'

'For one month only, subject to satisfactory progress being achieved. Then we will see.'

All else was forgotten in the relief at having achieved her objective. She was not to be sent back. Cassie let out a huge sigh. 'Thank you. Oh, thank you so much, I won't let you down, I promise.'

'I will hold you to that. I do not take kindly to those who do. We start for Daar in fifteen minutes.'

Jamil pulled back the curtains and strode out into the morning sunshine, calling for Halim. Cassie stood, gazing at the space he had occupied, her mind in a daze. She'd done it, she'd persuaded him. A smile spread over her face, and she gave a little skip of excitement. She was going to Daar. She was going to be Linah's governess. She was going to show Papa that she could do something worthwhile. She was going to show the little princess what love was, and she was going to teach the little girl's cold-hearted, autocratic, infuriating father how to love her back. Whether he wanted to or not.

This gave Cassie pause. She did not doubt that somewhere, buried very deep, was Jamil's love for his daughter, but uncovering it would take tact as well as patience. For some reason, he was very resistant to the idea. Yet cold as he was—as he liked to appear, perhaps?—he could not really be so. He cared enough about Linah to want to bring her up properly. And Cassie had her own reasons for knowing he wasn't incapable of emotion. Last night…

Stop! She wouldn't think about last night. Her own behaviour had shocked her. She just couldn't understand it. But Jamil—well, he was a man, after all. One to whom desire came easily. Cassie's skin prickled. He had seen her in a state of undress and he had wanted to…

It was her fault! He was hot-blooded. It must be the desert air, or the heat of the sun, or perhaps there was just something in the prince's culture that encouraged such behaviour. Celia had hinted at something she called sensuality, though she wouldn't explain, and to tell the truth, Cassie had been too embarrassed to ask. Whatever it was, it had to be said, there was something terribly romantic about desert princes. And Jamil was the epitome of a desert prince. A passionate sheikh with a strong sense of honour—look at the contemptuous way he had talked of Augustus! It made her feel just a bit better, to have him take her part. Sort of. Just a little.

But that didn't mean he would always be so understanding. She would do well indeed to forget all about last night, and all about Jamil as anything other than her exacting employer. She was done with romance. Done with giving her heart any say at all in matters. She was done, quite done, with men, whether traitorous poets or desert princes, romantic or otherwise.

Cassie made the journey to the city of Daar mounted on a snowy white camel, a rare breed, though its exclusivity did not, unfortunately, make it any more of a comfortable ride than its more dowdy brethren. The high-backed saddle was more splendid than the one on which she had arrived at Jamil's camp, but it was still basically a sparsely-padded wooden seat. As Jamil made a clicking noise at the back of his throat, and the beast knelt down to allow her to mount, Cassie's muscles protested by cramping. However, she climbed on to what passed for a saddle, pleased to discover that she did so with some semblance of grace, even more pleased to see the very brief look of approval that flitted across Jamil's face. He made the clicking noise again, and the camel got back to its feet. Cassie arranged her skirts and pulled the long veil, which she had attached to her little military hat, over her face. 'I'll take the reins, thank you,' she said, holding out her gloved hand.

Jamil hesitated. It was the custom for women to be lead and the white camel was not only extremely rare but extremely sensitive, with a mouth as soft as a thoroughbred horse. What if this woman was as impetuous a rider as she was in every other way? It would just take one jerk of the reins and she would end up thrown.

'You need not worry, I won't let him bolt and I won't ruin his mouth,' Cassie said, reading his thoughts a mite too easily for Jamil's liking. He surrendered the reins reluctantly, and, mounting his own camel with practised ease, headed the caravan east.

They had journeyed all day, save for a short break at the sun's zenith, and on into the night, too, for Jamil was anxious to be home. By the time they made camp, the stars were already luminous, stitched like jewels into the blue velvet blanket of the sky. Cassie sat a little apart on a little outcrop of rocks, next to the small drinking pool, watching them set up the tents. Leaning back on her hands, she threw her head back to gaze up at the night sky, which looked so vast compared to England, the stars seeming to hover so much closer to earth than they did at home. The desert, too, in daylight, was vast, undulating and unrolling in front of them in shades of ochre and rust, of gold and tawny brown, a landscape of barren beauty, so exotic in its fierceness, and so very different from England that she felt as if she were on another planet. Celia said it had intimidated her when first she came here, but Cassie found it invigorating and beguiling. She liked its very otherness. She even liked the way it put her firmly in her place, reminding her she was one tiny scrap of insignificance in the face of nature's magnificence.

It struck her that Jamil seemed the very physical embodiment of the desert's exotic charms. Perhaps that was why he integrated so seamlessly into the terrain. It certainly explained the ease with which he navigated the way across what looked to Cassie to be a vast expanse of nothingness. He was a product of the desert, yet not subjugated or intimidated by its harshness, seeming instead to dominate the sandy landscape.

Above her, two shooting stars streaked across the sky, one after the other. Her aches and pains forgotten, Cassie cried out with delight. *'Most glorious night! Though wert not sent for slumber!'*

'I beg your pardon?'

Cassie jumped. Jamil was standing beside her. How did he move so silently? 'It's Byron. An English poet, he—'

'You admire such a man, who has behaved so scandalously?'

'You know of him, then? I admire his poetry, regardless of his behaviour.'

'I forget, you have a weakness for poets, do you not? Or more accurately, perhaps, for poets who treat women with a callous disregard for honour. But it is much too beautiful a night for harsh words,' he added, noting her hurt expression, 'and in any event, you must be very tired, Lady Cassandra.'

'Cassie, please. My given name has too many unwarranted associations.'

'You don't see yourself as a prophetess, then?'

'Hardly.' When he smiled, as he was doing properly now, his expression softened, making him look much less austere. Cassie smiled back. 'If only I had been able to see a bit further into the future, I wouldn't have made such a fool of myself over Augustus.'

'But then you wouldn't have come here.'

'Very true.' Cassie tried to smother a yawn.

'You are tired, and no wonder, it has been a long day.'

'I am a little weary, I must confess.' Her head drooped. 'I should retire.' As she stumbled to her feet, a strong pair of hands circled her waist. 'I can manage,' she protested, but already she was falling asleep.

With an exclamation that could have been impatience, and might have been something more tender, Jamil scooped her up and carried her to her tent, where he laid her down on the divan. She was already deeply asleep. He hesitated before loosening the double row of buttons on her ridiculous little jacket, easing her carefully out of it, resisting the urge to look at the soft curves revealed under the flimsy material of her undergarment. Settling her carefully, he unlaced her boots, but left her stockings on. This much she might reasonably thank him for; any more would be a liberty.

He pulled a rug over her, tucking it securely in at the sides, for the coming dawn would be cold. She nestled her cheek into a cushion, her lips pouting into a little contented sigh. Long lashes, a darker gold than her hair, fanned on to the soft curve of her dusty cheek.

Her hair was a tangle, tresses curling down her neck, little tendrils clinging to her forehead. No doubt she would be horrified by her state of dishevelment, but to Jamil the imperfections enhanced her appeal. She was no goddess now, but mortal, flesh and blood, and possibly the most disturbing flesh and blood he had ever encountered. There was something about her that made him want to cradle her and ravish her at the same time.

'Governess, governess, governess,' he muttered to himself as he made his way to his own tent, matching the words to his stride.

They rode on the next day and the next. The land began to rise as they neared the mountains, which rose starkly in front of them like a painted theatre backdrop. They passed several small communities based round the oases. The houses were ochre-coloured, built into the rocks to which they clung precariously, like small children to a mother's side. As the caravan passed, the people threw themselves to their knees. Women abandoned their laundry, men stopped their tilling of the narrow strips of cultivated land, little children rushed excitedly towards the beautiful white camels, only to be pulled back by mortified mothers. Jamil nodded his acknowledgement, but made no move to stop. Looking back over her shoulder, Cassie caught a group of women staring and pointing at her, though they immediately dropped their gaze when they saw they had been spotted.

It was the same in the next village and the next, each one larger than the last, eventually joining up into a string of settlements linked by vibrant irrigated fields, before finally the walls of the city of Daar came into view. The scent of damp soil and ripe vegetation replaced the dry dusty smells of the desert. On the steep approach to the gate where the water from the main oasis had been channelled, the dates were being harvested from the palms that grew along the banks. Huge woven baskets sat under the trees, waiting to be filled and ferried into the city by a train of mules. Cassie watched in astonishment as the pickers shimmied down the trunks of the trees at a terrifying rate, to make obeisance to their returning prince.

She had fallen behind Jamil. With every step that took them closer to the city, he became more remote, almost visibly assuming the mantle of power. Under his head dress, which was no longer pulled over his face, his expression was stern, the little frown lines apparent. His shoulders were set. He was no longer Jamil, but Prince of Daar-el-Abbah. Behind him, Cassie felt lost and a little apprehensive. Their regal entrance into Jamil's city was quite sufficient to remind her of the true nature of their relationship,

Daar was built on a plateau. The city gates were emblazoned with a golden panther rampant and some Arabic script she assumed would spell *Invincible*, which Celia had told her was Jamil's motto. They passed through the large gates into a city which looked very much like Balyrma, with a network of narrow streets running at right angles to the main thoroughfare. Each alley was crowded with tall houses, overhanging more and more as they rose so that at the top they almost seemed to touch. A series of piazzas with a fountain at the centre of each linked the main thoroughfare, which she was surprised to see was cobbled. The air was redolent with a myriad of smells. The sharp, distinctive tang from the tannery mingled with the aroma of spices and roasting meat. The citrus perfume of lemons and oranges vied with the sweet heady scent from a white blossom Cassie did not recognise. A pungent, surprisingly familiar sheep-like smell emanated from a herd of penned goats. As they picked their way through the crowds, she barely had time to track down the source of one aroma before another assailed her senses.

Everywhere was colour: the robes of the women, the blankets that were being strung out to air across the alleys, the blue and red and gold and green tiles which decorated the fountains and the minarets. And everywhere was noise, too, the braying of the animals, the excited cries and laughter of the children, the strange ululating noise that the men made as they bowed. Captivated and overwhelmed, Cassie forgot her fears and surrendered herself to the magic of the East.

Towards the end of the plateau, nearer the palace, the alleys were gradually replaced by grander houses with white-tiled walls and keyhole-shaped doors, tall turrets marking the corners. The royal palace was built on the furthest part of the plateau, surrounded on three of its sides by the city walls, which formed a second layer of protection after the palace's own. The doors of the gatehouse were of a dark wood, fronted by a heavy portcullis that was being drawn up as they approached. The golden panther was emblazoned on a crest at the apex, and emblazoned, too, on the twin turrets that were built into the corners of the high white walls. An intriguing line of little ornamental towers stretched along the top of the wall, above an intricately tiled border of red and green and gold. Fascinated, Cassie slowed her camel in order to drink in the detail, unwittingly causing a minor traffic jam as the whole caravan halted behind her. Jamil, who had already passed through the doorway, quickly sent his gatekeeper out to lead her camel in.

'I'm sorry,' Cassie whispered, once she had finally climbed out of the saddle, 'your palace is so beautiful I stopped to get a better look.'

Jamil gave no acknowledgement, shaking out his cloak and making his way across the courtyard to where Halim awaited him. Cassie stood alone in the shadow of the gatehouse, wondering what she should do. Glancing around her, at the gatekeeper, the guards who stood with their arms crossed, she was met with blank expressions and downcast eyes. She took a hesitant step into the courtyard, then another, as far as the fountain, which was its centrepiece. Neither Jamil nor Halim gave any sign of noticing her. The water, which sprinkled from a smiling fish, looked lovely and cool. She stripped off her gloves and put back her veil, holding out her hands to let it drip on to them, then dabbed her wrists to her hot forehead. Heavenly! She sat down on the fountain's rim, and trailed her fingers in the water, smiling to see the little gold and silver fish that swam in the bowl. The sound of someone clearing their throat made her look up. She encountered the impassive gaze of Halim.

'Lady Cassandra, Prince Jamil has asked me to take you to Linah.'

'But—is the prince not going to introduce me to his daughter himself?'

'The prince has more important matters to attend to.'

Cassie got to her feet. 'Will the prince be visiting Linah later?'

'I am Prince Jamil's man of business, Lady Cassandra. He does not make a point of sharing his domestic arrangements with me.'

'I see,' Cassie said. Obviously this man was not happy with her presence here. As she followed Halim's rigidly disapproving back across the courtyard and along a seemingly endless corridor to the back of the palace, Cassie's confidence ebbed. Jamil hadn't told her anything of his domestic arrangements. She had no idea what her place was in the palace hierarchy.

Halim stood back to allow her to go through a door flung open by a guard. The door clanged shut behind her. She heard the gradually retreating sound of Halim's footsteps echo on the tiled floor on the other side of the door.

The room was small, a mere ante-chamber. Two of the walls were covered in mirrored tiles that reflected the beautiful enamelled vase which sat on a gilt table in the centre of the room. She passed through another doorway, lifting aside the lace and silk curtains, and found herself in the most unusual courtyard she had ever seen. It was not square but oval, with a colonnaded terrace curving all the way round, a series of connected rooms leading off it, with a second tier of rooms above. There were two fountains playing in harmony, one with the sun as its centrepiece, the other the moon. The courtyard was decorated with intricate mosaic, which featured a gold border interlaced with blue flowers, inside which was portrayed, to Cassie's delight, what looked like Scheherazade sitting at King Shahryar's feet. A spiral staircase set in the furthest end of the oval attracted her attention. Picking up her skirts, she climbed up to the second floor, which had a covered terrace, and upwards again, to the topmost part of the turret, where the stairs ended on a flat viewing platform like a English castle's battlement. Clutching the sides, for the height was dizzying, Cassie could see that her courtyard and terrace were set into the furthest part of the plateau. Below the white walls of the palace were the ochre ones of the city. Beyond that, the lush, green terraced fields fed by the oasis stretched out, and beyond that lay the desert and the mountains.

She stood there for some time, gazing out over Jamil's kingdom, oblivious of the baking heat of the sun, until a scuffling sound distracted her. Looking down into the courtyard, she saw a small, exquisitely dressed young girl gazing up inquisitively at her. 'Hello, Linah,' Cassie called down, for it could only be she, 'my name's Cassie and I'm your new governess.'

Chapter Four

Cassie's initial enthusiasm for her new role was very quickly tempered by the reality of the challenge facing her. Linah, an astonishingly beautiful child with soulful eyes the same shade as her father's, was also an extremely accomplished tyrant, ruling her miniature kingdom through a combination of endearing smiles and extraordinary tantrums, both of which she seemed to be able to turn on and off at will.

What Jamil had referred to as the schoolroom turned out to be an entire wing of the palace, formed around what Cassie called the Scheherazade courtyard. Here, Linah and her retinue of handmaidens and servants spent their days in almost complete indolence, free from supervision since the last in the series of women who had been employed to care for her had departed somewhat hastily after her charge introduced a large snake into her sleeping chamber.

Linah, as Cassie very quickly discovered, was an

extremely bright little girl. The combination, however, of bored intelligence and the complete deference in which she was held by the members of her miniature household meant she was also a little girl wholly lacking in discipline and accustomed to getting her own way. Cassie, calmly removing a series of small rodents from her shoes, her divan and even her dressing case, very quickly realised that Linah's reputation was well earned.

At first, the child was determinedly uninterested in Cassie's carefully planned lessons, drumming her fingers on the miniature desk, kicking her heels against the legs of her chair—for the room used for lessons had been kitted out, to Cassie's surprise, in a Western manner, presumably by Jamil and at great expense. There was a substantial oak desk for herself, a slate board and a large globe, all imported. When requested to desist, Linah would either roll her eyes and feign sleep, or simply throw the desk over and storm out, hiding herself within the ranks of her maidservants, a clutch of giggling, fluttery creatures who made Cassie think of a cloud of butterflies, who were only too keen to pander to Linah, soothing her with comfits, singing her to sleep in her favourite spot under the lemon tree by the fountain, so that no amount of coaxing or reasoning or even threats from Cassie could persuade her to return to the classroom. That the child was bored, Cassie could plainly see. That she had an excess of energy to fuel her regime of defiance was also obvious.

There had been some minor signs of improvement of late, but not sufficient, in Cassie's view, to yet be measured in any way as success. Linah occasionally paid attention during lessons, very occasionally she asked a question or deigned to do a few sums, but mostly she continued with her campaign of disobedience. After ten days, Cassie, having signally failed to exert her authority, was starting to wonder whether the task was beyond her.

It was evening, and she was taking refuge in her room—actually a suite of rooms, which took up the whole southern ellipse of the main courtyard, consisting of a day room that led to a sleeping chamber, a dressing room and a magnificent tiled bathing room. She'd been certain that all it would take was a little love and affection, but Linah responded to neither and Cassie, who was used to the security of her own loving little circle of sisters, was beginning to realise just how much she had taken the daily tokens of affection between them for granted—and how much they had sustained her, too, for without them she was beginning to feel as lost and unloved as poor little Linah.

Cassie sat up wearily, resolutely denying herself the solace of a good cry, and rubbed her eyes, though a few stray tears escaped. She was tired, she was a bit disillusioned and a bit homesick, that was all. With Jamil inexplicably absent, she had no one to talk her problems over with, no one to confide in, nor anyone to encourage her either. Cassie, used to the bustle of the Armstrong household where female company, whether in the shape of her beloved sisters or her formidable Aunt Sophia, was never in short supply, found herself longing even for such an unsympathetic ear as Bella's. She was lonely, and she was unsure of herself, and she was afraid of making mistakes.

Another tear trickled its solitary path down her cheek, and then another. Cassie sniffed. Crying was pointless, as was self-pity. If she was Celia—but she was not, and never would have her elder sister's calm assurance. How much she wished she was with Celia right now. Just a few moments in her company would restore her equanimity.

She sniffed again, but her tears gathered momentum. Bella was right. Aunt Sophia was right. Papa was right. She had been foolish beyond measure to think she could succeed where so many others had patently failed. Linah didn't even like her and Jamil quite obviously wasn't interested in his daughter. He'd told her as much, yet she hadn't listened, so determined had she been to hear only what she wanted to hear. Yet again.

She fumbled for her handkerchief, but the scrap of lace that her sister Caro had so carefully embroidered eluded her grasp, which made her tears flow faster still. She was useless! Linah could see that, and if an eight-year-old child could see that, it surely would not be long before her father did, too—if he ever deigned to visit them. Finally locating her kerchief, Cassie rubbed her cheeks furiously. She would not fail. She would not allow herself to fail. 'I'll show them, all of them,' she muttered, 'and in particular one uncaring man with autumn-coloured eyes who needs to be taught a lesson in love.'

Strengthened by this reviving thought, her mood lightened. The heat of the day had given way to the welcome cool of the desert night, the time she loved best. She kicked off her kid slippers, untied her garters, stripped off her stockings, and made her way out to the courtyard, wriggling her bare toes with relish on the delicious cool marble of the tiled floor. The air was lemon-scented, the moon a thin silver crescent. Making her way over to the minaret, she climbed the stairs, feeling her way with her toes in the dark. At the top of the tower, she sat, her arms clasping her knees, and gazed up at the stars, which seemed, tantalisingly, almost within reach.

Save for a fleeting visit a day after her arrival, she had not seen Jamil at all. He was away dealing with weighty matters, she had been informed by Halim, who greeted her ongoing enquires with disdain. Prince Jamil would return when Prince Jamil saw fit. It was unlikely, Halim said with a superior smile, that his first port of call would be the schoolroom. Prince Jamil was far too important, he clearly implied, to be wasting his time on English governesses and wayward daughters.

At first Cassie had been relieved not to have to face him—or at least that's what she told herself. Best not to be reminded of that kiss. Best not to be distracted by his presence. She didn't want to think of Jamil as anything other than her charge's father—though it was one thing to decide to think that way, quite another, she discovered, to do it. His absence was proving just as distracting as his presence would have been.

Throwing her head back, she looked up at the heavens. The vastness of the skies, the fierce beauty of the endless desert landscape, had an eternal quality. She could neither change nor conquer it, but what she could do was embrace it. There was nothing so pure or so perfect or so wildly exciting as nature in this raw state. It was intoxicating. The natural effervescence with which she used to embrace life began to return, and with it came a renewed determination to succeed in making Linah happy. Which meant confronting Jamil, an idea as exciting and intimidating as taking on the desert over which he alone was master. He was out there now, somewhere under the stars, perhaps surveying them just as she was. Perhaps looking at that particular one, just there. Perhaps he, too, saw the shooting star that blazed across the tip of the moon's crescent. Perhaps...

A noise in the courtyard below caught her attention. Thinking it might be Linah, who was prone to sleepwalking, Cassie got to her feet and leaned over the parapet, but the person looking up at her was most definitely not a child. A tall figure, lithe in his white robe, with eyes that glittered in the harshly beautiful planes of his autocratic face. Cassie gripped hold of the parapet, trying to ignore the absurd little flutter of excitement which rippled through her tummy. 'Your Highness—Jamil. You're back.'

'Lady Cassandra.' He made a small bow. 'Cassie. I am only just returned this past hour.'

Only an hour ago, and yet he had come here to see her! To see Linah—or at least to obtain a report on Linah, Cassie reminded herself sternly. 'I—we are flattered. I'm afraid Linah is asleep.'

'I should hope so. But you, I see, are not.'

'It's a beautiful night.'

Jamil stared up at her, what he could see of her above the parapet. The fiery tints of her hair and the pale material of her dress outlined her starkly against the night sky. He had forgotten how breathtakingly beautiful she was. She looked like a princess in a tower, awaiting rescue. 'Lovely,' he said softly.

Cassie leaned precariously over to obtain a better view. Jamil was barefoot and bare-headed, as she was. Even without the trappings of authority, his air of command was there in the way he stood, feet firmly planted, hands on his hips, head thrown back. He looked like the master of all he surveyed, she thought, then had to suppress a smile because of course he was, and there could be no mistaking the fact. Including her. Cassie shivered. It was a disturbing thought. She knew she shouldn't like it.

'If you lean over any further, you will fall,' Jamil said. 'Come down and tell me how you have been getting on with my daughter.'

His daughter. Of course, that's what he'd come to talk about. He wasn't interested in her. She had imagined the glint of smouldering desire in his expression. Reality broke into her fantasy of playing Juliet or Rapunzel, of Jamil mounting the tower—without using the stairs, of course—to come to her rescue. His daughter was his only concern. And should be *her* only concern!

Jamil watched her descend the lower, exposed staircase. He had forgotten how gracefully she carried herself, the way she seemed to glide rather than walk. He had forgotten that certain something about her which exuded sensuality, that certain something of which she seemed entirely unaware, and of which his own body was only too conscious. As she approached him across the courtyard, her progress marked by the silken rustle of her gown, his manhood stirred. He had thought absence would eliminate this inconvenient attraction, but it only seemed to have enhanced it.

Cassie curtsied. 'I trust the business that took you away from us was successfully concluded?'

'Eventually. I had not meant to be detained for so long.'

As he turned towards the cushions that lay in their habitual place scattered around the sun fountain, holding out his hand to allow her to precede him, Cassie noticed the scar, a long vicious slash running from his wrist to the inside of his elbow, angrily red, held together by some rather fearsome-looking stitches. 'Your arm! What on earth happened?'

'It's nothing. A skirmish on the border, a band of opportunistic brigands.'

'You fought them yourself? Did not your guards…?'

Jamil smiled, his real smile, the one that made her heart turn cartwheels. 'You think me incapable of defending myself against a few cutthroats?'

'I think you capable of taking on an entire army of cutthroats if you choose,' Cassie said frankly, 'I am just surprised that your guards allowed the men to get near you.'

'I was alone. I could not sleep, and had left the caravan behind.'

'Good God, Jamil, you should have more of a care. How many were there?'

'Four.'

It was hard not be impressed—he must be as fierce a warrior as his physical attributes suggested. But to have placed himself in such danger! 'You could have been killed.'

'But as you see, I am perfectly unharmed.'

'If you can call that unharmed,' Cassie replied tartly, pointing to the wound. 'Is it painful?'

'Not really.'

'Which means it is. Sit down, let me look at it.' In her concern, Cassie had once more forgotten all about the rules of propriety. She pushed Jamil on to the cushions and knelt before him, scrutinising his arm carefully. 'It looks angry, the skin is pulling where it has been stitched, but it's not infected,' she said finally. 'I have some lavender oil, it will take away the inflammation.'

She hurried off to retrieve the bottle from her dressing case, and knelt before Jamil again, dabbing the oil carefully on the scar, frowning with concentration as she bent over him. 'There.' She sat back to admire her handiwork, holding his arm in her lap, so intent upon her task that she did not notice his expression until she looked up. 'What is it?'

'You seem very knowledgeable.'

'Only a little. Mama was interested in healing herbs and plants, and when she died, she left me her recipe book—well, actually, she didn't quite leave me it, I sort of took it,' Cassie admitted, 'as something to remember her by. I made this oil myself, it's perfectly safe.'

Male eyes the burnished colour of an English autumn met female eyes the colour of turquoise. Jamil turned his injured arm over to clasp her fingers. Her knees were pressing into his thigh through her dress. He could see the rise and fall of her breasts through the lace that covered them. The material was pale blue, embroidered with tiny white flowers. The same tiny white flowers decorated the ruffle of lace at her arm.

She smelled of lavender and something else he couldn't name. Floral and heady. 'Thank you,' Jamil said again, lifting her hand to his mouth and pressing a kiss on the fragile pulse of her wrist. He felt it flutter under his lips. He heard the soft intake of her breath. Then he remembered.

Governess, governess, governess. It should not be so difficult to remember! He dropped her hand as casually as he could manage and sat back on the cushions, adjusting his position to put a little distance between them. 'Tell me about Linah.'

Cassie struggled to assemble her thoughts, which seemed to have scattered like dandelion clocks in the breeze. She tugged her skirts over her bare toes, trying to put from her mind the romantic picture they made, the two of them, sitting under the stars by the tinkling fountain, she and the desert prince.

Not the desert prince. Linah's father. Her employer. Who wanted to know about his daughter. That was all. That was absolutely all. 'Linah. Linah is—she and I are—I think we're making progress.'

She started to tell him, haltingly, of her trials and tribulations, of the breakthroughs and the setbacks, the small triumphs and the still-regular defeats. Tempting as it was to exaggerate her success, she knew better than to lie, remembering quite clearly Jamil's detestation of prevarication. 'She is learning to trust me a little, but it is early days yet. Linah is still testing the limits of her powers.'

'You mean she is still ungovernable.'

His voice contained not anger, but resignation. He thought she was failing. He had expected her to fail!

Cassie clenched her fists determinedly. 'Not at all, but Linah is a very clever little girl. All her experience has taught her that such strategies as she employs—'

'Such as?'

'Well, her temper tantrums. And her refusal to co-operate. And her hiding behind those maidservants of hers. And the practical jokes, of course.'

'Practical jokes?'

'Your daughter has an affinity with wildlife.'

'You will explain, if you please?'

'Mice, snakes and a whole host of other creatures I'm afraid I don't even recognise. Linah seems to be able to tame them, or mesmerise them in some way, it's really quite amazing. Then she puts them where they should not be—you know, divans, chests, cupboards. She put a toad in the tea samovar. Really, one has to give her credit for being inventive.'

'And cruel.'

'She's not cruel—or rather, she is but doesn't realise it, and once she realised that I was not alarmed—'

'Not alarmed?'

'Truly, Jamil, it didn't bother me at all. I was brought up in the English countryside where wildlife abounds. My sisters, you see, were wont to do much the same sort of thing to Celia and me when they were being naughty. I explained to Linah that she was frightening the poor creatures more than me, and she stopped.'

'Explained?' Jamil said ominously. 'You should have punished her for her actions. By failing to demonstrate your authority, you are showing weakness. She will exploit that, one way or another, if not now, then later.'

'She is not my enemy, Jamil. It was punishment

enough for her to know that she had caused distress without realising it,' Cassie explained patiently. 'And as I said, she hasn't done it since.'

'Can you be certain these unorthodox methods of yours will work?'

'Not entirely, not yet.' Cassie looked up from the intricate pattern she'd been weaving with her fingers in her lap. 'She is only eight, Jamil.'

'Old enough to understand right from wrong. Old enough to exert some control over her temper.'

'You expect too much. At her age, I am willing to bet you had a considerable temper.'

'By her age, I had already learned how to control it.' *Or to suffer the consequences.*

'At eight!' Cassie exclaimed. 'I don't believe it. Why, you must be at least twenty-eight now, and I have seen you lose your temper several times.'

She was smiling, meaning only to tease, but Jamil's lips thinned. It was true, Cassie seemed to bring out extremes in him that he had not thought himself capable of, but it was not anything of which he was proud. 'It may surprise you to know that I rarely lose my temper,' he said curtly. 'In fact, the *only* time I have lost it has been in your company. And that is not a compliment.'

'I didn't take it as such. Why are you so touchy? All I meant to say was that, as a little boy, you probably had just as many tantrums as Linah, only you don't remember.'

'You are quite mistaken,' Jamil said with an air of finality.

She opened her mouth to contradict him, saw the implacable look on his face, and something darker in his eyes, which gave her pause. He had not been a happy child, that much was obvious. She decided, wisely for once, to change the subject. 'I've been thinking, it would be a good thing for Linah to have more company her own age. She's lonely, she doesn't seem to have any friends. Children need the stimulation of others.'

'That is why she has you.'

'It's not the same. Surely you are not so old that you cannot remember what it was like to play with your friends?'

'I did not have any friends,' Jamil said starkly.

Cassie's mouth dropped open. 'What? Don't be silly, you must have. At school, and—'

'I did not go to school. It is the tradition with princes of the royal blood in Daar-el-Abbah to be kept in isolation so that others may not witness their early mistakes, their growing pains. That is why our motto is *Invincible.*'

'That must be hard to live up to.'

'A prince is the ultimate role model for his people; his behaviour must be beyond reproach.'

'But you are human, for goodness' sake, you're not flawless. No one is. I would have thought your people would see a few signs of mortality as a good thing.'

'You know nothing of the matter. That is not our way.'

Cassie stared at his bleak profile in astonishment. He had not be exaggerating, then, when he said he had no friends as a child. The isolation he mentioned, it was the literal truth. Aghast at the very idea of such an upbringing, she also felt an immense pity for the lonely little boy Jamil must have been. No wonder he had no idea about how to treat his own daughter. 'Is that what you wish for Linah,' she asked, trying desperately to keep the emotion she felt from welling up into her voice, 'to be raised in isolation, to be chastised when she shows any signs of normal, everyday emotion—what you call weakness?'

Jamil stared off into the distance, giving no sign that he had heard her. 'Jamil? Is that what you want?' Cassie demanded, in her anxiety to get through to him, once again forgetting all about restraint. 'Do you want your daughter to become just like you—cold-hearted and apparently incapable of showing affection even for her own children? Well? It's not right and it's not fair, Jamil. She may be a princess, but she's also a little girl.'

At some point in her last speech, Cassie had grabbed Jamil's sleeve in an effort to make him listen. At some point in her speech, it had worked. He was no longer staring off into the distance, but right at her, and he did not look happy. She tilted her chin defiantly.

Jamil carefully detached her hand from his arm. 'Once again,' he said stiffly, 'you overstep the mark. You talk about things which you have no understanding of. *None!*'

She flinched at the vicious tone in his voice, but refused to give ground. 'Linah—'

'Linah will not endure what I did. I will not inflict such a regime on her, but—and you will listen most carefully here, Lady Cassandra, for I do not wish to have to repeat myself again—she is of the royal blood, and though as a woman she is not required to be seen as invincible, her behaviour must be superior to all others.

She must learn to take control of her emotions. Do you understand me?'

'Yes, but she will learn how to do so much more easily if the discipline is inflicted by her peers. Little girls can be quite ruthless, you know, far more so than boys. If Linah misbehaves among her friends, she will be ostracised. She will learn quickly enough that she cannot do as she pleases.' Seeing that Jamil was struck by this, Cassie pushed home her advantage. 'As a princess, she must learn not just discipline, but kindness. Surely you agree she will be a better princess for having some understanding of her subjects?'

'I don't know. It is not the custom.'

'You keep saying that, but traditions are only traditions for as long as they are maintained. You are the prince; if you wish to change something, you can do so. Set your own traditions.'

Jamil's expressions softened into one of his near smiles. 'My Council—'

'You said yourself, your Council need to be brought into the nineteenth century,' Cassie pointed out quickly. 'Or at least,' she amended conscientiously, 'I think that is what you meant.'

Jamil's smile widened. 'I see now that you are indeed Lord Henry Armstrong's daughter.'

'I will take that as a compliment,' Cassie replied with one of her irrepressible smiles. 'A compliment from you is as rare an event as a rainy day in the desert. I shall cherish it. But seriously, will you think about it, Jamil. Please? For Linah's sake? You know it—'

'What I know, Cassie, is that a wise strategist knows when to retreat as well as when to advance,'

Jamil interrupted. 'Your point is well made and I will reflect on it, but you should stop now, before you lose the advantage you have gained.'

She did so most reluctantly as she had still not broached the subject of Jamil's contact with his daughter. Proud of her restraint, for it did not come at all naturally to her, Cassie nodded, fastening her lips together primly.

'I can see that you are making a significant effort on my behalf,' Jamil said, trying very hard not to laugh. Another thing he had forgotten about this beguiling creature was her more endearing qualities. She had the ability to throw him from one extreme to the other, in a way no one else could. Not that he was endeared. Just tired.

He had been away too long. The increasing demands of his kingdom were a sign of successful expansion, yet he did not feel rewarded. Halim had been appalled by the brigand attack just as much as Cassie, but for quite different reasons. Infallibility again. The shedding of blood was evidence of mortality. Halim feared for the prince, but Cassie feared for the man. No one else, it seemed to him, saw him in that way. Cared for him in that way.

'You have everything you need here?' he asked brusquely, getting to his feet.

'Yes, thank you. Linah's schoolroom is exceedingly well equipped.'

'I did not ask about Linah, I asked about you.' Jamil reached out his hand to pull Cassie up beside him. Instead of letting her go, he pulled her to him, the better to scrutinise her face. 'You look tired.' His eyes narrowed. 'Have you been crying?'

'No, I—it was nothing.'

'What have you not told me? If you are trying to protect Linah, let me tell you that—'

'No, Linah is not the cause, not really. I'm just feeling a bit sorry for myself, that's all.'

'You are unhappy here?'

'No, not unhappy but—well, being cooped up here all day, it can be a bit stifling,' Cassie replied with an apologetic look.

Jamil frowned. 'I should have thought about it before. Of course you are used to having a little more freedom. Would you like to ride?'

'Camels?'

Cassie's expression of dismay was so comical, Jamil could not restrain a bark of laughter. 'No, horses.'

He had a nice laugh, deep and infectious, extremely masculine. Cassie smiled back. Exercise, she realised, was what she needed to blow away the blue megrims, and maybe it would do Linah good, too. 'That would be wonderful. Does Linah ride?'

'It is considered improper for women here, unless they are led.'

'You are a prince—are not traditions yours to make or break as you wish?'

'Or as you wish? You tread a fine line, Lady Cassandra.'

The tone in his voice pulled her up sharply. Cassie's face fell. She dropped her eyes. 'I beg your pardon, Highness. I would not wish to place you in a difficult position. If it would cause too much offence…'

'As you point out, I am the prince,' Jamil said sardonically. 'I will arrange it, but it must be tactfully done. You may ride, and Linah, too, but you will need an escort.'

'I'm perfectly capable of looking after Linah and myself.'

'I am not talking about your riding skills, Lady Cassandra, I'm talking about your safety. There are those who will be offended by your embracing such freedom. You must promise me never to go out without an escort.'

'Yes. Very well, but...' Catching Jamil's ominous expression, Cassie caught her words just in time. 'I promise.'

'We will begin tomorrow morning. I will accompany you personally.'

'You! I assumed you meant a guard, or a groom.'

'When I am satisfied there is no risk. For the moment, I will personally supervise these excursions.'

If she was delighted, it was for Linah's sake. If she was already looking forward to it, that was for her also. Absolutely it was. 'Thank you,' Cassie said warmly, 'Linah will be thrilled.'

His proximity was making her blush. His almost palpable maleness accentuated her awareness of her own femininity. She should say goodnight now. Drop a curtsy to release herself from his hold and say goodnight, because if she did not...

'Goodnight, Lady Cassandra.' Jamil released her and walked off across the courtyard, his feet padding soundlessly on the tiles. The huge door swung inwards.

He was gone, in a flutter of white robes, before Cassie could reply, or even decide if she was relieved or not.

The prospect of a riding lesson in the company of her father sent Linah into paroxysms of excitement. She could barely be persuaded to eat, gulping down a mango sherbet and some pineapple, dancing anxiously from foot to foot while Cassie rummaged among her copious wardrobe for something suitable to wear. Terrified lest she be left behind, Linah insisted on watching while Cassie made her own *toilette*, laughing at Linah's fascinated inspection of her stays, stockings and boots.

The riding lesson went well, with Linah cowed into her best behaviour by her father's presence. Her natural affinity with animals allowed her to form an instant bond with the sprightly little pony Jamil had picked out for her. Cassie's own mount was a thoroughbred Arabian dappled grey mare, a flighty, highly strung beast that tried to throw her the minute she sat in the saddle. The mare reared up on her hind legs, and when this failed, spun round in tight circles before attempting to rear up again. Cassie, however, had had enough, and reined her in sharply, leaning over to whisper soothing words into her ear the minute she was under control. Jamil, watching with an open-mouthed Linah, was more impressed than he cared to admit. He had known her to be more than competent, and would not have seated her on the grey had he doubted her ability, but still, the grace with which she held her saddle, the way she gave her mount its head before reining it in, evidenced a horsewoman of rare ability.

'That was amazing, was it not, *Baba*?' Linah said,

her admiration for her most unusual governess rousing her from her shyness.

Jamil looked at his daughter in surprise. She had not called him *Baba* since she was a small child. His own father had banned the term. *I am a father to all my people, not just you*, Jamil remembered being told pointedly. 'Amazing, but rather ostentatious,' he agreed curtly, watching the light fade from Linah's eyes, ignoring the tight feeling in his chest, telling himself it was for her own good.

They rode out through the city gates, with Linah on a leading rein, to a sandy paddock enclosed by tall cypress trees. Tethering his horse, Jamil watched while Cassie taught her the rudiments of walking and trotting. His daughter was awkward at first, glancing over each time she made a mistake. Realising that he was making her nervous, Jamil removed himself from her sight. Watching from the cover of one of the trees, he saw her grow in confidence, soon able to attempt a trot round the paddock on her own.

'Did she not do well?' Cassie said, beaming at her charge, when they rejoined him back at the stables.

'She shows some ability,' Jamil agreed stiffly. He watched Linah's face fall, saw Cassie frown at him in vexation, and told himself once more that it was for the best, but still he felt unaccountably guilty.

'Thank your father for most graciously giving up his time,' Cassie said to Linah, 'for if you do not, he will think his presence unnecessary, and will not come again.'

'Oh, no, *Baba*, I would not like you to think that. Please will you come again tomorrow?'

'Affairs of state permitting. Fakir will show you how to rub down your pony,' Jamil said, nodding at his head groom. 'You must learn to take care of your horse if you are to become a real horsewoman.' When Cassie made to dismount in order to help, however, he shook his head. 'That mare of yours is still fresh, we'll go for a gallop before the sun is too high.'

Surprised and delighted at the opportunity to put such a beautiful animal through its paces, Cassie waited only until they were back out of the city gates to release her hold. The grey mare needed no urging, flying across the sand with Jamil, mounted on a magnificent black stallion, in hot pursuit.

They rode together again the following day, after Linah's lesson, and the next and the next. Away from the confines of the palace, Jamil was a different person. Not just more at ease in the wide, untrammelled space of his desert, but more approachable, too. They found they shared a passion for the natural world, and Cassie's obvious enthusiasm for the harshly vibrant beauty of the desert, so different from the soft green landscape of England, encouraged Jamil into increasingly ambitious expeditions in search of rare plants or obscure species. The time flew by with a speed that surprised them both. Several times Jamil had returned to the palace to find Halim in a lather of worry at his having kept some merchant or visiting dignitary waiting.

Halim did not approve of his prince taking time out from his formal schedule, not even if he did return looking refreshed. Especially, Halim did not approve of Jamil spending that time in the company of his daughter's English governess, though he was far too circumspect to give voice to such thoughts. People were talking. Such talk would end when Prince Jamil's betrothal to the Princess Adira was made public, so Halim devoted his energy to the arrangements for the ceremony. If they were watertight, this time the prince could not escape them. He would be wed and then life for Halim, and the whole of Daar-el-Abbah, would continue as it had always done.

Chapter Five

Cassie woke every morning looking forward to the coming day. Gone was her homesickness, banished were her doubts. Linah flourished under the combined regime of physical and mental exercise, her natural intelligence and surprisingly wry sense of humour were beginning to emerge. While she still shied away from any physical signs of affection, she had twice now allowed herself to be cuddled when waking from a nightmare, and once slipped her little hand into Cassie's on the journey to the stables. The tantrums had abated dramatically. The sulks were not gone, but had become rare. Her behaviour was improving, definitely improving with every passing day.

Though she was not aware of it, for she rarely bothered these days with her looking glass, Cassie, too, was improving every day. Her skin glowed with vitality, tinged with the sun, rosy with health. Her eyes sparkled, the azure of a summer sea with the sun glinting upon it. She walked with a lighter step. She hummed to herself when sitting sewing in the shade of the lemon tree. She was happy.

She was happy because she was making a difference to Linah. She was happy because she was doing something positive. She was happy because Jamil was pleased with her efforts. She was happy because in Jamil, the man she had come to know, if not yet fully understand, she felt she had found that rare thing—a true friend. The thought made her smile, for Jamil would have scorned it—had he not said that he did not want or need friends? But that made her smile all the more. Of course they were friends. What else could it be, this empathy that had grown up between them, the ease with which they talked, disputed, laughed, the way sometimes they did not even need to do that, content merely to be in each other's company?

'Friends.' She said the word aloud, as if tasting it, and again, this time more assertively. They could not be anything else. She did not wish it. He did not think of it. At least…

Sometimes, when they were alone in the desert, she caught him looking at her. Sometimes, she looked at him just like that, she suspected. Hungrily. Imagining. Trying not to imagine. Remembering. Trying not to remember. When their hands met accidentally, something akin to a shock surged through her, making her awkward, aware of something not right, something too right. She thought about that kiss in those moments. His lips on hers. His arms around her. She thought about it, then she banished it.

She banished it now, forcing her mind to focus on

her one other concern. Though she and Jamil might be friends, Jamil and Linah were not. Though his attitude towards his daughter had softened, and he showed a real interest in her progress, Jamil seemed to be incapable of showing her any sign of affection. He spoke to his daughter as to an adult. He was a perfectionist, and there was nothing at all wrong with that, save that he praised so rarely and criticised so frequently. Could he not see that the child worshipped the ground he walked on? That one sign of affection would make an enormous difference to her confidence? Tough as his own upbringing must have been, from the very little he had let fall about it, surely there must have been some tender moments for him to recall?

Casting aside her sewing, a sampler she had been making for Linah, Cassie got to her feet. It was mid-afternoon, the hottest part of the day, when everyone took respite in the cool of their rooms, but she was restless. The Scheherazade courtyard was eerily quiet. Looking for a distraction, she remembered that Linah had once mentioned gardens on the eastern side of the palace, old gardens gone to ruin. The idea of a secret wilderness, a neglected and forgotten hideaway, appealed strongly to the romantic side of Cassie's nature. Opening the huge door that led to the corridor, nodding in a friendly way to the guards, she set off in search of it.

Jamil could not concentrate on the papers before him. The complicated series of commercial transactions began with the trading of Daar-el-Abbah's diamonds upon the lucrative Dutch market and ended with the import of some of the new spinning equipment from the British cotton mills. Bills of lading, interest calculations, net costs, gross costs, profit and conversions from one currency to another danced before his eyes. The end result was positive. It always was.

Jamil rolled his shoulders in an attempt to ease the tension there. This morning he and Cassie had ridden out to a nearby oasis with Linah, his daughter permitted for the first time to handle her pony without the leading string. She'd done well, sitting straight-backed and riding light-handed, in an excellent imitation of her teacher. He'd been proud of her, but though he formed the words of praise, he could not speak them. Cassie had been unable to hide her disappointment; he saw it in the downturn of her mouth, in the tiny frown instantly smoothed between her fair brows.

Jamil cursed softly under his breath. He would not let this woman's disapproval dictate his actions. He had learned the hard way just how important it was not to let anyone know what he was feeling—that he even had feelings—for feelings could be exploited. They were a weakness. For her own good, Linah should be taught the same lesson.

But, increasingly, he found it hard not to show just the sort of weakness his father had been so keen to eradicate. It had been easier, when Linah was not so often in his company. Now, with his daughter's endearing personality imprinting itself upon him every day, thanks to Cassie, it was proving difficult to maintain the barriers that had been so hard built. Sometimes he felt as if Cassie was determined to remove them brick by brick. To expose him. Sometimes he appalled himself by wanting to help her.

Abandoning his papers, Jamil got to his feet and wandered out into the courtyard. The heat was stifling. Even the ever-industrious Halim had retired for the afternoon. In search of distraction, he found himself wandering in the direction of the schoolroom, only to be informed by the guards that Cassie had left, half an hour before. It was not like her to go off unchaperoned like that. Slightly concerned, Jamil set off in search, tracing her meandering path through the endless corridors of the palace by way of the various sets of guards she had passed.

The trail went cold at the entrance to the east wing, where he paused, his frown deepening. The large oak door with its heavy iron grille was closed. There was no reason to think she would have opened it, save the fact that he knew there was no other way for her to have gone without being noticed. No guard stood at this door. No one, to Jamil's knowledge, had passed beyond the door for years. Eight years. Eight years, six months and three days to be precise. Since the day Jamil had come to the throne of Daar-el-Abbah, exactly one week after his father had died.

Just looking at the implacable door made Jamil's heart pound as if his blood were thick and heavy. There was no reason for Cassie to have entered the courtyard. No reason for him to have expressly forbidden it, either. He had locked the memories away long since. But now, looking through the grille to the dusty ante-room beyond, he knew that was exactly what she had done.

He didn't want to go in there. He really, really didn't want to. But he didn't want Cassie there, either. His palms sweating, his fingers shaking, Jamil opened the door and stepped in, back, over the threshold of his adulthood into the dark recesses of his childhood.

She'd found the door after following many false trails and dead ends. She'd known it must be the one, from the rusty look of the key. That there had been a key in the lock at all surprised her. That it turned, gratingly and reluctantly, had excited her, but then she stepped inside and the overpowering air of melancholy descended like a thick black cloak.

It was a beautiful place, a completely circular courtyard with a dried-up fountain, the marble cracked and stained, the ubiquitous lemon trees grown huge and wild, jasmine and something that looked very like clematis, but could not be, flowering with wild abandon around the courtyard's colonnaded terrace. Dried leaves covered the mosaic floor. She heard the unmistakable scuttling of small creatures as she crossed it slowly. The fountain's centrepiece, which she had at first thought to be a lion cub, she now realised must be a baby panther. She had not seen the panther fountain in Jamil's private courtyard, but he had once described it to her, mockingly. This must be its counterpart, which meant that this must be the rooms of the young Crown Prince Jamil, shut up and left to crumble into ruin, as if he had turned his back not only on his childhood, but his past.

Cassie shuddered. The stark contrast of the dull tiles, the weeds that grew between the cracks in the floor, the general air of sullen neglect, with the rest of the pristinely cared for palace, was unbearable. Sensitive as she was to ambiance, she could almost taste the ache of unhappiness in the air. Wandering over to another solid-looking door, she peered through the grille and caught a glimpse of the secret garden. Far from the pretty wilderness she had imagined, this one was barren, arid, with skeletal trees, the bark shed in layers like skin, with thickets of some barbarous thorny shrub covering the entire ground area, like a spiky, mottled carpet.

She should not be here. It was too private a place, too redolent with intimate memories. Instinctively, she knew that Jamil would be mortified by her presence. Yet instinctively, too, she felt that here lay the key to his relationship—or lack of it—with his daughter. If she could find it—if she could understand—then surely...

Holding the hem of her gown clear of the detritus that covered the courtyard floor, Cassie picked her way carefully to the doorway of the apartments. Like all the palace suites, they followed the shape of the courtyard, a series of rooms opening out, one on to the other. The divans had been abandoned, their rich coverings simply left to rot. Lace, velvet, silk and organdie lay in tatters. The mirrored tiles of the bathing room were blistered, the huge white bath, sunk into the floor, yellowed and cracked. She found a silver samovar with a handle in the shape of an asp, tarnished and bent. A notebook, the pages filled with a neat, tiny hand in Arabic, which stopped abruptly half-way down one page. When she picked it up, the spine cracked, the cover page separated.

Careless now of her gown, overcome with the

melancholy of the place, Cassie wandered into the last room. A sleeping divan, the curtains collapsed on the bed. An intricately carved chest. On the wall above it, hanging on a hook, what looked like an ornamental riding crop. She took it down, admiring the chased-silver handle decorated with what looked like emeralds. Obviously ceremonial. How had it come to be left here?

'What in the name of all the gods do you think you're doing? Put that down immediately.'

Cassie jumped. The riding crop fell to the ground with a clatter. Jamil kicked it under the carved chest. His face looked thunderous, brows drawn in a straight line, meeting across his nose, his mouth thinned, the planes of his cheekbones standing out sharply, like the rugged contours of the desert mountains.

'Well?'

'I thought—I heard about a secret garden. I wanted to see it.'

'Well, now you have, so you can leave.'

His eyes blazed with anger, though his tone was icy cold. She was afraid. Not of him, but of the pain she could see etched into his handsome countenance. 'Jamil…'

'You should not have come here.'

His tone was bleak, his eyes echoing his mood. She could see the tension in the set of his shoulders, in the tightness of his voice. 'They were yours, these rooms, weren't they?' Cassie asked softly.

'These are the traditional apartments of the crown prince. Mine. Before me, my father's. And before him, my grandfather's.'

'So this is one tradition you definitely intend to break with?'

'What do you mean?'

'You obviously don't intend any son of yours to stay here, or else you would not have allowed the place to fall into such decline,' Cassie said, with a sweeping gesture towards the derelict courtyard.

'If—*when*—I have a son, he will have—he will be given...' Jamil faltered, swallowing hard. 'No.' He shook his head, shading his eyes with his hands. 'No. As you say, this is one tradition that ends with me.'

'I'm glad.' Cassie laid a hand tentatively upon his arm. 'This is not a happy place, I can tell.'

'No,' Jamil replied with a grim look, 'happiness was a commodity in short supply here.' The hand he used to run his fingers through his auburn hair was trembling. 'Discipline, honour, strength—they are what matter.'

'Infallibility.'

'Invincibility. My motto. My fate.' His shoulders slumped. He sank down on to the lid of the chest suddenly, as if his legs would no longer support him. 'Here is where I was taught it. A hard lesson, but one I have not forgotten.' He dropped his head into his hands.

Jamil was a man who had until now appeared as invulnerable as a citadel, with all the power of an invincible army. Seeing him so raw, so exposed, all Cassie yearned to do was to comfort and to heal. Careless of all else, she crouched down and cradled his head, smoothing the ruffled peaks of his hair back into a sleek cap, stroking the cords of tension in his neck, the knotted sinews of his shoulders, his spine. Jamil stilled, but did not move. She drew him closer, wrapping her arms around him, oblivious of the awkwardness of her own cramping limbs, thinking only somehow to ease the hurt, the deep-buried hurt that clung to him now like a dark aura.

She whispered soothing nothings and she held him close, closer, pressing tiny fluttering kisses of comfort on to the top of his head, enveloping his hard, tense lines with her softness. They stayed thus for a long time, until gradually she felt him relax, until he moved his head, and she realised, almost at the same time as he did, that it was nestled against her breasts. She became conscious of his body not as something to be comforted, but as something to be desired. Her own body responded alarmingly, heating, her nipples hardening. He stirred in her arms and she released him, blushing, looking away, concentrating on standing up, shaking out the leaves and twigs and dirt from her skirts.

'I must apologise,' Jamil said, rising slowly to his feet.

'There is no need,' Cassie said quickly.

'A moment of weakness. I would be obliged if you would forget you witnessed it.'

Cassie chewed on her lip, knowing that further probing might well anger him. 'Jamil, it is not weakness to admit to having been unhappy—rather the opposite.'

'What do you mean?'

'Something horrible happened here, I can sense it.' She shuddered, clasping her arms around herself. 'Don't you see that by refusing to acknowledge it, you are granting whatever it is the victory of silence?' She clutched at his sleeve to prevent him from turning away.

'You exaggerate. As usual.'

'No. No, I don't. Jamil, listen to me, please.' She gazed desperately up into his face, but the shutters were firmly back in place. 'Why can you not tell Linah how you feel about her?'

The directness of the question took him by surprise. Jamil raised a haughty eyebrow.

'I know you care for her,' Cassie continued recklessly. 'I know that you're proud of her, but you can't bring yourself to tell her. Why not?'

Jamil pulled himself free. '*Show thine enemy a heart, and you hand them the key to your kingdom.* My father taught me that lesson here in this very room with the aid of a very persuasive assistant,' he said fiercely, stooping to retrieve the riding crop from under the chest.

'He beat you! My God! I thought that thing was ceremonial.'

Jamil's laughter was like a crack from the whip he held. 'In that you are correct. The ceremony of beating the weaknesses out of the crown prince was one that took place on a regular basis.'

Cassie's face was ashen. 'But why?'

'To teach me to conquer pain. To ensure that I understood extreme emotions well enough to abandon them. To make me what Daar-el-Abbah requires, an invincible leader who relies upon no-one else.'

'There is no such thing,' Cassie said passionately. 'You are a man, not a god, no matter what your father thought, no matter what your people think. Everyone needs someone. For heaven's sake, Jamil, that is absolutely ridiculous. You are a man, and you have feelings, you can't pretend they don't exist.' Even as she spoke the words, Cassie realised that that was exactly what Jamil did. The appalling nature of his upbringing struck her afresh. Her fury at Jamil's father knew no bounds. 'What about your mother? Where was she when this was happening?'

'I was not permitted to see her, save on ceremonial occasions, once I was established here.'

'That's what you meant about losing her at an early age?'

Jamil nodded.

'What age, precisely?'

'Five.'

Cassie's mouth fell open. 'That's barbaric!'

'Unfamiliar customs often seem barbaric. We are an ancient civilisation, much older than yours.' Cassie's utter horror was written plain on her face, making Jamil deeply uncomfortable. Having locked up these rooms, he had persuaded himself he had also locked away what had happened here. Only in moments of weakness, in the dark of night, did the memories intrude, scurrying out from the crevices of his mind, like scorpions in the desert after dark, to sting him. He dealt with them as his father had taught him to deal with any weakness, by ruthlessly suppressing them. Now, seeing his childhood experiences through Cassie's eyes, he felt cornered. He had endured, but never questioned. What he had been taught here formed the foundations of his entire life. He did not want to have to scrutinise them. He did not want to even think about whether they were wrong. 'It is the way of things here,' he said, annoyed to find that his voice contained just a hint of defensiveness, even more annoyed to find himself wondering whether Cassie might have a point.

'Well, if the result of your traditions is a long line of cold, unfeeling, *invincible* rulers like you,' Cassie responded heatedly, 'then I'm glad I'm not part of it. And I'll tell you something, Jamil, I think deep in your heart, you don't want to be part of it either.'

'You know nothing about—'

'You've already admitted you won't be treating your son in the same way,' Cassie interrupted ruthlessly, desperate to find a way to get through to the man she now realised was barricaded up inside a coat of armour forged from pain and suffering. 'You told me that you wanted things to be different for Linah, too. You want a different life for your children, you're even prepared to face the wrath of your Council to provide it, but can't you see the place you need to start is with yourself? Jamil, your father was so wrong.' Her eyes were wide with unshed tears. 'To care is not a weakness, it's a strength. To stand alone, to say you don't need anyone, that's simply a lie. Everyone needs someone to love, everyone needs someone to love them, don't you see that?'

'Your love for your poet—did that strengthen you or weaken you?' Jamil asked coldly. It was a cruel remark, he knew that, but he was hurting.

Cassie flinched. 'I did not love Augustus.' Not at all, she realised suddenly. She had been in love with the idea of love only.

'You told me yourself, the first time that we met, that what you felt was humiliation as a result of this so-called love.'

He was just lashing out, she knew that. This place held such awful memories for him, it would be a miracle if he did not. And what he said was true, after all, even if it was said to divert her. To divert him. Cassie laced her fingers together, then unlaced them. Then laced them again, frowning hard. 'You're right, I did feel humiliated,' she admitted, 'but not by being in love, by being so mistaken. I was humiliated and ashamed of my stupidity, my wilfulness.'

She stared at him hopelessly. An immense pity for the lonely boy he had been, for the solitary man he had been forced to become, washed over her. How to get through to him, she had no idea, especially since he seemed intent on preventing her. This was a pivotal moment, she felt it. If she did not make him see now, he never would. 'You are missing out on so much by denying yourself.'

'You cannot miss what you have never had,' Jamil replied curtly. 'In any case, I am not *denying* myself. I am protecting myself. And my kingdom.'

'By refusing to allow yourself to feel! To love! Do you deny your people such things?'

'Love! Why must you always bring that up? It doesn't exist, save in those pathetic poems you are forever reading.'

Seeing his determinedly set face, Cassie almost despaired. His knuckles were white around the horse whip. A horse whip, for God's sake. His father had trained him in the same way as he trained his thoroughbreds. A flash of rage gave her a surge of strength. She grabbed the riding crop from Jamil and, bending it over her knee, snapped it in two. 'There! That is what I think of your father's methods, and that is what I think of your stupid traditions,' she declared, panting with the exertion. 'Do you really want this thing to dictate your entire life?' She threw it with all her might out into the desolate garden. 'What he did to you was cruel. Disgustingly, horribly cruel, but he is dead now. You are your own man, not your father's. He was wrong, Jamil, wrong. Allow yourself to feel, allow yourself to love, and you will see for yourself how happy it can make you.'

'It did not make you happy,' Jamil retorted pointedly.

'Oh, why must you keep bringing Augustus into everything?' Cassie exclaimed. 'I'm beginning to feel as if I'll never be rid of him.' But at least Jamil was looking at her properly now. He was listening. Cassie took a deep breath. 'When you love someone, really love someone, you can feel it here...' she pressed a hand to her bosom '...or here.' She touched her stomach. 'I've never felt that, I admit it. Few people do, but when they do, they just know. That is the kind of love that makes you strong.'

'That kind of love is a myth.'

'No. No, it's not. It's just rare,' Cassie said, surprising herself now, for it turned out she did believe in love after all. 'But when you find it, as my sister Celia has, it is the greatest source of strength in the world. Far, far greater than the sword, or scimitar or whatever. It's not that you depend upon someone, it's that you have someone else to depend on. Oh, why can't you see that?'

'Perhaps I would give your little flights of fancy more credence if you spoke from a position of experience,'

Jamil replied. 'But since you have already admitted that you do not...' He shrugged.

Cassie gave a rather undignified squeal of frustration. 'You don't have to have experienced something to know it exists, believe it exists! In here!' she exclaimed, pressing her hand to her breast.

Her face was flushed. Her bosom heaved with indignation. A long tress of fiery gold hair had come undone and lay over the white skin of her shoulder, where her dress had slipped. Her eyes sparkled a blue that put turquoises to shame. The maelstrom she had stirred up was suddenly too much for Jamil to cope with. Resorting to one of the few ways he knew of to express himself, he pulled her roughly into his arms, and silenced her in the age-old way, with a passionate, angry, famished kiss.

Cassie struggled only briefly, her hands flailing against his chest in an ineffectual attempt to free herself. It was a kiss meant to punish, she knew that, knew, too, that she had pushed him to his limit. It meant nothing, she told herself, nothing more than a show of strength, but still, the touch of his lips on hers, the lean length of his body held close, but not close enough to the soft yieldingness of hers, was beginning to work its magic. Cassie stopped struggling. Her body seemed to melt into his. Her lips parted. Her skin heated. Her heart began to pound.

It was over too quickly. With a hoarse cry, Jamil pushed her away, glaring at her as if it were her fault. As it was, Cassie could see quite clearly why he would think so. For long moments they simply stared at each other, breathing, lost in a tangled jungle of emotions, unsure about which path to take to regain solid ground. It was Jamil who broke the silence, his voice harsh, edged with something less certain that gave Cassie a tiny cause to hope.

'I will not apologise for that, it was your own fault. Once again, you dare to intrude on matters that do not concern you. You should not have entered here. I wish that you had not. This place...'

'You should reclaim it. Banish the ghosts, take it back. Until you do, it's like a dark secret, brooding away.'

'This place,' Jamil continued, ignoring her interruption, 'is none of your business. I don't want you coming here again and I certainly don't want you bringing Linah here.'

'Of course not. Jamil, you could make Linah so happy if you showed her just a little bit of affection. Loving her could make you happy.'

Jamil sighed heavily. 'You just don't give up, do you?'

Cassie took his hand and pressed it to her cheek. 'It takes courage to change the habits of a lifetime, but courage is something you have in abundance.'

Jamil's smile was twisted. 'I'm not the only one. You have the courage of your convictions.' He kissed her knuckles. 'I'll think about your suggestion.'

'That's all I ask.'

'For the moment, at least,' he said wryly. 'Come, let us leave this place.'

Turning the key in the lock of the outer door, Jamil removed it and secreted it in his robes. Cassie watched him stride down the corridor, his tunic rippling in the slight breeze caused by his rapid gait. Poor, tortured Jamil. If he could but make a start by loving Linah, then maybe some day he would be capable of real love.

Why was that thought making her uncomfortable?

She had an absurd urge to run after him, missing him more with every step he took away from her, a premonition of a time when he would be gone from her for ever. She hadn't thought about that until now. Until today. She didn't want to think about it now.

It would have been naïve to expect that Jamil would be transformed overnight, but from that day on, Cassie did detect a marked difference in him. Awkwardly at first, but with increasing confidence as Linah responded, he began to allow his feelings for his daughter to show. Cassie looked on with a pride she took care to disguise. Knowing that she had been instrumental in effecting this change was enough; she did not want his gratitude, and she most certainly did not want Linah to guess the part she had played. Besides, it was a painful enough process for Jamil to override the years of pain that had beaten his reserve into him. She did not want him worrying about her witnessing his metamorphosis.

She was watching him with Linah one day. Jamil was standing in the middle of a bathing pool, teaching his daughter to swim. He had abandoned his cloak and *igal*, but retained his tunic. The water came up to his waist. Linah, lying supported in his arms, was giggling at something he had said. He looked over at Cassie and smiled. Their eyes met and her heart did a little flip flop. His tunic, damp from Linah's splashing, clung to his body like a second skin, showing off his muscles, the width of his shoulders, the dip of his stomach. His hair was sticking up in endearing spikes. His eyes sparkled with good humour.

Father and daughter together. It was exactly the tableau Cassie had dreamt of creating, but though it was of her making, she felt excluded. Father and daughter. The obvious gap opened up before her like an abyss. They had been playing happy families, the three of them, but she was not really part of it. And yet she wanted to be, she realised. She wanted to be a lot. Because she loved Linah now, too. But mostly because she was in danger, in very real danger, of feeling something she should not feel for Linah's father. And that would be a mistake.

Cassie turned away from Jamil's beckoning smile, busying herself with packing away the lunch things. It was not too late. She had caught herself just in time. It was not too late.

'The Council await you, Highness.'

Jamil looked up from the document he'd been perusing and gazed blankly at his man of business, who was hovering in the open doorway.

'The betrothal contract,' Halim prompted anxiously. 'You rearranged the signing for today. It must be witnessed by the Council, so I took the liberty of organising the gathering. They are ready.'

'The betrothal contract.'

'Yes, Highness. You said—'

'I know what I said. This alliance is advantageous to us, it is to be welcomed.' But Jamil did not want to be married. He did not want to even have to think about marriage, about siring an heir with a female he had absolutely no interest in whatsoever. The idea of it filled him with repugnance. He was sick and tired of having to think about the endless matters of state that obtruded on his day, and sick and tired of having to spend his time resolving them, one problem after another. Sometimes it felt as if he was the only person in the whole kingdom of Daar-el-Abbah capable of making decisions. Jamil rubbed the bridge of his nose with long, elegant fingers. It had always been thus— why was it bothering him so much now?

With some caution, Halim approached the desk behind which his master sat. The prince had been behaving strangely of late, spending much time with his daughter and that English governess of hers. 'You must be heartened by the improvement in your daughter's behaviour,' he said carefully, 'the whole palace is talking about the change in her.' *And the change in Prince Jamil!* 'You will be able to hand over Princess Linah with confidence now.'

'Hand her over?' Jamil looked confused.

Halim laughed nervously. 'Well, you will hardly require the services of the English governess when you are married, Highness. Your daughter will be in the care of your new wife, as is right and proper.'

'Eventually, perhaps, when I am actually married.'

'But with the betrothal papers signed, there will be no reason to delay.'

No reason, save his own reluctance. 'I've only met Princess Adira once, remember.'

Halim beamed. 'And the next time you meet her will be on your wedding night, as is the tradition.'

Jamil thumped his fist down on the desk. 'No!' He pushed his chair back and got to his feet. 'It is time both you and the Council recognised this is the nineteenth century, not the thirteenth. I won't have my wife brought to me painted and veiled like some offering. I am not a prize stud camel, I don't perform to order. And she—Princess Adira—she's barely exchanged two words with me.'

'You are hardly marrying her for her conversational skills,' Halim said with a smirk, 'she will be first wife, not first minister.'

'First and only wife. Therefore it is, even you will admit, preferable that at the very least we do not hold one another in dislike.'

'Indeed, but the Princess Adira—'

'I am sure she has many excellent qualities, but that's not what I'm talking about.'

'What *are* you talking about, Prince Jamil?'

A beautiful face, a pair of turquoise eyes, a coral mouth curved into a welcoming smile.

'Master?'

Someone to depend upon. Someone who would share and not just take. Cassie! The beautiful creature who had created a sanctuary in Linah's apartments where he could be free from the cares of the world. Who saw him not as Prince Jamil, ruler of Daar-el-Abbah, nor as a provider, nor as a peace maker, neither as an enemy nor an ally. Who called him Jamil in that soft husky voice of hers with the quaint English accent. Who saw him as a man, not a prince. Who talked to him as a friend. Whose delicious body and delightful scent and coral-pink mouth haunted his dreams.

It would be pleasant there in the courtyard as dusk began to fall. An oasis of calm and peace, of seclusion from the world, even if it was just an illusion. He would go to her once he had, yet again, done his duty by signing away the little he had left of himself. He would go to her, and she would soothe him just by talking about the mundane details of her day. He would let her voice wash over him, and he would forget about everything else for a few precious moments.

The thought was enough of an incentive to force him into action. 'Very well, let's get this over with.' Jamil grabbed the ceremonial gold-and-emerald cloak that lay waiting on the divan under the window and fastened it around his neck with the ornate emerald pin. The sabre next, then the ring and the head dress and the golden band. He straightened his shoulders and tugged at the heavy belt holding the sabre in place. Then he nodded at Halim, who flung open the door to the prince's private apartments, and clicked his fingers to summon the honorary guard.

Six men, dressed in pristine white, formed up in the corridor behind their ruler. Halim himself picked up the trailing edge of Prince Jamil's cloak, and the party set off for the throne room at a swift pace.

The double doors of the magnificent room were already open in readiness. Two rows of Royal Guards formed a pathway to the dais, their scimitars raised, points touching. Rays from the sinking sun slanted through the high windows and glinted on the polished steel. The waiting Council of Elders made obeisance as Jamil strode by, remaining on their knees, heads bowed, eyes averted, until he ascended the steps to the throne and bowed solemnly in greeting. The contract lay before him on a low table along with a selection of quills and a bottle of ink. Jamil picked up a pen, dipped it in the ink and signed his name, waiting impatiently for Halim to heat the wax before imprinting the seal from his ring.

It was done. His duty was done. He would not think of it now. He would not allow himself to dwell on the consequences. Jamil scattered sand over the wet ink and pushed the document aside. He got to his feet so quickly that he was already halfway back down the length of the throne room before Halim and the Council realised he was going.

'Highness, the celebrations,' Halim shouted after him.

'I am sure you will enjoy them all the more for my absence,' Jamil called over his shoulder. In other circumstances, the startled look on Halim's face would have amused him. Right now, he could not have cared less. Without bothering to change out of his formal robes, Jamil took the now very familiar route to the schoolroom.

Chapter Six

As he had expected, he found Cassie sitting alone by the sun fountain. They ate early here in the schoolroom apartments and the remnants of dinner had already been cleared. Linah would be asleep upstairs, he knew, so familiar was he now with his daughter's routine. With her governess's routine.

She was sitting on the cushions with her book. Her feet were tucked out of sight, but he knew they would be bare. She relished the coolness of the tiles on her toes. He liked to see them peeping out from under the hems of her English dresses. He had not thought feet could be so sensual.

Engrossed in a volume of Mr Wordsworth's poems, Cassie had not noticed the courtyard door opening and did not look up until he was almost by her side. 'Jamil,' she said, closing the book and rising gracefully from the cushions, shaking out the folds of her gown. 'I wasn't expecting you. Linah is in bed.'

'I know.'

He looked different. Not angry but—different. His eyes were stormy. A flush stained his cheek bones. He was looking at her strangely. 'Have you eaten?' she asked. 'I could ring for some food, if you like.'

'I'm not hungry.'

She hovered uncertainly on the edge of the cushions. During the day it was just about possible for her to disguise the pleasure she took in his presence, the attraction to him that she continued to deny, but in the evening, alone with him like this, it was much more difficult. Try as she might, she could not see him as a prince, only as a man. An incredibly attractive man, who, at the moment, looked as if he carried the weight of the world on his shoulders. 'You're wearing your official cloak,' she said. 'Have you come from the Council?'

'Yes.' Jamil tugged at the emerald pin that held the heavy garment in place. He'd forgotten all about it, another heirloom passed on from his father, who had received it from his. It fell with a soft whoosh on to the tiled floor of the courtyard. The priceless emerald pin he dropped with a careless clatter on top of it.

'It will crease if you leave it there,' Cassie said, stooping to retrieve it. 'Let me—'

'Leave it.'

Startled by the harshness of his tone, which she had recently so rarely heard, Cassie did as he bid her. 'Is there something wrong?'

Jamil shrugged. 'Nothing more than usual.'

'Do you want to talk about it?'

'No.'

She could not read his mood. He had his Corsair face, impenetrable and remote. 'I was thinking—wondering—if you had considered what I was saying about Linah. About her having some friends of her own age, I mean. I think she's ready for it now, she hasn't had a tantrum in ages, and it will do her good to have someone other than you and me to talk to.'

'Is she bored with my company already?'

'Of course not, I didn't mean that.' Cassie smiled, but it was a nervous smile, her lips trembling. She sat down on the edge of the fountain and trailed her hand in the cool water, trying to regain control of herself. He looked so careworn, she wanted more than anything to comfort him, but did not know how to start when he was in such a strange mood. She stretched out her hand invitingly. 'Sit with me a while. You don't have to talk, just sit and enjoy the night. Look up, the stars are coming out, they're lovely.'

But Cassie herself made too lovely a picture for Jamil to be interested in the stars. Her dress was made of lemon-yellow silk, with some sort of complicated trimming on the ruffle at the hem. The colour brought out the fiery lights in her hair. The sleeves were shorter than she usually wore during the day, finishing just above her elbow, though a fall of cream lace covered her forearm. There was cream lace at the neckline, too, almost the same colour as her skin. An evening gown, intended to be worn in the formal drawing rooms of London and yet looking perfectly at home here, in the stark wildness of the desert. He could see the roundness of her bosom, rising and falling beneath the creamy lace. He could see one bare foot peeping out, balancing her on the edge of the fountain. He moved towards her, took the hand she was holding out, but didn't sit down. It was a delicate hand, lost in his. Easily crushed. For some reason, this made him angry. He let it go, and regretted it as soon as he had done so, and that made him even more angry.

'Perhaps it is you who are bored with my company,' he said harshly. 'Are you missing your poet, Cassie? Are you missing the simpering compliments and admiring glances of your gaggle of gallants? I warned you that life with Linah meant seclusion.'

Turquoise eyes turned on him, dark with hurt. He hadn't meant to lash out, but he couldn't seem to stop. 'My daughter is a princess of royal blood. She must learn there is a price to be paid for that privilege. And so must you.'

'Jamil, why are you being like this? It's not like you.'

'But you are wrong, Lady Cassandra, it is very like me. You don't really know me at all.'

'I don't agree. In these last few weeks, I think I have come to know you very well.'

'You see only one aspect of me. You know nothing of my life as a ruler.'

'Perhaps, but I know what you are like as—as…'

'As?'

'A man.'

'You think so?'

He took a step closer to her. The air seemed to crackle with tension. Cassie's hand lay so still in the water of the fountain that one of the little golden fish which lived there brushed against it. She couldn't understand how the conversation had taken this turn, nor why it felt so—so…precarious? Precipitous? Was that even a word? Pre-emptive? But of what?

'Tell me, then, what am I like, Cassie. As a man?'

Jamil had taken another step towards her. In fact, he was standing so close to her his knees were brushing her thigh. She could almost feel the anger pulsing from him, and something else burning there behind his tawny eyes that gave her goose bumps. 'Jamil, stop this.'

'Stop what, Cassie?' He pulled her to her feet, holding her there, almost in his embrace, with his hands lightly on her waist. 'Stop pretending that I don't find you attractive? Stop pretending that I don't think of you as I first saw you in the tent in the desert? Stop pretending that I don't remember our kiss? Stop pretending that I don't want to kiss you again? That every time I see you I see only an English governess? Why should I? Was it not you who told me I should acknowledge my feelings?'

'I didn't mean that. Please don't do this.'

'Why?' He pulled her closer. She did not resist, nor did she comply. She dropped her gaze, closed her eyes. He didn't want that. He gave her a tiny shake. 'Look at me, Cassie. Tell me honestly that you don't feel it, too. Tell me that you don't think of these things. Tell me you don't want me and I'll let you be. Only, look at me when you say the words.'

For a long moment she did not move. Then, with a small sigh that could have been resignation, but might have been something quite different, she met his gaze, and all the secret thoughts, the shameful night-time dreams that she bundled up and held securely in the back of her mind during the day, tumbled forth as if the knot that held them had been untied. He knew. He saw it in her eyes. His gaze raked over her, her eyes, her mouth, her breasts, then her mouth again.

He was going to kiss her, unless she stopped him. He was going to kiss her and she couldn't stop him. She wanted him to kiss her again, she had been wanting him to ever since that last unsatisfactory, cut-short kiss, though God knew she had tried not to.

'Cassie.' He pulled her close, his hands tight around her waist, pressing her hard against him. 'Cassie, let us have no more of this pretence.'

She closed her eyes in an effort to try to regain some sort of hold on reality, but it was already too late. Too late for calm, rational thinking. Too late to release herself from his hold. Too late to think about how wrong, how utterly wrong, this would be. It couldn't be wrong, not when it felt like this. Not when she had been wanting this, just this, for weeks now. There was no point in pretending any more that the pleasure she took in his company was for Linah's sake. No point in pretending that the urgent ache consuming her, the thing that held her fast to him, made her lips long to cling to his, was anything other than base desire. He wanted her. Her wilful heart wanted him. 'Yes,' she whispered, not really knowing what she was agreeing to, save only that she was agreeing. 'Yes.'

Jamil hesitated. Lovely, delicious, irresistible as she was, honour and duty dictated resisting. But for once, for just this moment, Jamil had had a surfeit of honour and duty. He wanted the pleasure she could give him and he wanted the oblivion such pleasure would grant him. To be, just for a while, merely a man, not to have to think, lost in the sweet delight of a woman. This woman. He tilted her chin up with his finger. Angled his mouth towards hers. And kissed her.

He kissed her softly, lingering on the soft pillow of her luscious lips, tasting her. She was so sweet. So heady. Like peaches and English strawberries, laced with fire. His kiss deepened. His manhood hardened. Pliant in his embrace, she was soft, lush and ripe for the taking. He kissed her harder.

Cassie moaned softly under the onslaught. Kisses such as she could never have imagined, dark delights such as she could never have dreamed, consumed her. Her body was on fire. His kiss demanded things from her she didn't know how to give, though she wanted to. She wanted to so much. His lips moulded hers into a response she hadn't known she could make. She opened her mouth and his tongue slid in, touching hers, sparking like a shooting star, sending echoing shivers out to the extremities of her body. Her fingers curled into his robe, her toes into the cushions on which she stood. Now she knelt as he eased her down, now she lay as he eased her further, still kissing, kissing, kissing, dark and hot and velvety.

Little kisses on her eyes now, then her throat and her neck. Her hands fluttered over the breadth of his shoulders, feeling the heat of his skin through his tunic. Daringly, she pushed his head dress back, touching his hair, then his cheeks, with their faint traces of stubble.

His lips fastened on hers again and Cassie closed her eyes. His hands traced the line of her waist through the silk of her gown, making her shiver with expectation.

She could feel his legs pressing against hers now. She could feel something building inside her, a knot of something that wanted to unravel. His tongue touched hers again, and she bucked under him. He pressed her back against the cushions, stroking her, her waist, the side of her breast, making her jump again, making her nipples ache in the confines of her chemise, her stays, her dress. Her clothes felt too tight, she felt too hot. His tongue touched hers again. *Should she like it so much?*

She didn't care, she did like it. His hand moulded her breast now, and she liked that, too, though her nipples strained, hard, tingling, exciting. *Should she feel that? Like that? And that?*

She didn't know. All she desired was that he do it again. Fingers brushing her breasts, lingering on the place where her nipples pressed into the fabric. More sparks. More yet as he stroked down, over her belly, her thighs, cupping the roundness of her, as if to show her how different she was, for at the same time her own fingers were boldly exploring his back, his arms, the dip of his stomach, wondering at the sheer delight of male heat and male muscle and male otherness. He was so different. So very, delightfully, different. She felt as if she was melting.

Jamil kissed the mounds of her breasts, but the lace of her dress got in the way. The fastenings were at the back. Complicated fastenings. Too complicated for now. Need, raw need was taking a hold on him. He kissed her with a new urgency. He was hard, more than ready. Still kissing, he found the hem of her dress and pushed it roughly out of the way. Toe. Ankle. Calf. Knee. The skin so soft, the shape so curvaceous. She was panting under him, her hands clutching at his robe, seeking skin. Above her knee was some sort of undergarment. He hadn't expected that. Her thigh beneath the cotton was smooth and creamy. His hand roamed higher, to the apex, and found to his surprise the undergarment was split. Curls. Damp and warm and inviting.

Through the delicious haze of her growing excitement, the words leapt unbidden into Cassie's head, delivered in that familiar clipped, censorious tone. *Remember, child, once a female has abandoned her corsets, there is no saying what else she will abandon.* Aunt Sophia's parting words to her. The effect was instantaneous; the fire of Cassie's passion was extinguished as effectively as if she had been doused in cold water. 'No! Stop!'

Jamil froze.

Cassie began to wriggle free of his intimate embrace. He released her immediately. She pulled her dress down over her legs and sat up, her breath coming fast and shallow. 'I'm sorry—I…'

Jamil got to his feet, tugging his tunic back into place. Sitting before him on the cushions, her hair falling down in long golden tresses over her breast, Cassie looked a picture of abandon. He had never wanted anyone so much in his life, never felt such frustration.

'Jamil, I didn't mean to—I'm sorry.'

But he was in no mood to listen. He was in no mood, either, to question his own motives. 'There is no need to apologise,' he said, gathering up his cloak, his head dress, his emerald pin. 'You have my gratitude, you have spared us an experience we would both ultimately regret,' he said tersely, as he strode off.

The doors closed behind him with a snap. Cassie made no attempt to stand up. Her knees wouldn't hold her. She was appalled. Not at Jamil, but at herself. The liberties she had granted him. The liberties she still wanted to grant him. The wanton way he made her feel, as if to abandon all restraint was her heart's desire. She was mortified. She sank slowly back down on to the floor and covered her head with her hands.

'Ah, Henry, my dear fellow, how the devil are you?' Lord Torquil Fitzgerald strode over to where his old friend was seated alone in the library of Boodle's, enjoying an after-dinner snifter of brandy. 'Haven't seen you for an age.'

'I've been in Lisbon for the last three weeks, at Castlereagh's behest. He has some notion of possible unrest in Portugal.'

'More radicals!' Lord Torquil exclaimed, his eyebrows shooting up alarmingly, making him look like a startled rabbit, and betraying the accuracy of his old Harrovian nickname.

Lord Armstrong had know Bunny Fitzgerald since their schooldays. He shrugged. 'Liverpool is reading conspiracy into everything, since Cato Street. I don't think it will come to anything. Managed to pick up a barrel or two of port while I was out there though, so it wasn't exactly a wasted journey.'

'Heard congratulations are in order, by the way. A son after all this time. You must be mightily relieved.'

'James. A fine boy.' Lord Henry smiled proudly.

'A toast to the whippersnapper, then,' Lord Torquil said, helping himself to another snifter. 'Be nice to have another man around the house, I'll wager. Quite over-run with all those daughters of yours till now. Which reminds me,' he said, thumping his forehead with his glass, 'bumped into Archie Hughes the other day, he was telling me that the fair Cassandra is rusticating.'

Lord Henry's genial expression faded. 'Cassandra is visiting her sister in Arabia. I would hardly call it rusticating.'

'A bad business, that entanglement with the poet. You must have been sick as a dog. Little beauty like that, she'd have gone off well.'

'Cassandra will still go off well enough,' Lord Henry said determinedly. 'When she returns, she will be betrothed to Francis Colchester. It is not quite the brilliant match I had intended, but it will do well enough.'

'Colchester? That the boy who was one of Wellington's protégés? A younger son, I think, but a sound choice. He's predicted to go far. Provided, of course, you can tear her away from that sheikh of hers,' Lord Torquil said with a throaty chuckle.

'Your brain's befuddled as usual, Bunny. *Prince* Ramiz of A'Qadiz is married to my eldest daughter, Celia. Had you forgotten?'

''Course not. Rich as Croesus, has that port in the Red Sea you did the deal on. No, I'm not talking about him. It's another one. Hang on a minute, it'll come to me. Jack—no—Jeremy—no—Jamil! That's it. Sheikh Jamil al-Nazarri. Principality next to A'Qadiz, I believe.'

'I have no idea what you're talking about,' Lord Henry exclaimed. 'What has this to do with Cassandra?'

'Well, I heard it from Archie, who was just back from a stint in Cairo, and he got it from old Wincie himself—though how he knew I'm not sure. But anyway, upshot is that the fair Cassandra is apparently cooped up in this sheikh's harem.'

'What!'

'For God's sake, Henry, keep your wig on, only passing on what I heard. Sorry to have dropped the cat among the pigeons, thought you knew. I'm sure it's all very innocent, though it doesn't look too good, does it?'

'I beg your pardon?'

'Well. Cassandra's a lovely girl. Stuck alone out in the desert with a man who owns all he surveys. *Droit de seigneur,*' Lord Torquil whispered, tapping his nose.

Lord Henry drained his glass of brandy and got to his feet. 'If you value our friendship, sir, you will keep this news to yourself. My daughter is visiting her sister Celia. When she returns, she will be married to Francis Colchester. Do you understand?'

'No need to—that is, of course,' Lord Torquil blustered.

'Then I will bid you goodnight.' Accepting his hat and cane from the major-domo, Lord Henry demanded a hack and instructed the driver to take him to Grosvenor Square. It was late, but that was of no matter. His sister, Lady Sophia, was forever informing him of her inability to sleep. If anyone knew what was what, and what was to be done, it would be Sophia. Strangely, it did not for an instant occur to Lord Henry to consult Bella, his wife.

Cassie endured a restless night after Jamil stormed off, her mind circling endlessly between anger, mortification and regret as she tossed and turned end-lessly on her sleeping divan. She was furious with her-self for having succumbed to her own base desires, for had she not promised herself over and over again that she would not. And now she had made a complete fool of herself.

At this point mortification took the upper hand. She had more or less thrown herself at Jamil! Celia would be horrified. Aunt Sophia would—no, she could not begin to contemplate what Aunt Sophia would think—accuse her of casting off her morals with her stays, for a start. Not that she had cast off her stays, or anything else for that matter. In fact, apart from her stockings and slippers, which she had discarded earlier, she had remained fully dressed. Yet she might as well have been naked.

Oh God! Cassie's face burned at the recollection of Jamil's touch, her own uninhibited response. She was shocked, not by what she had done, but by how much she had enjoyed it, relished it. More, even, than she had imagined in those feverish dreams that had haunted her since first she had met Jamil. Dark, erotic dreams where his hand did more than rest, as it had earlier, so tantalisingly briefly on that most intimate part of her. Dreams where he kissed her more intimate-ly, too, touched her more intimately, where his lips, his tongue, roused her to a shameless yearning for more. Dreams that made her nipples ache, which brought to life a throbbing pulse deep inside her. Dreams in which she and Jamil were naked, their bodies shockingly entwined. Dreams where Jamil—where she and Jamil…

She was a complete wanton!

She must be. Jamil obviously thought so. By kissing him in such a way she had quite obviously led him to expect—to expect more. Whatever more was. And she, she had been too caught up in the sating of her own passions to think about the fact that her behaviour could—should—be taken for encouragement.

That very first time they had met, all those weeks ago in the tent, Jamil had taken her for a woman who belonged not in the schoolroom but the harem. She had seen it for herself, in her reflection in the mirror, but had stubbornly chosen to believe that the real Cassie was Linah's responsible governess. She had been deluding herself.

She had not been fooling Jamil, though. He had known the truth all along. Cassie threw off the thin silk sheet that was her only cover and, wearing only her nightgown, padded out to the courtyard again. The sun and moon fountains tinkled at each other. A moonbeam shafted down, bathing Scheherazade's tiled image in ghostly light. The air was completely still.

The same illicit thoughts that had been keeping her awake at night had clearly been occupying Jamil's mind, too. Despite everything, Cassie found the idea exciting. The strength of his passion was so powerful, so all-consuming. He was not some weak, foppish excuse of a poet like Augustus, who expressed his emotions in sentimental doggerel, but a man of the desert, whose desires were as raw and fiery and elemental as the landscape he inhabited.

Regret came now. She would never be desired in such a way again, for she would never again meet someone like Jamil. She wished she had not stopped him. She almost wished he had ignored her protestations. But of course he had stopped, the moment she asked him to. He, who was master of all he surveyed, would not stoop to take by force. He, who could so easily have overcome her resistance, had chosen not to. The latent power in that lithe body of his was kept firmly leashed.

Cassie shivered. What would it feel like were he to unleash it? Dear heavens, what would it be like to be the subject of such an onslaught, helpless to do only as he commanded? She shivered again, and felt the knot of excitement that had not quite unravelled tense again in her belly, felt the tinge of heat between her legs return. Was this what Celia saw in Ramiz? Did submission bring with it the sleepy, sated look she had observed on her sister's unguarded countenance? No wonder Celia preferred her desert prince to any Englishman. If Jamil had not left the courtyard, if she had not asked him to stop, would she, too, be feeling that way?

Oh, God! There was no point in such thoughts. The chances were that in the morning Jamil would send her ignominiously packing. Though really, looking back, she remembered that he had been the one to initiate things. Such a strange mood as he had been in. Momentarily distracted, Cassie frowned. He had almost been intent on picking a fight with her.

Cassie recalled her sister's warning not to become either too involved or too attached and wished she had paid heed to it. As ever, Celia had been right. Why could she not be more like Celia?

Exhaustion hit her like a cold flannel. She stumbled

back to her divan and pulled the sheet up. Almost instantly, she fell into a troubled sleep, haunted by dreams in which she was pursued relentlessly by ravening wild animals, desperate to consume her.

Jamil had stormed back to his private rooms, angrily casting the wretched state cloak and head dress on to the floor of his dressing room. He paced the perimeter of the courtyard around which his apartments were built. It was twice the size of any other in the palace, with four fountains and an ornate pagoda-like structure in the centre built around a fifth, much larger fountain, on top of which perched, rather incongruously, a statue of the royal panther.

Prowling dangerously in a manner very like that of the big cat, first in one direction and then in the other, Jamil swore colourfully in his native language and then, when this proved insufficient, resorted to summoning up curses in the other six languages in which he was fluent. It didn't help. His heart still pounded too fast. His fingers still curled tight into fists. His shoulders ached with tension. He flung himself down on the curved bench in the middle of the pagoda and made a conscious effort to still the emotions raging inside him.

Anger was a weapon, one which Jamil had been taught to harness. He was not a man given to losing his temper easily, yet of late it was becoming much more of an effort to control it. Everything frustrated him or irked him or felt like too much effort. His life, which had been tolerable until Cassie came along, now seemed burdened with more cares than he wished to carry.

Had he ever been content? Jamil cursed again, more

viciously than before. Cassie again. Why must she question everything? Why must she force *him* to do the same, to confront things long buried? Since that day in the east wing, more and more memories of his childhood had begun to rear their ugly heads, not just in the middle of the night, but at odd times during the day. He remembered, as he had not allowed himself to do before, the overwhelming loneliness of his childhood. He remembered how much he had missed his mother. He remembered crying, alone in the panther cub courtyard, when everyone else was asleep, not for the pain his father had inflicted with his whip, but for the deeper hurt of feeling himself unloved. He remembered. He tried not to, but he did. And that was Cassie's doing.

Anger, his habitual release, helped only fleetingly. After anger came the bitterest doubt. That his suffering had a purpose had been his consolation. That it might have been unnecessary made him furious, for he had no way to revenge himself. His father was dead. The damage—if damage it was—was done. Jamil was the man his father had made him, moulded in his image. He could not change. *And why should he want to?*

He was confused, and he had no way of achieving understanding. To discuss with Cassie the turmoil she had stirred up in him was unthinkable—he had neither the words, nor could he consider the blow to his dignity such a discussion would entail. But sometimes, more and more often, that is what he longed to do. She had started it. It was up to her to help him end it. She *owed* him the succour he sought.

Jamil got to his feet again and resumed his relentless pacing. If he was honest—and Jamil prided himself on his utter honesty—it was not really Cassie's fault, save indirectly. He had not realised, until she had rejected him, just how badly he wanted her. His anger should be directed not at Cassie, but himself.

What had he been thinking! His ways were not hers. Even before he succumbed to the temptation of kissing her, he had known it would be a mistake, but he had chosen not to listen to the warning bells ringing in his mind. For once, for perhaps the first time since he was a child, he had allowed his passions to hold sway. There was no way of avoiding it. Unless he apologised to her, she would leave, and he did not want her to leave. For Linah's sake, obviously.

No, not only for Linah's sake. With a heavy sigh, Jamil retired to his divan, a huge circular bed with gilded clawed feet covered by day in green velvet edged with gold *passementerie*. The organdie curtains hung from a coronet suspended from the ceiling, forming a tent-like structure. Jamil cast aside his tunic and slippers and threw himself naked on to the soft silk sheets, but he could not sleep. Images of Cassie pliant in his arms heated him. Her untutored kisses and beguilingly naïve touch had aroused him as no other woman ever had. The combination of innocence and sensuality promised untold delights. Delights which would, for him, have to remain for ever unsavoured. He knew that, how could he not, after tonight. But still, he groaned in frustration.

Cassie was no coquette, but she was no strait-laced English rose either. Underneath the layers of buttons and lacings that guarded that delicious body of hers slumbered a soft, sensual woman with a passion crying out to be awoken. Jamil's manhood stirred into life once more. The fleeting touch of her damp sex on his hand was seared into his memory, rendering all other future pleasures pale by comparison. He must not tread that path, could not tread that path if she was to stay, and she must stay. He was not ready for her to leave. Though he was not prepared, either, to question why.

In a few hours from now the three of them would head out for their customary early morning horse ride. After his daughter's lesson, when he and Cassie were alone in the desert, he would explain, put her mind at rest. Satisfied with this, Jamil lay awake, counting the hours until dawn.

Cassie was awoken by Linah, who was already dressed, proudly sporting her new riding habit, which Cassie had made with her own clever needle. Her governess having overslept, the little girl was anxious lest they miss their riding lessons. 'Hurry, or *Baba* will think we are not coming,' she said, tugging the sheet back.

'I think it best if you go yourself today, Linah. I will ask one of the maidservants to take you to your father.'

'What is wrong? Are you ill?' The child looked at her anxiously. 'Are you missing your sisters, is that it? Do you need a hug?'

'I'm not sad,' Cassie said, smiling as the little girl put her arms around her neck of her own accord, 'but I am a little out of sorts. I don't think I can face riding today.'

A few weeks ago, the words would have sparked a tantrum. Indeed, for a few moments Linah's lip trembled and her eyes widened, but then she straightened her shoulders and gave a little nod, a gesture that was so wholly her father's that Cassie almost laughed. 'I will stay with you, if you are ill. I will bring you sorbet and tea and I will ask cook to make your favourite pastilla, and—'

'Stop, stop. I'm getting up. Such devotion deserves a reward, Linah.'

'So you'll come riding with *Baba* and me after all?' The child clapped her hands in delight.

'Yes.' She must face Jamil some time; it might as well be now. 'Go and wait for me outside, I won't be long.'

But when they arrived at the stables, it was to be informed that Jamil would not be joining them today, and the groom was to accompany them instead. 'Did he say why?' Cassie asked, but the man only shook his head and said that the prince was otherwise engaged.

Cassie was immensely relieved to have been granted such an unexpected reprieve, but Linah was hugely disappointed and became increasingly distracted and fractious during the lesson. They were practising jumping small fences, and Linah twice lost her temper when her pony refused, the second time raising her whip angrily.

'Don't take your own incompetence out on the horse,' Cassie said sternly, staying Linah's hand before the whip made contact. 'It is spiteful to do so and a sure sign of poor horsemanship.'

'Let me go,' Linah shouted, trying to shake herself free.

'When you calm down I will do so, not before.'

'Let me go. How dare you lay a hand on me, I am a princess of the royal blood. No one may touch me. Let me go. *Now!*'

'Linah!'

'I hate you. I hate you. Go away. Go back to England, I don't want you here any more.'

'Linah, you don't mean that. Calm down, and we will…'

But it was too late. Linah kicked her heels into her pony's flank and spurred the beast forwards at a gallop. She crossed the paddock and sailed in a perfect jump over the fence before Cassie could remount. By the time Cassie arrived back at the stables, Linah had already stormed off in the direction of the schoolroom.

Satisfied that the girl was safe within the palace, Cassie decided it would be better to give her time to cool down. Though she knew Linah did not mean her hurtful words, still she was stung by them. Her spirits sank into her riding boots. Now Jamil would have no reason at all to give her another chance, for why keep a wanton, wilful governess whose only charge hated her?

Thinking only of the enticing prospect of a temporary release from her cares, not for a moment considering how her actions would be interpreted by a small, contrite, eight-year-old girl, never mind her autocratic prince of a father, Cassie wheeled her grey mare round and headed out of the city gates at a gallop, without so much as a backward glance.

Chapter Seven

Jamil had risen when dawn broke, to be met with a crisis of state that threw his plans into disarray, obliging him to attend emergency Council meetings for many long, tedious hours until the sun was already high in the sky. Knowing that Linah was accustomed to take a nap after the noon meal, he made his way to the school room, expecting to find Cassie in her usual position in the shade of the lemon tree by the sun fountain, quietly engrossed in one of her many books of poetry. Instead he entered the courtyard to be met by a scene of chaos and Linah, surrounded by her bevy of maidservants, sobbing as if her heart would break. The porcelain shards of a shattered jug were scattered across the mosaic of Scheherazade, the mango sorbet it had held spreading out in a sticky pool over the fairytale princess's hair. The real-life princess who ran, shrieking *Baba*, pushing aside the maidservant who would have restrained her, was in an equally dishevelled state, her hair damp and tangled, her cheeks streaked with tears.

'*Baba*, *Baba*, you must get her back,' Linah said, throwing herself at her father, hot little hands clutching insistently at his tunic.

'What in the name of the gods is going on?' Jamil demanded, taking Linah's hand, but addressing the gaggle of servants, who immediately threw themselves on to their knees, faces hidden, gazing at the tiled floor.

'It is Cassie,' Linah said, tugging at his belt in order to get his attention.

'What about her?'

'She has gone, *Baba*.'

Jamil had never felt fear, but now he felt something very like it clutch its icy fingers around his heart. 'Gone where?'

'It is my fault, *Baba*. I ordered her to go.'

Jamil picked up his clearly distraught daughter and carried her to a low stool in the shade of the terrace where she sat on his knee, racked by incoherent sobs. Eventually, after promising several times that her confession would not result in any punishment, Jamil extracted the story of the morning's dramatic events from Linah.

'I told Cassie I hated her, and I said I wanted her to go back to England, and she looked so sad, *Baba*, and I—I was pleased she looked sad because I knew that she would go back to England soon anyway and I didn't want her to leave me—and now she's left anyway.'

'When did she leave? How?'

'According to the groom, she rode off on her horse, master,' one of the women said, 'into the desert.'

Jamil got to his feet, but Linah clung to him pathetically. 'Please don't be angry, I didn't mean it. I promise I'll be good, *Baba*, if only you will bring her back.'

'Listen to me, Linah,' he said gently. 'Soon I will be taking a new wife. You will have a new mother, maybe brothers and sisters in time. Then you will not need Cassie. She must leave eventually.'

Linah's tear-stained face brightened. 'You could marry Cassie instead. That would solve everything.'

Jamil smiled wryly. 'Life is not so simple, child. My new wife—your new mother—has already been chosen.' Jamil turned to leave but before he did so, he stooped to give Linah a brief hug. 'Don't worry. I'll find Cassie. No harm will come to her, I promise.'

He found her horse first, less than ten miles out into the desert. She had been heading due east and he picked up the trail fairly easily, the distinctive marks of the horse's shoes being quite different from those of camels or mules. She'd taken the route to the Maldissi Oasis, and it was here he found the grey mare cropping in an unconcerned manner at the shrub by the edge of the main pool, but there was no sign of Cassie. The horse had not been tethered. Its sleek coat was warm, but not overheated—it had obviously been at the oasis for a while. It had been at least five hours since Cassie had left the palace and, according to his head groom, she had no water or any other form of supplies.

Securing the mare under the shade of a palm tree and quickly removing the tack, Jamil tried to ignore the knot of anxiety forming in his stomach. He needed to think rationally. Cassie was an excellent horsewoman;

if she had suffered a fall, it must have been serious for her to have let go of the reins. The alternative, that she had wandered off without first tying up the mare, was unthinkable. Leading his own stallion, Jamil traced his way slowly around the perimeter of the oasis, searching the sand for hoof marks, but Cassie's mount had wandered around aimlessly, circling from one pool to another and back again, and the sand on the outer reaches was soft and churned up. The air was still, too still. Shading his eyes with his hand, Jamil squinted up at the sky, all his senses on alert. There was a sandstorm coming, not a shadow of a doubt, he could smell it.

With a new sense of urgency, he resumed his scanning of the terrain underfoot, finally tracing the path of the mare's incoming hoof prints. His own horse was frisky now, sensing, as he did, the imminent change in the weather. Keeping an iron grip on the reins, Jamil followed the tracks for two slow miles. He was heading towards the ochre plateau, which was the first of the flat-topped mountains known to his people as the Seats of the Gods. A mile further on, the clouds began to gather, still high in the sky, roiling an angry shade of red with the glow of the sun behind them. Another half-mile and the trail stopped dead.

Dismounting from his stallion, Jamil pushed his dusty head dress back from his face and, scanning his surroundings anxiously, called Cassie's name. His voice echoed round the rocky foothills, but there was no reply. He called again. No answer.

Screwing his eyes up in the fierce glare of the sun, Jamil spotted something that might be footprints veering off to his left. They were faint and intermittent, due to the wind, which had picked up and was causing the sand to ripple one way then the next, like waves breaking on the shore. His heart pounding, his desert-tuned senses horribly aware that the storm was only minutes away, Jamil followed the faint track. His cloak flapped in the breeze. He pushed the *igal* that held his head dress more firmly into place and called out again.

The stallion heard her first, his sensitive ears pricking back. Then Jamil heard her, too, her voice faint but distinctive, and he sprinted towards the sound, relief at having found her tempered by fear. He knew only too well how harsh the desert environment could be. He prayed she was unharmed.

She lay huddled in a fissure between two rocks, which offered her some meagre protection from the elements. Her face was tear-streaked, her eyes dark with fright, though she made a feeble effort to smile. It was this, such a vulnerable, wobbly little smile, which made his heart contract, made his voice harsh as he called her name, pulling her ruthlessly from her pitiful hiding place and hugging her tightly to his chest. 'Cassie, by all the gods in the heavens! Cassie, do you have any idea of the worry you have caused, running off like that? You could have perished out here.'

She trembled, clutching feebly at his arms, allowing herself to acknowledge the truth only now that he was here. She could so easily have died if he had not found her. She could have died without ever seeing him again. 'I'm sorry. I'm so sorry.' Her words were a whisper. Shaking, she clutched at him, feverishly running her hands over his arms, his back, pressing her face into his chest, drinking in the warm, musky, male scent of him, breathing it in as if it was her life's breath, terrified that if she let him go he would prove to be a mirage. 'I'm sorry,' she muttered again. 'I've been so foolish. I didn't think. I just…' Her voice became jagged as tears of remorse and relief began to flow. She trembled violently, stumbling a little, and gave a yelp of pain. She would have fallen if he had not caught her to him.

'Are you hurt?'

She bit her lip, stoically ignoring the searing pain. 'It's nothing. My ankle, I've twisted it. Such a stupid thing to happen, a snake spooked the mare and she reared. I let go of the reins and she threw me and then bolted. It's nothing,' she said again, trying bravely to test putting her weight on her ankle, but the pain was excruciating. Her face turned ashen.

'You are lucky to have escaped so lightly,' Jamil said curtly, scooping her up into his arms. Now that he had found her relatively unscathed, the full horror of what might have been was making him feel sick.

'Jamil, I'm so sorry to have put you to such trouble. If I had only thought…'

His arms tightened around her. 'But you never do, do you?' he said with a ghost of a smile. 'Stop struggling.'

'I'm—'

'Save your apologies. You are safe, that is all that matters.' He looked up at the lowering sky, frowning. 'Later, there will be time enough later for apologies and recriminations; for the moment, we have to find somewhere sheltered to sit out the storm.' Scanning the surrounding rocky outcrops, he saw a darker, deeper fissure that he fervently hoped might be a cave. Holding

Cassie securely in his arms, with his horse following obediently, Jamil made his way quickly towards safety.

His instincts proved to be correct. A narrow passageway, just large enough for the horse to pass through, opened out into a deep cave. It was dark and cool inside, the direction of the entranceway fortunately at the correct angle against the prevailing wind to keep them safe from the worst of the sand, which was already beginning to blow around. 'Stay there while I see to the horse,' he commanded, lowering Cassie to the ground. She sank onto the sandy earth, easing out her cramped muscles, trying to assemble her thoughts into some explanation for her actions that sounded reasonable. Actions, she was beginning to realise, that were not only foolish, but could have been potentially fatal.

Jamil stripped his horse of its tack and retrieved from the saddle the two goatskin water flasks he always carried with him, along with a blanket. The cave was almost dark now, the sun's light having been almost obliterated by the dark storm clouds. There was an air of stretched-taut tension, which always preceded a sandstorm, but it seemed to him there was another layer to it today. What had she been thinking of to behave so irresponsibly? His temper quivered on the edge of fury, like a bow strung tight for battle, his relief at finding her safe giving way to anger at the danger in which she had placed herself.

He made his way carefully across to where she sat, exactly as he had left her. Draping the blanket around her, he felt her shoulders shaking. 'You are trembling.'

Cassie nodded. 'It's the shock, I think. My own fault,' she whispered, teeth chattering. 'Sorry.'

'Here, drink this.'

He took the lid off his goatskin flask and held it to her mouth. Her skin was dry, dusty, heated. 'Slowly, slowly.'

She sipped, spluttered, sipped, then coughed. 'I lost my hat and veil in the fall. I must look a fright,' she said with a vain attempt at humour.

In the dim interior of the cave her face was a ghostly shadow, her hair a contrasting golden halo. The rest of her, in her dark habit and tan gloves, now cloaked in the blanket, blended into the background, accentuating the fragile beauty of her face. He held the flask to her lips again and she sipped slowly, though he was close enough to sense the effort it took for her not to grab the flask and gulp greedily.

'Thank you,' she said, her voice croaky.

'I'm going to examine your ankle now. It will mean taking off your boot, and it's unlikely you'll be able to put it back on again.'

'Can't it wait until we get back?'

Jamil shook his head. 'I need to make sure it's not broken.' Before she could object further, he picked up her foot and began, with great delicacy, to unlace her riding boot.

She bore his examination bravely, biting her lip as he manipulated her foot first one way and then the other, distracted by the heat of his hands as he moved them gently over the arch of her foot, her swollen ankle, her calf. His touch was expert and business-like, but she could not help remembering last night, his hands roaming over her in quite a different way, and in remembering she could feel her body flush with embarrassment and something else.

'Nothing broken, but it will have to be bound.'

'I'll do that. I can use my stocking.'

But he was already untying her garters, a breathtakingly intimate gesture in any other circumstances, first one, then the other, using both stockings to form a tight bandage, before fastening them with the pin from his cloak.

'Thank you,' Cassie said shakily. She rubbed her eyes and face in a futile attempt to wipe some of the sand away. It was stuck fast, as if baked on.

Jamil shook off his head dress and poured a little of the precious water on to a corner of the silk. 'Here, let me.' He tilted her face towards him and gently stroked away the worst of the dirt. Then he let her drink a little more. 'Better?'

Cassie nodded. She was still shaking, but not so violently. 'Yes, though I don't deserve to be. I'm so sorry. I know I've been stupid.'

'Extremely.'

His voice was uncompromising, though his touch had been tender. She couldn't see his expression, could make out only the white shape of his robes. Was he angry? Probably. She deserved that. Whatever happened now, the inevitable result must be her return to England in disgrace. She had, by her own foolish actions, proved to be a most unreliable governess. 'I'm sorry,' she said again. 'The last thing I intended was to put you in harm's way.'

Jamil's teeth showed white. 'You did not. I know this desert like my own body. But you—you could easily have died had I not found you. What on earth possessed you? Was it Linah? She told me what she had said to you.'

'It wasn't really Linah's fault,' she said in a very small voice. 'That was just the final straw. Last night—I should not have allowed you to—encouraged you to—I should not have. I'm so ashamed. I'm sorry.'

'You are sorry! It is I who should apologise to you. I took advantage of your innocence and of your situation. It was wrong of me.'

'You didn't take advantage.'

'I would have,' Jamil said harshly, 'if you had not asked me to stop.'

'But you did stop, Jamil. Immediately. I'm such a stupid fool, I didn't realise that a kiss could lead to such—because I have never…' Cassie faltered to a halt, sensing, rather than seeing, Jamil's intense gaze upon her. She had been rehearsing her apology over and over while huddling in the shelter of the rocks, for it kept her from panicking about the possibility that no one would find her and she would perish in the desert, but what had seemed so clear was now hopelessly muddled. Jamil did not blame her, but himself. Had she not, then, behaved wantonly?

'Do you regret what happened?' She blurted the words out without thinking. The question hung in the air between them, heavy with implications. 'I should not have asked you that, you don't need to…'

'No.'

'What?'

'No, I do not regret it.' The truth, but was it wise to have spoken it? His anger had fled, sped on its way by

Cassie's unexpected and wholly disarming honesty. His own honour dictated a matching of the truth with the truth, no matter that it revealed more of himself than he intended. In the dark of the cave, such revelations were, in any case, somehow easier. Jamil found her hand and clasped it between his. 'I cannot regret it, though honour decrees that I should, for you were in my care.'

She thought about this for some moments. 'You were not shocked by my behaviour?'

Jamil laughed softly. 'On the contrary. I thought it was obvious that I was excited by it. As you were by mine at first, were you not?'

The conversation had taken off into wholly unchartered territory. It was not a conversation Cassie could ever have imagined. Such intimate feelings were the domain of the great poets, but she had never encountered a poem that came close to expressing what she was experiencing at this moment. Aunt Sophia would be utterly appalled. But Aunt Sophia was thousands of miles away in England and Cassie was in the middle of a desert, quite alone with a desert prince, and what precedent was there for that situation? None. So…

'It frightened me a little,' she confessed in a whisper.

'What did?'

'The strength of feeling it evoked in me. It was as if—as if I were caught in a whirlpool and could do nothing to escape.'

'And yet you wanted it to overwhelm you?'

Cassie nodded, then realised he probably couldn't see her doing so. 'Yes,' she admitted. 'Was that wrong?'

'On the contrary, it was very right. In my country,

Cassie, it is not only permissible but expected that women enjoy the sharing of passion as much as men.'

'Oh.'

'They can, you know, I promise you.'

'Can they?' A new idea. An exciting one. Illicit? In England maybe, but not here. Jamil was still holding her hand. Somehow, Cassie didn't know how, she had edged so close to him that they were sitting with their legs touching, thigh to thigh. She felt safe. Jamil had already proved himself entirely honourable. But in another sense she wasn't safe at all, because she didn't want to be.

'In my country,' Jamil continued, 'it is in fact expected that women experience pleasure. It is a man's responsibility to ensure that she does.'

This statement, so loaded with unimaginable possibilities, was also entirely contrary to the little Cassie knew about intimate relations. Aunt Sophia had quite clearly implied that such duties were unpleasant. Celia, on the other hand, seemed to enjoy hers. Pleasure was not a word that Cassie had given much thought to. She found reading pleasurable, and walking in the countryside, and dancing, but she hadn't ever associated it with love-making before. Did this mean then, that pleasure and love-making were actually quite separate things? Could one take pleasure without first giving one's heart? Was *not* giving one's heart perhaps a prerequisite? With only Augustus as an example, Cassie was forced to conclude that this might well be true. She had foresworn love, but Jamil was not talking about love and seemed to be implying that she need not foreswear pleasure. *What did he mean?*

'Can one—can a woman, then—are there different ways of taking pleasure?' she asked, shocking herself and throwing caution to the winds at the same time. If she did not ask, she would never know, and it was not likely that there would ever be anyone she could ask again, under cover of the dark, cut off from the disapproving glances of society.

Jamil smiled in the darkness. 'There are infinite ways of taking pleasure, and infinite ways of giving it.'

'Oh.' In truth, she was already beyond reason. Last night Jamil had opened a door for her. She had taken a step over the portal and what she had seen had awed her, tempted her, thrilled her, but frightened her a little with its very newness. An unknown world was not, after all, to be entered without a little trepidation. She had turned her back on it last night with one word. No. But today? Today she wanted to experience that forbidden world, for if she did not, it would not exist tomorrow.

She was under no illusions about that. Jamil would not tolerate the blurring of the two worlds if she were to return to look after Linah, nor would she wish it. Though he had not actually said he would show her, she knew from the sound of his voice, from the tension in his body, touching but not touching hers, that he would if she asked him to. He had not said so, but he did not need to. All she had to do was ask. Her throat was dry, though not from thirst. She moistened her lips. 'Jamil, would you show me…?'

Her voice did not sound like her own, it was too husky, almost croaky, but he understood her all the same. 'Do you want me to?' he asked.

'Yes. Do you want to?'

'Very much.'

Very much. It was that, his wanting her, rather than the promise of what he would show her, that swayed Cassie. She had never been wanted in such a way. Not for her looks or for her family, but just for herself. The words, spoken in a soft growl, gave her delicious shivers. He wanted her. Just her. Though what he wanted to do to her—and what she was to do in return—she had no idea.

'You need do nothing, but enjoy,' Jamil said, as if he had read her thoughts. 'My pleasure will be in pleasuring you; I ask nothing in return. What I really want, my lovely Cassie, I cannot have. What I can have must suffice instead.' It was no lie. Though he ached to possess her, to do so would be a transitory relief compared to the guilt such dishonourable behaviour would inflict upon his soul. He would give, and she would receive, and he would therefore always be her first. That, no one could ever take from him.

'I don't understand.'

'But you will,' Jamil said confidently.

Then he kissed her, and the flames that had been subdued last night flickered immediately into life. The touch of his lips upon hers kindled a fire, the tangle of his tongue with hers stoked it, the stroking, soothing, rousing feel of his hands on her neck, her arms, her back, made a furnace of her. Cassie took no persuading to abandon all maidenly modesty. Jamil kissed her and she stepped boldly into the palace of pleasure.

He kissed her deeply, but with restraint. She sensed the leashing of his passion in the tension in his shoulders. His kisses roused and enticed, but did not savage. He set her free, with his tongue and his hands and his lips, but he did not permit himself the same liberties. The pins were tugged from her hair, his fingers running through it, fanning it out over her shoulders. He helped her shrug free of her jacket, untied the fall of lace at her throat and kissed the rise and fall of her breasts. The sensation of his mouth on her flesh made her sigh and moan as her hands roamed over the muscles of his arms, his shoulders, his chest, until he stilled them, reminding her that this was about her pleasure, entreating her to be still.

So she was. He eased her back onto the sandy floor of the cave, careful of her bandaged ankle. He kissed her neck, soft plucking kisses that raised little bumps of sensation. He kissed the valley between her breasts and the knot in her belly began to tighten. Cursing softly under his breath, he freed her from the restraints of her corset and took her nipples in his mouth, one then the other, sucking and licking, circling, causing such sweet shards of delight to pierce her that another knot, different in tension, tingling and aching, began to tighten between her legs, as Jamil suckled and sucked and she began to feel herself unravel.

He kissed her mouth again, her breasts again, and then he eased up her skirts and kissed her knees, her thighs. She tensed, uncertain, unsure, not frightened, but she had never thought—kissing there? He touched her, stroking from her knee to her thigh, her thigh to her knee, up, down, up, down, and she relaxed. He kissed the crease at the top of her thigh and she tensed in quite a different way. His fingers now, stroking into the crease, then fluttering over a more intimate fold, and she understood then, that this was the centre of her tension, and she wanted him to release it, needed him to ease it, couldn't bear for him not to as his fingers stroked and then he kissed her there again—or at least it felt like kissing—his tongue just easing a tiny fraction into her, making her clench her fists, arch up, making her call out *please, please, please,* because if she didn't he might not and then she would surely die.

'Please,' she said again as he braced her, his hands on her thighs. 'Please,' she panted as he kissed her intimately, his mouth on her moist core and then finally, deliciously, his tongue flicked inside, and the pleasure was unendurable, but she endured it because she knew that there was more to come. He licked her again, slowly, as she arched under him until her whole body was a knot of tension screaming for release.

It came so suddenly that she gasped and bucked and gasped again. A violent explosion that shattered her as if she were glass, sparkling diamond fragments of pleasure-like crystal, flying, floating, soaring, until she was engulfed by it, coated in it, lying panting, mindless and oblivious on the sandy floor of a dark cave in the middle of the desert.

Jamil held her, pulling her into his arms to cradle her, to stroke her hair, to kiss her neck, relishing the shivering, pulsing, shaking aftermath of her climax, deeply satisfied on one level that he had given her this gift, struggling on quite another with the unexpectedly primal urge to give her more. His shaft was hard and heavily aching. His entire body was rigid with need, pulsing with anticipation, aching with pleasure denied.

Cassie, slumberous and soft and infinitely desirable, was also, in her current state, infinitely compliant. Her fingers plucked at his tunic, her body nestled closer into his. His erection pressed demandingly against her. Her mouth, her lips, were soft on his neck. He longed to feel her skin on his. He knew she wanted it, too.

But she wanted it because of what he had done. And he had promised himself, as well as her, to keep her safe. It was enough. It would have to be. Jamil tried to ease himself away, but Cassie mumbled a soft protest, snuggling agonisingly closer. He could not bring himself to make the final break, not yet. 'Sleep,' he said, hushing her, soothing her hair, 'sleep.' She mumbled his name, but, drowsy with satisfaction, made no further protest. Cassie slept. Outside the cave, the storm raged. Inside the cave, Jamil waited for a different tempest to subside. It took a long, long time to do so.

She awoke in his arms. For a few delicious moments, almost afraid to breathe lest she disturb him, Cassie allowed herself to wonder what it would be like to wake in his arms every morning. To feel safe, and wanted, and cherished. To feel this delightfully floaty, blissful, can't-tell-which-bit-is-me feeling. To have her body melded into his like this every day. What would that be like? And what would it be like if he had truly made love to her? Would she feel even more blissful?

Was it possible to feel even more blissful?

Ought she not to be feeling rather the opposite?

No. She would not regret, and she would not allow herself to feel shame. What had happened had been wonderful. More than wonderful. She would not allow its memory to be tainted, or the colours dimmed—it was too precious. It felt too right.

Right?

But it could not be right. It must be wrong, it must be—every tenet of her upbringing ought to tell her that! And if it did not yet, then surely it would soon. Very soon. Just as soon as she left this dream-like experience behind and returned to real life. As Jamil's daughter's governess, not his—his doxy!

The word made her smile, such a picture of decadence as it conjured up. But then her smile faded. She might not be a painted harlot, but that is surely how she had behaved, how the world would view it, even if she did not. If the world ever found out. Which it would, of a surety, if it happened again, and it would happen again because there was no getting away from the simple, plain fact that she found Jamil irresistible, and now that he had introduced her to the delightful world of sensuality, she would find it impossible to refuse his invitation to join him there again. And the world would know, for it would be writ large on her face, for everyone to see: Cassandra Armstrong, fallen woman.

She would be disgraced. She would have disgraced her family. And Celia, too, for she could not stay in the palace under such circumstances, with everyone thinking her Jamil's concubine. Neither could she continue to serve as Linah's governess, since the occupant of that position must, as Jamil never tired of pointing out, have a stainless reputation. But the thought of leaving here made her panic. She most certainly did not want to leave.

Not yet. Not yet. Not yet.

Which meant this intimacy must not be repeated. Ever. This was the first time. And the last time. It had to be. Determined to imprint it for ever on her mind, Cassie turned her face into Jamil's chest, rubbed her cheek on the rough hair there and drank in that tantalising scent that was him. Just him. Outside, the storm had abated. Let him not wake, not yet, she thought, but even as she did so, he stirred.

For a fleeting moment, his arms tightened around her. She felt the whisper of his kiss on the top of her head. Or she hoped she did. Then he gently put her from him and got to his feet, straightening his robe. 'The storm has passed,' he said brusquely, heading for the mouth of the cave. 'When you are ready, we will be on our way.'

Jamil did not look at her, or speak to her again, waiting outside while she righted her clothing, the short distance between them seeming, after such intimacy, more like an unconquerable gulf than a mere few yards. Despite her resolution to create just such a distance, Cassie was hurt by it. Too caught up in the novelty of her own feelings, she had not had a chance to analyse his, but now it struck her forcefully that she had no clue at all about them. His face was impassive. The shutters were closed. *Did he even care?*

Outside, the desert seemed to have shifted its contours, with new dunes formed where none had been, flat rippled sand where before there had been rolling hills. A landscape as altered as Cassie's own feelings, as alien to her as Jamil's. Sitting astride the black stallion in front of him, her back pressed close against his chest, his arm tight around her waist, she looked around her in bewilderment. 'How do you know which way to go?' she asked, relieved to be able to break the ominous silence that was growing between them. 'It looks so different.'

'A man who navigates by the shifting sands is like to be a dead man,' Jamil replied, his voice cold as he urged his horse into motion. 'I set my course by the stars.'

Night was falling, but the storm-cleared sky was lit by an almost-full moon. As they headed back towards the oasis where Cassie's horse was tethered, the silence between them became tangible. The oppressive heat had given way to more balmy conditions. Save for the soft fall of the horse's hooves on the sand, the occasional scuffle of some night creature, silence reigned. The journey should have been the very essence of romance, just the two of them on a black stallion galloping across the desert under the stars, bathed in the warm glow of sated passion, she held close in the arms of the man who was, just for the moment, her desert prince. It should have been romantic, but Cassie was aware, horribly aware, that this journey marked not a lovers' meeting, but a lovers' parting.

Not that they had been truly lovers. How she wished they had. But she must not wish that. If only she knew what *he* was thinking. Except maybe she didn't really want to know. Cassie sighed wearily.

Jamil tightened his arm around her distractedly. He had not planned what had happened. Despite the fact that, from that very first encounter in the tent, he had been unable to banish his desire for Cassie, he had until now at least succeeded in constraining it. The position she held in the royal household, coupled with a conviction that the reality of her would never live up to his imagination, had ensured he did so. Now, he had abused one and proved conclusively the falseness of the other, rousing unfamiliar emotions he had no precedent for dealing with.

He wanted her. More than ever. Giving her pleasure had given him pleasure. A strange satisfaction it had been, unsated, but satisfaction nevertheless. Jamil cursed himself for a fool. He shifted in the saddle, trying to create even a fraction of distance between himself and the distractingly soft bundle he was holding, but it was to no avail. The horse's gentle jogging brought Cassie's delightfully rounded bottom immediately back into contact with his embarrassingly persistent erection. What was it about this infuriating Englishwoman that so got under his skin? He could have any woman he desired and yet he was drawn to this one, a woman who had the ability to confuse him, rouse feelings in him he had spent a lifetime subduing. Well, he would put an end to it. It was time to re-establish order and control in his life. Enough of this mawkish dabbling in emotions. No matter how much he wanted her, the simple fact was that Cassie must remain strictly out of bounds.

They had arrived at the Maldissi Oasis. The grey mare whinnied a welcome as they approached. Jamil dismounted and helped Cassie down. She winced as she put weight on her injured ankle, but shook her head at his offer of support. 'I can manage.' The pain that shot up her leg from her injury had jolted her into reality.

Jamil's silence spoke volumes. She sensed a speech coming and braced herself.

'What transpired between us must not happen again,' Jamil said.

She hung her head, lest he see the foolish tears that sprang to her eyes. That he was right, that it was just what she'd thought herself, did nothing to alleviate the stab of what felt decidedly like rejection.

'Cassie, you do see that?' Jamil said, tilting her chin up with his finger.

'I know, I know,' Cassie interrupted, jerking her face away, 'No doubt you bitterly regret it.'

Jamil hesitated, then shook his head. 'I don't, I cannot.'

She couldn't help it, her heart gave a little flutter. 'Nor can I,' Cassie said softly, just touching his arm with her hand.

He grasped her hand firmly. 'I am—relieved,' he said picking his words with care, 'but it changes nothing. Our actions must not be repeated, you understand that, Cassie?'

She forced herself to smile, though it felt very much like a grimace. 'I understand, Jamil, completely. And I want you to know that I'm very conscious of the… the honour you do me in investing such…such trust in me—and I can assure you that I will do my very best to make sure it is not misplaced.'

Once again, her willingness to shoulder the whole burden of responsibility touched him, where recriminations, probably quite justified recriminations, would have set his back up. Jamil's smile was wry. 'I am sure you will, but I think it best if our noble intentions are fortified by some more practical considerations. There are conditions attached,' he said, thinking bitterly that his whole life seemed to have conditions attached. 'We must not be alone in each other's presence. Any contact must be in relation to Linah only. I require these terms to be strictly observed. You do see that it's for the best, don't you?'

'Of course. Absolutely. Definitely.' Stoically ignoring the ominous sinking feeling in her heart, Cassie took a deep breath and held out her hand. 'In my country, we shake hands on a treaty.'

Jamil took her hand, but instead of shaking it, pressed a kiss. On her wrist. Then on her palm. Then on each of her fingertips. 'I am not in your country, more's the pity,' he said enigmatically. 'You, on the other hand, are in mine.'

Settling herself in the saddle, trying to be pleased by the bargain she had just struck, which had, after all, granted her exactly what she wished, Cassie cast a longing eye back at the sandy blue waters of the Maldissi Oasis. Another opportunity for a midnight dip gone. She was beginning to doubt there would be another.

Chapter Eight

For the second time in his life, Peregrine Finchley-Burke, formerly, for an embarrassingly brief period, of the East India Company, currently acting in a junior capacity within the large confines of the British Consulate in Cairo, found himself in the unenviable position of being required to assist the estimable Lord Armstrong in the recovery of one of his daughters. For it to happen once, Peregrine considered himself unlucky. For it to have happened a second time, he began to consider himself cursed.

'Why the blasted fellow had to have so many of 'em, and why he ain't able to keep them closer to home, I don't know,' muttered Lord Wincester, the Consul General, known to Lord Henry Armstrong and his other fellow Harrovians as Wincie. 'First it was the eldest getting herself kidnapped...'

'Not actually kidnapped, my lord,' Peregrine reminded him gently, 'Lady Celia was being held for her own safety in the royal palace at Balyrma.'

'Aye, so you told me, and to be fair you were directly involved,' Lord Wincester agreed testily, 'but I'm pretty certain, despite all the hush-hush afterwards, that there was a damn sight more to it than that.'

'Lady Celia's marriage to Prince Ramiz was an excellent alliance for the crown, my lord,' Peregrine said tactfully.

It was undoubtedly true that Prince Ramiz's principality of A'Qadiz was endowed with a most convenient port on the Red Sea, a port that had already proved invaluable to Britain in opening up a faster route to India, but Peregrine was not telling, as Lord Wincester suspected, the whole truth. Even now, two years after the event, the memory of that trip to Balyrma with Lord Armstrong could still make Peregrine sweat. His journey to take up his position with the East India Company had been fatally interrupted by the affair and he had been offered a posting with the diplomatic service as a reward, Lord Armstrong had made clear, for his continued discretion. And Peregrine had in turn remained obdurately discreet. He had not spoken, not once, not even in his letters to his dear nanny, Lalla Hughes, about that scene in the royal palace harem, a fact for which Lord Wincester had not quite forgiven him.

Though Peregrine had dreamed of diplomatic glory in Cairo, operating at the hub of British relations with the crumbling Ottoman Empire, it had been mundane diplomatic graft that had sustained him over the last years. Humble had been his beginnings in the Consulate, and humble they remained. Peregrine was Lord Wincester's preferred dogsbody, for which role he was rewarded by also serving as the butt of Lord Wincester's rather cumbersome wit. The kind of Old Harrovian wit that found the placing of a pig's bladder filled with water under Peregrine's pillow, or the replacement of snuff with pepper, hysterically funny. Peregrine endured such japes with unabated good humour—being an Old Harrovian himself, he had, in fact, made a career out of providing his school fellows with a willing victim—but the truth was that he would take them in even better part if only his genial suffering were complemented by even the tiniest element of progression in his diplomatic career.

Lord Wincester drummed his fingers on the walnut veneer of his imposing desk, and frowned over the communiqué, sent express in the diplomatic bag, from Lord Armstrong. 'Nothing for it, Perry, but you're going to have to go and fetch the damned girl,' he said. 'She's in Daar-el-Abbah, can't quite remember where that is.'

Peregrine rolled to his feet and studied the large map of Arabia which was laid out upon one of the long side-tables under the window. 'Here, just next to A'Qadiz,' he said.

'Hmm. Might make sense for you to take a detour then. Consult her sister, Lady Celia.'

'May I ask, my lord, what exactly it is I am required to do?' Peregrine asked tentatively.

Lord Wincester's copious eyebrows shot up in surprise, looking rather like two furry caterpillars. 'Do? Haven't I just told you, go and fetch the girl.'

'But which girl? Lord Armstrong has five daughters.'

'Lady Cassandra. You surely remember her—quite

a little beauty, as I recall, even if she was prone to fits of histrionics.'

Peregrine paled. Lady Cassandra was the most beautiful woman he had ever met, and quite the most intimidating. It had been she who had persuaded him to escort her and her father and that terrifying aunt of hers across the desert. Persuaded him with those big blue eyes and those big luscious… He coloured, coughed and shuffled forwards to position himself in the shade of the map table. 'Lady Cassandra. How—what…?'

Lord Wincester chuckled. 'Locked up in Sheikh al-Nazarri's harem, or so Henry seems to think. Don't believe a word of it myself—though mind you, if I was the sheikh and she was in my palace—but there, I'm sure Henry's exaggerating. Don't need me to tell you, mind, that if he's not, the utmost discretion is needed. Henry's marked her down for one of Wellington's protégés, don't want the goods tainted. At least,' Lord Wincester added with a chuckle, 'if they're tainted, don't want any word of it getting back to Blighty. Do you understand me, Perry?'

Peregrine goggled.

'Right. Expect you'll want to be off in jig time,' the Consul General said, rubbing his hands together in a gesture that made Peregrine think ominously of Pontius Pilate. It was a gesture of which Lord Wincester was rather fond. He slapped Peregrine's back in what he hoped was a reassuring manner, handed him Lord Armstrong's epistle and exited in search of much-needed refreshment in the form of his latest shipment of port, which had arrived with the diplomatic bag from Lisbon.

Alone in the office, Peregrine sank on to the

extremely uncomfortable gilded chair that faced the great man's desk, and perused the letter with a growing sense of horror. Clutching his pomaded locks in his sweaty palms, he grasped at the only straw he could think of. 'Lady Celia,' he said fervently to himself. He sincerely hoped she would prove the answer to his prayers.

Back in Daar, both Cassie and Jamil strictly observed their new rules of engagement. Superficially at least, it seemed to work. Cassie thought of life in the royal palace of Daar as being like a Persian carpet, the surface depicting their day-to-day life, but underneath the strands were stretched and tangled with the multi-hued threads of desire. And then she would chide herself for her overheated romantic sensibilities and concentrate on the task in hand.

She continued to enjoy every day spent with Linah, whose new-found thirst for knowledge was second only to her new-found hunger for the company of her beloved pony and adored *Baba*. Linah was a rewarding pupil. She would always be highly strung, her temper would never be anything other than volatile, but with the correct balance of mental and physical exercise, the days of her tantrums were finally, truly in the past. Everyone in the palace commented on the changes in her, and while Halim was reluctant to grant Cassie any credit, preferring to attribute this to the time his master spent with his daughter, Jamil did not stint in his admiration for Cassie's talents as a governess. He had even permitted a select group of other little girls to visit the palace. Linah was finally making friends.

Cassie should be pleased, thrilled even to receive such an endorsement of support from a man whose standards in all things were of the highest. She had proved herself, exactly as she had hoped. Her own papa, Aunt Sophia, even Celia would surely be impressed. But the satisfaction such an achievement should have given her eluded her. She never saw Jamil, except in company. They were never alone. He no longer visited the Scheherazade courtyard save at times he could be sure of Linah's presence. She missed their talks and their laughter and their outings. She missed him terribly, and no matter how many times a day she reminded herself it was for the best, every day she missed him more.

Jamil had, for a few precious moments out in the desert, been her lover, and because of that, he was now a stranger to her. It wasn't fair. It wasn't right. And yet anything else would be wrong. The conflicting thoughts fought for attention in her head. She could not sleep for thinking of him, for speculating in lurid, shocking and exciting detail what exactly were the many ways of giving pleasure he had spoken of. And the many ways of receiving. But in her dreams such thoughts would have to remain. Restless and aching with unfulfilled desire, she spent many hours pacing the perimeter of the courtyard in the star-strewn hours of the night.

Jamil, too, took to pacing his own private courtyard at night. He thought of Cassie more than he had thought it possible to think of anyone. He, who had never before had any problems in denying himself, was now tossed on a stormy sea of need, frustration and unsated passion.

The same arguments that rolled and roiled around Cassie's head played havoc with his orderly mind. He caught himself staring into space in the middle of Council. When setting off for the stables or the throne room or his own courtyard, he often found himself standing outside the schoolroom doors, as if his feet had a mind of their own, as if his entire body was conspiring against him in its efforts to slake its need. He knew Halim was worried about him. He was worried about himself. He had no solution, save to stay resolute in the hope that it would pass, comforted in the belief that at least Cassie remained oblivious, but perversely not comforted by that at all. For some reason, her thinking him indifferent was unacceptable, yet her thinking him indifferent was surely the point.

He had not realised, until it was denied him, how much he had come to enjoy her company. Cassie was witty, she was endearing and, most of all, she was never predictable. She made him laugh and even made him angry sometimes, when she disagreed with him, just to see how he reacted, and that made him laugh, too. While she was never anything but deferential upon the rare occasions they were together in the public eye, in private she was not afraid to call him to account. She would not tolerate what she had confessed to calling his Corsair behaviour. He had never had a friend, a true companion, or wanted one. As a woman, Cassie could not possibly fulfil such a role, but it was exactly in that role that he missed her. Though not only in that role. There were other parts he wished her to play. Other lines he wished her to recite. Other deeds he would have her perform. If only.

* * *

He came upon her one day, walking in the palace rose garden. Her golden hair, burnished by the sun, was arranged in a simple knot on the top of her head, long tendrils curling down over her shoulders, flaxen wisps caressing her forehead. As usual, when alone, her head was uncovered. Her dress, palest lemon with a white sash tied at the waist, showed her curves to perfection. The sun had given her pale English skin a warm glow, an endearing scatter of freckles on her turned-up little nose.

From under cover of the terrace, hidden by a colonnade, he watched her. She tripped gracefully along the little paths between the rose beds, stooping every now and then to smell a bloom. This she did, as she ate, with relish, closing her eyes, her coral-pink mouth pouted into a delicious smile, completely unaware that she was being watched. She moved with the sensuous grace of a dancer. She looked so delectable that he could not be anything else but aroused by her as she flitted between the flowers, overshadowing their beauty, no English rose but something far more exotic. Jamil's manhood stirred, stiffened.

A statue of Ra, the Egyptian Sun God, stood at the centre of a riot of pink and peach, a gift to his mother from one of her relatives. Here, Cassie stopped and consulted what looked like a sheaf of papers. To his surprise, she threw her head back to look into the eyes of the marble god, casting an arm dramatically wide as if she were on the stage. She was clearly in what she had once told him, laughingly, her sister Celia referred to as her 'full Cassandra mode'. Intrigued, Jamil made his way around the terrace until he was behind her, then padded closer, the better to hear her performance.

'For Cassandra, upon the occasion of her accepting my hand,' Cassie intoned. Momentarily abandoning her pose, she addressed the statue in her normal voice. 'Would that I had not, for then in his misery perhaps Augustus would have been inspired to write something a little more accomplished.' She cleared her throat and began again.

Delectable gaoler, thou doth guard my faint heart,
In that most tempting of prisons, from where love doth start.
The bars that contain me from gossamer are made,
Manacles of beauty on my ankles are laid.

Cassie giggled. 'Poor Augustus, it really is quite dreadful,' she said to Ra. 'I'm not surprised you're looking so pained. I'm afraid there's more, though.

Trapped in my cell by thy loving embrace,
The key to my freedom is in thy sweet face.
A lifetime sentence will be mine 'ere long,
When I make you my bride, Cassandra Armstrong.

She finished with a deep curtsy. Standing only a few feet away, Jamil struggled to contain his laughter, resisting the urge to applaud only because he wished to see what she was going to do next—for he realised this was not just a performance, but a rite.

Cassie emerged from her curtsy with a regal nod

at the sun god. 'I was going to read them all, but you know, I don't think I can bear it, and I see no reason why you should have to endure it either,' she told the statue. She shuffled the sheaf of paper, upon which, Jamil could now see, were numerous poems, all written in the same rather untidy scrawl.

Cassie took the first, and began to tear it into strips, then into scraps. 'Cast yourself upon the winds and fly,' she declaimed. 'Begone, ghost, begone.' With one extravagant gesture, she threw the shredded pieces of poetry into the air, twirling round as she did so, and coming face to face with Jamil. 'Oh! What a fright you gave me.' Colour flooded her face. 'How long have you been there?'

'Long enough to work out that your Augustus was not only a despicable man, but a truly mediocre poet.'

'Do you know, Jamil, I am positively glad now that he did abandon me. Only think, if he had not I may have had to listen to such doggerel every morning over the breakfast cups.'

'That would indeed have been tragic, though I would have thought that such a romantically inclined person as yourself would have been happy to listen to poetry at any time of the day.'

She slanted a look up at him from under her lashes. If she did not know him better, she would have said he was flirting with her. She could not resist being charmed, so beguilingly handsome was he, and so delightfully romantic the setting. 'True, but it depends upon the quality of the poetry.'

'I hope you find this to your taste,' Jamil said sweeping her theatrically into his arms. '"Shall I compare thee to a summer's day? Thou art more lovely, and more temperate." Your Mr Shakespeare's lines, but they could have been written for you, most lovely Cassandra.'

He kissed her then, what was meant to be a courtly kiss, a stage kiss, but the touch of her lips, warm and soft and yielding, lit a fire in him. Pulling her upright and close into his arms, he kissed her passionately and, with a soft moan of long pent-up need, she twined her arms around his neck and kissed him back with equal fervour. The heady scent of the roses wafting up as their clothes brushed the petals, the arid heat of the desert sun brightly blazing down upon them, the bitter-sweetness of the forbidden, gave to their kisses a romantic, never-to-be-repeated edge. Their lips drank deep, for they knew they would not drink again. They kissed, and kissed again, and again, until finally Jamil drew away. He was breathing heavily. His face was flushed, his eyes burning dark and golden.

'To quote another of your poets,' he said huskily, "'Since there's no help, come let us kiss and part."'

"'Nay, I have done,"' Cassie finished, with a sad little smile, "'you get no more of me."'

Picking up her skirts, she made her way swiftly out of the garden. The heavy door into the palace swung shut behind her. Jamil stood among the roses, as still and impassive as the statue of Ra. On the ground, unnoticed in the heat of passion, the torn remains of Augustus's poems swirled aimlessly in the breeze.

It was the time of the annual ceremony of Petitions, the traditional handing out of alms to the nomadic tribes. The week in the desert amongst his people, resolving disputes and acting as mediator in marriage negotiations, was usually one of Jamil's favourites, but this time he found himself unable to concentrate, wishing himself back at the palace. He missed Linah. He missed Cassie more—much, much more than was good for his peace of mind. He wondered if she missed him, too, and chastised himself for such mawkish thoughts, but could not banish them. Her face hovered before him each night as he drifted off into a troubled sleep. His body ached with unfulfilled longings. In the midst of a crowded tent filled with grateful tribesmen, in the middle of a celebration around a camp fire, surrounded by his loyal and adoring people, Jamil felt lonely. He was tired of being a prince, weary of being the all-seeing, all-knowing ruler. Cassie, only Cassie, saw him as a man. A man with flaws.

He was not invincible, and he was beginning to wonder why he had ever aspired to be so. Feelings, vague longings, long-suppressed emotions he hadn't even realised were there, seemed to be uncurling themselves, as if they had been hibernating and were now emerging blinking into the light, seeking a voice. But it was a voice only she could hear, and so it remained unspoken. And the silence hurt him. He missed her. It gradually dawned on him that only she could ease him. Whatever it was that ailed him.

Returning to Daar in the cool of the evening, his first impulse was to seek her out, but, knowing his daughter would be sleeping, and therefore unable to perform her role as unwitting chaperon, Jamil resisted the urge with immense difficulty. This self-imposed treaty of theirs was proving to be an agonising burden. Truthfully, he knew it would take very little temptation to break it. Very truthfully, what he wished was for something or someone to put temptation in his way.

Wearily, wishing he were headed in quite the opposite direction, Jamil made for the hammam. A long relaxing steam bath was just what he needed. At least, if it was not what he needed, it was what he could have.

Though each of the main palace courtyards had their own bathing chambers, the hammam was housed in a separate building. It consisted of a series of interconnected rooms, each with a domed roof. Only the first, the changing room, had windows set high into the walls; the rest were completely enclosed. Impatiently dismissing the servants who would normally oversee the bathing ritual, Jamil stripped off his tunic, head dress and slippers and headed naked into the hot room. The plunge pool, a tiled bath of cold water constantly refreshed from a spring located deep underground, was octagonal in shape and formed the room's centrepiece. Ignoring the steps, Jamil launched into the icy depths, relishing the shock as the cold water enveloped his body, taking his breath away.

Emerging shivering, he threw himself down on one of the full-length marble tables which were arranged around the hot room, interspersed with little basins with gold taps which were built into niches in the round walls. Lying on his stomach, he closed his eyes, allowing the steam to envelop him, willing the heat to lull him into a much-needed torpor. Eventually, it did.

* * *

It had been Linah's suggestion that her governess make herself some looser-fitting clothes more appropriate to the desert climate. Cassie, who was heartily sick of the way her English garments, and in particular her English undergarments, clung to her skin, eagerly made the expedition to the souk for materials, accompanied by one of Linah's handmaidens. She did not know if Jamil would approve, but Jamil was not here to ask. His week-long absence attending the Petitions ceremony should have been a relief, a period for sensible reflection and acceptance of the boundaries that constrained their relationship, but though she tried— *how she tried*—it just wasn't working.

The more she tried not to think of him, the more she did. The more she told herself, sternly, that to think of *such* things was wrong, the more they crept, with startling, arousing clarity, into her dreams. Invoking Aunt Sophia made no difference. Telling herself the sacrifice was worth it for Linah's sake made no difference either, Cassie was ashamed to admit. What had happened in the cave had changed her for ever. She could not now un-know. She could not help wanting to know more. She could not—would not—have it undone. And she was pretty certain that Jamil felt the same.

That was the difficult part. She caught him watching her, time after time, when he thought himself unobserved. She saw the look of naked desire on his face and it made her own flare and flame. She recognised it from her mirror, that desire. It was not only she who was denying herself. She *could* deny herself, but how she wanted. Ached. Yearned. Pined, wickedly wished for the fates to throw them together, alone, just once more. She would not resist the fates. She was pretty certain Jamil would not either. But the fates, unfortunately for Cassandra, seemed quite oblivious of her wishes.

As usual, everyone save her was asleep. As usual, Cassie was restless. Deciding to take a walk around the palace grounds, she donned one of her new outfits for the first time. A pair of loose pantaloons, which Linah told her were called sarwal or harem pants, pleated at the waist, billowing out over her legs, then gathered in at her ankles with a beautifully worked piece of braid studded with little pearls, they were made of dark blue gauzy material, which rustled alluringly when she walked. Over these rather daring items, she wore a long silk caftan in her favourite cerulean blue, slit almost to the top of her legs to allow ease of movement, with long, loose sleeves, finished with the same braiding that ornamented her sarwal pants and fastened down the front with a long row of tiny pearl buttons. Little slippers, also pearl-studded, of the softest leather she'd ever come across, covered her feet. Aside from a tiny scrap of silk like a sleeveless shirt, she wore nothing else. No stays, no chemise, no petticoats, no stockings. Her hair was combed down, held back from her face with a tortoiseshell clip, a gift from Linah.

Looking at herself in the mirrored tiles of her bathing chamber, Cassie was confronted by an exotic creature, the curves of her body quite clearly defined through the softly draped clothes, though in fact there was little actual flesh on show, and the neckline of her caftan was much higher than her day dresses. Despite this, she knew Aunt Sophia would be shocked, not just at her lack of English corsetry, but by the way such a lack allowed her body to move freely, and for the movements to be quite apparent as she walked.

Was she verging on the indecent? Aunt Sophia would say so, but Celia would not—Celia herself dressed all the time in just such garments. And Linah's servants, too, though their clothes were plainer, wore no more than these three items of clothing and slippers. When in Rome, and all that. In any case, no one would see her, not at this time of night. It was just a question of becoming accustomed to unfamiliar garments, and she could not do that if these lovely new clothes lay unworn in the chest in her sleeping chamber.

Reassured, Cassie opened the door of the courtyard. The guards were too well trained to display any reaction, and, as she had hoped, she met no one else. With the rose garden strictly out of bounds in her mind, Cassie wandered off to the opposite end of the palace, where a strangely shaped building stood surrounded by shady palms. Intrigued by the series of little domed-roof rooms, assuming from the lack of guards that it was some sort of summer house or perhaps even a plant house, Cassie opened the large door and stepped inside.

The walls of the changing room were not marble, but tiled, Roman-style, with intricate mosaic pictures of various gods, some of whom she recognised, some not. The images were what Aunt Sophia would most decidedly have called *warm*. Men and women entwined in any number of embraces. Cassie, examining them more closely, found herself blushing. And wondering. These images were designed to stimulate, and they did, providing her with some astonishingly arousing images of herself and Jamil doing those very same things.

Captivated, entranced by now being able to give some form to her own already fevered imagination, Cassie followed the mosaics round the room, growing more and more heated as she tried to picture Jamil doing *this*, or herself doing *that*. By the time she came to a break, formed by the door opposite the one by which she had entered, she was flushed, and not particularly from the heat of the room. Realising now that she must be in the Roman-style baths the locals called a hammam, she hesitated with her hand on the handle, but no one would be taking a steam bath at this time of night. Besides, there had been no sign of the attendants, and she wanted to see more of these mosaics. She suspected that in the next room they would have progressed to even more compromising positions, the kind of compromising positions Jamil called pleasure. If she could not experience, at least she could understand.

The door opened silently. Closing it behind her, Cassie's vision was momentarily obscured by the cloud of steam that rose up to meet the cooler air. The room was fiercely hot, the air damp and extremely humid, lit by oil lamps built into the walls. Her silk tunic began to mould itself to her skin.

She didn't notice him at first. The plunge pool attracted her attention. Stopping down, she dipped her fingers in the icy water, dabbing some of it on to her temples. Standing up again, slightly giddy with the cloying heat, she saw that someone was lying flat on a marble bed. A man. A naked man. With an exclamation of dismay, she was about to head quickly out of the room, when he looked up. Autumn eyes. Even through the haze there was no mistaking them, or their owner.

'Jamil!'

He had been dreaming of her, and now here she was, clad most alluringly in silk and organdie, the damp material clinging deliciously to her curves. She stood rooted to the spot, her eyes wide, fixed upon him. He remembered he was naked, save for the small strip of towel upon which he lay. His robe was in the changing room. The larger bathing towels were kept in the warm room. There was no way to avoid her seeing him. Part of him relished the prospect.

This thought startled him, for though many women had admired his body, Jamil was very far from being a vain man. Cassie looked delectable, with her skin flushed and her hair clustering in damp tendrils on her brow. The caftan suited her. The sarwal pants showed her shapely legs to perfection. 'Cassie.' Desire gripped him. She was here, just as if the gods had gifted her to him, dressed as if they had done so for his pleasure. This time, he would not—*could not*—resist.

'Jamil. I didn't know anyone was here.'

'You look delectable.'

A blush stole over her already heated skin. She stared at him, as if mesmerised. Had she not been wishing, only a few moments ago, for just this? Had the fates finally thrown her an opportunity? If so, would it be wrong to ignore it? 'I should go,' she said uncertainly.

'*No!* Don't go. No one will disturb us here. Stay.' Jamil held out his hand towards her.

She didn't seem able to move, in any case. Her feet in their seed-pearl slippers seemed to have taken root on the tiled floor. Her eyes were riveted on his body. She could not force them to look away. She had seen naked statues and she had seen paintings of naked gods, but nothing had prepared her for the reality of this man. He was quite beautiful, and so very, very different from her. The breadth of his shoulders tapered down to a trim waist. His back was muscled, his buttocks taut, his legs long, rough with hair. His skin was the same golden colour all over. All around him, on the walls, the gods sported together, coupling intimately. The steam was making her light-headed. She was hot, her clothes were damp and clinging. She couldn't seem to breathe properly.

She wanted to touch him. She wanted to run her fingers down the long line from his neck down his spine to the slope of his buttocks. 'I really ought to go,' she said breathlessly, but still made no move.

'No,' Jamil said softly. 'This was meant. You see that, don't you?'

She nodded, and with her nod cast farewell to the last of her reservations. It was meant. It was inevitable and they both knew it.

'Come here, Cassandra,' he commanded.

She did. As if in a trance, she skirted the pool and stood beside him, looking down at him. Her eyes were wide, her pupils dark. Her lips were plump and ripe. Beneath her caftan, her nipples peaked against the silk.

He did not want to frighten her, but he could not lie here for ever. Jamil sat up swiftly, deftly wrapping the towel around his waist, covering up the all-too-obvious evidence of his arousal. It was enough, barely.

'I was looking at the pictures on the walls,' Cassie

said, still gazing at the far more beguiling picture in front of her.

'Touching is much more sensual than merely looking,' Jamil said, taking her hands and placing them on his shoulders.

She ran her fingers down his arms, to where the soft downy hair began, back up to his shoulders, following the contours of his muscles, down to the swell of his chest. There she stopped, unsure, shocked, aroused. 'I can't,' she whispered, all the time thinking, *can I*?

He took her hand between his, pulling her closer so that she was standing between his legs. Slowly, he undid her caftan, making a play of each button, giving her time to move, to leave, holding his breath lest she did. The final button ceded to him. The tunic fell in a crumpled heap on to the floor. She stood before him, blushing wildly, but holding his gaze, her excitement mirroring his in the rapidity of her breathing, in the swelling of her nipples, clearly visible now through the thin layer of silk that covered them.

Jamil bent his head to envelop one hard bud with his mouth, breathing through the silk on to her skin. She moaned, and slumped forwards, supporting herself on his shoulders. He did the same to the other nipple and was rewarded with another soft little moan. 'Touch me, Cassie,' he whispered huskily, taking her hand and placing it on his chest, untying the silk top at the same time to release her breasts to his ministrations. 'Make me feel what you are feeling.'

Jamil stroked the creamy skin of her breasts, cupping their weight in his hands, suckling with his mouth, tugging and licking and caressing. Heat that had nothing to do with the steam room flushed her skin as her body remembered and rejoiced and then began to clamour for more. More of his touch. More of hers. She ran her hands over his chest, smoothing them against the hard wall of muscle, dipping down, to the concave of his stomach under his rib cage. His skin felt so different. His touch made her shiver and heat and shiver. The yearning she'd felt since the last time he'd touched her, which she thought sometimes she'd been feeling since she'd first set eyes on him, made it impossible to do anything other than comply with his wishes. For they were her wishes, too.

He kissed her passionately, his tongue tangling with hers, his hands on her waist, pulling her closer, crushing her breasts against his chest. His hands skimmed her hips, loosening the sarwal pants. Eager to please, eager to learn, eager for his touch, she kicked off her slippers and stepped out of the pantaloons. She was completely naked. She was hardly ever naked, save in the privacy of her own bath. She should have been embarrassed, but the sharp intake of breath, the blaze of something primitive in Jamil's eyes, told her that she pleased him.

Shyly, she stood while he freed her hair from the clip that held it, smoothing it out over her shoulders, each touch, each look, telling her how much he liked what he saw, giving her confidence, feeding the fire in her belly, making her quiver with what she now realised was desire. Byron's *effusions that spring from the heart*, which truly did *throb with delight*.

'Beautiful,' Jamil whispered into her ear, and then words in his own language she could not understand, though she did not have to, for they curled round her like wisps of smoke. He stood and the cloth that covered him dropped to the floor between them. Automatically, Cassie looked down, flushed fiery red at what she saw and looked away.

'Don't be frightened,' Jamil said.

'I'm—I'm not.' She wanted to look again, she wanted to look at him as he looked at her, but it was shameful, surely? The statues she had seen had been either discreetly draped or—or—or not at all like Jamil.

He tipped her chin up with his finger, forcing her to meet his gaze, a smouldering blaze of gold. 'We have five senses, Cassie. We can touch.' His thumb grazed the tip of her nipple. 'We can smell.' He nuzzled her neck. 'We can hear,' he whispered, licking the shell of her ear. 'We can taste,' he said, licking into her mouth, 'and we can see. Each adds to the pleasure of the others. Don't you want to look?'

He took a step back from her, and Cassie looked. From his handsome countenance, her eyes travelled down, his shoulders, his chest, his belly, faltered at the thin line of hair arrowing down, then followed it, to the scimitar arc of his erection. Such strength. She could not imagine how—but already, thanks to the mosaics, she was imagining.

He pulled them both onto the tiles so that they sat facing each other, legs entwined, close enough to touch, and to kiss. Smothering kisses. Flesh on flesh. Damp skin on damp skin. Hot steam, hotter passion. His hands were on her thighs now, on her flank, then on the soft skin on the inside, stroking into the source of heat nestled between them. She could feel the same mounting, clutching tension as before, only this time it was not frightening. This time she embraced it, welcomed it, sought it. His fingers slipped inside her, and softly caressed the hardening source of it all.

When Jamil spoke his voice was ragged, as if, like she, he was having difficulty breathing. 'Do you like this, Cassie?'

'Yes.'

'And this?'

'Yes.' His touch, stroking and circling and thrusting, was taking her to the precipice over which she longed to jump, but this time she wanted more. She wanted to take him with her. She wanted him to fall into the dark abyss of pleasure, too. 'Jamil, can I—will you let me...?'

'Yes. Yes, touch me, Cassie.' He placed her hands on his manhood. Unexpectedly smooth, silky smooth and hard. 'Like this,' Jamil said, showing her how to stroke him, his breath coming faster, showing her that she pleased him. A small groan escaped him. She stroked again, and he groaned again, and then he resumed his stroking, too, and almost immediately it started, the slow build, the faster climb, the pause, the excruciatingly exciting pause at the top as he held her there, touching but not enough, and her own inexpert touch on his shaft became more confident, and she felt him tighten and swell, echoing a swelling and tightening in her, and she stroked again and heard his low guttural cry of release mingle with her own soft, wild cries, his hot seed spilling onto her hand, and then she fell, fell, fell, and floated like before, only more because this time she was not alone. She had pleasured and was pleasured in return. Here in the steam room surrounded by images of pleasure, she had opened another new door.

'Byron was right,' she murmured rather incoherently into Jamil's shoulder, lying damp and sated, clasped tight.

Chapter Nine

Jamil did not want to move. Once his needs were slaked, he usually desired to be alone, for a melancholy stole over him that he never wished to share. This time, however, the familiar ennui failed to appear. The pulsing pleasure of his climax held him headily high, then floated him gently back to earth as if on a magic carpet. His body felt heavy, his limbs reluctant to move. Limp and damp and warm in his arms, Cassie felt every bit as delightful as he had imagined. His release had come with more force than he had ever experienced before, but, amazingly, his manhood was stirring again.

'Hot,' Cassie murmured, opening her eyes, gazing up at him with the unmistakable look of a sated woman.

Jamil's erection hardened. Instead of sadness, he felt a sudden, unexpected surge of joy. 'How hot?'

Cassie stirred, easing herself away with some difficulty, for their skin was slippery with sweat. 'Too hot.'

Jamil got lithely to his feet, pulling her with her. 'So you want to cool down?'

Confused by the laughter in his eyes, by the smile she could see trembling on his kiss-frayed lips, Cassie eyed him uncertainly. 'What do you mean?' Catching the direction of his glance, she saw the plunge pool and remembered its icy feel. 'No,' she squealed, but it was too late. Before she could stop him, he picked her up and jumped in, holding her close, laughing as she screamed when the water hit her, kissing her protesting mouth into submission as they emerged, standing shivering in the waist-high pool, Cassie still clasped tight to his chest, kissing until desire took them once more, and Jamil carried her up the shallow steps and through the next door into the warm room. The place the Romans called the *tepidarium* was designed for cleansing, and was amply supplied with scented oils and fragrant soaps. It was also equipped with an ingenious device that sprinkled warm water over the body. Designed like a fountain, the water shot out from the mouths of a shoal of little golden fishes built into a niche in the wall, controlled by a tap in the form of a conch shell.

Cassie jumped when the first jets of water sprinkled her body, and then, as the warm water drenched her, smiled with delight at its soothing touch. Picking up an enormous sponge and lathering it with jasmine-scented soap, Jamil stepped into the jets with her and began another long, slow onslaught of her body. He might not be able to take her in the way he most wanted, but he could ensure that she never forgot him. The sponge swept over the delightful curves of her, down her spine, the slope of her bottom, up to her breasts, where the nipples peaked rosily, begging for his attention. The sponge fell to the floor as Jamil fell upon her hungrily.

She couldn't believe it could happen again so quickly. Kissing, touching, wanting, starting slowly before becoming more urgent. She could feel Jamil's erection pressing into her thigh. She could not help wondering how it would feel pressing inside her. He was kissing her mouth again now, his lips ravaging her, devouring her, as their bodies twined closer and closer, and all the time the warm soothing water cascaded over them. She was leaning against the tiled wall of the fountain, clutching on to one of the golden jets for support when Jamil knelt to kiss her thighs, her sex, and she came suddenly and violently, crying out his name. He held her until the storm of her orgasm passed, before standing up, his erection standing proud, nudging insistently into her thigh.

What he made her feel, surely he should feel, too? What he had given, surely she could return? Without giving herself time to think, filled with a desire only to please as he had pleased, Cassie slid down on to her knees, just as Jamil had done. She kissed his thighs, just as he had done.

'Cassie.'

The rough edge of his voice told her she was right. The solid, curving heft of his manhood confirmed her thoughts. She touched it, marvelling at the silken hardness of it. Jamil groaned. A surge of desire, a different kind of desire, heated her. She wanted to please him. She hoped this would provide pleasure for both of them.

Gently she cupped him before taking him in her mouth. The result was beyond her wildest hopes.

Later, they lay entwined on one of the wooden beds used for massages, allowing the gentle warmth of the air to dry them, too sated to speak. It was Cassie who moved first, aware that it must be nearly time for the palace household to be stirring. 'I must go. If I am seen leaving...'

'You are worried about what people will say of you?'

'No, I'm worried about what they'll say of you,' Cassie retorted. 'You're the one who has been at immense pains to tell me how important it is that I behave with discretion, remember? The Council...'

'The Council are my subjects, just like everyone else. I won't tolerate gossip!'

Cassie could not but smile at this. 'You may be a prince, but you can't actually stop people talking.' Her smile faded as reality began to creep in. 'They will say I am your concubine.'

For some reason, the truth of this enraged him. Jamil's eyes darkened. 'Any man who implies any such thing...'

'But they will, and it is the truth and...' Then the truth, the real truth, hit Cassie with a shock that made the icy plunge into the pool earlier feel like a hot bath. She was in love with him.

'Cassie?'

She was in love with Jamil, Prince of Daar-el-Abbah. 'Cassandra?'

Of course she was in love with him. Why else would she have behaved like a strumpet? *Her foolish, foolish heart had done it again, only this time she knew it was profoundly different!* True, undying, eternal love. The kind of love she had always dreamed of, just as she had described to Jamil that day in the secret garden. A love that made her feelings for Augustus seem absurdly trivial. She was in love with Jamil, Sheikh al-Nazarri. In love, in love, in love.

'Cassie! What in the name of the gods is wrong with you? Why are you looking at me like that?'

'Jamil.' She took a step towards him, holding out her hands as if in supplication.

'I will ensure your reputation is protected, if that is what you are worried about.'

'It's not that. I don't care about that.'

Despite the heat, the colour from her cheeks had faded. Despite what she said, she clearly did regret their lovemaking, Jamil realised. Her regret pained him, as did the need for secrecy, for it placed the last few hours in a sordid light that made him uneasy. What had happened was not sordid. It was nothing to be ashamed of. In fact, quite the opposite. He *wanted* the world to know. That she did not, that she was right not to wish such a thing, only served to make him rail all the more at the situation. Why did it all have to be so complicated? Why could she not have kept her feelings to herself? She had pierced the bubble of their interlude, forcing him to step back into reality, out of the oasis of wonder they had temporarily created. 'You are ashamed,' he said harshly, 'I should have known.'

'*No!* Jamil, don't.' Cassie dashed a hand over her eyes. The euphoria that had enveloped her, clouding reality in a rosy pink hue, had vanished. 'Please don't think I wish we hadn't—please don't. You don't understand.'

'Then explain to me!'

'I can't.' She wrenched herself from his grasp and ran for the steam room. Grabbing her sodden clothes, she scrabbled into them and, wrapping one of the dry towels from the changing room around her like a cloak, made it somehow back to her own rooms undetected.

Stripping off her damp clothes, Cassie lay shivering under the thin silk sheet and finally gave way to tears. She was in love, and it should feel like the best feeling in the world, and it did. But it also felt like the worst. She buried her head beneath a heap of satin cushions and prayed in vain for sleep to take her.

Back in the hammam, Jamil jumped into the plunge pool, but the icy water did nothing to cool his ire. How did she do that so effortlessly, turn his emotions upside down? He, who had been taught at such an early age to exercise iron control? And why, despite having experienced the two most amazing climaxes of his life, was he still burning with desire for her?

Cassie was obviously not a woman easily tired of. In fact, right now, Jamil could not imagine tiring of her at all. Despite her English reserve, she was in spirit a true wild flower of the desert. He could teach her not to be ashamed. He could show her real passion, real fulfilment, in the joining of their bodies. He could teach her that there were some feelings he knew more about than she.

But he could not have her, honour forbade it. There were some boundaries he could not cross. Unless…

Unless honour was first satisfied.

Something Linah had said the day Cassie had gone missing in the desert popped into his mind. He smiled. Out of the mouths of babes and innocents. It was ridiculous, of course. The barriers he would have to demolish. The diplomatic hoops that would have to be jumped through. And there was the not insignificant obstacle of the already signed agreement. Jamil frowned heavily as he towelled himself dry and donned his tunic.

But as Cassie had pointed out, he was a prince. If he could not do as he wished, who could? Had he not, for some time, been fretting at the ties that bound him to duty, the burdens of state that were becoming so onerous? Could not this really rather enticing solution provide him with renewed enthusiasm for serving his kingdom? In fact, were the advantages of such an alliance, bringing as it did such excellent connections, not actually something for which his people should be thankful?

It would take some thought, and a great deal of negotiation, but he had Halim, that master of tact, and he had precedent, too, in the shape of Lady Celia. And, most of all, it was what he wanted. For the first time in his life, he would be taking what was right for him. Jamil nodded emphatically to himself as he strode across the gardens from the hammam to the palace. He would think it over tonight. And then, in the clear light of day, he would act.

Time after time, when some minor catastrophe struck, Celia's best advice to her sisters was to sleep on it. 'Things always look better in the morning,' she would say, 'then we will know what to do.'

Usually she was right. Solutions to problems that had seemed insurmountable would be resolved with a clear head and a fresh day. But as she made her *toilette* the morning after running away from Jamil in the hammam, back in her corsets and one of her muslin dresses, Cassie frowned. This particular problem would not be so easily resolved. Pinning up her hair into a tight chignon on top of her head, bereft of any of her usual defiant curls, she bit her lip hard to stop the tears from falling.

This time, the advice had failed her. She had woken with no idea of what to do. No, she did not for a moment regret coming here, how could she, for otherwise she would never have met Jamil. She loved him. She would have realised it sooner or later, even had she not surrendered to the passion he roused in her. She loved him, would always love him, would never have truly loved had she not met him. Fate, something in which Cassandra had always been inclined to believe, a tendency for which she was indeed most aptly named, had brought them together. She would not have had it any other way. She was made to love him.

Despite the dilemma that hung, like the desert storm clouds, lowering and ominous, over her, Cassie smiled. She loved him so much. She loved the proud hauteur that kept him apart from other mortals, but what she loved most about him was the man beneath the princely cloak. The man only she knew. The man no one else would ever know—for despite the advances he had made with his daughter, Jamil had not changed at all, when it came to the most important thing in the world. Love. He did not believe in it, and who could blame him, given his upbringing? Even if he did allow himself to come out from behind that armour of invincibility long enough to allow it to happen, would he even know how?

The idea of Jamil in love with anyone else was too awful to contemplate. The idea of him finding another confidante to replace her was awful, too. Except if he didn't, he'd be lonely again, and she didn't want that either. What she wanted was for him to be happy.

She could make him happy. 'I could, I really could,' she told her reflection. But she couldn't.

Could she?

Celia had done it. Celia was happy. Very happy. The happiest person Cassie knew, in fact. But the difference was, Ramiz loved Celia. Jamil only desired Cassie, and that was not enough. 'Because desire can fade without love to sustain it,' Cassie said sadly to the mirror, 'and I could not bear that.'

It seemed the night had, after all, brought wise council. All her instincts told her that she should leave. To stay would be to destroy something, for she would not be able to resist Jamil, and he would surely tire of her eventually. Unless…

At this point, the vicious circle of Cassie's rather illogical reasoning was interrupted by an unusual summons. Prince Jamil wished to have an audience with her. The formality of the request set her heart beating wildly in her breast. This was the end. The decision had been made for her. Perhaps his Council had spoken.

Telling herself it was for the best—was it not exactly

the conclusion she had reached herself?—Cassie finished her *toilette*. The white muslin dress with its close-fitted sleeves and lace-covered neckline was plain and sombre, eminently suitable for the occasion. She picked out a white Brussels lace scarf, a birthday present from her sisters, and fixed it on her hair with more pearl-headed pins, pulling it down to veil her face. It would serve the dual purpose of disguising her reactions and covering the distress that would inevitably result from her dismissal. She did not wish Jamil to see how upset she was. She would not cry. She would not!

The walk to the state rooms felt like it would never end. Balling her hands into fists in an effort to stop them trembling, Cassie followed the male servant along long marble corridors to a small ante-room tiled in the royal emerald. The double doors were flung open. A seemingly endless narrow green carpet led towards a dais. The chamber—it must be the throne room—was sparkling with light, the sun bouncing off the immense crystal chandeliers which put even those at the Brighton Pavilion to shade. The doors swung shut behind her. Her escort, along with the two guards, remained on the other side. The room was empty, save for one person seated on a strange and rather hideous golden throne set upon the dais. Jamil.

Cassie began the journey towards him. Part of her, the Cassandra part of her, rather relished the dramatic scene: the ornate room, the waiting prince, the green carpet, herself all in white, making her steady way to her fate. But Cassandra could not compete with Cassie. Cassie was terrified and horribly nervous, and on top of it all, seeing him again, knowing just how much she loved him, she had to fight the urge to run all the way to the dais, cast herself at his feet and beg him to love her in return.

Or maybe that was Cassandra, too? Then she got to the first of the shallow steps of the dais and looked up at Jamil, and Cassandra melted silently into the wings. Cassie it was who took centre stage, shaking like an actress with first-night nerves.

He was dressed in formal robes, much more ornate than any she had seen him wear before. A head dress of gold silk edged with emerald, the *igal* that fastened it made of gold thread. His tunic was of the same green, the heavy gold belt buckle decorated with an enormous emerald surrounded by yellow diamonds, the like of which she had seen only once before, in the dazzling crown jewels that Ramiz had worn on his wedding day. A golden cloak, heavily braided and jewelled, pooled at Jamil's feet and trailed down the steps of the dais. It would take at least four pages to bear. It was fastened with another fantastically ornate piece of jewellery, the panther emblem in gold, a yellow diamond for his glinting, impassive eye.

Cassie curtsied low, taking advantage of her veil to survey Jamil's expression. He was not frowning, but not smiling either. Inscrutable. His Corsair look. *Why did he have to be so very handsome?*

'Your Highness.'

'Lady Cassandra.'

'You desired an audience with me, your Highness?' She was relieved to hear her voice sounded almost normal. Almost.

Jamil nodded. 'I have some important news to impart to you.'

Cassie's knees began to shake. The moment she'd been dreading had arrived.

'I have decided,' Jamil continued, 'that it would be in the best interests of my kingdom for you to become my wife.'

Once, years ago, a friend of her father's who had been to the South Seas had brought back a huge pink conch shell. 'Listen, and you can hear the sea,' he'd said to Cassie. She had, and had heard not the familiar sound of the sea, but a rushing, whistling kind of sound. She heard the same thing now, and her mouth went dry. The green carpet beneath her, Jamil's golden cloak on the steps, began to shimmer in front of her eyes, as if in a heat haze. 'Your wife?' she said, her voice trembling on the edge of hysteria.

'I have decided we are to be married,' Jamil said, frowning. 'Obviously, there will be obstacles to be overcome.'

'Obstacles?' Cassie repeated blankly.

Why was she not smiling her joyful acceptance? They were alone, he had broken with tradition to ensure that they would be. *Why was she not embracing him?* 'Nothing that cannot be overcome, I assure you. The advantages of this match over the one that my Council has arranged—'

'What?'

'Obviously, that contract will have to be nullified before we can marry.'

Cassie hastily put back her veil. 'What are you talking about, Jamil? What contract? Are you saying that you are already betrothed?'

Save for a bright slash of colour across her cheek-bones, and the luminous blue of her eyes, her face was as alabaster white as the dress she wore. 'It is nothing,' he said dismissively, 'a prior commitment arranged by my Council.'

'Nothing! You call the fact that you are formally betrothed nothing! Why did you not tell me before?'

'Why on earth should I? It was none of your concern.'

'Good grief! Of course it concerns me. It concerns me very much that you were engaged to be married when you were—when you and I were...'

'What you and I were doing had nothing to do with the Princess Adira.'

'Princess Adira! So you at least know her name.'

'I know her name, I know her family, I know what the alliance will bring in tangible terms of gold, silver and diamonds,' Jamil said angrily, 'and I also know what breaking it will cost me in terms of ill will from my Council and from Princess Adira's kinfolk, but I am prepared to endure all that in order to take you as my bride.'

They were words that Cassie had not dared hope to hear, not even in her wildest dreams, and yet they rang hollow. He had not said the most important words of all. *I love you.* 'Why?'

'I beg your pardon?'

'Why do you want to marry me?'

'There are all sorts of sound reasons. For a start, your own strategic connections to the British Empire far outweigh any offered by Princess Adira's family, and though your dowry will be negligible compared to hers, it will not matter, for my own personal wealth is more than sufficient.'

Cassie stared at him, open-mouthed. 'You talk about marriage as if it were some sort of commercial contract or diplomatic treaty. In fact, you sound *exactly* like my father.'

Jamil made a little bow. 'Thank you.'

'I did not mean it as a compliment.' She dashed a hand across her eyes. The man she loved had asked her to marry him. It should be the happiest moment of her life. It was turning into the worst. 'I can't believe this is happening,' she said, a stray tear trembling on the end of her eyelash.

Jamil, who had been about to clasp her in his arms, paused. Somehow he knew these were not tears of joy. 'It is not just a matter of your valuable connections,' he said, 'it is the fact that your English heritage brings with it modern ideas. You will be an ideal role model for the women of Daar-el-Abbah. Much admired and copied.' He smiled encouragingly. 'Then there is Linah. You have been an excellent influence on her. I would wish that to continue; anyway, I know you have grown very fond of each other. This way the bond need not be broken.'

'All sound practical reasons, I grant you,' Cassie sniffed, 'but what about the most important one of all?' It was a faint hope, but she had to know.

Jamil smiled. 'You mean my need for an heir. Naturally, that is of prime importance. After yesterday, I have no doubt that we will both find the execution of that particular duty a delightful and continued pleasure.'

Now she knew! 'Execution of duty! That is what you call it! I can't believe what I'm hearing.'

'Come, Cassie, our countries may be thousands of miles apart, but the customs are not so dissimilar. People of our class and rank marry for two reasons— mutual benefit, and the continuance of the line—you know that as well as I do. Are you not the great Lord Armstrong's daughter? Has he not approved just such an alliance for your sister? It is serendipitous that another such alliance will bring you and me great enjoyment.'

'You may think so, Jamil, and no doubt so, too, may my father, but I am sorry to inform you that I do not.' Just for a moment she had allowed herself to hope. Just for a moment she had allowed herself to dream. Yesterday, she had been making love to Jamil while Jamil had merely been taking pleasure. That is all he would ever do. The realisation was like a kick in the stomach from a mule. Disappointment made her reckless. She felt as if he had taken her most cherished romantic dream and trampled on it. 'I'm sorry, Jamil, but I can't marry you. You do not want a wife, you want a brood mare.'

She had gone too far. She knew that, in the way his face set, his eyes narrowed, in the way he withdrew, mentally and physically, retreating up the stairs of the dais to stand over her, every inch of his rigidly held stature emanating cold fury. 'I had thought you had outgrown such intemperate remarks,' Jamil said. 'I had given you credit for having acquired, in your time here in Daar, a little of the sound judgement you told me at the outset you lacked. Obviously I was wrong.'

'Obviously!' Cassie threw at him. She didn't care now. She had nothing left to lose.

'I see now that you are quite undeserving of the honour I was willing to bestow on you,' Jamil said, bowing stiffly. 'I will make the preparations for your departure. In the meantime, you will consider yourself confined to your quarters.'

He strode down the steps of the dais. Maybe there was something to be said for abiding by tradition after all. A lesson learned. As well for him that it had been one taught in private. Cassie was staring at him, her eyes wide with unshed tears. Something told him he was missing something vital, but his pride, which had ruled him from such an early age, was in no mood to explore what it was. His father was right after all! To expose a need is to expose a weakness. One alone is better than many. Or even two. Jamil walked quickly up the length of the room. The extravagantly long state cloak stretched out behind him. With an exclamation of annoyance, he undid the clasp and let it fall.

The doors slammed shut behind him. The huge room was eerily silent. Cassie's knees finally gave way. She sank down on to the lowest step of the dais and dropped her head into her hands. Tears trickled in a steady flow down her pale cheeks. She sat there, a solitary ghostly white figure, for more than an hour. When she finally rose, cramped and shivering despite the heat of the day, she was resolved. Her heart was broken, but her spirit was not. She must leave this place before that, too, succumbed and was shattered into a thousand pieces.

* * *

Jamil's fury knew no bounds as he made his way to his own apartments. That she had dared turn him down! And in such a way!

He could not believe it.

He could not understand it.

He would not accept it!

And still he wanted her. Having decided to make Cassie his wife, no other would now do. He did not know why that was the case, but it was. The fates had sent her to him for a reason. Not that he believed in the fates, but in this instance—in this instance, it felt *right*. Cassie was meant for him. He would not be denied her.

Jamil changed hurriedly out of his formal state clothes, cursing in any number of languages, none of them bringing him any relief at all. That he, Sheikh al-Nazarri, Prince of Daar-el-Abbah, should have been refused by a mere woman! The same woman, moreover, who had betrothed herself to a penniless poet in the teeth of her family's opposition.

He paused in the act of pulling one of his favoured simple white tunics over his head. Perhaps that was where he had gone wrong, not proposing through the correct channels? Hastily fastening the collar of a plain *thoub* of white cotton round his neck and ramming his head dress in place, he made his way out of his apartments to the stables, deep in thought. Having incurred her father's wrath as a result of her incomprehensible misalliance with the poet, Cassie was not likely to defy him a second time, he realised, springing into the saddle and spurring his horse into motion.

But she would not need to. She must surely know, as

he himself did, that Lord Armstrong would welcome this alliance with open arms. Her sister's marriage to Prince Ramiz had been a great diplomatic success. Cassie's marriage into the royal family of Daar-el-Abbah would consolidate Britain's position of influence in Arabia, protecting the vital fast-trade route to India. Lord Armstrong would do everything in his power to bring that about, were it proposed. Including bringing his daughter to heel.

But for some reason, this made Jamil uncomfortable. He did not want Cassie to be brought to heel. He wanted her to come to him of her own accord. More than that, he wanted her to come to him willingly. Yesterday, in the hammam, she had shown herself more than willing. Why then had she refused him?

Riding out at a gallop over his beloved desert, past the Maldissi Oasis in the direction of the cave in which he and Cassie had taken shelter from the storm, Jamil's anger dissipated as he pondered this most perplexing of questions. Cassie was wilful, he knew that. Truth be told, it was one of the things he liked about her, for it was part of her passionate nature. She spoke without thinking. If she was ordered to do one thing, the chances were she would choose to do the opposite, not because she was contrary, but because it was in her nature to resist having her will subverted to another. A little like him. Jamil smiled wryly. A lot like him. He had handled her badly, he could see that now. He should have allowed her the pretence of considering instead of presenting her with a *fait accompli*.

There was more to it than that, though. What was it she had said? The most important thing.

The most important thing to him was her. Startled by this thought, Jamil reined in his horse and took a long swig of water from his goatskin flask. The best interests of his kingdom, which had until now always been his primary consideration, no longer felt quite so important. He had never felt like this before and it was all Cassie's fault, Cassie who had awoken these feelings, Cassie who had made him see that such feelings were not wrong.

The most important thing to Cassie, Jamil realised hot on the heels of this revelation, was romance. Hearts and flowers and pretty speeches. What she called love. True love, such as she had described so fervently to him that day in the ruined east wing. Jamil's lip curled. Love. Upon that subject she had not changed his mind. Love of that kind was a myth dreamed up by those damned poets she favoured to explain away passion, nothing more. Poor, deluded Cassie—could she not see that the desire that flamed between them was far more tangible and even more long-lasting? Past experience should have taught her that much.

Jamil's fists clenched. No matter how shallow were her feelings for the man to whom she had been betrothed, he did not like to think of her feeling anything for anyone but him. A simple, primal possessiveness gripped him. She must be made to see that what they had together was something much more tangible. It was not love that made the heart beat faster, but desire. If he could make her see that, if he could show her how real could be a body's fulfilment, she would have no need for empty declarations. If he could show her that, she would see that what they had between them was more than most had. He would prove it to her. He was already looking forward to proving it.

As soon as he got back, he would talk to Halim about the cancelling of his current betrothal. It had been a mistake from the start. He should have known, from his own uncharacteristic prevarication, that it was wrong. It would be messy, and would cost him dearly, but he cared naught for that. He would not marry Princess Adira. Cassie or no, he doubted he would ever have married the Princess Adira. Thank the gods for Cassie.

Turning his horse for home, Jamil smiled to himself. For once his own desires and those of his kingdom were in harmony. He could hardly wait to claim her. Blood rushed to his groin at the thought of finally thrusting into Cassie's warm, yielding flesh. To spend himself inside her. To feel her velvet heat sheathing him. To plant his seed in her garden of delights. Such rapture, he was certain they would experience such untold rapture. His erection curved hard against his belly. Soon she would be his, and no one else's.

Spurring his horse into a gallop, Jamil headed back to Daar, his head full of delightful plans for Cassie's deflowering.

Chapter Ten

Peregrine Finchley-Burke's journey by dhow down the Red Sea to A'Qadiz had provided blessed relief from the claustrophobic heat and dust of Cairo. He had enjoyed his time on board immensely. Watching the pretty coral reefs and the local boys diving for pretty coloured fish took his mind off the tribulations of his diplomatic career, which was also pretty. Pretty disastrous, that is. Lying in the back of the little craft under the shade of the canopy, idly trailing his hands in the water, with his neckcloth loosened and his waistcoat unbuttoned, Peregrine imagined himself as a pharaoh of ancient Egypt, waited upon by sultry-eyed slaves, who would bow and scrape at his feet and pander to his every whim. It was a beguiling fantasy, one with which he happily whiled away the hours as the dhow made its meandering way south, allowing him to forget all about the travails which undoubtedly lay ahead.

Until, that is, they joined the swarm of river traffic

that made negotiating their way into the ever-expanding port of A'Qadiz a most hazardous affair. Peregrine kept his eyes tight shut amid the chaotic bustle until a gentle prod from the boatman indicated that they were safely berthed. He stepped gingerly ashore into the fray of braying mules and bleating camels and gesticulating, sweaty stevedores and clawing, insistent hawkers offering him everything from a new camel to a new wife, most of which, fortunately, he did not understand. A tiny sand-cat kitten, its ringed tail twitching in terror, was placed into his hands. A small child held determinedly on to his cutaway coat, tugging at one of the decorative silver buttons in a most alarming way. Attempting to brush the child away, Peregrine dropped the kitten, which landed, claws out, on the left leg of his dove-coloured pantaloons. Peregrine shrieked. The kitten hissed. The small child laughed. A man selling incense took advantage of the pause in the procession to douse Peregrine liberally with something that smelled distinctively of old dog, and waited, hand extended expectantly, for payment.

With a sigh of resignation, Peregrine reached into his pocket for the inexhaustible supply of pennies he had learned, in Cairo, to keep there for just such occasions. His dream of himself as King Akhenaton vanished in the puff of noxious smoke emanating from the incense bowl. 'Balyrma,' he announced, to no one in particular, followed by the very few words of the language he could command. *Camel. Tent. Guide.* Few words, but sufficient, for within an hour, after some haggling, entered into with gusto on the part of the would-be guide, with resignation by his customer, Peregrine was seated uncomfortably upon a camel headed east.

Three hot dusty days later, he arrived at Balyrma to be greeted with some surprise by Prince Ramiz and his wife, Lady Celia, formerly Armstrong, now Princess al-Muhanna.

'Mr Finchley-Burke,' Celia said, handing him a glass of iced tea, 'what an unexpected pleasure, I hope you are well.'

Although he was used to the Eastern habit of sitting on the floor, it was not a position in which Peregrine was ever comfortable. The not-insubstantial bulk of his stomach made it difficult for him to do anything more dignified than loll, and he was—correctly, as it happened—rather horribly afraid that he looked more like a grounded walrus than a man of fashion. 'Oh, tolerably well, thank you,' he said, wriggling his ample buttocks on to a large—but not quite large enough—satin cushion. 'Can't complain, you know.'

'And you are enjoying your new career at the Consulate?' Lady Celia continued politely, trying not to catch her husband's eye.

'Absolutely,' Peregrine said, smiling bravely.

'I'm sure you must have made yourself quite indispensible to Lord Wincester by now.'

Peregrine blushed. Despite having over a year of sound British diplomatic training under his belt, lying did not come naturally to him. 'Well, as to that—well.' He took a sip of tea.

'You are too modest,' Celia said with a smile. 'Why

else would Lord Wincester send you here to us on what I am sure must be most important business?'

'Yes, just what exactly is this mission of yours?' Ramiz asked pointedly. 'I was not informed of your impending visit.'

'Ah.' Peregrine took another sip of tea. 'Thing is, not actually an affair of state. At least, not strictly...'

Intrigued, Celia set down her own glass and cast her husband an enquiring look. 'You have come here, perhaps, on business of your own?'

'No, no. Lord, no. Don't get me wrong,' Peregrine said, flustered, 'I mean lovely to be here and all, lovely to see you both again, but—no. Fact is,' he blurted out, diplomacy forgotten, 'it's about your sister.'

'My sister!' Celia paled, and sought her husband's hand. 'Which one? Has there been an illness at home? Why has not my aunt, or my father—? Peregrine, please tell me you are not here to inform me that there has been a tragedy.'

'No, no. Nothing like that. Not involving one of *those* sisters any road. I'm talking about the one here in Arabia. Lady Cassandra.'

'Cassie! What has happened to Cassie?'

'I beg you to be calm, Lady Celia. Didn't mean to alarm you.'

'Then you will tell us, if you please, exactly what it is you have come here to discuss, and you will tell us quickly without further prevarication,' Ramiz said in clipped tones, all amusement gone as he pulled his wife protectively towards him. 'Don't worry,' he said to Celia, 'if Cassandra had come to any harm, we would have heard it direct from Prince Jamil before now. I am sure of it.'

'Of course. Of course,' Celia said. 'Silly of me.' She turned her attention once more to Peregrine. 'Please explain, Mr Finchley-Burke, you have my full attention.'

But when Peregrine finished his halting and somewhat expurgated explanation, Celia was more confused than enlightened. 'But I don't understand—why is my father is so keen to have Cassie return to England forthwith?' she asked.

Peregrine shrugged embarrassedly. 'Mine is not to reason why. I suspect he is concerned for her—ahem—safety.'

'But that doesn't make any sense. I wrote to Papa when Cassie left for Daar to inform him that she was taking up the role of governess there with my full approval, but he must have sent his communiqué to Cairo before that. How, then, did he know of Cassie's presence there? And more to the point, *what* precisely does he think she is doing there?'

'Ah,' Peregrine said, shuffling uncomfortably on his cushions.

'Ah?'

'Suspect he thinks it's a little less above board than—you know how these rumours fly at the Foreign Office, Lady Celia.'

'I do indeed, Mr Finchley-Burke,' Celia replied acerbically. 'Let me assure you, my sister and I have been in regular correspondence since she went to Daar, and she is not only perfectly happy there, she is very well thought of, and is making an excellent fist of her role as governess. Prince Jamil is her employer, nothing more.'

'I'm sure, I'm sure. But regardless of that, I'm still under strict instructions to facilitate her immediate return to England,' Peregrine said despondently, 'whether the young lady wishes it or not. It is not a task I relish, I can tell you, but there you have it, needs must. I will rest here tonight, with your permission, then set off for Daar tomorrow.'

Celia turned to her husband. 'Perhaps it is for the best if I accompany him, dearest? I am overdue a visit to see Cassie, and Bashirah is weaned now. I'm sure there is nothing at all wrong, but I would rather see that for myself, just to make sure.'

Ramiz nodded. 'It would make sense.'

'Then it is settled. I will accompany you to Daar, Mr Finchley-Burke, if you have no objection.'

'Objection? My dear Lady Celia,' Peregrine said with enormous relief, 'that is a most capital idea, a most capital idea indeed. Your assistance in this matter would be most gratefully received.'

Clearly buoyed, Peregrine left for 'a bit of a wash and a brush up' as he put it, and Celia turned to her husband. 'I just need to make sure this ridiculous man doesn't upset Cassie unduly, that's all. She is still recuperating emotionally from this Augustus business. I don't want a combination of Papa and Mr Finchley-Burke setting her back. I'll only be gone a few days.'

'One day is too many,' he replied, kissing her deeply. 'I will have the caravan readied for the morning. Hurry back, my beloved.'

'Don't worry, I won't be away from you a day more

than I have to,' Celia replied, melting into his arms. 'Anyway, I am already looking forward to you welcoming my return.'

Upon his return to the palace later that same morning, Jamil wasted no time in summoning Halim and informing him briskly of his decision to terminate his betrothal to the Princess Adira. 'I want you to work out suitable terms,' he said, glancing through the stack of papers that Halim had left for him to sign. 'Be generous, I don't want her father to bear us any ill will.'

'Not bear us any—but, Highness,' Halim exclaimed, aghast, 'you cannot have considered the consequences of such a rash course of action.'

'Of course I have,' Jamil replied impatiently. 'It will be a tricky challenge, but one I am sure you are more than capable of meeting. I have every faith that you will be able to redraw the marriage agreement in the form of an alliance treaty, and...'

Under any other circumstances, Halim would have blossomed under the rays of such warm praise, but these were not any other circumstances. Never before, to his knowledge, had a betrothal been broken without a war resulting. 'Prince Jamil, I beg you to reconsider...'

'I have considered. I'm sick of considering. I have never, as you perfectly well know, wanted to marry Princess Adira, and I have decided now that I shall not do so. Come, my friend, you underestimate your powers of negotiation.'

Jamil smiled, one of his rare smiles, but Halim was too distraught to respond, rocking back and forwards on the balls of his feet. 'Yes, yes, I am flattered you have such faith in me—but no amount of negotiating on my part can produce an heir for Daar-el-Abbah, Highness.'

'An heir. Yes, I know how much you are worried about my heir, but there's no need to.'

Halim stilled. 'You have another bride in mind?'

'I do.'

'Another from the Council list?' It was said hopefully, but Halim was experiencing a rather horrible sensation. He felt as if his stomach was creeping slowly towards his knees.

'No. It is Lady Cassandra.'

Halim crumpled to the floor and began to beat his breast. 'No, Jamil—Prince Jamil, I beg of you.'

'Get up. For the sake of the gods, Halim, get up and stop sobbing like a woman. I know you don't approve of Cassie, but—'

'Don't approve! She has no royal blood, she brings with her no lands. She is not even one of us.'

Jamil had taken Halim's understanding for granted, just as he had taken for granted his support. Now he realised that his man of business was in his own way just as blinkered as the Council. So, mustering his patience, he explained at some length just why it was that his marriage to Lady Cassandra would be even more advantageous for Daar-el-Abbah than his marriage to Princess Adira or any other of the Arabian princesses on the Council's list.

Halim remained deeply skeptical, but neither his rational counter-arguments, nor his pointing out that tradition decreed the prince's marriage to be subject always and completely to the Council's approval, made any difference. The prince merely reiterated his own point of view again with renewed force. Nothing he said would persuade him to change his mind. Prince Jamil, Halim realised with sudden clarity, though he did not know it, had completely fallen under the spell of a pair of blue eyes. This was not about breaking tradition or advantageous alliances, this was about a young English governess. Halim sighed. He did not like to see his prince brought low by a mere woman like this, but the only course of action open to him now was damage limitation. 'If you were to visit the Princess Adira's family yourself, Highness, inform them in person of the change in your plans, it would be less of an insult,' he suggested tentatively.

'There is no insult to the Princess Adira. You yourself told me that I was one of five men being considered for her. She did not choose me, any more than I chose her.' Jamil ran his fingers through his hair, dislodging his head dress. *Why was nothing simple in his life?*

'You would not wish Daar-el-Abbah to go to war over a mere woman,' Halim said, playing his last card.

Jamil gave a growl of exasperation. 'Summon the Council now. I want this over, and I want it over now. But be assured, I will not permit Princess Adira to be the cause of us going to war.'

'She is not the woman I was referring to,' Halim muttered to himself as he bowed and slowly backed out of the room.

Cassie endured a horrid night. No matter that she returned to the schoolroom apartment determined to leave just as soon as arrangements could be made, no matter that her head told her quite unequivocally that to do so was the one and only sensible course open to her, her heart refused to listen.

The idea of being married to Jamil, of being his wife, of sharing his bed, if not his heart—oh, it was so very tempting. She loved him. Of course she wanted to marry him. To bear his children. To share his life.

But he did not love her. Perhaps if she loved him enough, then surely he would come to love her, too? But it did not work that way, even the poets agreed on that topic. He would not come to love her and when his passion for her faded—what then?

No, love for her had to be not just unequivocal, but utterly reciprocal. And love was an integral part of marriage. So in the end, it was simple. She could not marry Jamil, no matter how tempting the compensations. And since she loved him and only him, it meant she would never marry anyone and was doomed to remain childless.

A spinster.

A virgin.

She would never experience true love-making with him. And could not, with anyone else.

When dawn broke, Cassie rose wearily from her divan, dressed in one of her English muslin gowns, and dejectedly began to pack. If she could be ready to leave as soon as arrangements were made, it would all be for the best. A clean break from Linah. From Jamil. From her heart. It was for the best.

But the day passed, with Linah subdued, sensing something was wrong and obviously afraid to ask, and still no word came from Jamil or any of his officials.

The Council were in session, one of Linah's hand-maidens informed her, and Cassie assumed that state business had taken precedence—as it always would. Nevertheless, she resented being ignored. Obviously she was being taught a lesson as to her irrelevance in the grand scheme of things. So it was, when the summons came for her to join his Highness in his private courtyard, Cassie was inclined to reject it.

But of course she did not. Instead, she donned one of her most elegant of evening gowns, a cream crepe slip worn under an overdress of gold spider-gauze. It had a low décolleté, too low for her to have worn it in public here in Arabia for it showed rather a generous amount of Cassie's creamy bosom, but if this was the last time she was going to see Jamil she wanted to look her best. Between the tiny puff sleeves and the long, elegant cream kid gloves was just a hint of dimpled flesh. She wore her locks up, braided into an elaborate coronet on top of her head, and affixed her diamond earrings, a coming-of-age gift from Aunt Sophia, to her ears. Her neck she left unadorned. Cream silk stockings with gold clocks, which she'd never before worn, cream kid slippers and a matching shawl of gold spider-gauze, completed the ensemble. A quick glance in the mirrored tiles of her bathing chamber satisfied her. Despite the sleepless night, she looked passable.

The servant attending her hurried her along the corridors. She was late. Belatedly, Cassie realised that while she considered the time well spent, there was a chance Jamil might not agree with her. Still, at least he intended to communicate the arrangements for her departure in person, rather than have some lackey do it. That, at least, was something.

Heart pounding, head held high, determinedly ignoring the fluttering in her stomach and the trembling in her knees and the flush that she just knew stained her cheeks, Cassie stepped into Jamil's private courtyard. He was standing by the fountain, dressed in a plain caftan in emerald silk. His feet were bare, his head uncovered, an endearing lick of auburn hair standing up over his brow. Without his robes of state, he was not the Corsair, but simply the most handsome man she had ever seen. Or would ever see.

Cassie could not help it, her eyes positively ravished him, the fierce little frown between his brows, the sharp cheekbones, the almost-tilt of his lips, the burnish of his autumn eyes. He was watching her impassively, but she could feel the hunger in his gaze. Her nipples tightened in response. She thanked heaven that she had her corsets and her chemise and her underdress on to disguise this blatant physical response. He must not see. She must not falter.

But already she was faltering. Imagining the touch of his fingers on her skin. Her own on his. The soft folds of his caftan showed off his perfect physique. She wondered if he wore anything beneath it. She wished she hadn't wondered. Then she couldn't help but wonder. Then she remembered how angry he had been yesterday, and though there was no trace of it now, she would do well to be cautious. 'Your Highness,' she said stiffly.

'Jamil.'

'You wanted to see me?' Her voice sounded all wrong. She compensated for its breathiness by glaring.

Jamil spread his hands. He smiled at her, partly to reassure her, for she looked like she was walking on broken glass, and partly because he was simply glad to see her. More than glad. 'You are looking quite ravishing tonight, Cassie,' he said, taking her hand and pressing a kiss on her palm. 'Do you know, you are quite the most beautiful woman I've ever known? And the most desirable.'

Why was he speaking to her like this? He never spoke to her like this! *Why was he making it so difficult for her?* 'Please don't say such things.'

Jamil caught her in his arms. 'Why not, when they are true?'

'Because I—because we—just because. Let me go, Jamil.' But her body was already yielding, melting into the hard planes of his.

He pulled her closer, effortlessly stilling her attempt to free herself, and tilted her chin up. 'I don't intend to let you go, Cassie.'

His voice was husky. His eyes glowed fiercely as they rested on her face, on her heaving breast. Her heart was pounding, slow and heavy, thump, thump, thump. She was afraid to ask what he meant. Afraid she would be wrong. Men like Jamil did not change overnight. But she so much wanted to be right. *Oh God, she was weak.* 'Jamil…'

'Cassie, about yesterday. When I asked you to marry me, I did not make the nature of my feelings clear.'

She felt faint. Were it not for his embrace she would surely slip to the floor. 'Feelings?'

Jamil smiled wryly. 'Don't look so surprised. You were right, I do have some.'

Hope began to tap its way out of the shell in which she had encased it, like the frantic pecking of a baby bird. 'What—what feelings?'

'I have never desired anyone more than you.' He would not make her pretty speeches, but he could speak the truth of what he felt; she had taught him the value of that. Though he had never before made any such admission, curiously it felt liberating rather than destructive. The truth of how he felt. Surely not something she could resist? 'I have cancelled my betrothal to the Princess Adira. I cannot marry her. I cannot marry anyone but you.'

The egg shell cracked. The fledgling that was hope peeped through.

'Yesterday,' Jamil continued, 'I spoke of practical reasons, advantages. Those remain valid, but they are not the most important thing. The most important thing is what we have together, the special emotion we feel for each other.'

Cassie waited, scarce able to breathe.

'Passion,' Jamil said firmly.

The fledgling paused in the act of spreading its wings. 'Passion?' Cassie repeated.

'What you call love, Cassie, does not exist, save on the pages of a book or in a poem. Pretty words and sentimental nonsense, they mean nothing. Hearts do not speak, but bodies do,' Jamil said, too caught up in the unexpected relief of finally speaking his mind aloud to notice that he was making what, to all intents and purposes, was a pretty speech. 'What we feel for each other is real. More than most can aspire to. More than I have ever experienced, or ever hoped to have. We can share that, surely that is enough?'

She wanted to believe him. She wanted to be persuaded. If he could speak as he just had, if he could admit to so much that he had never before admitted to, and speak of it, too—she wanted so much to hope that *this* would lead to *that*. She knew she should resist, but that was the one thing she did not want to do. She was in danger of being swept away. Oh, lord, how much she wanted to surrender to the surging tide of her love for him. 'I—Jamil, I…'

'Cassie. Cassie, Cassie, Cassie. I want you so much. Let me show you how much,' he said urgently, pulling her close, moulding her body into his, smoothing his hands over her back, down her spine to the delightful little curve where it ended at her bottom. 'Let me prove to you that passion is enough, more than enough, to base a marriage on. Let me show you that *this* is what really matters.' He nuzzled the tender skin behind her ear lobe, licking into the crease there.

She wanted to be persuaded. She wanted to give him every chance. She wanted, wanted, wanted. His hands were trailing heat. His mouth was plucking desire from deep within her, raising it to the surface so that her skin burned with it. How could she resist?

'Cassie?'

She could not deny him. She could not deny herself. He was sure he was right? But how could she prove to him that she was right? 'Make love to me, Jamil.' She kissed his neck, the hollow of his throat, relishing the tangy, masculine scent of him. 'Make love to me.' *Please, please, let me be right. Let it be love.*

She tilted her head back so that he could kiss her throat. His lips trailed heat down to where her breasts rose and fell from her décolleté.

'I have waited so long for this moment,' Jamil murmured huskily.

He placed little fluttering kisses on the pulse at her collar bone, up to her ear, round to her mouth, making her thirsty for his, making her moan and clutch at him, until finally, finally, he kissed her, and she was lost. She had never tasted such kisses, could not ever imagined having enough of such kisses, thought she would die if she did not have more.

He kissed her and, somehow, she did not know how, he had loosened her dress, and now he was kissing her breasts, sucking hungrily at her nipples, tugging kisses, first one, then the other, and then the first one again, so that she could not think, could not think of anything save the aching pull that connected Jamil's mouth, his hands, her breasts, the throbbing, swelling pulse between her legs.

She was lying on a divan now, though she had no memory of getting there. Her dress was loose. Her slippers were gone. Her skirts were rucked up. Jamil's kisses were hard, demanding, his fingers stroking at the heat between her legs, making her buck under him, making her body clamour for satisfaction, for gratification, for him. 'Please,' she said, 'please.' *Please love me. Please don't ever leave me. Please.* She clung to him and her climax neared, neared, neared, came, making her cry out.

Barely had she floated back to earth than she became conscious of him naked beside her, his erection proud

and curved and frighteningly large. He was arranging
her on the divan, placing pillows under her, murmuring soothing phrases, promising her it would not hurt.
What would not hurt?

He looked at her, barely able to believe it was finally
about to happen. He ached with need, was heavy with
the seed he was desperate to spend inside her. And she
was so ready for him, so wet and pink, still pulsing
from her climax. He angled himself carefully over her.
Not his favourite position, but the one least likely to
hurt her. And he wanted to see her face. His manhood
nudged at her entrance. By the gods, let him be able
to control himself. He kissed her deeply, slowly, and
slowly began to nudge inside her, almost crying out
aloud at the delight of it.

He pushed gently, deeper, testing for the point where
her maidenhood would end, meeting it, readying himself to thrust, so taut with the strain of controlling his
own urge to pound into her that he could barely breathe.
'I will try my best not to hurt you, trust me,' he said,
and thrust.

A sharp pain, like the tearing of cloth. Cassie tensed,
but it was gone almost as quickly as it happened, sub-
merged in the waves of something much more piercing.
He was inside her. She could feel him, shaped into
her, the most wonderful, unbelievable, indescribable
feeling, as if he were made for her. Who would have
thought? She opened her eyes, a hazy smile on her
bruised lips, to tell him, and saw the strain of his control etched on his beautiful face. Instinct took over.

Cassie arched her back the tiniest bit to encourage
him. 'Please,' she whispered, this time in no doubt

of what she wanted. Jamil tilted her towards him. He kissed her, tongue pushing into the heat of her mouth, and his manhood pushing into the heat of her sex. Like petals unfolding, like leaves unfurling, she felt herself give and give as he moved ever deeper into her, so slowly she felt every tiny fraction of him easing his way until he was sheathed. Ripples of sensation made her cling to him. She felt him pulsing as she clung, and clung all the more fiercely to him.

Ecstasy. She was ecstatic with sensation. Jamil withdrew and then pushed back inside her, like an ebb and a flow, more decisive now, as if the tide were turning as she tightened around him. She arched her back and he plunged ever deeper. She could hear his little grunts of effort, heard her own strange mewling response, felt his shaft swell and thicken, felt herself tensing again, and, as he cried out his gratification as he surrendered suddenly to the intensity of his own climax, she felt her own surge and swirl around her again and again, catching her up and casting her adrift, lost in a world that was only she and he and the one that they had become. Who would have believed it? Cassie thought, clinging and clinging to him, holding him to her, inside her, feeling the last ripples of his orgasm send responding echoes of her own shivering through her, until she thought she would die of pleasure.

Jamil rolled over on to his back, pulling her with him, reluctant to disconnect from her, already wanting more. It was all he had dreamed. All he had fantasised. More. He had never felt so—satisfied? Not just that. Sated? Not yet. Whatever it was, he wanted more. And he could have it now. Any time. Every day. Cassie was his. With a lazy smile of satisfaction, he twisted a long golden curl of her hair, which had escaped its elaborate braid, around his finger. Jamil was not a possessive man, but there was something primal about his feelings for this wilful, beautiful Englishwoman that made him want to mark her as his own. His woman. His wife.

Cassie opened her eyes to find Jamil gazing down at her, his eyes glowing with satisfaction and intent. 'A penny for them,' she said, smiling up at him.

He looked quizzically at her. 'An English saying,' she explained. 'It means tell me what you are thinking.'

Jamil's laugh was a low growl of intent. 'I'm thinking that, having made my point so eloquently, I would like to make it again. Right now.'

She could feel his stiffening manhood nudging against the small of her back. He was indeed more than ready to take his pleasure. To give her pleasure. To make love? A crushing weight of disappointment hovered like a cloud, waiting to envelop her in its gloom. He had not said it. The words, which she was having to almost physically swallow, were never going to touch his tongue. She had poured her love over him, on to him, into him, in the hope that it would rouse the same feelings in him, but it had not. It had not. *Had it?*

She had to know. 'Jamil, don't you feel any different, now that we have…?'

He nuzzled her neck. 'Feelings, always feelings with you, Cassie. You know how I feel.' He took her hand and placed it on his manhood. 'This is what I feel for you.'

Passion. Desire. Not love. It would never be love. She had her answer. *What a fool she had been! What a complete and utter fool!* She felt the little fledgling of hope drop broken-winged to the ground. Jamil did not love her. Jamil would never love her. Worse! He'd made it clear, perfectly, abundantly, unequivocally clear, that he did not want her love. He wanted her body. It was all he'd ever want from her. She'd hoped he'd wanted her, Cassie, the person inside, not the packaging. She felt sick. And angry. And cheated. The pain enveloped her, a dense black mass of despair. She had to get out of here, away from him, before he saw, because that would be the ultimate humiliation. Pushing herself free from his embrace, Cassie sat up. 'No!'

Jamil tried to pull her back down again. 'Did I hurt you? Next time, I promise it will not…'

She struggled frantically to release herself, terrified lest her love, her poor wounded love, would clutch at the crumbs he offered, pleading that they would be enough, knowing they were not. She had to get away. 'Leave me alone. Get off me.' She struggled to her feet, breathing harshly.

'Cassie, I didn't mean to hurt you.'

'You didn't hurt me. And there won't be a next time.'

'If you mean you wish to wait until after we are married, then I would respect your wishes,' Jamil said reluctantly. It would be a compromise. A severe compromise, but the rites could be arranged quickly. Well, relatively quickly. Six weeks. The very notion of waiting six weeks filled him with horror.

'We're not getting married.'

Her words had a finality to them that cut into him like a dagger. For a few moments Jamil could only stare at her in stupefaction as Cassie began to right her clothing. 'You are being ridiculous,' he finally managed. 'I thought you understood. Tonight—'

'I do understand. I wish I didn't, but I understand. You've made it perfectly clear.' She was trembling. Her fingers could not manage her buttons. She could not tie her lacings. Hastily clutching her dress together anyhow, she clenched her fingers into little fists and folded her arms across her chest, partly to steady herself, partly to hide her anguish from Jamil. If only he would not look at her so. If only...

She steeled herself. *If only* belonged in the world of fairytales and poetry. This was the real world. 'I'm sorry,' she said, her voice cracking, 'I can't marry you.' He looked so thunderstruck that she could not resist touching him, putting her little clenched fist to his arm, but Jamil shook her off angrily.

'You still insist on love, Cassie? You are deluded, for you are looking for something that does not exist. You will not find it. Here or anywhere else.'

Cassie flinched. *I have found it, I have.* But it was no use. 'I'm sorry,' she said again, for there was nothing more to be said.

He felt as if the world was coming crashing down around him. All his certainties. All his plans. Gone, in an instant. Suddenly, it was too much. 'Get out!' he roared. 'Get out of here, and never let me set eyes on you again.'

She had the distinct impression that her heart was breaking, something that turned out to be no poetic licence. Not just her heart. Her world. She was on the brink of a precipice. The urge to hang on with her fingers was so strong she almost followed it. To have just a little was surely better than to have nothing?

Cassie wavered. To be his wife, to be desired, if not loved—surely that was still worth having? But one look at Jamil's face told her that option was no longer open to her. And anyway, in her heart, that poor, wounded heart of hers, she knew it would be wrong. She loved him absolutely. Nothing else would suffice.

Jamil's skin was pale, his lips two thin lines. Almost, Cassie did not recognise him. 'I'll bid you goodbye then.' Her voice wobbled. She waited, but Jamil made no reply, staring resolutely over her head, as if she did not exist. Cassie turned, with a heavy heart, and made for the courtyard door.

After it closed behind her, Jamil retrieved his scimitar from the ceremonial case in which it lay glittering wickedly. Returning to the courtyard, with a fierce intake of breath, he lifted it high over his head and brought it down in a series of smooth, vicious arcs, neatly slicing through a row of ornamental bay trees, leaving the tops of the bushes lying like the heads of decapitated soldiers on a battlefield.

Chapter Eleven

Jamil left Daar-el-Abbah early the next morning. Cassie had dealt a bitter blow to his pride, but the knowledge, lurking in the dark recesses of his mind, that it was not sufficient to quell his overwhelming need to make her his, was what made it necessary for him to leave the royal palace. Knowing she was there, within its walls, was too much of a temptation. He would not beg, he would not demean himself by showing such weakness, but Cassie had the ability to scramble his senses so effectively he decided not to take the risk. Taking decisive action would help restore his shattered equilibrium. He decided to act on Halim's advice and deliver the news of the broken betrothal to Princess Adira's family in person.

He rode out on his white camel at the head of a small caravan. At least, it was what Halim called a small caravan, for it consisted of ten guards, about the same number of servants, and twenty mules carrying, in addition to the tents and hangings, a number of valuable gifts for the princess and her family. Jamil did not wish to be accused of a lack of generosity. Most certainly he did not want to risk offence. Though no one, he thought cynically, could possibly be offended by such an excessive hoard of gold and precious jewels.

He had no real reason to break the betrothal now, but he was more convinced then ever that he could not take the Princess Adira or the Princess Anyone as his wife. In fact, the very notion of a wife at all filled him with repugnance. With one exception. But *that* he would not think about.

Yet later, unable to sleep, padding silent as a panther beyond the perimeter of the camp, Cassie was all Jamil could think about. That he still wanted her with an unabated passion, he could not understand. She had rejected him not once but twice. That fact alone should be enough to tear her from his thoughts, to rip all desire for her from his body, but it was not. He could not fathom it, any more than he could understand Cassie's refusal. Her passion for him was as strong as his for her, there was no mistaking that. She had given herself with an abandon that fired his loins, had relished their union every bit as much as he. She would have given herself again with very little persuasion, he was sure of that, yet she would not take him as a husband. It was ironic—not that he was in the mood for irony—that all he believed of Englishwomen previously was proving quite untrue. They had a reputation for being keen to snare a husband, but less than enthusiastic about activity in the marital bed afterwards. Cassie, unfortunately, was proving to be the exception.

Jamil sat down on a large boulder at the furthest edge of the oasis and watched morosely as two scorpions carried out an elaborate mating dance on the sand. Ritual and instinct. The dance. The copulation. The production of young. Not so very different from the way he had been raised to think of his own marriage. The wedding contract and formal rites. The mating. The production of heirs. The separation of the harem, of women and children from men. As in the world of the scorpions, so in the world of the royal palace. He had his role. His wife had hers. So it had always been.

Not any more. He did not want it. He would not have it. Traditions had often irked him, but until recently he had not been inclined to challenge them. It was Cassie who had questioned, Cassie who had given him pause, Cassie who had, without him noticing, subtly altered his whole way of thinking. And Cassie who had made him realise how lonely life as a prince could be. She had taken away that loneliness, too.

Everyone needs someone! A curse upon her! If she had not challenged and provoked and forced him to see his life through her eyes, then he could have carried on as he was. As he had always been. If not happy, then content.

But that was a lie. He had not been content; she was right about that, too. His past had always haunted him. He realised with a start that it no longer did. The dreams, the memories that had tortured him, had gone since that day she had broken his father's whip over her knee. Cassie had performed some sort of exorcism.

She did not deserve his curses, she deserved his admiration for the way she had adapted to a foreign land, one with a fierce climate and an alien tongue. Had thrown herself with gusto into the fray, transforming his daughter in the process, demonstrating a love of the desert and Daar-el-Abbah's history that rivalled his own. She had even begun to master the rudiments of the language. Underneath that beautiful and desirable exterior lay a quite remarkable person, Jamil could now see.

He smiled, thinking of the many occasions upon which she had blurted out her thoughts, the way she would cover her mouth with her hand as if to push the words back, the endearing combination of guilt and defiance in her big blue eyes. The memories triggered others. The fearless way she rode, the endless patience she displayed with Linah, the care she put into the smallest of tasks, the way she smiled and the way she laughed and the way she frowned, chewing on her lower lip when she was thinking something over. The way she clasped her hands when she was nervous. The tender way she talked about her sisters. The hurt she tried to hide when talking of her father. She never lied, or even prevaricated. She said what she thought, often—too often, maybe—regardless of the consequences. She would not be ordered, but she would be guided. And she listened. She really listened, in a way that no one else did. She wore her feelings plainly on her beautiful face.

The scorpions had gone. The oasis was perfectly still. Above him, a crescent moon shone weakly through an unusual covering of light cloud. Jamil picked up a handful of sand and let it sift through his fingers. He had made no arrangements for her departure, but he had given no commands to prevent it, either. That note of finality in her voice could not be ignored. She would go, might even be gone by the time he returned. He should be pleased. Temptation would be removed. But as he watched the sand trickle from his palm, Jamil felt a piercing sadness. Closing his fingers, he tried to catch the last few grains, but it was too late. His hand was empty. Beyond the oasis, the vast plain of the desert stretched. His desert. His kingdom. His life. Empty.

There was a time for enduring alone, a time for nursing one's feelings back to health without anyone ever knowing they had been hurt, a time for trying to prove that one could rise above one's reputation as the flighty, irresponsible one of the Armstrong girls. And then there was a time to seek solace with the person who had been her chief comforter and solid supporter since Mama died. Cassie's first action the morning after making love to Jamil was to write to Celia, urging her to send someone to fetch her as quickly as possible. She must get away, and until she did, she must stay clear of Jamil. After last night, she was under no illusions about her strength of will. She would surrender herself to him whenever he asked. Her body was his—and he knew it. Her heart, too, though that, he did not know and must not. And her soul. That, she must keep safe, for both their sakes.

It would take ten days, she calculated, for the letter to reach Celia and for her requested escort to arrive. When Linah informed her that Papa was gone, and would be away for at least three nights, she should have been relieved, but was contrarily first offended that he had left without taking his leave of her, then simply hurt and very lonely. She missed him as if he had become part of her. His absence was like a permanent ache that served to emphasise the need to leave this place, for the more she had to endure his presence, the harder would their parting be. But part they must. And she must find the strength to get herself through the next ten days without betraying herself.

Tears, which had come so easily to her in the past, now refused to flow. Her grief was too great for such gratuitous expression; the devastation she was enduring at the destruction of her world was too fundamental a pain to articulate with extravagant gestures. The dramatic and flamboyant Cassie of old would not recognise this quiet, withdrawn and unutterably sad creature.

She endured. For Linah's sake, she even managed to put on a brave face. Though her smile felt rigid, and every movement was an effort, she managed it—or thought she did. She smiled and shook her head dismissively when Linah asked what was wrong. Then she claimed a headache. Then Linah stopped asking, and took to staring at her in a disconcertingly worried way, holding her hand tightly. She did not like to let Cassie out of her sight.

That, too, Cassie endured. At times she felt as if she were watching herself in a play. She wanted to scream at the fates for the unfairness of it all. Why could not Jamil love her? Why not? Why not? Tears would have been a relief then, but still they did not come. She felt as if she were hewn from stone.

* * *

What did arrive, unexpectedly, was Celia. While Cassie was sitting in the courtyard staring absently into space, the heavy door was flung open to reveal the familiar figure of her beloved sister.

'Celia! Oh, Celia, I can't tell you how good it is to see you,' Cassie said, throwing herself with relief into her sister's arms. 'But how do you come to be here so quickly? I only despatched my note the other day. And Mr Finchley-Burke,' she exclaimed, catching a glimpse of Peregrine, hovering uneasily in the background. 'Quite a delegation!'

Peregrine stepped forwards and made an elegant bow. 'Lady Cassandra. Pleasure to see you again.'

'Are you here in some official capacity? Is something wrong? Have you a message from home? One of my sisters? Oh goodness, is it Papa?'

'No, no, do not be alarmed,' Celia said, 'it is nothing like that.'

'Then what—oh, I beg your pardon, I am being most remiss, you will be wanting tea after your journey. Won't you come and sit down?'

With resignation, Peregrine followed the two sisters over to the ubiquitous heaps of cushions, lowering himself down carefully. While Cassie poured tea, and Celia took covert note of the dark shadows under her sister's eyes, Peregrine prayed for guidance. Warring tribes and broken treaties were one thing, but affairs of the heart and young lady's delicate sensibilities were quite another. A specialised field, in his experience. A field he had become bogged down in before. He need not have worried, as it turned out. His plea for divine intervention seemed to have been answered.

'I am so glad you have come, Celia,' Cassie said, ignoring her own tea, 'I wish to leave here as soon as possible.'

'Leave!' Celia exclaimed in surprise. 'But I thought you were so happy here?'

'Leave!' Peregrine exclaimed in relief, 'Excellent news. Capital!' He was suddenly aware of two pairs of Armstrong eyes viewing him with disapproval. 'Obviously hope there's nothing wrong. Didn't mean to imply—simply meant I'd be delighted to help in any way. Get you home, that is.'

Cassie addressed her sister. 'I was happy. Very happy.' Her voice trembled, but she took a quick breath, and straightened her shoulders. 'I just—things have become complicated—I just need to leave.'

Peregrine clapped his hands together. 'Righty-ho. What say we just turn the caravan around immediately? Camels will barely be in the stables. If I just pop round now,' he said, creaking to his feet, 'we can be on our way in jig-time.'

'No, wait. I can't go today.'

'Nonsense. Best not to put it off,' Peregrine said with an encouraging smile.

'I can't. I have to say goodbye to Linah properly. Tomorrow, maybe, or…' *The next day. When Jamil might be back.*

'Tomorrow's not looking so good,' Peregrine said, dismayed by the sudden indecision in Lady Cassandra's voice. 'Storms forecast apparently,' he said, quite untruthfully. 'Best to go now.'

Seeing that her sister was in the grip of strong emotion, Celia put an arm around her. 'Tomorrow will be soon enough,' she said firmly to Peregrine, 'but there is nothing stopping you leaving today and returning to Cairo. After all, your mission would appear to be successfully completed without any need for your intervention.'

Cassie gave herself a little shake and freed herself from Celia's embrace. 'Mission? Precisely why are you here, Mr Finchley-Burke?' she asked.

Faced with piercing eyes every bit as blue as he remembered, and a figure every bit as luscious and distracting, too, Peregrine felt his eloquence desert him. 'I—your father, that is—worried about your safety, you know,' he spluttered. 'Thought you'd be keen to get back to England—enough of the heat and the flies and what not,' he added, shuffling his feet.

'As it happens, I do want to leave Arabia,' Cassie told him with a wobbly smile, 'though how my father…'

'Oh, you know Lord Armstrong,' Peregrine told her bracingly, 'always one step ahead, always knows what's best.'

'Cassie? Are you sure you really want to go back to England?' Celia said.

Cassie nodded. 'I must.'

Peregrine rubbed his hands together and began to shuffle backwards towards the courtyard door. 'So, in that case I'll be off then, back to Cairo. Secure you a place on a ship. Or I could stay and escort you, if you wish.'

'No. Really, Mr Finchley-Burke,' Celia interposed,

'my husband will wish to make those arrangements personally.'

Peregrine had reached the doorway now and made a bow from the safety of the other side. 'As you wish, happy to oblige. Lovely to see you again, Lady Cassandra. Your humble servant, Lady Celia. If I can't be of any further service then? No. Right. Well. I'll bid you adieu.' With a final flourish of his hat, Peregrine Finchley-Burke concluded his visit to Daar. An hour later, anxious to be off before either Armstrong sister could dream up another commission for him, he was seen heading out into the desert with only a guide, a mule and a camel for company.

'How very strange that Papa should have sent for me at this time,' Cassie said to her sister, back in the Scheherazade courtyard. 'I suppose I should not be surprised; he never wanted me to out come here in the first place.'

'And I thought you did not want to leave,' Celia said. 'Your letters have been so full of Linah this and Linah that. Where is she, anyway?'

'Visiting friends. She is permitted to do so once a week now.' In the excitement of Celia's unexpected arrival, and the need to preserve face in front of Mr Finchley-Burke, Cassie's woes had retreated to the back of her mind, but now they returned to her with full force. 'I sent you a note,' she said, slumping back down on to the cushions by the fountain. 'You obviously haven't got it yet. I'm so glad you're here, anyway.'

'No.' Now that they were alone, Celia took the opportunity to look more closely at her sister. It was not just the dark shadows, but the lack of animation in her beloved sister's face that worried her. Cassie's eyes were dull, her attention seemed to be turned inward. When she smiled, as she was trying to do now, it looked more like a grimace. Something had hurt her; her misery was obvious in the tense way she was holding herself. But to hold a tight rein on her emotions—that wasn't like Cassie. Nor was the distinct lack of tears. Her sister was being most un-Cassandra-like, Celia noted with growing alarm. 'What is it, dearest? Tell me what on earth has been going on. And no shilly-shallying, if you please, I want the truth.'

Under her sister's concerned gaze, Cassie's throat clogged. She shook her head, avoiding eye contact. 'I can't. You will think I'm so foolish. And you're right, Celia, I *am*.'

'Please, Cassie, tell me what's wrong. I can't bear to see you like this. You look as if someone has died.'

Cassie's chin wobbled. 'Not someone, but something. Crushed to death. I love him so much, Celia.'

'Love him? Who?'

'Jamil. Prince Jamil. I am in love with him.' Her confession came out in a rush.

'Oh, dear.'

Her fingers plucked feverishly at the embroidery on one of the satin cushions. It was almost a relief to say it. 'I know. I know. I know. And he wants to marry me, and he's so angry that I said no, and now he's gone away and he hates me. He hates me, Celia, and I love him so much.'

'Marry you!'

'It was the most awful thing. He sounded like Papa, and he said it would be a pleasant duty for him to produce an heir, and he said that his betrothal to the Princess Adira didn't matter, and…'

'He is already betrothed!'

'Not any more. He's off breaking the news to her family at the moment. And now he won't have anyone to give him an heir. And I don't want anyone else to give him an heir. Except I don't want him to be alone either.' Cassie gave a hysterical little laugh. 'Oh, Celia, it's hopeless, all of it. I must get away from here, you see that, don't you? I can't see him again, but I can't bear the thought of never seeing him again. I can't. I just can't. Please, please, please, just take me away.'

At this point, Cassandra would normally have thrown herself on to her sister's shoulder and sobbed, but she did not. Cassie simply resumed her frantic plucking, unravelling a beautiful fringe of emerald-and-gold *passementerie*, winding the strands around and around her fingers, rocking back and forth, staring off into space with an expression of misery on her face that Celia had not seen since their mother died. Then, Cassie had not cried either. With a sense of foreboding, Celia began patiently to extract the story. From the things Cassie left out, together with her own experience of just how very seductive the desert and its princes could be, she surmised with some accuracy the full extent of Cassie's indiscretions. She could not blame her, having been just as indiscreet herself when first she met Ramiz, but nor could she see a way out of the tangle. Nothing Cassie said gave her the slightest hope that Prince Jamil loved her. And on this matter the sisters were in complete accord. Without love, Cassie could not—should not—marry.

'So you'll take me away from here?' Cassie said, looking at the carnage she had wreaked on the cushion with some surprise. 'Tomorrow. Only I must stay to see Linah first. She will be so upset; we have become very close. My only consolation is that I have done some good there. Jamil—Jamil—he loves his daughter, and she loves him.'

'Then you have indeed done some good, and should be proud of yourself,' Celia said bracingly. 'Tomorrow, then, we'll start back to Balyrma. If you're sure.'

White-faced but determined, Cassie nodded.

But Linah took the news very badly indeed, and Cassie's self-control was tested to the limit. The child was distraught, blaming herself, pleading with her governess to stay, promising never to misbehave again. Touched to the core by this evidence of her affection, Cassie was overwhelmed with guilt.

Broken-hearted, Linah begged for one final outing on horseback together. Desperate to make amends, Cassie agreed. But when they arrived at the stables the next morning as dawn was breaking, they discovered that Jamil's groom, who always accompanied them when he was not able to do so himself, was smitten by a fever. Linah's disappointment knew no bounds. Cassie was powerless against her frantic pleas. Though she knew it was forbidden, she decided just this once to take Linah out alone.

They set out at a slow trot through the city, out of the gates and into the desert, taking the familiar route to the Maldissi Oasis, where they stopped for a refreshing drink of water. The sun was rising in the azure-blue sky. They sat in the shade of a cluster of palm trees and sipped from a goatskin flask, dangling their bare feet in the shallows of the pool.

Anxious not to be away too long from the palace, Cassie put her stockings and boots back on, and helped Linah into the saddle, but the little girl wasn't ready for her treat to end and begged that they go on just a little bit, that they have a race. Cassie agreed, unwilling to deny Linah on this their last ever day together. They set off, Cassie giving Linah a head start.

Spurring her pony into a gallop, the little girl headed due east, directly into the sun. Cassie's stirrup had come loose. She took some time to adjust it, and by the time she was back in the saddle, Linah was lost in the dazzle of the sunlight. A knot formed in Cassie's stomach. She should not have let her out of her sight. Pulling on the reins, she set off towards the speck in the distance that must be her charge. How had the child got so far so quickly? Urging her grey mare into a gallop, Cassie called her name, but Linah either ignored her, or her voice was lost in the wind. She called again, and saw the speck slow. Relieved, she began to do the same.

She was only two hundred yards from Linah when three men on camels appeared from behind an outcrop of ochre rock directly into their path. The child pulled her pony up so quickly she tumbled off, and Cassie gave a cry of dismay. Leaping down from the mare almost before she came to a halt, she gathered Linah to her, relieved to find her dazed and bruised, but with no broken bones.

'Thank you,' she said to the nearest man, who had a hold of the pony's reins, but when she made to take them from him, he growled and snatched them back, spitting an oath. The pony shuffled nervously in the sand. Linah shrank against her side. Cassie looked from one man to the other, noting the ragged clothing, the straggling beards, the hungry look in their eyes beneath their red-and-white chequered head dresses. Brigands.

Fear ran like an icy river down her spine, but she knew better than to show it. Cassie cast the man holding the reins a haughty look. He had a vicious scar running from his ear down to his neck. 'Thank you for your kind help,' she said again, holding out her hand imperiously. 'I will take these now.'

The man growled something incomprehensible. Linah whimpered and huddled into Cassie's skirts. Cassie's mare was some fifty yards away now, for she had let her go in her rush to get to Linah. She surveyed the motley group. The other two men were watching the one with the scar, obviously taking their cue from him. Each man wore an unsheathed scimitar tied around his waist. She had no weapon but surprise.

Without giving herself time to think, Cassie made to snatch the pony's reins. The scarred man leapt from his camel, pulled a dagger from behind his back and grabbed her. She did not know whether they meant to rob or murder her; her only thought was to get Linah to safety. As the thin point of the blade made contact with her neck, Cassie dealt him a vicious kick on the shins. He yelped and dropped the reins.

'Run, Linah, run,' Cassie screamed, pushing the little girl towards her pony, grabbing the man's belt and digging her heels in to prevent him from giving chase, at the same time sinking her teeth into the hand that held the knife. The scarred man howled, his two henchmen dismounting in order to come to his aid, were already on the sand when Linah scrabbled into her saddle and spurred her pony into a wild gallop. As Cassie kicked and bit and threw sand indiscriminately at each of the men, she caught a glimpse of Linah's terrified face looking over her shoulder. 'Ride!' she screamed. Then a vicious blow to her temple from the hilt of a scimitar knocked her unconscious to the sand.

She awoke to darkness and agony. Her mouth was dry; it felt as if it had been washed out with sand. Her head was a ball of fire, centred on her right temple. She tried to sit up. White light blazed, a searing pain, and she lost consciousness. Some time later, she came to again and this time lay completely still, trying to assess the situation The ache was now a dull throb. Her mouth was almost glued shut with thirst. She was lying on her back in the sand, in what appeared to be a cave. She wriggled her toes, then tried to move her feet, only to find them bound. Her arms, too, were tied at the wrists and bound to a stake in the ground. She had only a groggy memory of how she had come to be here.

'Linah?' Her voice was the merest croak, echoing eerily into the darkness. No reply. 'Linah,' Cassie said again. Nothing. Good, she had escaped. Or else she was being held separately. Or else—*no, no, don't think that.*

Time passed. She had no idea how long. She lay fitfully between sleeping and waking, waiting, trying not to wonder, for to wonder was to panic. Linah had escaped. She would fetch Jamil. No, Jamil was not there. She would fetch Halim. Not there either, he was with Jamil. The guards then. Or—or Peregrine Finchley-Burke. Light-headed with dehydration, Cassie giggled as she tried to picture apple-shaped Peregrine riding to her rescue. He would not get even as far as the Maldissi Oasis. And even if he did, how would he know where to look next? He did not know the desert. Besides, he was probably halfway to Cairo by now. Only Jamil knew this desert well enough. And Jamil probably didn't care. And even if he did, he wasn't there. And...

Tears rolled down Cassie's cheek. She could taste them, salty and hot on her tongue. They made her even thirstier. What would she rather die of—thirst or whatever the brigands had planned for her? A thousand cuts? Were they going to stake her out in the heat of the sun and leave her to the predators? Or maybe they would first ravish her. Maybe they intended not death, but life as some sort of slave. She recalled the hungry look in their eyes and shivered so hard her bonds dug into her wrists. If only she had not read all of those tales in *One Thousand and One Nights*. To think that she used to believe them romantic, even the most bloodthirsty. She did not want to die like a heroine. She had a sneaking suspicion that she was not going to make any real sort of heroine anyway. A real one would surely have found some way of freeing herself by now.

Cassie strained, but the ropes merely cut deeper into her wrists and her ankles. They must have taken her boots. How dare they take her boots! And her stockings, too—her feet were bare. Somehow, this minor violation was the one which offended her most, and fed her courage. Cassie took a deep breath and screamed at the top of her voice.

'Help! Help! Help!' Her screams resounded and echoed. 'Help! Help! Help!' She was giving herself a headache. She tugged frantically at her bonds, wriggling and squirming in the sand in an effort to pull the stakes free, but to no avail. Exhausted, her head pounding like a smithy's anvil, Cassie lay panting and attempted to reason. If they wanted her dead, they would not have staked her out like this. Therefore they wanted her alive. Therefore they would be back, soon maybe. She must conserve her energy. She must try to reason with them. If not reason, she must fight. She did not want to die, but she *would* not submit.

At first, they could make no sense of what Linah said, for the child, having mustered all her strength and courage to get back to the royal palace, collapsed in a state of shock, muttering Cassie's name over and over. It was Celia who finally coaxed the story from her, and Celia who dispatched two servants hot foot, one in the direction of Prince Jamil, the other to her husband.

Even allowing for a child's natural tendency to exaggerate, what Linah told her of the kidnap was terrifying. Sick with dread, she resisted, with extreme difficulty, the completely useless but wholly natural impulse to rush out into the desert and search for Cassie herself. Instead, she interrogated Prince Jamil's head groom and with his help organised a search party consisting of palace guards. They were out all day, and into the night, but though they found the spot at which the kidnap had taken place, there was no sign of tracks leading from it, and no one in all of Daar seemed to have any knowledge of where the brigands came from, what tribe they might belong to.

Celia spent the night pacing the floor, trying not to imagine what fate Cassie had met. That they had not murdered her on the instant was her only consolation, and it was a poor one, augmented only by the lack of a body, alive or—but, no, Celia refused to think of that.

Linah had woken several times in the night, hysterical with fear. Morning brought neither a ransom demand nor any sign of Prince Jamil. In despair, Celia consulted with the groom over another search party. Then she set about pacing the floor, wringing her hands and telling herself not to panic.

Meanwhile, Jamil had concluded the better part of the treaty negotiations. The Princess Adira had graciously accepted his apologies for the inconvenience and, with even more alacrity, accepted his gifts of jewels and precious stones. The concessions that Jamil had prepared in advance with Halim, he allowed her father to barter hard over. Honour was finally satisfied. The old man's sensibilities were further oiled by the gift of an unusual rose-coloured diamond. The celebratory feast was an elaborate affair. Tables groaned with food and drink, musicians played in the background. The festivities were in full flow when the messenger bearing the letter summoning Jamil home arrived. Reading it with numb disbelief, Jamil felt as if his own senses had been kidnapped. Abandoning his caravan and his host summarily, and leaving Halim to smooth things over, he selected the best of his guards and set out in the dark. Stopping only for water, he rode the whole long night and morning before reaching Daar.

Let her be alive.

Let her be safe.

Cassie. Cassie. Cassie. He muttered her name to himself like a talisman as he urged his camel to a speed that even his pedigree beast found difficult to sustain. He prayed. He bartered with the gods. He prayed again. He offered himself in her stead. He would have offered his kingdom. That was when he realised. He would have given anything to have her back and safe. She was more important to him than life itself.

He loved her.

This need for her. This passion. This urge to keep her only to himself. The desire always to be by her side. The way he wanted always to talk to her, to ask her opinion. The way her face was etched in his mind. The feeling he had, that part of him was missing when she was not there. He loved her.

Not in a flowery, sentimental way either, but in a profound, deep-rooted way. What he felt for her, he felt in his bones. In his soul. In his heart. Truly, in his heart, just as Cassie had described it. That aspect of what the poets said was true. He thought of her and his heart ached.

He loved her. He was in love with her. In love. The realisation brought with it an elation and an enormous sense of relief, as if he were breaking free from a prison, the prison of his tormented past. He was not alone. He did not have to stand alone any longer. With Cassie by his side he was strong enough to conquer the world.

By his side. If she died—if she died so, too, would
he. He loved her so much. He would not let her die.
Cassie. Cassie. Cassie. On and on Jamil rode, the beating of his camel's hooves pounding out her name, his
love, her name, his love, over the miles of desert that
separated him from Daar.

He would not believe she was dead. He would know.
He would feel it. Here, in his heart, he would feel it.
He would know. He told himself that as the grey light
of dawn broke and despair began to rise with the sun.
He would know. Of a certainty he would know.

That they had parted in anger he could not bear to
think about. That they had parted without him telling
her how he felt, he could not abide.

He loved her. And she loved him. *How could he have
been so blind?*

That was why she would not marry him. Not because
she didn't love him, but because she did. Believing him
to be indifferent, she knew only unhappiness could
result. He would change all that. He would make her
happy. He would make her happiness his life's work.
By the gods, let her be alive. Let him have the chance
to put things right.

'I love you.' He said it under his breath. The words
sounded strange, but pleasing. 'I love you,' he said,
looking up at the fading sky. Altair, the eagle star, one
of the brightest, could just be made out. Jamil closed
his eyes and wished on it, just as he had as a child,
mindless of how nonsensical it was. 'Be safe, Cassie,'
he wished. 'I love you.'

As he spurred his flagging camel towards the Seats
of the Gods mountain range that marked the home

strait, Jamil, Sheikh al-Nazarri, Prince of Daar-el-Abbah, felt a tightening in his chest. *I love you.* The words, in Cassie's breathy voice, were so clear he had to check over his shoulder to make sure they hadn't been carried to him by the wind.

She was alive. He would find her if he had to rake the desert inch by inch with his bare hands.

He reached the royal palace mid-morning and headed straight for the schoolroom courtyard where he found Celia pacing the oval perimeter and muttering to herself.

'Thank God,' she exclaimed, all formalities abandoned as she rushed towards the prince with whom she was barely acquainted. 'Oh, thank heavens you have come. My sister…' Celia stopped, her voice weighted with tears. She blinked rapidly, taking several deep breaths. 'I'm sorry. I just—I have been so worried. But then so must you. Linah. Your daughter, she's all right. Cuts and bruises, nothing more. She's still very upset, not surprisingly. But she was very brave, she rode all the way back on that little pony of hers, you must be so proud of her. You'll want to see her, of course.'

He was pale, coated from head to foot in dust, his mouth a thin, set line. His eyes—such striking eyes, she had forgotten—were fixed piercingly on her. 'In a moment. First, tell me exactly what happened,' he said curtly.

She did, as succinctly as possible, gathering all the salient facts and placing them before him in a logical, orderly manner, from the kidnap to the various searches she had organised. Later, her handling of the situation would earn his admiration, but at present, he was impatient for her to be finished.

'You say they have found no trace?'

'Nothing. No trail, nothing. No one knows who they might be, nor does anyone claim to have seen them before. Have you any enemies, someone who bears you a grudge?' she asked.

Jamil shook his head. 'None that would dare encroach upon my territory. The culprits are more likely to be opportunistic brigands. They probably don't even know Linah and Cassie belong to the royal household or else they would not have dared attack them.'

'Perhaps when they realise the error of their ways they will release her,' Celia said hopefully.

'Perhaps, but I do not intend to leave that to chance. In saving Linah, Cassie has placed her life in danger. I warned her—more than once, I warned her not to go out without an escort.' Jamil ran his fingers through his hair and sank on to the wall of the sun fountain. 'I should not have left. We argued.'

'She told me,' Celia said gently, perching beside him.

'What did she tell you?'

'Enough.'

'I see. You must think me an arrogant fool.'

Celia smiled. 'You will forgive my presumption in the circumstances, but I think you no fool, merely a man in love.'

Jamil rubbed his knuckles in his eyes. 'Cassie always said you were the clever one. It seems you knew before I did.'

'The main thing is you know now. Now go and find

my sister, Prince Jamil. Bring her back safe and well, I beg of you, for both our sakes.'

He grasped her hands between his. 'By all that is sacred, I promise that I will.'

He left immediately, pausing only to hug his daughter fiercely to his chest, to tell her she was as brave as a panther, to promise her, to fervently promise her, that he would bring Cassie back.

Chapter Twelve

The brigands brought her water. She remembered, just in time, Jamil's warning not to drink too thirstily and forced herself to sip it slowly. They untied her and watched impassively as she struggled to her feet, her ankles throbbing painfully as the blood returned to them. To her utter relief, they allowed her to remain upright, though she was still hobbled like a camel. The air in the dank cave was fetid.

'What do you want of me?' she asked in her faltering Arabic.

The man with the scar, clearly the leader, leered and rubbed his thumb and fingers together. 'Money. Someone will pay a fine price for a pretty filly such as you.'

'It is you who will pay the price when Prince Jamil hears of this.'

'What has the prince to do with it?' the scarred man snarled.

'You don't know what you've done, do you?' Cassie

replied triumphantly. 'The little girl with me? She was Princess Linah. I am her governess. Prince Jamil will have you hunted down and killed like dogs if any harm comes to me.'

'Numair,' one of the other men said, his voice tinged with fear, 'I want no part of this. Let her go now or Prince Jamil's wrath will descend on all our heads.'

'Silence, you spineless cur,' Numair said. 'I need time to think.' They left Cassie alone in the cave.

Later, she woke from a light-headed doze to hear raised voices outside. Creeping cautiously towards the cave's entrance, which seemed rather strangely to be uphill, she listened hard.

One of the others seemed to be arguing for her release. 'Gold is no use to a dead man,' she heard quite distinctly. 'He will show us no mercy. We have offended his household. I say let her go.'

But the man called Numair shook his head vehemently. 'No. We have hooked a bigger fish than we intended, that is true. But if we keep our heads then the price of our catch will be higher, too.'

Something alerted them to her presence. Numair stood up and grabbed her, holding his knife to her throat. Cassie felt it graze the skin. 'You were spying on us,' he said. 'Maybe it would be better to kill you, cut our losses.'

'I won't say anything,' Cassie said, her voice a mere thread. 'Please, just let me go and I promise I won't say anything.'

Numair simply snarled and pulled her clear of the cave's entrance, which turned out to be no more than a hole in the ground, forcing her to her knees in front of him. 'Move another muscle, and I will make sure you never speak again. Maybe I should sample this fine catch of ours first, make sure it is of the requisite quality.'

With a swift movement, he cut the front of her riding habit open with his knife. Cassie screamed, piercingly loud. She was released so suddenly she fell to her knees. Numair laughed contemptuously. 'Not yet, not yet, perhaps. But soon, you have my word on it.'

Jamil patted the glittering scimitar which he wore unsheathed in his belt. Not the ornamental weapon of state, but a working sword, with a chased silver hilt and a steel blade freshly sharpened that morning. His dagger, he wore in the classic position for war, strapped between his shoulders, and tucked into his boot was another, smaller dagger with an ivory handle.

He rode out on a fresh camel, the royal colours of emerald green and gold flying like a flag from the saddle covers, his emerald cloak and head dress a challenge in themselves. He was the Prince of Daar-el-Abbah and he wished the scum who had kidnapped Cassie to know who they were dealing with.

The search parties had tried all the obvious places, but no one knew this desert—*his desert*—like he did. Putting himself in the minds of the brigands, it came to him. The Belly of the Vulture, an hour beyond the Maldissi, where there were a set of underground caves formed by a long dried-up oasis. An obvious place, if you knew about it. Few did.

As he neared the desolate location, Jamil's hands tightened on the reins of his camel, slowing the beast down to a walk, anxiously scanning the barren remnants of the well. Hoof prints. Feet. Three sets. He saw them, cowering behind a rock, near the entrance to the cave. *Bastards.*

Raising his scimitar, he drew his camel to a halt a few yards in front of them. Already, two were shuffling backwards, fear in their eyes. They would cause him no problems. The other one, the one with the scar, looked like more of a challenge. A heavy-set man, but muscled. Jamil's blood lust rose. *Bastards.*

He addressed himself directly to the leader. 'Where is she?' His voice was cool, steady as a rock. Show the enemy no fear.

'Safe enough where she is,' the man replied, spitting contemptuously on the ground.

'Bring her out.'

'For a price. One might even say a princely sum.' He smiled, showing yellow, uneven teeth.

'I do not pay scum like you,' Jamil snarled. 'Bring her out,' he said to the other two, *'now!'*

They did as he bid them, ignoring their leader's protests, too overcome with awe and fear to do otherwise. Bowing and scraping, they disappeared into the depths of the cave, emerging almost immediately with a bedraggled figure, bound at the ankles and wrists.

'Cassie.' In an instant Jamil dismounted from his camel and strode over to her, scimitar drawn, though it was not needed, for the men made a final obeisance before taking advantage of his distraction to turn on their cowardly tails. Gathering her close, keeping one eye on the scarred leader, Jamil looked anxiously at Cassie. 'Are you harmed?'

She gazed up at him in stupefaction. Three days without food, only a minimum of water, and her hold on reality was extremely loose. 'Jamil?'

'Cassie, have they harmed you?'

She must be dreaming. Only in her dreams did he look at her so tenderly. Only in her dreams did he gaze at her in just this way, as if she were the sun and moon and stars to him. As he was to her. She must be dreaming. 'Jamil.' She clutched at his arm. It felt real. 'You came.'

Her voice was no more than a whisper. There was dried blood on her neck. A huge purple bruise on her temple. Her skin was hot and dry, her eyes glazed. A cold fury such as he had never known possessed him. Gently, he laid her down by the cave's entrance, hastily cutting her bonds, handing her his flask before turning his full attention on her captor.

The scarred man, realising he had been abandoned, was himself trying to back away, frightened now, alarmed by the murderous look on his prince's face. 'She took no harm, Highness,' he said, raising his hands as if in surrender.

A thirst for vengeance swelled within Jamil, granting him the power of a hundred men. He seemed to visibly grow with it. 'No harm! You call that no harm,' he growled, releasing the catch on his cloak, testing the weight of his scimitar, slicing it over his head.

'Highness,' the scarred man said, 'forgive me.' He made as if to throw himself on the ground, but in the same movement drew his own sword. He had nothing to lose now. With a guttural cry, Numair launched himself at his prince.

* * *

Cassie couldn't understand what was happening. She wasn't in the cave any longer. She had been dreaming that Jamil came to her rescue. Jamil, in an emerald cloak, looking so fierce and so angry. Because she had disobeyed him by taking Linah out alone. Because he had been put to the effort of rescuing her. *I'm sorry*, she wanted to tell him. *I love you*, she longed to say.

But it was a dream. And now he wasn't there and she was sitting outside in the sun, leaning against a rock. Her head was buzzing. She raised a hand to rub her brow and realised she was no longer bound. Dazedly, she looked down at her ankles. Free.

Just in front of her, there was a flurry of movement. Two men. Fighting with scimitars. She couldn't focus. She could hear the hiss as the blades arced through the air, she could hear heavy breathing, and the scuffling noise of feet in the sand. She got shakily to her feet. The scarred man. Numair. And Jamil.

She almost called his name. Luckily it stuck in her throat. She almost ran towards him. Luckily she stumbled. Luckily, for just then the scarred man raised his sword and were Jamil's attention not completely focused he would have been slain there and then.

Cassie watched, scarcely able to breathe as the battle raged. The men were well matched, but Jamil fought with the skill and determination of a man possessed. It felt like for ever, but it was over in minutes. A feint. A side step. A movement of the arm that was almost balletic, and Jamil's scimitar sliced through Numair's shoulder, neatly disabling the arm. Blood spurted, crimsoning on the sand. Numair fell to his knees, screaming in agony, his own scimitar dropping useless to the ground.

Cassie tottered towards Jamil, calling his name. He turned towards her. She was almost beside him, her arms held out, thinking only that it really was him, it really was, thinking of nothing else, when the glint of steel caught the corner of her eye. Numair had drawn a knife, was holding it in his left hand, was aiming it high, into the middle of Jamil's back.

Cassie screamed and threw herself between them with all her remaining feeble force. The cold kiss of steel pierced her as easily as a needle through silk. Blood blossomed on her dusty habit. She looked at it in astonishment, for she felt no pain. In slow motion, she saw Jamil, his face rigid with horror, pull a small vicious dagger from the strap around his ankle. He sank the dagger deep into Numair's chest. The brigand fell back on to the sand. Blood trickled from his mouth. Jamil turned to her. He was saying something. It sounded like her name. It sounded like 'I love you'. So this was a dream after all, then. It was a dream and now she was very, very tired. She had to sleep. 'I love you,' she said to Jamil before she sank into the blissful, black-velvet oblivion of unconsciousness. 'I love you.'

He feared for her life. The blood loss, combined with her weakened state from lack of sustenance, would make it a close-run thing. Though he bound it as best he could, and made the journey back across the desert to Daar at a painstakingly slow pace in order to prevent any jolting causing the wound to open again, by the time Jamil handed Cassie over into the care of her sister, she looked so lifeless that he could not help thinking the worst.

He paced nervously up and down all through the long night. He prayed as he had never prayed before. He watched, feeling completely helpless, as Celia changed the blood-soaked bandages, changed the sweat-drenched sheets in which Cassie writhed. He listened terrified to Cassie's feverish ramblings. He knelt by her divan, clasping her hot, dry hands in his, willing some of his own life-force to transfer itself to her, offering it all if only she would live.

Still Cassie's fever raged. Not even Prince Ramiz's arrival, along with her infant daughter, could lift Celia's mood.

On the fifth night, Jamil rode out alone into the desert, to the sanctuary of the ancients. The ritual was described in one of the oldest texts and kept under lock and key in the vaults of the palace, for its profane practices contravened all the sacred laws. But Jamil was desperate.

The moon was full, a good omen. He took the ring, the great seal of Daar-el-Abbah, from his finger, a symbol of what had been most precious to him. His kingdom. He offered it up as a sacrifice for something more precious still. Cassie.

He laid the ring on the stone boulder that had been used for centuries as an altar. He tore open the front of his tunic to reveal his bare chest. Then he took his dagger and made a cut over his heart, murmuring the ancient words. Blood dripped down his torso on to the altar. Throwing his arms wide, Jamil looked up at the moon and made his fervent wish. For love to heal.

Dizziness caught him unawares. A rushing in his ears. A blackness, like a thick blanket. He tumbled forward on to his knees. Blood dripped from the cut over his heart, crimson drops on to the silver sand. He fell. As he lost consciousness, a white owl, the traditional messenger of the ancients, hovered overhead, watching.

In the royal palace of Daar, Cassie stirred and opened her eyes.

He arrived back at dawn to find the palace in an uproar. Such an uproar he thought at first that Cassie had died, until he saw that Celia, rushing to meet him, was crying from happiness, and that she was smiling. 'The fever broke in the night,' she said, clutching at his sleeve in a most un-Celia-like manner. 'She's sleeping now, a proper, restful sleep. Oh, Jamil, I think she's going to live.'

He watched from the curtained doorway of Cassie's chamber, too afraid to wake her, so shaken with love and tenderness that he could not, in any case, trust himself with more for the present. Beside him Linah tucked her little hand into his. 'She's going to get better, *Baba*,' she whispered. 'Now you don't have to be sad any more.'

Jamil stooped down to give his daughter a hug, holding her fiercely close. 'No, now none of us need be sad any more,' he said gruffly.

He watched for hours. He had no comprehension of time. Cassie slept. Jamil stood guard. He was almost asleep on his feet when she spoke.

'Jamil.'

Her voice was so faint he barely heard it. Instantly, he was at her side, gazing anxiously into her beloved face, so pale and wan. Her eyes though, her beautiful turquoise eyes, no longer had the opaque glaze of fever.

Cassie blinked. She was so tired. How could she be so tired, when she felt as if she had been sleeping for ever? 'Jamil. What are you doing here? What happened? Why can't I move my arm?'

'The brigand stabbed you. You saved my life.'

She remembered. Vague pictures, becoming clearer. 'You killed him.'

'Yes,' Jamil said tersely.

'I'm glad. He was going to kill you. I couldn't bear that. Is Linah…?'

'She's all right. You can see her later.'

'I had the strangest dream about a white owl. When I woke up I found this in my hand.'

She handed him his ring. The ring of Daar-el-Abbah, with the seal. The ring he had left on the altar of the ancients. Jamil stared at it in astonishment.

'In my dream, your heart was bleeding,' Cassie told him. 'You'll think that's silly. Hearts don't bleed, you'll say.'

'No. I was wrong. I know now they can and they do.'

He had not intended to declare himself like this. Though Cassie was still weak, he found he could wait no longer. Kneeling down on the floor, he took her hand in his. 'My heart was bleeding for you. I love you, Cassie. I was wrong. It exists. True love. Real love. One love. I love you with all my heart.'

'Jamil!' A single tear trickled down her pale cheek.

'Don't say it unless you really mean it. Please, I don't want you to say it just because you think it's what I want to hear. Or out of honour or duty because you think I saved your life. Or because you feel sorry for me. Or because—'

'Darling Cassie,' Jamil said with a smile, 'I am saying it only because it is true. You will forgive me for not saying it earlier, but I didn't realise I was in love with you. Halim did. And Celia did, too. I was too blind, too stupid to see it, but now I do.'

'Please tell me this isn't a dream.'

'It is no dream. Or if it is, it is the most wonderful one, one we will never wake up from.'

'Jamil,' Cassie said softly, 'I love you, too.'

'My darling.' He kissed her. Gently, a whisper of his mouth on her cracked lips. He held her tenderly against his heart, felt the faint flutter of her own against his chest, and felt a settling take place inside him as if something was finally resolved, concluded. As if something had taken root. Happiness.

He held her until she fell asleep, her head nestled into the crook of his arm. He held her while she slept, and he was still holding her when she woke again, ready to reassure her, to tell her how much he loved her, how much he would always love her, how he already loved her more than when he had first told her and how he would love her more again the next time she asked.

Ten days later, Cassie's strength was fully returned. She and Celia were sitting by the sun fountain. Linah was taking an afternoon nap. With baby Bashirah asleep in her basket in the same room, the sisters were free to talk confidentially.

'We thought we were going to lose you,' Celia confessed. 'I even wrote to Papa, to prepare him for the worst.'

'Lord Armstrong will have had a surfeit of mail from Arabia then, because I, too, wrote to him,' a strong male voice said.

'Jamil,' Cassie said, jumping to her feet.

'Cassie. You look well.'

'I am well. I'm very well. I've never been healthier,' she said fervently. 'In fact, I am completely recovered, am I not, Celia?'

Celia, too, got to her feet, shaking out her caftan. 'Completely,' she said with a smile.

'No small thanks to you, Lady Celia. You have my eternal gratitude. But your work here is done and you must be anxious to be reunited with your husband.'

'I confess I am.'

'As you should be,' Jamil said with a smile. 'I have taken the liberty of readying your caravan. Your maidservants have just finished your packing. My guards will escort you to the border, where your husband will be waiting to meet you. He will be as pleased to see you both as you are to see him, no doubt.'

'He is a good husband and a fine father. I am blessed,' Celia replied.

'He is to be envied,' Jamil said.

'I am sure one day soon you, too, will make an admirable husband and father,' Celia said, with a sidelong glance at Cassie.

'Jamil,' Cassie said quickly, embarrassed by her

sister's blatant probing, 'You mentioned writing to my father. What about?'

'We will discuss it later,' he said with an enigmatic smile. 'First you must say your farewells to your sister. If you will excuse me, I have some things to take care of.' He raised her hand to his mouth, and planted a kiss on her palm.

Cassie stared after him in consternation. 'What...?'

Celia chuckled. 'What do you think? He wants to be alone with you. Now come and help me change into my travelling clothes.'

Celia left just an hour later with Bashirah strapped, Bedouin-style, across her chest. The caravan disappeared out of the palace gates, leaving Jamil and Cassie alone. She was nervous. So, too, it seemed, was he, though she could not understand why.

'I have a surprise for you,' he said, taking her by the hand and leading her to the eastern wing of the palace. She had been there just once before, but she had never forgotten it. The door to the courtyard had been newly painted. It stood ajar. She looked up at Jamil questioningly, but he said nothing, only urging her forwards, into the ante-room.

White tiles, with a mosaic pattern of emerald-and-turquoise. The sweetest smell of orange blossom and something more familiar. Lavender, that was it.

Cassie took a tentative step through and into the courtyard. It had been transformed. Gone was the panther-cub fountain. In its place, a new fountain tinkled, with a mermaid as its centre piece. Outside, the garden had been replanted. Bay trees and lemons, oranges and figs. Gone was the air of desolation. Gone were all traces of Jamil's boyhood quarters. The place had been transformed into a riot of colour and light.

A little stream meandered into a pool where water lilies floated and silver fish darted in the green depths. A delightful little pavilion was tucked into another corner, jasmine and honeysuckle mingling on its trellis. The jasmine flowers were closed with the rising heat, allowing the sweet scent of the honeysuckle dominance. Delighted, Cassie smiled up at Jamil. 'The hedgerows in England are a riot of honeysuckle in the early summer. How did you know I loved its scent—oh, Celia, I suppose. There's a lane going down to the mill pond at home, I used to sneak out of the house before any of my sisters were awake, to walk there—and sometimes if there was no one around I would bathe. Jamil, this is beautiful. It's wonderful. How did you manage to do all this without my knowing?'

They wandered arm in arm through each of the rooms, Cassie's fingers trailing over delicate hangings, her slippered feet curling into rich carpets. The bathing chamber had the most enormous bath she had ever seen. Sunk into the floor, with two steps leading down into the tub, it had gold taps in the shape of fishes. 'Big enough for two,' Jamil said with a smile that made Cassie shiver in anticipation. The whole place gleamed with vibrant colour; it sang with vibrant life.

'You like it?' he asked when they had finally completed the full circuit of the rooms.

'I love it. It's magical.'

'Our own quarters. Yours and mine. I wanted to make a break with tradition, I don't want to spend any more time apart from you than I have to.' Jamil led her back to the fountain. 'This is one tradition—an English tradition—I want to respect, though.' Dropping gracefully to his knees, he took her hand. 'You can do me no greater honour than to be my wife, Cassie. You can make me no happier than to say you will spend your life with me. All I have is yours. I offer you my heart. That, too, is yours, always. Say you'll marry me.'

Cassie dropped to her knees beside him. 'Oh, Jamil, yes. Yes. For you have my heart, too, my dearest, darling Jamil. My own desert prince.'

His kiss was resonant with love. Always, afterwards, Cassie would associate lavender and jasmine with the most extreme happiness. For the first time ever, he kissed her as a lover, as if she were the most precious thing in the world, and the most desirable. Tenderly and passionately he kissed her, as if it were his first kiss, as if he had never kissed, as if he would never leave off kissing. Her lips. Her lids. Her cheeks. Her ears. Her throat. Murmuring his love. Whispering her name. He kissed her, and she returned his kisses, as lovers do, with adoration and fervour, just exactly as if they had never kissed, and always would.

He picked her up in his arms and carried her to the sleeping chamber. Placing her on the divan, he kissed her while he removed each scrap of her clothing. Kisses that coiled their wispy magic around her, raising her pulse, heating her blood, so gradually she did not notice at first. She lay spread before him naked, relishing the reverence in his face, in his touch, on his lips, relishing the way he looked and tasted and touched, anxious to do the same, tugging at his caftan until he lifted it over his head and stood before her proudly erect, magnificent.

He kissed her thighs, then licked into her sex. 'Wait, wait, wait,' she said, tossing and turning, clutching, trying to hold on, but he would not let her. He kissed her and she came, wildly, jerked into paradise with the force of it, clutching his shoulders for fear of being lost, saying his name over and over.

Even as the pulsing shook her, he pulled her on top of him, easing her down on to the long silken length of him, his face etched with the pleasure of it. Even as the throbbing receded and began to build again, he lifted her, showing her how to sheathe him and how to unsheathe, to move to a rhythm that was just theirs, only theirs, lost in the power of his thrust conjoined with her own, lost in the beauty of him, below her, inside her, swelling and pulsing until he came, crushing her to him, holding her tight against his chest, his heart beating the same wild rhythm as her own.

Her fingers traced the small scar above his heart. The place where he had bled for her. His fingers traced the deeper scar on her arm, where she had bled for him. 'You were right. To embrace true love is a sign of strength, not of weakness. You make me stronger. I love you, Cassie. I will always love you,' Jamil said hoarsely. 'I will never, ever tire of making love to you.'

'I know,' she said. Because she did.

Epilogue

London—two months later

'Henry, haven't seen you in ages.' Lord Torquil 'Bunny' Fitzgerald strode across the salon and helped himself to a glass of their hostess's rather poor claret and plonked himself down opposite his old friend. 'Frightful squeeze this, only came because I heard Wellington was bound to drop by. Didn't realise we'd be subjected to some damned caterwauling female though.'

'La Fionista,' Lord Henry said. 'If you've seen her, you'll realise why Wellington's here—you know how much he likes a good vibrato!'

The two men chuckled heartily. 'Saw your good lady wife somewhere,' Bunny said, flicking open his snuff box. 'Here with one of your daughters—sorry, can't remember her name. The plain one, intimidating gal, bookish.'

'Cressida.'

'Aye, that's the one. Pity she took after your side of the family. T'other one now, she's a fine-looking girl. Cassandra.' Bunny lowered his voice confidentially. 'Last time we met she was in a bit of a spot—assume you got it all sorted, right and tight?'

Lord Henry took a generous pinch of snuff, inhaled it, sneezed twice, wiped a few specks from his coat sleeve and drained his glass. 'I suppose you could say that,' he said, waving the waiter over and telling him to leave the bottle. 'Aye, you could say that, though, by God, Bunny, for a while there it was all hell to pay. After we last spoke, you should know I acted pretty sharply. Sent off a despatch to Cairo; there's a chap there owes me a favour, bit of a bumbler but reliable enough. So I sent him off to fetch Cassandra home.'

'And?' Scenting scandal, Bunny pulled his chair a little closer.

'Well, next thing is, I get a letter from Celia—my eldest, married to Prince al-Muhanna—usually very level-headed gal. Chip off the old block and all that. Anyway, she informs me that Cassandra has taken it into her head to become a governess. For this other sheikh. Al-Nazarri. Something about proving herself, I don't understand it—but all perfectly respectable and above board according to Celia.'

Bunny shook his head. 'And this sheikh, is he…?'

'Rich as Croesus.'

Bunny drew in his breath. 'Tricky.'

'Very. Of course, I sent another despatch to Cairo, but it was too late, Finchley-Burke had already gone. No post for weeks. No idea what was happening, then I got three letters all at once. Cassandra blithering on the way she does about what a marvellous job she's doing teaching the Prince's brat—dismissed that, needless to say. Then one from Celia telling me that Cassandra has been kidnapped and stabbed and not likely to survive. Well…' Lord Henry drank deep. 'You can imagine how that went down with the other girls. Hysterical, they were. Had to call in Sophia. Bella no use whatsoever, burning feathers and drumming her heels. Took myself off to Boodle's pretty damn smart.'

'My God, I should think so. Another snifter?'

'Wouldn't say no. Then I read the other letter…' Lord Henry chortled '…turns out it's from this prince chappie, Prince Jamil al-Nazarri, demanding Cassandra's hand in marriage.'

'Good lord. But I thought you said she was dying.'

'No, she rallied. She's all right now. Fully recovered. Funny, it took Sophia quite a while before she could laugh about it. So there you are,' Lord Henry said with what in a lesser man would have been described as a grin. 'I've two pet princes in the family now, helped my standing in the Foreign Office no end.'

'But what about the other one—the chap you were so set on Cassandra marrying—Wellington's protégé?'

Lord Henry guffawed. 'Another funny thing. Dead. Malaria. Touch of good fortune for me, because I'd as good as promised her. So there you go, all's well in the end.'

'A toast,' Bunny said, rather sloppily tipping the dregs of the not-so-bad-after-all claret into their glasses. 'To your new sheikh.'

'Prince,' Lord Henry corrected.
'Whatever. Cheers.'

The preparations for the wedding of the Prince of Daar-el-Abbah could not be hurried. Everyone wished to pay their respects and their dues. Men of import and influence, heads of tribes, neighbouring princes, distant kith and kin all wished to take part in the celebrations. Not even Halim could find a way of speeding the proceedings along. They went at the pace they needed to go at. It was the tradition. Jamil, conscious of the fact that he was breaking almost every other tradition, determined to give his beloved bride every possible chance of being accepted by his people, had reluctantly accepted the fact that the wedding would take six weeks to organise. In fact, it took eight. Eight long weeks during which he and Cassie spent an agonising amount of time apart. Eight long weeks in which they both counted the days, the hours, until they were formally united. Eight long weeks of nothing but snatched kisses to fuel their passion.

Eight long weeks, but finally the waiting was over. The betrothal ceremony, the day before the wedding itself, also followed tradition, with the women in one part of the palace, and the men in the other. Celia, who had recently discovered she was expecting her second child, was not present for the celebrations, it being the storm season and Ramiz having too much care for her well-being to allow her to travel. The loving letter she sent was gift enough for Cassie, though. In truth, Cassie would not have cared if they had taken their vows with no one else present at all. All they needed was each other.

The bride-to-be's hands and feet were painted in henna, her hair braided and oiled, and the women danced together. At this point, tradition would end, for the wedding day was to be spent celebrating the future, which meant, Jamil had informed his shocked Council, that the rites would all be new.

The morning saw the bride and groom take breakfast together in the company of their most honoured guests, the women sitting at table with the men, partaking of food from the same dishes. From behind her veil, Cassie's eyes followed her husband-to-be with a longing that was almost tangible—to Jamil, at least. Though this was the most important day of his life, he could not wait for it to be over.

Cassie's wedding gown represented a mixture of east and west. A half-robe of golden silk, with an overdress of gold lace, with long, tight-fitting sleeves, puffed at the shoulder, but instead of an underdress or petticoats, she wore harem pants of gold, generously pleated and caught into her ankles, trimmed with little gold bells that tinkled when she walked. A long cloak of gold lace trailed out behind her, also trimmed with little bells, carried by six little girls at either side, orchestrated by a proud Linah bringing up the rear. On her head, Cassie wore a golden tiara over which another lace veil was suspended, with her long hair brushed into a cloud, cascading freely down her back. On her feet, she wore soft kid slippers edged with diamonds.

Trembling with anticipation, she made the seemingly

never-ending journey down the emerald green carpet from the entrance of the throne room. The guests were so numerous that they filled the ante-room at the back, and spilled out into the corridors, but Cassie looked neither to the right nor to the left, for her eyes were focused firmly to the front where Jamil waited for her, wearing a plain silk tunic, a long gold cloak to match her own and a golden head dress. His scimitar gleamed. On his belt was one of the famous yellow diamonds of Daar-el-Abbah. A matching diamond sat on Cassie's finger. As she reached the bottom of the dais, Jamil stepped down to meet her and put back her veil.

'You look like a goddess come down from heaven,' he whispered. 'My beautiful bride. How I have longed for this moment. I can't wait for tonight.'

'Jamil.' She clutched at his hand, grateful for the support, suddenly unbearably nervous. But he smiled at her, his own particular smile, and she took courage and smiled back.

Their vows were said clearly and with a simple sincerity that made the women weep and the men harrumph.

'I now declare you my wife,' Jamil said, gazing deep into her eyes.

'I now declare you my husband,' Cassie replied, dimly conscious of the cheering as Jamil kissed her firmly on the lips.

The wedding banquet was a feast of delights, but she could barely eat. She and Jamil did not dance, but sat watching, their hands entwined, waiting. Finally, Halim stood before them, and informed them that the caravan was ready. 'My very best wishes, Lady Cassandra,' he said, bowing low. Halim was too wise a man to do anything other than accept Cassie wholeheartedly into the palace. In time, he would even begin to think, grudgingly, that the influence she had on Daar, and on its prince, was positive.

Climbing on to the high wooden seat of the white camels, Cassie and Jamil showered the cheering well-wishers behind them with gold coins, and were in turn showered with rose petals and orange blossom. They made the short journey to the Maldissi Oasis in a silence stretched taut with anticipation. The tent stood in the lee of the palms—a huge tent, an opulent tent with an enormous round divan taking pride of place. It was hung with garlands and strewn with more rose petals.

'Darling. My own darling wife. Tonight I will love you as I have never loved you,' Jamil said, scooping Cassie into his arms and carrying her over the threshold. 'And tomorrow, I will love you more.'

He laid her down on the divan and began to do just that. And later, when they embraced naked in the pool of the oasis, they made love again. The cool of the water and the heat of their skin and the velvet hardness of Jamil thrusting inside her made Cassie certain that she had indeed arrived in paradise.

As he gathered her into his arms and spent himself high inside her, as her own climax pulsed around him, she tilted her head back and saw the stars. So close, they were. It felt as if she and Jamil had taken their place among them, where their love would burn brightly for all eternity.

* * * * *

Rake with a Frozen Heart

MARGUERITE KAYE

Chapter One

Sussex—May 1824

The early morning mist was just beginning to clear as he turned Thor, his magnificent black stallion, towards home, taking the shortcut through the long yew-tree walk that bordered the formal gardens of Woodfield Manor. The bright sunlight of an early English summer shafted down through the tall trees, causing the dew on the grass to sparkle as if strewn with a myriad of tiny diamonds. The earthy scent of freshly disturbed soil and roots churned up by Thor's prancing hooves mingled with the heady perfume of the honeysuckle, which roamed untrained around the trunks of the stately yews. It was a perfect morning, the prelude to what would undoubtedly be a beautiful day.

The Right Honourable Rafe St Alban, Earl of Pentland, Baron of Gyle and master of all he surveyed was, however, completely oblivious to the glories of nature, which assailed him from all sides. Mentally drained after another sleepless night, physically exhausted after his strenuous early morning gallop, his only interest was in falling into the welcoming arms of Morpheus.

Reining his horse in, Rafe dismounted to unlatch the wrought-iron gates, which opened on to the gravelled side path leading directly to his stables. The tall, perfectly proportioned man and the huge ebony horse made a striking pair, each in their own way glorious examples of blue-blooded pedigree, perfect specimens of toned and honed muscle and sinew at the peak of physical perfection. Rafe's skin glowed with a healthy lustre. His raven-black hair shone in the sunlight, the severe lines of his Stanhope crop emphasising his faultless profile, the angle of his cheekbones highlighted by the flush of exertion from the break-neck gallop across the downs. The bluish hue of stubble only served to accentuate a strong jaw and very white teeth.

Byronic, is how one infatuated young lady had breathlessly described him, a compliment that Rafe dismissed with his customary crack of sardonic laughter. Though his handsome countenance and fabulous wealth made him one of society's most eligible bachelors, even the most determined ladies on the catch wilted under his aloof stare and acerbic wit—which suited Rafe very well, since he had no interest at all in leg-shackling himself for a second time. He'd had enough of marriage to last him a lifetime. Several lifetimes, in fact.

'Nearly home now, old friend,' he murmured, patting the horse's sweating flank. Thor tossed his massive head, expelling a cloud of warm air from his nostrils, as anxious as his owner for the warmth of his sleeping quarters. Deciding to walk the short distance to the house rather than remount, Rafe shrugged off his riding coat and slung it casually over his shoulder. Having no expectations of meeting anyone this early, he had come out wearing neither hat, waistcoat nor neckcloth. The clean white folds of his linen shirt clung to the perspiration on his back, the open neck at the front revealing a sprinkling of hair on a muscled chest.

The gate swung soundlessly back on its well-oiled springs and Rafe urged his horse forwards, but Thor pawed at the grass and snorted. In no mood for playfulness, Rafe tugged on the reins again, more sharply this time, but the stallion refused to move, giving a high whinny.

'What's spooked you?' Scanning their immediate surrounds in the expectation of seeing a rabbit or a fox peering out from the deep ditch that ran parallel to the path, instead he saw a shoe. A lady's shoe. A small leather pump, slightly scuffed at the toe, attached to a very shapely ankle clad in eminently practical wool. With a muffled exclamation, which expressed more annoyance than concern, Rafe looped his horse's reins round the gatepost and strode over to peer into the ditch.

Lying lengthways on her back, and either dead or deeply unconscious, was the body of a young woman. She was clad in a serviceable round gown of brown worsted, buttoned high at the neck. She wore no hat or pelisse, and her chestnut hair had unravelled from its pins to fan out behind her, where the ditchwater had soaked it, turning its curling ends almost black, like a dark halo. The face revealed, when Rafe cautiously brushed back the obscuring reeds, was stripped of colour, marble-white and ghostly. With her arms folded protectively over her bosom, the overall impression she gave was of a prosaically dressed effigy, the image marred only by the awkward angle of the little foot that had first betrayed her presence.

Casting his coat aside, Rafe knelt down at the edge of the ditch, noting with irritation the water seep into his riding breeches. He could detect no movement, not even a flicker from beneath the closed lids. Leaning over further, he tentatively lowered his head to place his ear close to her face. A faint whisper of breath on his cheek betrayed the first glimmer of life. Grasping one slim wrist, he was relieved to find a pulse beating, faintly but steadily. Where had she come from? More importantly, what the *hell* was she doing lying in his ditch?

Rafe got to his feet again, absently noticing the green patches on his breeches, which would have his valet tutting in dismay, and pondered his options. The easiest course would be to leave her here, return to the house and send a couple of the stable hands to recover her. He eyed the recumbent form appraisingly, his frown accentuating the upward slant of his brows. No, whatever she was doing here, he could not in conscience walk away from her. She looked like Ophelia. Something about the angle of that little foot of hers made her seem horribly vulnerable. And she was but a slight thing, after all, hardly worth the trouble of summoning two men when he had his horse. Resignedly, Rafe set about removing her from her temporary resting place.

'That will be all, thank you, Mrs Peters. I'll call if I need any further assistance.'

The words, so faint they seemed to be coming from the end of a long tunnel, penetrated the dense fog engulfing Henrietta's mind. She moaned. It felt as if someone was squeezing her skull with some medieval instrument of torture. She tried to raise her hand to her forehead, but her arm would not comply, lying heavy on her chest as if weighted down. White-hot sparks of stabbing pain forced her eyelids open, but the swirling collage of colour that she then encountered made her close them again immediately. Now her head felt as if it were being pounded by a blacksmith's hammer. The painful throbbing was unbearable.

A welcome coolness descended on her brow and the pain abated somewhat. Lavender, she could smell lavender. This time when she tried to move, her arm cooperated. Clutching the compress, Henrietta opened her eyes again. The world tilted and the room swam before her. She scrunched her eyes closed, then, breathing deeply and counting to five, resolutely opened them, ignoring the siren call of black, comforting unconsciousness.

Starched sheets. Feather pillows. A warming pan at her feet. Damask hangings overhead. She was in bed, but in a bedchamber that was completely foreign to her. A bright fire burned in a modern grate and light streamed in through a small gap in the curtains which had been drawn across the windows. The room was furnished in the first style of elegance, with pale-yellow tempered walls and darker-gold window hangings. A lurching wave of nausea swept over her. She *could* not be sick in such pristine surroundings. With a truly heroic effort of will, Henrietta swallowed hard and forced herself upright.

'You're awake.'

She started. The voice had a rich, deep timbre. A seductive quality. It was unequivocally male. Obscured by the bed curtain, she had not noticed his presence. Shrinking back against the pillows, Henrietta pulled the covers high up to her neck, realising as she did so that she was clad only in her undergarments. The compress dropped from her head on to the silk coverlet. It would stain, she thought rather distractedly. 'Don't come any closer or I'll scream.'

'Do your worst,' the man replied laconically, 'for all you know I may already have done mine.'

'Oh!' His tone was amused, rather than threatening. Completely disconcerted, Henrietta blinked owlishly. Then, as her vision cleared, she gulped. Standing in front of her was quite the most beautiful man she had ever seen. Tall, dark and really quite indecently handsome, he was a veritable Adonis. Ink-dark hair ruthlessly cropped revealed a bone structure flawless in its symmetry. Winged brows. Hooded eyes that were a curious shade of blue—or was it grey? Like the sky on a stormy night. He was in shirt sleeves and had not shaved, but this slightly dishevelled state served only to emphasise his physical perfection. She knew she was staring, but she could not tear her eyes away. 'Who are you? What on earth are you doing here in this—this bedchamber? With me?'

Rafe allowed his gaze to drift over the damsel in distress. She was clutching at the sheet as if it were her last defence, looking at his coatless body as if he were half-naked, her thoughts written large on her face.

He could not resist toying with her. 'I can't imagine. Can you?'

Henrietta gulped. The obvious answer was shockingly appealing. She was in her underwear. He looked as if he had not finished dressing. Or undressing? Did he mean it? Had they—had *he*? A *frisson*, a shiver of heat, made her close her eyes. No! She would have remembered *that*! Not that she had much idea what *that* was precisely, but she was certain that she would have remembered it. He was unforgettable.

So he was teasing her, then? *Wasn't he?* She slanted him a look from under her lashes. Her gaze clashed with his and she looked hurriedly away. No. Greek gods did not descend from the heavens to seduce slightly plump young ladies with hair hanging down their backs like rats tails and smelling—Henrietta sniffed cautiously—yes, there was no getting away from it, smelling slightly of ditch water. Absolutely not. Even if they did imply…

As his gaze drifted deliberately down to where the sheet was tucked under her chin, Henrietta felt heat flood her cheeks. A quirk of his eyebrow and his eyes met hers. Her blush deepened. She felt as if she had just failed some unspoken test and couldn't help wishing that she hadn't. She tilted her chin defiantly. 'Who are you?'

He raised an eyebrow. 'Shouldn't I be asking you that question? You are, after all, a guest, albeit an uninvited one, in my home.'

'Your home?'

'Precisely. My home. My bedchamber. My bed.' Rafe waited, but to his surprise the young lady seemed to have done, for the moment, with acting the shrinking violet. 'You are in Woodfield Manor,' he conceded.

'Woodfield Manor!' It was the large estate that bordered her employer's. The large estate owned by— 'Good grief, are you the earl?'

'Indeed. Rafe St Alban, the Earl of Pentland, at your service.' Rafe made a sketchy bow.

The earl! She was in a bedchamber with the notorious earl, and she could quite see, could see very, very clearly, just exactly why his reputation was so scandalous. Henrietta clung to the bedclothes like a raft, fighting the impulse to pull them completely over her head and burrow deep down in the luxurious softness of the feather bed. 'I am pleased to make your acquaintance, my lord. I am Henrietta Markham.' The absurdity of the situation struck her suddenly. She felt an inappropriate desire to laugh. 'Are you sure you're the earl, only—no, of course if you say you are, you must be.'

Rafe's mouth twitched. 'I'm fairly sure who I am. What makes you think I might not be?'

'Nothing. Only—well, I did not expect—your reputation, you know...' Henrietta felt her face colouring.

'What reputation would that be?' He knew perfectly well, of course, but it would be amusing to see just how, exactly, she would phrase it. There was something about her that made him want to shock. To disconcert. Perhaps it was her eyes, wide-spaced and clear-gazing, the colour of cinnamon. Or was it coffee? No, that wasn't right, either—chocolate, perhaps?

Rafe settled himself casually on the edge of the bed. Henrietta Markham's eyes widened, but she didn't shrink away as he'd expected. There was just enough space between them to seem at the same time too much and not enough. He could see her breasts rising and falling more rapidly beneath the sheet.

She wasn't what received wisdom would call beautiful. She lacked inches, for one thing, and could not by any stretch of the imagination be described as willowy. Though her skin was flawless, her mouth was too generous, her eyebrows too straight and her nose not straight enough. Yet now that some colour had returned to her cheeks and she no longer resembled a marble effigy, she was—no, definitely not beautiful, but rather disturbingly attractive. 'What, Miss Markham, at a loss for words?'

Henrietta licked her lips. She felt like a mouse being toyed with by a cat. No, not a cat. Something much more dangerous. He crossed one leg over the other. Long legs. If she were sitting where he was on the edge of the bed, her feet would not touch the ground. She was not used to sitting so close to a man. Had not ever—in bed—on bed—whatever! She had not. It was— She couldn't breathe. She was not frightened exactly, but she was intimidated. Was that his intention? Henrietta sat up straighter, resisting the impulse to scuttle over to the other side of the bed, confused by the contrary impulse to shuffle closer. Dangerously close. She decided she would not allow him the upper hand. 'You must know perfectly well that you are notorious,' she said, her voice sounding near enough steady for her to be quite pleased.

'Notorious for what, precisely?'

'Well, they say that—' Henrietta broke off, rather unusually at a loss for words. There were grass stains on the knees of his breeches. She caught herself staring at them, wondering precisely how they had come to be there and whether they were anything to do with her. Realising he had noted her blatant gaze, she blushed yet again, pressing on. 'Not to put too fine a point on it, they say that you are—only I am sure it is nonsense, because you can't possibly be as bad as—and in any case, you don't look at all like I imagined one would look like,' she said, becoming quite flustered.

'I don't look like *what* one what would look like?' Rafe said, fighting the urge to laugh.

Henrietta swallowed. She didn't like the way he was looking at her. As if he might smile. As if he might not. Appraising, that was the word. If it was a word. Once again, she worried about being found lacking. Once again, she chided herself for such a pathetic response, but he was so overwhelmingly male, sitting far too close to her on the bed, so close that her skin tingled with awareness of his presence, forcing her to fight the urge to push him away. Or was that just an excuse to be able to touch him? That crop of raven-black hair. It looked like it would be silky-soft to the touch. Unlike the stubble on his cheek, which would be rough. 'A rake,' she blurted out, now thoroughly confused by her own reactions.

The word jarred. Rafe got to his feet. 'I beg your pardon?'

Henrietta blinked up, missing the warmth of his presence, at the same time relieved that he had moved, for his expression had altered subtly. Colder. More distant, as if he had placed a wall between them. Too late, she realised that calling someone a rake to their face, even if they *were* a rake, wasn't perhaps the most tactful thing to say. She squirmed.

'Pray enlighten me, Miss Markham—what exactly does a rake look like?'

'Well, I don't know *exactly*, though I would say someone not nearly so good-looking for a start,' Henrietta replied, saying the first thing that popped into her head in her anxiety to make up for her lapse of manners. 'Older, too,' she continued, unable to bear the resultant silence, 'and probably more immoral looking. Debauched. Though to be honest, I'm not entirely sure what debauchery looks like, save that you don't. Look debauched, I mean,' she concluded, her voice trailing off as she realised that, far from appeasing him, the earl was looking decidedly affronted. Both his brows were drawn together now, giving him a really rather formidable expression.

'You seem quite the expert, Miss Markham,' Rafe said sardonically. 'Do you speak from personal experience?'

He had propped his shoulders up against the bedpost. They were very broad. Powerful. She wondered if perhaps he boxed. If he did, he must be good, for his face showed no marks. *Her* face was level with his chest now. Which also looked powerful, under his shirt. He had a very flat stomach. She hadn't really thought about it before, but men were built so very differently from women. Solid. Hard-edged. At least this man was.

Henrietta chewed on her bottom lip and tried hard not to be daunted. She wouldn't talk to his chest, but she had to crane her neck to meet his eyes. Slate-grey now, not blue. She swallowed again, trying to remember what it was he'd asked her. Rakes. 'Personal experience. Yes. I mean, no, I haven't previously met any rakes personally, at least not to my knowledge, but Mama said—my mother told me that…' Once again, Henrietta trailed into silence, realising that Mama would prefer not to have her past held up for inspection. 'I have seen the evidence of their activities for myself,' she said instead. Her voice sounded horribly defensive, but little wonder, given the way he was standing over her like an avenging angel. Henrietta bristled. 'In the Parish Poor House.'

The earl's expression was transformed in an instant, more devil than angel. 'If you are implying that I have littered the countryside with my illegitimate brats, then you are mightily misinformed,' he said icily.

Henrietta quailed. The truth was, she had heard no such thing of this particular rake, though, of course, just because she had not heard did not mean—but really, he looked far too angry to be lying. 'If you say so,' she said deprecatingly. 'I did not mean to imply…'

'None the less you did, Miss Markham. And I resent the implication.'

'Well, it was a natural enough assumption to make, given your reputation,' she retorted, placed firmly on the back foot, a position to which she was most unused.

'On the contrary. One should never make assumptions until one has a full grasp of all the facts.'

'What facts?'

'You are, as you point out, in my bed, in your underwear, yet you have been neither ravaged nor despoiled.'

'Haven't I? No, of course I haven't. I mean—do you mean that you're not a rake, then?'

'I am not, Miss Markham, in the habit of defending

my character to you, or anyone else for that matter,' Rafe said, no longer amused but furious. He might indeed be a rake, though he despised the term, but he was very far from being a libertine. The notion that he would wantonly sire children in pursuit of his own pleasure was a particular anathema to him. He prided himself on the fact that his rules of engagement were strict. His raking was confined to females who understood those rules, who expected nothing from him. His encounters were physical, not emotional. Innocents, even if they were wide-eyed and lying half-naked in his bed, were quite safe. Not that he was about to tell this particular innocent that.

Henrietta cowered against the pillow, taken aback by the shift in mood. If he was the rake common knowledge called him, then why should the earl take such umbrage? It was well known that all rakes were unprincipled, debauched, irresponsible....

But here her thoughts stuttered to a halt, having come full circle. He might be a rake, but he hadn't—though perhaps that was because he didn't find her attractive enough? A strangely deflating thought. And a ridiculous one! As if she should mind at all that a notorious rake thought so little of her that he hadn't tried to seduce her. Which reminded her. 'How did I come to be in your—I mean, this bed?' she asked, grasping at this interesting and unanswered question with some relief.

'I found you quite unconscious. I thought you were dead at first, and despite what you have been imagining, Miss Markham, I much prefer my conquests both *compos mentis* and willing. You can be reassured, I made no attempt to molest you. Had I done so, you would not have readily forgotten the experience. Something else I pride myself upon,' Rafe said sardonically.

Henrietta shivered. She had absolutely no doubt that he was entitled to boast of his prowess. His look told her he had once again read her thoughts. Once again she dropped her gaze, plucking at the scalloped edge of the sheet. 'Where *did* you find me?'

'In a ditch. I rescued you from it.'

This information was so surprising that Henrietta let fall the bedclothes shielding her modesty. 'Goodness! Really? Truly?' She sat up quickly, forgetting all about her aching head, then sank back on to the pillows with a little moan as the pain hit her. 'Where?' she asked weakly. 'I mean, where was this ditch?'

'In the grounds of my estate.'

'But how did I come to be there?'

'I rather hoped you could tell me that.'

'I don't know if I can.' Henrietta put her fingers carefully to the back of her head where a large lump was forming on her skull. 'Someone hit me.' She winced at the memory. 'Hard. Why would someone do that?'

'I have absolutely no idea,' Rafe replied. 'Perhaps whoever it was found your judgemental attitude tedious.' The hurt expression on her face didn't provide the usual sense of satisfaction he experienced when one of his well-aimed barbs struck home. On this occasion something more like guilt pricked him. She really was looking quite pale, too. Perhaps Mrs Peters was right, perhaps he should have summoned the local quack. 'Apart from the blow to the head, how are you feeling?'

The true answer was awful, but it was obvious from the falsely solicitous tone of his voice that awful was not the answer he wished to hear. 'I'm quite well,' Henrietta said, striving and failing to keep the edge out of her voice, 'at least I'm sure I will be directly. You need not concern yourself unduly.'

He had been ungracious, not something that would normally bother him, but her *not* pointing it out somehow did. Rather too quick with her opinions she most certainly was, but Henrietta Markham was not capricious. Her frankness, when it was not rude, was refreshing.

The memory of her curves pressed against him as he had lifted her from the ditch crept unbidden into his mind. Awareness took Rafe by surprise. It irked him that he remembered so clearly. Why should he? 'You may, of course, take as long as you require to recuperate,' he said. 'What I want to know right now is who hit you and, more importantly, why they abandoned you on my land.'

'What you really mean is, why didn't they pick somewhere less inconvenient to dump me?' Henrietta retorted. She gasped, pressed her hand over her mouth, but it was too late, the words were out.

Rafe laughed. He couldn't help it, she was amusing in a strange kind of way. His laugh sounded odd. He realised it was because he hadn't heard it for such a long time. 'Yes, you are quite right,' he said. 'I would have happily seen you abandoned at the very gates of Hades instead, but you are here now.'

He had a nice laugh. And though he might be ungracious, at least he was honest. She liked that. Henrietta smiled tentatively. 'I didn't mean to be quite so frank.'

'You are a dreadful liar, Miss Markham.'

'I know. I mean— Oh dear.'

'Hoist with your own petard, I think you would call that.'

The band of pain around Henrietta's head tightened, making her wince. '*Touché*, my lord. You want me gone, I am sure you have things to do. If I could just have a moment to collect myself, I will get dressed and be out of your way directly.'

She had turned quite pale. Rafe felt a twinge of compassion. As she had so clearly refrained from pointing out, it was not her fault she had landed on his doorstep, any more than it was his. 'There is no rush. Perhaps if you had something to eat, you might feel a little better. Then you may remember what happened to you.'

'I would not wish to put you out any more than I have already done,' Henrietta said unconvincingly.

Once again, he felt his mouth quirk. 'You are as poor a prevaricator as you are a liar. Come, the least I can do is give you breakfast before you go. Do you feel up to getting out of bed?'

He was not exactly smiling at her, but his expression had lost that hard edge, as if a smile might not be entirely beyond him. Also, she was ravenous. And he did deserve answers, if only she could come up with some. So Henrietta stoically told him that, yes, she would get out of bed, though the thought of it made her feel quite nauseous. He was already heading for the door. 'My lord, please, wait.'

'Yes?' She had dropped the sheet in her anxiety to call him back. Long tendrils of chestnut hair, curling wildly, trailed over her white shoulders. Her chemise was made of serviceable white cotton. He could plainly see the ripe swell of her breasts, unconfined by stays. Rafe reluctantly dragged his gaze away.

'My dress, where is it?' Realising that she had dropped the sheet, Henrietta clutched it up around her neck, telling herself stoutly there was nothing to be ashamed of to be found to be wearing a plain white-cotton chemise which, after all, was clean. Nevertheless, clean or no, she couldn't help wishing it hadn't been quite so plain. She wondered who had removed her gown.

'My housekeeper undressed you,' the earl replied in answer to her unasked question. 'Your dress was soaking wet and we did not wish you to catch a chill. I'll lend you something until it is dry.' He returned a few moments later with a large, and patently masculine, dressing gown, which he laid on the chair, informing her breakfast would be served in half an hour precisely, before striding purposefully out of the room.

Henrietta stared at the closed door She couldn't fathom him. Did he want her to stay or not? Did he find her amusing? Annoying? Attractive? Irksome? All or none? She had absolutely no idea.

She should not have mentioned his reputation. Though he hadn't exactly denied it, she could very easily see just how irresistible he could be, given that combination of looks and the indefinable something else he possessed which made her shiver. As if he was promising her something she knew she should not wish for. As if he and only he could fulfil that promise. She didn't understand it. Surely rakes were scoundrels? Rafe St Alban didn't look at all like a scoundrel. Rakes were

not *good* people, yet he must have some good in him—
had he not rescued her, a noble act?

She frowned. 'I suppose the point is that they must be
good at taking people in, else how could they succeed
in being a rake?' she said to herself. So was it a good
thing that he hadn't taken her in? She couldn't make up
her mind. The one thing she knew for certain was that
he was most eager to be rid of her. Henrietta tried not
to be mortified by that.

Perhaps he just wanted to know how she had come
to be on his estate in the first place? She'd like to know
that herself, she thought, touching a cautious finger to
the aching lump on her head. Last night. Last night.
What did she remember of last night?

That dratted pug dog of Lady Ipswich's had run off.
She'd entirely missed her dinner while looking for it,
no wonder she was so hungry now. Henrietta frowned,
screwing her eyes tightly shut, ignoring the dull ache
inside her skull as she mentally retraced her steps. Out
through the side door. The kitchen garden. Round to
the side of the house. Then…

The housebreaker! 'Oh, my goodness, the housebreaker!' Her mind cleared, like the ripples of a pool
stilling to reveal a sharp reflection. 'Good grief! Lady
Ipswich will be wondering what on earth has happened
to me.'

Gingerly, Henrietta inched out of the luxurious bed
and peered at the clock on the mantel. The numbers
were fuzzy. It was just after eight. She opened the curtains and blinked painfully out at the sun. Morning.
She had been gone all night. Her rescuer had clearly
been out and about very early. In fact, now she had a

chance to reflect upon it, he had had the look of a man who had not yet been to bed.

Raking, no doubt! But those shadows under his eyes spoke of a tiredness more profound than mere physical exhaustion. Rafe St Alban looked like a man who *could* not sleep. No wonder he was irritable, she thought, immediately feeling more charitable. Having to deal with a comatose stranger under such circumstances would have put anyone out of humour, especially if the aforementioned stranger looked like a—like a—what on earth *did* she look like?

There was a looking glass on top of the ornately inlaid chest of drawers in front of the window. Henrietta peered curiously into it. A streak of mud had caked on to her cheek, she was paler than normal and had a lump the size of an egg on her head, but apart from that she looked pretty much the same as always. Determinedly un-rosebuddish mouth. Eyebrows that simply refused to show even the tiniest inclination to arch. Too-curly brown hair in wild disorder. Brown eyes. And, currently in the hands of the aforementioned Mrs Peters, a brown dress.

She sighed heavily. It summed things up, really. Her whole life was various shades of brown. It was to her shame and discredit that no amount of telling herself, as Papa constantly reminded her, that there were many people in the world considerably worse off than her, made her feel any better about it. It was not that she was malcontent precisely, but she could not help thinking sometimes that there must be more to life. Though more of what, she had no idea.

'I suppose being thumped on the head, then being

left to die of exposure, to say nothing of being rescued by a devastatingly handsome earl, counts as a burst of genuine excitement,' she told her reflection. 'Even if he is a very reluctant knight errant with a very volatile temperament and an extremely dubious reputation.'

The clock on the mantel chimed the quarter-hour, making her jump. She could not possibly add keeping the earl from his breakfast to her other sins. Hastily, she slopped water from the jug on the nightstand into the prettily flowered china bowl and set about removing the worst of the mud from her face.

Almost precisely on time, Henrietta tripped into the breakfast parlour with her hair brushed and pinned, her body swathed in her host's elegant dressing gown of dark green brocade trimmed with gold frogging. Even with the cuffs turned back and the gown belted tightly at her waist, it enveloped her form completely, trailing behind her like a royal robe. The idea that the material that lay next to her skin had also lain next to his naked body was unsettling. She tried not to dwell on the thought, but it could not be said she was wholly successful.

She was nervous. Seeing the breakfast table set for just two made her even more nervous. She had never before had breakfast alone with a man, save for dear Papa, which didn't count. She had certainly never before had breakfast with a man while wearing his dressing gown. Feeling incredibly gauche and at the same time excruciatingly conscious of her body, clothed only in her underwear, handicapped by the voluminous folds of the dressing gown, Henrietta tripped into the room.

He didn't seem to notice her at first. He was staring into space, the most melancholy expression on his face. Darkly brooding. Formidable. Starkly handsome. Her pulses fluttered. He had shaved and changed. He was wearing a clean shirt and freshly tied cravat, a tightly fitting morning coat of dark blue, and buff-coloured pantaloons with polished boots. The whole ensemble made him look considerably more earl-like and consequently considerably more intimidating. Also, even more devastatingly attractive. Henrietta plastered a faltering smile to her face and dropped into a very far from elegant and certainly not, she was sure, deep enough curtsy. 'I must apologise, my lord, for being so remiss, I have not yet thanked you properly for rescuing me. I am very much obliged to you.'

Her voice dragged Rafe's thoughts back from the past, where he had once again been lingering. Be dammed to the precious title and the need for an heir! Who really cared, save his grandmother, if it was inherited by some obscure third cousin twice removed? If she only knew what it had cost him already, she would soon stop harping on about it. He gazed down at Henrietta, still smiling up at him uncertainly. Holding out his hand, he helped her back to her feet. 'I trust you feel a little better, Miss Markham. You certainly look very fetching in my robe. It is most becoming.'

'I'm perfectly all right, all things considered,' Henrietta said, grateful for his support as she got up from her curtsy, which had made her head swim. 'And as for the robe, it is very gallant of you to lie, but I know I must look a fright.'

'Frightfully nice, I'd say. And you must believe me, for I am something of an expert in these matters.'

His haunted look had disappeared. He was smiling now. Not a real smile, not one that reached his eyes, but his mouth turned up at the corners. 'I think I've finally remembered what happened,' Henrietta said.

'Yes?' Rafe shook his head, dispelling the ghosts that seemed to have gathered there. 'It can wait. You look as if you need food.'

'I *am* hungry—a dog made me miss my dinner.'

For the second time that morning, Rafe laughed aloud. This time it sounded less rusty. 'Well, I am happy to inform you that there are no dogs here to make you miss your breakfast,' he said. The dressing gown gave Henrietta Markham a winsome quality. It gaped at the neck, showing far too much creamy bosom, which she really ought to have had the decency to confine in stays. She looked as if she had just tumbled from his bed. Which in a way, she had. He realised he'd been staring and looked away, slightly disconcerted by the unexpected stirrings of arousal. Desire was usually something he could conjure up or dispense with at will.

Helping her into a seat, he sat down opposite, keeping his eyes resolutely on the food in front of him. He would feed her, find out where she had sprung from and return her there forthwith. Then he would sleep. And after that he must return to town. The meeting with his grandmother could not be postponed indefinitely. An immense malaise, grey and heavy as a November sky, loomed over him at the thought.

So he would not think of it. He need not, not just yet, while he had the convenient distraction of the really quite endearing Henrietta Markham sitting opposite him, in his dressing gown, with her tale to tell. Rafe poured her some coffee and placed a generous helping of ham on to her plate along with a baked egg and some bread and butter, helping himself to a mound of beef and a tankard of ale. 'Eat, before you faint with hunger.'

'This looks delicious,' she said, gazing at her loaded plate with relish.

'It is just breakfast.'

'Well, I've never had such a nice breakfast,' Henrietta said chirpily, at the same time, thinking *be quiet*! She was not usually a female who wittered, yet she sounded uncommonly like one this morning. Nerves. Yet she was not usually one to allow nerves to affect her behaviour. Off balance. He disconcerted her, that's what it was. The situation. The dressing gown. The man. Definitely the man. This man, who was telling her, with a quizzical look that meant she'd either been muttering to herself or allowing her thoughts to be read quite clearly on her face, that it would be a nice cold breakfast unless she made a start on it.

She picked up her fork. Was he just teasing, or did he think she was an idiot? She sounded like an idiot. He had the ability to make her feel like one. Taking a bite of deliciously soft egg, she studied him covertly from under her lashes. The dark shadows were clearer now in the bright morning light that streamed through the windows. He had a strained look about his mouth. She ate some more egg and cut into a slice of York ham. He was edgy, too. Even when he smiled, it was as if he were simply going through the motions.

Clearly not happy, then. Why not, she wondered, when he had so much more than most? She longed to ask, but another glance at that countenance, and the question stuck in her throat. More than anything, Henrietta decided, what Rafe St Alban was, was opaque. She had no idea what he was thinking. It made her want, all the more, to know, yet still—quite unusually, for Henrietta had been encouraged from a very early age to speak her mind—she hesitated.

A tiny *frisson*, this time excitement mingled with fear, caused goose bumps to rise on the back of her neck. He was not just intimidating. He was intimidatingly attractive. What was it about him that made her feel like this? Fascinated and frightened and—as if she were a rabbit faced with a particularly tasty treat, though she knew full well it was bait. She was beginning to see Rafe St Alban's reputation might well be deserved, after all. If he set his mind to something, she would be difficult to resist.

She shivered again and told herself not to be so foolish. He would not set his mind on her! And even if he did, knowing the type of man he was, being fully aware of his lack of morals, she would have no difficulty at all in resisting him. Not that he had made any such attempt, nor was likely to.

More to the point, why was she wasting her time thinking about such things? She had much more important matters to attend to now that she remembered the shocking events of last night. Even before that, she must attend to her stomach, else she would be fainting away, and Henrietta, who prided herself on her pragmatism, would not allow herself such an indulgence. With resolution, she turned her attention more fully to her breakfast.

Chapter Two

When they had finished eating, Rafe stood up. 'Bring your coffee. We'll sit by the fire, it will be more comfortable there. Then you can tell me your tale.'

Awkwardly arranging the multitudinous folds of silk around her in the wing-backed chair, Henrietta did as instructed. Across from her, Rafe St Alban disposed his long limbs gracefully, crossing one booted foot over the other. She could see the muscles of his legs move underneath the tight-fitting material of his knitted pantaloons. Such unforgiving cloth would not show to advantage on a stouter man. Or a thinner one. Or one less well built.

'I'm a governess,' she announced, turning her mind to the thing most likely to distract her from unaccustomed thoughts of muscled thighs, 'to the children of Lady Ipswich, whose grounds march with yours.'

'They do, but we are not on calling terms.'

'Why not?'

'It is of no relevance.'

Anyone else would have been daunted by his tone,

but Henrietta's curiosity was aroused, which made her quite oblivious. 'But you are neighbours, surely you must—is it because she is a widow? Did you perhaps call when her husband was alive?'

'Lord Ipswich was more of an age with my father,' Rafe said curtly.

'He must have been quite a bit older than his wife, then. I didn't realise. I suppose I just assumed....'

'As you are wont to do,' Rafe said sardonically.

She looked at him expectantly. Her wide-eyed gaze was disconcerting. Her mouth was quite determined. Rafe sighed heavily, unused to dealing with such persistent questioning. 'His lordship passed away under what one might call somewhat dubious circumstances, and I decided not to continue the acquaintance with his widow.'

'Really?'

'Really,' Rafe said, wishing he had said nothing at all. The poor innocent obviously had no idea of her employer's colourful past and he had no intention of disclosing it to her. 'How came you to be in Helen Ipswich's employ?' he asked, in an attempt to divert her.

'There was a notice in *The Lady*. I happened to be looking for a position and Mama said that it all looked quite respectable, so I applied.'

'Your previous position was terminated?'

'Oh, no, this is my first experience as a governess, though not, I hope, my last,' Henrietta said with one of her confiding smiles. 'I am going to be a teacher, you see, and I wished to gain some practical experience before the school opened.' Her smile faded. 'Though from what Mama says in her latest letter, that will be quite some time away.'

'Your mother is opening a school?'

'Mama and Papa together—' Henrietta frowned '—at least, that is the plan, but I have to confess their plans have a habit of going awry. The school is to be in Ireland, a charitable project for the poor. Papa is a great philanthropist, you see.'

Henrietta waited expectantly, but Rafe St Alban did not seem to have a burning need to comment on Papa's calling. 'The problem is that while his intentions are always of the best, I'm afraid he is not very practical. He has more of a care for the soul than the body and cannot be brought to understand that, without sustenance and warmth, the poor have more pressing needs than their spiritual health, nor any interest in raising their minds to higher things. Like statues of St Francis. Or making a tapestry celebrating the life of St Anthony—he is the patron saint of the poor, you know. I told Papa that they would be better occupied making blankets,' Henrietta said darkly, too taken up with her remembered resentment to realise that she was once again rambling, 'but he did not take my suggestion kindly. Mama, of course, agreed with him. Mama believes that distracting the poor from their situation is the key, but honestly, how can one be distracted when one is starving, or worried that one is expecting another child when one cannot feed the other five already at home? The last thing one would want to do is stitch a figure of St Anthony voyaging to Portugal!'

'I don't expect many of the poor even know where Portugal is,' Rafe said pointedly. Papa and Mama

Markham sounded like the kind of do-gooders he despised.

'Precisely,' Henrietta said vehemently, 'and even if they did—are you laughing at me?'

'Would you mind if I were?'

'No. Only I didn't think what I was saying was particularly droll.'

'It was the way you were saying it. You are very earnest.'

'I have to be, else I will never be heard.'

'So, while Mama and Papa pray for souls, you make soup—is that right?'

'There is nothing wrong with being practical.'

'No, there is not. If only there was more soup and less sermons in the world....'

'My parents mean well.'

'I'm sure they do, but my point is that meaning well is not the same as doing well. I come across many such people and—'

'I was not aware you had a reputation for philanthropy.'

'No, as you pointed out,' Rafe said coldly, 'my reputation primarily concerns my raking. Now you will tell me that one precludes the other.'

'Well, doesn't it?' Henrietta demanded. Seeing his face tighten, she hesitated. 'What I mean is, being a rake presupposes one is immoral and—' She broke off as Rafe's expression froze. 'You know, I think perhaps I've strayed from the point a little. Are you saying that you *are* involved in charitable work?'

She was clearly sceptical. He told himself it didn't matter a damn what she thought. 'I am saying the world is not as black and white as either you or your parents seem to think.' His involvement with his own little project at St Nicholas's was extremely important to him, but he did not consider it to be charitable. With some difficulty, Rafe reined in his temper. What was it about this beguiling female that touched so many raw nerves? 'You were telling me about the school your parents want to set up.'

'Yes.' Henrietta eyed him uncertainly. 'Have I said something to offend you?'

'The school, Miss Markham.'

'Well, if—when—it opens I intend to be able to contribute in a practical sense by teaching lessons.' Practical lessons, she added to herself, remembering Mama's curriculum with a shudder.

'Lessons which you are trying out on Helen Ipswich's brats?'

'They are not brats,' Henrietta said indignantly. 'They are just high-spirited boys. I'm sure you were the same at their age, wanting to be out riding rather than attending to your studies, but—'

'At their age, my father was actively encouraging me to go out riding and ignore my lessons,' Rafe said drily. 'My tendency to bury my head in a book sorely disconcerted him.'

'Goodness, were you a scholar?'

'Another thing that you consider incompatible with being a rake, Miss Markham?'

He was looking amused again. She couldn't keep pace with his mood swings, but she couldn't help responding to his hint of a smile with one of her own. 'Well, to cut a long story short, which I'm sure you'll be most relieved to hear I intend to do, I like being a governess and I like the boys, even if their mama is a little—well—high-handed. Not that I really see that much of her, governesses clearly meriting scant attention. Anyway, I'm sure there are worse employers, and the boys do like me, and if—*when*—the school is opened, I am sure the experience will stand me in good stead. It is due to do so in three months or so, by which time my current charges are destined for boarding school, anyway, so hopefully they won't miss me too much. Not anything like as much as I shall miss them.'

'There, we must agree. Small boys, in my experience, are remarkably fickle in their loyalties.'

'Do you think so?' Henrietta asked brightly. 'I think that's a good thing, for I would not wish them to become too attached to me. What experience have you of such things? Have you brothers?'

'No.'

His face was closed again, his expression shuttered. 'I take it, then, that life as Helen Ipswich's governess has fulfilled your expectations?'

'Yes, it has served its purpose admirably.'

'How fortunate for you. Now, if you don't mind, we will return to the more pressing subject of how you came to be in my ditch, then you may return to these duties you enjoy so much. No doubt your employer will be wondering what has become of you.'

'That is true. And the boys, too.' Though the notion of returning to Lady Ipswich's home was less appealing than it should be. Another of a rake's skills, no doubt, to beguile you and make you want to spend time in his company. Henrietta sat up straight and tugged at the dressing-gown belt. 'Well, then, to return to the subject, as you wish. Last night. Well, what happened last night was that I was knocked on the head by a housebreaker.'

'A housebreaker!'

Gratified by her host's reaction, which was for once just exactly what she had anticipated, Henrietta nodded vigorously. 'Yes, indeed. At least,' she added, incurably truthful, 'I am almost certain that is what he was, though I didn't actually see him steal anything. I was looking for Lady Ipswich's horrible dog, you see.'

'The dog who deprived you of your dinner?'

'The very same. I heard a noise coming from the shrubbery, so I went to investigate it, thinking, you know, it might be Princess—that's the pug's name—and then I heard glass breaking. I held up the lantern and saw him as clear as day for just a split second, then he leapt at me and hit me on the head. The next thing I remember is waking up here.'

Rafe shook his head slowly. 'But that's nonsensical. Even if it was a housebreaker, why on earth would he go to the trouble of taking you with him? It takes time and effort to heft a body on to a horse.'

Henrietta coloured. 'I am aware that I am not exactly a featherweight.'

'That is not at all what I meant. It is women who consider stick-thinness the essence of beauty. Men actually prefer quite the opposite. I find your figure most pleasing on the eye.' Rafe was not in the habit of encouraging young ladies with compliments, for they were likely to be misconstrued, but Henrietta Markham was so different from any young lady he had ever met that he spoke without considering the effect his words would have. 'It was no hardship to get you on to my horse. I meant merely it would be awkward if the man were slight, or elderly.'

Or one less muscled, Henrietta thought, her gaze lingering on her host's powerful physique. It hadn't occurred to her until now to wonder how, exactly, he had retrieved her from the ditch. Had he pulled her by the wrist or the ankle? Held her chest to chest, or maybe thrown her over his shoulders? And when she was on his horse, was she on her front with her bottom sticking up? With her petticoats on show? Her ankles? Worse? Feigning heat from the fire, she frantically fanned her face.

Rafe followed the train of her thoughts with relative ease, mirrored as they were in her expressive face, recognising the exact moment when she tried to imagine how she had been placed on Thor's saddle. Unfortunately, it turned his mind also to that moment. He had lain her crossways on her stomach with her bottom pointed provocatively up to the sky. Her dress had ridden up a little, exposing her ankles and calves. At the time, he had not been aware of noticing. Yet now, in his mind's eye, he found he could dwell appreciatively on the inviting curves of her voluptuous body as if he had drunk in every inch of her.

'Why,' he said tersely, reining in his imagination, once again disconcerted by having to do so, 'having gone to all that effort to abduct you, did your housebreaker then change his mind and abandon you in my grounds?'

'I don't know,' Henrietta replied. 'It doesn't make

any sense, I can see that. Perhaps he had evil designs upon my person and then changed his mind when he got a better look at me,' she said with a wry smile.

'If that was the case, then his taste was quite at fault,' Rafe said impulsively, bestowing upon her his real smile.

It quite transformed his face. Henrietta blushed rosily, but even as she struggled for a response, the smile was gone, as if a cloud had covered the sun. Utterly confused, she folded her arms defensively. 'You don't really believe a word I've said, do you?'

The dressing gown gaped. Rafe caught a glimpse of creamy flesh spilling from a plain white cotton undergarment. The rake in him would have allowed his glance to linger. He wanted to look, but it was his wanting that made him look resolutely away. *Nothing touches you any more.* The memory of his friend Lucas's words made Rafe smile bitterly to himself. True, thank God, if you didn't count the all-pervading guilt. He had worked very hard to ensure it was so and that was exactly how he intended it to continue. Wanting was no longer part of his emotional make-up. Wanting Henrietta Markham, he told himself sternly, was completely out of the question.

'You have to admit that it sounds a tall tale,' he said to her, his voice made more dismissive by the need to offset his thoughts, 'but my opinion is of little importance. I would have thought the more pressing issue for you is whether or not Lady Ipswich believes you.' He got to his feet purposefully. Henrietta Markham had been a very beguiling distraction, but the time had come to put an end to this extraordinary interlude and for them both to return to the real world. 'I will arrange for you to be taken back in my carriage. Your dress should be dry by now.' He pulled the bell rope to summon the housekeeper.

Henrietta scrabbled to her feet. He was quite plainly bored by the whole matter. And by her. She should not be surprised. She should certainly not feel hurt. She was, after all, just a lowly governess with a preposterous story; he was an earl with an important life and no doubt a string of beautiful women with whom to carry on his dalliances. Women who didn't wear brown dresses and who most certainly didn't lie around waiting to be pulled out of ditches. 'I must thank you again for rescuing me,' she said in what she hoped was a curt voice, though she suspected it sounded rather huffy. 'Please forgive me for taking up quite so much of your time.'

'It was a pleasure, Miss Markham, but a word of warning before you go.' Rafe tilted her chin up with the tip of his finger. Her eyes were liquid bronze. Really, quite her most beautiful feature. He met her gaze coolly, though he didn't feel quite as cool as he should. He wasn't used to having his equilibrium disturbed. 'Don't expect to be lauded as a heroine,' he said softly. 'Helen Ipswich is neither a very credulous nor a particularly kind person.' He took her hand, just brushing the back of it with his lips. 'Good luck, Henrietta Markham, and goodbye. If you return to your room, I'll send Mrs Peters up with your dress. She will also see you out.'

He could not resist pressing his lips to her hand. She tasted delightful. The scent of her and the feel of her skin on his mouth shot a dart of pleasure to his groin.

He dropped her hand abruptly, turned on his heels and left without a backward glance.

Just the faintest touch of his mouth on her skin, but she could feel it there still. Henrietta lifted her hand to her cheek and held it there until the tingling faded. It took a long time before it finally did.

Molly Peters, Rafe's long-suffering housekeeper, was an apple-shaped woman with rosy cheeks. Her husband, Albert, who alone was permitted to call her his little pippin, was head groom. Molly had started service in the previous earl's day as a scullery maid, ascending by way of back parlourmaid, chambermaid and front parlourmaid, before eventually serving, briefly and unhappily, as lady's maid to the last countess. Upon her ladyship's untimely death, Master Rafe had appointed Molly to the heady heights of housekeeper, with her own set of keys and her own parlour.

Running the household was a task Molly Peters undertook with pride and carried out extremely competently. Indeed, she would have executed it with gusto had she been given the opportunity, but even when the last countess had been alive, Woodfield Manor had seldom been used as a residence. As a result, Mrs Peters had little to do and was frankly a little bored. Henrietta's unorthodox arrival provided some welcome excitement and consequently induced an unaccustomed garrulousness in the usually reserved housekeeper.

'I've known Master Rafe all his life, since he was a babe,' she said in answer to Henrietta's question. 'A bonny babe he was, too, and so clever.'

'He has certainly retained his looks,' Henrietta ventured, struggling into her newly brushed, but none the less indisputably brown dress.

Mrs Peters pursed her lips. 'Certainly, he has no shortage of admirers,' she said primly. 'A man like Lord Pentland, with those looks and the Pentland title behind him, to say nothing of the fact that he's as rich as Croesus, will always attract the ladies, but the master is—well, miss, the truth is…' She looked over her shoulder, as if Rafe would suddenly appear in the bedchamber. 'Truth is, he's the love-'em-and-leave-'em type, as my Albert puts it, though I say there's little loving and a darn sight more leaving. I don't know why I'm telling you this except you seem such a nice young lady and it wouldn't do to— But then, he's not a libertine, if you know what I mean.'

Henrietta tried to look knowledgeable, though in truth she wasn't *exactly* sure she understood the distinction between rake and libertine. Certainly Mama had never made one. She was attempting to formulate a question that would persuade Mrs Peters to enlighten her without revealing her own ignorance when the housekeeper heaved a huge sigh and clucked her teeth. 'He wasn't always like that, mind. I blame that wife of his.'

'He's married!' Henrietta's jaw dropped with shock. 'I didn't know.' But why should she? Contrary to what his lordship thought, Henrietta was not a great one for gossip. Generally speaking, she closed her ears to it, which is why Rafe St Alban's accusations had hurt. In fact, she had only become aware of his reputation recently, a chance remark of her employer's having alerted her. But if he was married, it made his behaviour so much worse. Somewhat irrationally, Henrietta felt a little betrayed, as if he had lied to her, even though it was actually none of her business. 'I hadn't heard mention of a wife,' she said.

'That's because she's dead,' Mrs Peters replied quietly. 'Five years ago now.'

'So he's a widower!' He looked even less like one of those. 'What happened? How did she die? When did they marry? Was he—did they—was it a love match? Was he devastated?' The questions tripped one after another off her tongue. Only the astonished look on Mrs Peters's face made her stop. 'I am just curious,' Henrietta said lamely.

Mrs Peters eyed her warily. 'Her name was Lady Julia. I've said more than enough already, the master doesn't like her to be talked about. But if you're ready to go, I can show you a likeness of her on the way out, if you want.'

The portrait hung in the main vestibule. The subject was depicted gazing meditatively into the distance, her willowy figure seated gracefully on a rustic swing bedecked with roses. 'Painted the year she died, that was,' Mrs Peters said.

'She is—was—very beautiful,' Henrietta said wistfully.

'Oh, she was lovely, no doubt about that,' Mrs Peters said, 'though handsome is as handsome does.'

'What do you mean?'

Mrs Peters looked uncomfortable. 'Nothing. It was a long time ago.'

'How long were they married?'

'Six years. Master Rafe was only a boy, not even

twenty, when they were wed. She was a few years older than him. It makes a difference at that age,' Mrs Peters said.

'How so?'

Mrs Peters shook her head. 'Don't matter now. As Albert says, what's done is done. The carriage will be waiting for you, miss.'

Henrietta took a final look at the perfect features of the elegant woman depicted in the portrait. There could be no denying the Countess of Pentland's beauty, but there was a calculating hardness in the eyes she could not like, a glittering perfection to her appearance that made Henrietta think of polished granite. For some ridiculous reason, she did not like to imagine Rafe St Alban in love with this woman.

Taking leave of the housekeeper, she made her way down the front steps to the waiting coach, unable to stop herself looking back just in case the earl had changed his mind and deigned to say farewell to her himself. But there was no sign of him.

A large fountain dominated the courtyard, consisting of four dolphins supporting a statue of Neptune. Modelled on Bernini's Triton fountain in Rome, Henrietta's inner governess noted. Beyond the fountain, reached by a broad sweep of steps, pristine flower beds and immaculate lawns stretched into the distance. Like the house she had just left, the grounds spoke eloquently of elegance, taste and wealth.

The contrast with her own childhood home could not be more stark. The ramshackle house in which she had been raised was damp, draughty and neglected. A lack of funds, and other, more pressing priorities saw to that. Any spare money her parents had went to good causes. An unaccustomed gust of homesickness assailed Henrietta. Hopelessly inept her parents might be, but they always meant well. They always put others first, even if the others weren't at all grateful. Even if it meant their only child coming last. Still, she never doubted that they loved her. She missed them.

But she had never been one to repine her lot. Henrietta straightened her shoulders and climbed into the waiting coach with its crest emblazoned on the door, already preparing herself for the forthcoming, almost certainly difficult, interview with her employer.

Rafe watched her departure from his bedroom window. Poor Henrietta Markham, it was unlikely in the extreme that Helen Ipswich would thank her for attempting to intervene—if that is what she really had done. He felt oddly uncomfortable at having allowed her to return on her own like a lamb to the slaughter. But he was not a shepherd and rescuing innocent creatures from Helen Ipswich's clutches was not his responsibility.

As the carriage pulled off down the driveway, Rafe left the window, stripped off his boots and coat, and donned his dressing gown. Sitting by the fireside, a glass of brandy in hand, he caught Henrietta's elusive scent still clinging to the silk. A long chestnut hair lay on the sleeve.

She had been a pleasant distraction. Unexpectedly desirable, too. That mouth. Those delectable curves.

But she was gone now. And later today, so too would he be. Back to London. Rafe took a sip of brandy. Two weeks ago he had turned thirty. Just over twelve years now since he had inherited the title, and almost five years to the day since he had become a widower. More than enough time to take up the reins of his life again, his grandmother, the Dowager Countess, chided him on a tediously regular basis. In a sense she was right, but in another she had no idea how impossible was her demand. The emotional scars he bore ran too deep for that. He had no desire at all to risk inflicting any further damage to his already battered psyche.

He took another, necessary, sip of brandy. The time had come. His grandmother would have to be made to relinquish once and for all any notion of a direct heir, though how he was going to convince her without revealing the unpalatable truth behind his reluctance, the terrible guilty secret that would haunt him to the grave, was quite another matter.

By the time the coach drew up at her employer's front door, Henrietta's natural optimism had reasserted itself. Whatever Rafe St Alban thought, she *had* tried to prevent a theft; even if she hadn't actually succeeded, she could describe the housebreaker and that was surely something of an achievement. Entering the household, she was greeted by an air of suppressed excitement. The normally hangdog footman goggled at her. 'Where have you been?' he whispered. 'They've been saying—'

'My lady wishes to see you immediately,' the butler interrupted.

'Tell her I'll be with her as soon as I've changed my clothes, if you please.'

'Immediately,' the butler repeated firmly.

Henrietta ascended the stairs, her heart fluttering nervously. Rafe St Alban had a point—her story did seem extremely unlikely. Reminding herself of one of Papa's maxims, that she had nothing to fear in telling the truth, she straightened her back and held her head up proudly, but as she tapped on the door she was horribly aware of the difference between speaking the truth and actually being able to prove it.

Lady Helen Ipswich, who admitted to twenty-nine of her forty years, was in her boudoir. She had been extremely beautiful in her heyday and took immense pains to preserve the fragile illusion of youthful loveliness. In the flattering glow of candlelight, she almost succeeded. Born plain Nell Brown, she had progressed through various incarnations, from actress, to high flyer, to wife and mother—in point of fact, her first taste of motherhood had preceded her marriage by some fifteen years. This interesting piece of information was known only to herself, the child's adoptive parents and the very expensive *accoucheur* who attended the birth of her official 'first-born', Lord Ipswich's heir.

After seven years of marriage, Lady Ipswich had settled contentedly into early widowhood. Her past would always bar her from the more hallowed precincts of the *haut ton*. She had wisely never attempted to obtain vouchers for Almack's. Her neighbour, the Earl of Pentland, would never extend her more than the commonest of courtesies and the curtest of bows. But as the relic of a peer of the realm, and with two legitimate children to boot, she had assumed a cloak of respectability effective enough to fool most unacquainted with her past—her governess included.

As to the persistent rumours that she had, having drained his purse, drained the life-blood from her husband, well, they were just that—rumours. The ageing Lord Ipswich had succumbed to an apoplexy. That it had occurred in the midst of a particularly energetic session in the marital bedchamber simply proved that Lady Ipswich had taken her hymeneal duties seriously. Her devotion to the wifely cause had, quite literally, taken his lordship's breath away. Murder? Certainly not! Indeed, how could it be when at least five men of her intimate acquaintance had begged her—two on bended knee—to perform the same service for them. To date, she had refused.

The widow was at her *toilette* when Henrietta entered, seated in front of a mirror in the full glare of the unforgiving morning sun. The dressing table was a litter of glass jars and vials containing such patented aids to beauty as Olympian Dew and Denmark Lotion, a selection of perfumes from Messrs Price and Gosnell, various pots of rouge, eyelash tints and lip salves, a tangle of lace and ribbons, hair brushes, a half-empty vial of laudanum, several tortoiseshell combs, a pair of tweezers and numerous cards of invitation.

As Henrietta entered the room, Lady Ipswich was peering anxiously into her looking glass, having just discovered what looked alarmingly like a new wrinkle on her brow. At her age, and with her penchant for younger men, she could not be too careful. Only the other day, one of her lovers had commented that the unsightly mark left by the ribbon that tied her stockings had not faded by the time she rose to dress. Her skin no longer had the elastic quality of youth. He had paid for his bluntness, but still!

Finally satisfied with her reflection and her coiffure, she turned to face Henrietta. 'So, you have deigned to return,' she said coldly. 'Do you care to explain yourself and your absence?'

'If you remember, ma'am, I went looking for Princess. I see she found her way back unaided.'

The pug, hearing her name, looked up from her pink-velvet cushion by the fireside and growled. Lady Ipswich hastened to pick the animal up. 'No thanks to you, Miss Markham.' She tickled the dog under the chin. 'You're a clever little Princess, aren't you? Yes, you are,' she said, before fixing Henrietta with a baleful stare. 'You should know that while you were off failing to find my precious Princess, the house was broken into. My emeralds have been stolen.'

'The Ipswich emeralds!' Henrietta knew them well. They were family heirlooms and extremely distinctive. Lady Ipswich was inordinately fond of them and Henrietta had much admired them herself.

'Gone. The safe was broken into and they were taken.'

'Good heavens.' Henrietta clutched the back of a flimsy filigree chair. The man who had abducted her was clearly no common housebreaker, but a most daring and outrageous thief indeed. And she had encountered him. More, could identify him. 'I can't quite believe it,' she said faintly. 'He did not look at all like the sort of man who would attempt such a shocking crime. In actual fact, he looked as if he would be more at home picking pockets in the street.'

Now it was Lady Ipswich's turn to pale. 'You saw him?'

Henrietta nodded vigorously. 'Indeed, my lady. That explains why he hit me. If he were to be caught, he would surely hang for his crime.' As the implications began to dawn on her, Henrietta's knees gave way. He really had left her for dead. If Rafe St Alban had not found her... Muttering an apology, she sank down on to the chair.

'What did he look like? Describe him to me,' Lady Ipswich demanded.

Henrietta furrowed her brow. 'He was quite short, not much taller than me. He had an eyepatch. And an accent. From the north somewhere. Liverpool, perhaps? Quite distinctive.'

'You would know him again if you saw him?'

'Oh, I have no doubt about that. Most certainly.'

Lady Ipswich began to pace the room, clasping and unclasping her hands. 'I have already spoken to the magistrate,' she said. 'He has sent for a Bow Street Runner.'

'They will wish to interview me. I may even be instrumental in having him brought to justice. Goodness!' Henrietta put a trembling hand to her forehead in an effort to stop the feeling of light-headedness threatening to engulf her.

With a snort of disdain, Lady Ipswich thrust a silver vial of sal volatile at her, then continued with her pacing, muttering all the while to herself. Henrietta took a cautious sniff of the smelling salts before hastily replacing the stopper. Her head had begun to ache again and she felt sick. It was one thing to play a trivial part in a minor break-in, quite another to have a starring role in sending a man to the gallows. *Oh God, she didn't want to think about that.*

'You said he hit you?' Lady Ipswich said abruptly, fixing her with a piercing gaze.

Henrietta's hand instinctively went to the tender lump on her head. 'He knocked me out and carried me off. I have been lying unconscious in a ditch.'

'No one else saw him, or you, for that matter?'

'Not that I'm aware of.'

'In fact,' Lady Ipswich said, turning on Henrietta with an enigmatic smile, 'I have only your word for what happened.'

'Well, yes, but the emeralds *are* missing, and the safe was broken into, and so—'

'So the solution is obvious,' Lady Ipswich declared triumphantly.

Henrietta stared at her blankly. 'Solution?'

'You, Miss Markham, are quite patently in league with the thief!'

Henrietta's jaw dropped. Were she not already sitting down, she would have collapsed. 'I?'

'It was you who told him the whereabouts of the safe. You who let him into my house and later broke the glass on the window downstairs to fake a break-in. You who smuggled my poor Princess out into the night in order to prevent her from raising the alarm.'

'You think—you truly think—no, you can't possibly. It's preposterous.'

'You are his accomplice.' Lady Ipswich nodded to

herself several times. 'I see it now, it is the only logical explanation. No doubt he looks nothing like this lurid description you gave me. An eyepatch indeed! You made it up to put everyone off the scent. Well, Miss Markham, let me tell you that there are no flies on Nell—I mean, Helen Ipswich. I am on to you and your little game, and so, too, will be the gentleman from Bow Street who is making his way here from London as we speak.' Striding over to the fireplace, she rang the bell vigorously. 'You shall be confined to your room until he arrives. You are also summarily dismissed from my employ.'

Henrietta gaped. A huge part of her, the rational part, told her it was all a silly misunderstanding that could be easily remedied, but there was another part that reminded her of her lowly position, of the facts as they must seem to her employer, of the way that Rafe St Alban had reacted to her story. What she said wasn't really that credible. And she had no proof to back it up. Not a whit. Absolutely none.

'Did you hear me?'

Henrietta stumbled to her feet. 'But, madam, my lady, I beg of you, you cannot possibly think…'

'Get out,' Lady Ipswich demanded, as the door opened to reveal the startled butler. 'Get out and do not let me see you again until the Runner comes. I cannot believe I have been harbouring a thief and a brazen liar under my roof.'

'I am not a thief and I am most certainly not a liar.' Outrage at the accusations bolstered Henrietta's courage. She never told even the tiniest, whitest lie. Papa had raised her to believe in absolute truth at all costs. 'I would never, ever do such an underhand and dishonest thing,' she said, her voice shaking with emotion.

Lady Ipswich coldly turned her back on her. Henrietta shook her head in confusion. She felt woozy. There was a rushing sound like a spate of water in her ears. Her fingers were freezing as she clasped them together in an effort to stop herself shaking. She wished she hadn't left the sal volatile on the chair. 'When he hears the truth of the matter, the magistrate—Runner—whatever—they will believe me. *They will.*'

Lady Ipswich's laugh tinkled like shattering glass as she eyed her former governess contemptuously. 'Ask yourself, my dear, whose version are they more likely to believe, yours or mine?'

'But Lord Pentland…'

Lady Ipswich's eyes narrowed. 'What, prey, has Lord Pentland to do with this?'

'Merely that it was he who found me. It was his carriage which brought me back.'

'You told Rafe St Alban this ridiculous tale of being kidnapped?' Lady Ipswich's voice rose to what would be described in a less titled lady as a shriek. Her face was once again drained of colour.

Henrietta eyed her with dismay. Her employer had not the sweetest of tempers, but she was not normally prone to such dramatic mood swings. The loss of the heirloom had obviously overset her, she decided, as her ladyship retrieved the smelling salts, took a deep sniff and sneezed twice. 'It is not a ridiculous tale, my lady, it is the truth.'

'What did he make of it?' Lady Ipswich snapped.

'Lord Pentland? He—he…' He had warned her. She

realised that now, that's what he meant when he told her not to expect to be treated as a heroine. 'I don't think—I don't know exactly what he thought, but I suspect he didn't believe me, either,' Henrietta admitted reluctantly.

Lady Ipswich nodded several times. 'Lord Pentland clearly attaches as much credence to your tale as I do. You are disgraced, Miss Markham, and I have found you out. Now get out of my sight.'

Chapter Three

Wearily climbing the stairs to her attic room, Henrietta struggled with the resentment that welled up in her breast. She was furious and shocked, but also ashamed—for soon it would be common knowledge in the household. Most of all, though, she was petrified.

Sitting on the narrow bed in her room on the third floor, she stared blindly at the opposite wall while pulling a perfectly good cotton handkerchief to shreds. She had been dismissed from her post. Lady Ipswich had branded her a thief. Heaven knows what Rafe St Alban would make of that. Not that it mattered what Rafe St Alban thought. Not that he'd actually give her a second thought, anyway, except maybe to congratulate himself for not becoming embroiled.

'Oh, merciful heavens! If I am brought to trial, he would be called as a witness.' He'd see her clapped in irons in the dock, wearing rags and probably with gaol fever. She knew all about gaol fever. Maisy Masters, who had been teaching her how to make jam from rose-

hips, had described it in lurid detail. Maisy's brother had spent six months in prison awaiting trial for poaching. Normally the most taciturn of women, Maisy had been almost too forthcoming on the subject of gaol fever. There was the rash. Then there was the cough and the headaches and the fever. Then there were the sores caused by sleeping on fetid straw and being bitten by fleas. Oh God, and the smells. She would *smell* in the dock. Maisy told her that the lawyers all carried vials of perfume, it was so bad. She would be shamed. Even if she was found innocent, she would be ruined. And if she was not found innocent, she might even be headed for the scaffold. Maisy had told her all about that, too, though she'd tried very hard not to listen. They would sell pamphlets with lurid descriptions of her heinous crime; they would come to watch her, to cheer her last few moments. Mama and Papa would…

Deep breaths.

'Mama and Papa are in Ireland,' she reminded herself, 'and therefore blissfully unaware of my plight.' Which was a blessing, for the moment, at least.

More deep breaths.

They wouldn't find out. They wouldn't ever know. They absolutely could not ever be allowed to know. She must, simply must, find a way to clear her name before they returned to England. Even more importantly, she must find a way to avoid actually being clapped in irons, because once she was in gaol she had no chance of tracking down the real culprit.

Though how she was going to do that she had no idea. 'No matter how you look at it,' she said to herself, 'the situation does not look good. Not good at all.' Just because she had truth on her side did not mean that justice would automatically follow. Malicious or not, Lady Ipswich's version of events had an authentic ring. And she had influence, too.

'Oh dear. Oh dear. *Oh dear.*' Henrietta sniffed woefully. She would not cry. *She would not.* Blinking frantically and sniffing loudly, she wandered about the confines of her bedchamber. She stared out of the casement window on to the kitchen gardens and wondered who was looking after her charges. They would be missing her. Or perhaps Rafe St Alban was right and they would quickly forget her. Though perhaps she would be too notorious for them to forget about her, once they heard that she was a thief. Or in league with one. Worse. Boys being boys, they might even admire her in a misguided way. What kind of example was that to set? She must speak to them somehow, explain. Oh God, what was she to do? What on *earth* was she to do?

Helplessly, Henrietta sank down once more upon the bed. Perhaps by tomorrow Lady Ipswich would have come to her senses. But tomorrow—maybe even by the end of today—would come the Bow Street Runner. And he would take her away to gaol until the next Quarterly Assizes, which were almost two full months away. She could not wait two full months to clear her name. And even if she did, how could she hope to do so with no money to pay anyone to speak on her behalf? She didn't even know if she was permitted to employ a lawyer and, even if she was, she had absolutely no idea how to go about finding one. The authorities would most likely summon Papa, too, and then...

'No!' She couldn't stay here. Whatever happened,

she couldn't just sit here and meekly await her fate. She had to get out. Away. Now!

Without giving herself any more time to think, Henrietta grabbed her bandbox from the cupboard and began to throw her clothes into it willy-nilly. She had few possessions, but as she sat on the lid in a futile effort to make it close, she decided she must make do with fewer still. Her second-best dress was abandoned and the bandbox finally fastened.

She spent a further half-hour composing a note to her charges. In the end, it was most unsatisfactory, simply begging their forgiveness for her sudden departure, bidding them stick to their lessons and not to think ill of her, no matter what they heard.

It was by now well past noon. The servants would be at their dinner. Lady Ipswich would be in her boudoir. Tying the ribbons of her plain-straw poke bonnet in a neat bow under her chin, Henrietta draped her cloak around her shoulders and cautiously opened the door.

Stealing down the steps in a manner quite befitting the housebreaker's accomplice she was purported to be, she slipped through a side door into the kitchen garden and thence on to the gravelled path that led from the stables, without once allowing herself to look back. At the gates she turned on to the road that led to the village. A short distance further on, Henrietta sat down on an inviting tree trunk with her back to the road and indulged in a hearty bout of tears.

She was not given to self-pity, but at this moment she felt she was entitled to be just a little sorry for herself. Already she was regretting her impulsive behaviour.

All very well to make her escape with some vague idea of clearing her name, but how, exactly, did she propose to do that?

The dispiriting truth was that she had no idea. 'And now that I have run away, they will think it simply confirms my guilt,' she said to her shoe. A large tear splashed on to the ground. 'Stupid, stupid, stupid,' she muttered, sniffing valiantly.

She had not a soul in the world to turn to. Her only relative, as far as she knew, was Mama's sister; Henrietta could hardly turn up on the doorstep of an aunt whom she had never met and introduce herself as her long-lost niece and a fugitive from the law, to boot. Besides, there was the small matter of the rift between Mama and her sibling. They had not spoken for many years. No, that was not an option.

But she could not go back, either. She had been badly shaken by the ease with which her employer had accepted her guilt, and that, on top of Rafe St Alban's scepticism, made her question whether anyone would take her side without proof. No, there was no going back. The only way was forwards. And the only path she could think of taking was to London. Such distinctive jewellery must be got rid of somehow and London was surely the place. She would head to the city. And once there she would—she would— Oh, she would think about that, once she was on her way.

What she needed to think about now was how to get there. Henrietta rummaged in her bandbox for her stocking purse and carefully counted out the total of her wealth, which came to the grand sum of eight shillings and sixpence. She gazed at the small mound of coins, wondering vaguely if it was enough to pay for a seat on the mail, realised she would be better keeping her money to pay for a room at an inn, returned them to the purse and got wearily to her feet. She could not remain on this tree trunk for ever. Picking up her bandbox, with the vague idea of obtaining a ride in the direction of the metropolis, she set off down the road towards the village.

The fields that bordered the wayside were freshly tilled and planted with hops and barley, sprouting green and lush. The hedgerows, where honeysuckle and clematis rioted among the briars of the blackberries, whose white flowers were not yet unfurled, provided her with occasional shade from the sun shining bright in the pale blue of the early summer sky. The landscape undulated gently. The air was rent with birdsong. It was a lovely day. A lovely day to be a fugitive from justice, she thought bitterly

For the first mile, she made good progress, her head full of fantastical schemes for the recovery of Lady Ipswich's necklace. The illicit hours she had devoted to reading the novels of the Minerva Press had not been entirely wasted. Before long, however, reality intervened. The straps from her bandbox were cutting into her hand; her cloak, the only outerwear she possessed, was designed for the depths of winter, not to be combined with a woollen dress in early summer. Her face was decidedly red under her bonnet and she could not conceive how such a few necessities as she carried could come to weigh so much. A pretty copse, where foxgloves and the last of the bluebells made vivid splashes of colour, failed to fill her with admiration for the abundant joys of nature. She was not in the mood to appreciate rural perfection. In fact, it would not be inaccurate to say that Henrietta's temper was sadly frayed.

By the time she finally approached her destination she was convinced she had a blister on her foot where a small pebble had lodged inside her shoe, her shoulders ached, her head thumped and she wanted nothing more than a cool drink and a rest in a darkened room.

The King George was a ramshackle inn situated at a crossroads on the outer reaches of Woodfield village. The weathered board, with its picture of the poor mad king, creaked on rusted hinges by the entrance to the yard, where a mangy dog lazily scratched its ear beside a bale of hay. Dubiously inspecting the huddle of badly maintained buildings that constituted the hostelry, Henrietta was regaled by a burst of hearty male laughter that echoed out from behind the shuttered windows. Not a place to trust the sheets, never mind the clientele, she concluded. Her heart sank.

The front door gave straight into the taproom, which she had not expected. The hushed silence that greeted her entrance proved that she had taken the patrons equally by surprise. For a moment, Henrietta, clutching her cloak around her, stared at the sea of faces in front of her like a small animal caught in a trap and the men stared back as if she were a creature fished from the deep. Her courage almost failed her.

When the landlord asked her gruffly what she wanted, her voice came out in a whisper. His answer was disappointing. The mail was not due until tomorrow. The accommodation coach was fully booked for the next two days. He looked at her curiously. Why hadn't she thought to enquire ahead? Was her business in London urgent? If so, he could probably get her a ride with one of his customers as far as the first posting inn, where she could pick up the Bristol coach that evening.

Suddenly horribly aware that the less people who knew of her whereabouts, the better, Henrietta declined this invitation and informed the landlord that she had changed her mind. She was not going to London, she informed him. She was definitely not going to London.

With a mumbled apology, she retreated back out of the front door and found herself in the stable yard, where a racing carriage was tethered, the horses fidgeting nervously. There was no sign of the driver. The phaeton was painted dark glossy green, the spokes of its four high wheels trimmed with gold, but there were otherwise no distinguishing marks. No coat of arms. The horses were a perfectly matched pair of chestnuts. Such a fine equipage must surely be London-bound.

Henrietta eyed it nervously, a reckless idea forming in her head. The seat seemed a very long way from the ground. The rumble seat behind, upon which was stowed a portmanteau and a large blanket, was not much lower. The hood of the phaeton was raised, presumably because the owner anticipated rain. If he did not look at the rumble seat—and why would he?—then he would not see her. If she did not take this chance, who knew what other would present itself? The spectres of the Bow Street Runner and Maisy Masters's tales of prison loomed before her. Without giving herself time to think further, Henrietta scrambled on to the rear seat of the carriage, clutching her bandbox. Crouching down as far as she could under the rumble seat itself, she pulled the blanket over her and waited.

She did not have to wait long. Just a few minutes later, she felt the carriage lurch as its driver climbed aboard and almost immediately urged the horses forwards. Only one person? Straining her ears, she could hear nothing above the jangle of the tack and the rumbling of the wheels. The carriage swung round past the front of the King George and headed at a trot out of the village. Sneaking a peak out of the blanket, she thought they were headed in the right direction, but could not be sure. As they hit a deep rut in the road, she only just stopped herself from crying out and clutched frantically at the edge of the rumble seat to stop herself from tumbling on to the road.

The driver loosened his hold on the reins and cracked the whip. The horses made short work of quitting the environs of Woodfield village. As they bowled along, Henrietta tried to subdue a rising panic. What had she done? She could not be at all sure they were headed towards London and had no idea at all who was driving her. He might be angry when he discovered her. He might simply abandon her in the middle of nowhere. Or worse! She did not want to think about what worse was. *Oh God, she had been a complete idiot.*

The carriage picked up speed. Hedgerows fragrant with rosehip and honeysuckle flew past in a blur as she peered out from under her blanket. Beyond, the landscape was vibrant with fields of swaying hops. She glimpsed an oast house, its conical roof so reminiscent of a witch's hat. They passed through a village, no more than a cluster of thatched cottages surrounding a water

mill. Then another. Farms. The occasional farmer's cart
rumbled past heading in the opposite direction. On a
clear stretch of road, they overtook an accommodation
coach with a burst of acceleration that had Henrietta
grabbing on to the sides of the phaeton. The driver of
the coach raised his whip in acknowledgement.

Jolted and bruised, cramped and sore, her head
aching again, Henrietta clung to the seat and clung also
to the one reassuring fact, that at least she had avoided
Lady Ipswich's Bow Street Runner. She found little
else to console her as they sped on through unfamiliar
countryside and soon gave up trying. The events of the
past twenty-four hours finally took their toll. Exhausted,
shocked, bruised and confused, Henrietta fell into a
fitful dose.

When she awoke, it was to find that the carriage
had slowed. They seemed to be following a river, and
it seemed wide enough to surely be the Thames. She
tried to stretch, but her limbs had gone into a cramp.
She was weighing up the risks of emerging from under
the seat when they turned off the road through a gap in
the hedgerow.

A swathe of grass rolled down to the wide, slow-
moving river. Henrietta's heart began to pound very
hard and very loud—so loud she was sure it could
be heard. Should she huddle down further or make a
break for it? Should she stay to brazen it out, perhaps
even request to be allowed to complete the journey? Or
should she take her chances with her very limited funds
and even more limited knowledge of where she was?

The chassis tilted as the driver leapt down. He was

tall. She caught a glimpse of a beaver hat before he disappeared round to the front of the horses, leading them down to the water and tethering them there. It was now or never, while he was tending to them, but panic made her freeze. *Get out, get out*, she chided herself, but her limbs wouldn't move.

'What the devil!'

The blanket was yanked back. Henrietta blinked up at the figure looming over her.

He was just as tall and dark and handsome as she remembered; he was looking at her as if she were every bit as unwelcome an intrusion into his life as she had been this morning. 'Lord Pentland.'

'Miss Markham, we meet again. What the hell are you doing in my carriage?'

Her mouth seemed to have dried up, like her words. Henrietta sought desperately for an explanation he would find acceptable, but the shock was too much. 'I didn't know it was yours,' she said lamely.

'Whose did you think it was?'

'I didn't know,' she said, feeling extremely foolish and extremely nervous. His winged brows were drawn together in his devilish look. Of all the people, why did it have to be him!

'Get out.'

He held out an imperious hand. She tried to move, but her legs were stiff and her petticoats had become entangled in her bandbox. With an exclamation of impatience, he pulled her towards him. For a brief moment she was in his arms, held high against his chest, then she was dumped unceremoniously on to her feet, her bandbox tumbling out with her, tipping its contents—its very personal contents—on to the grass. Her legs gave way. Henrietta plopped to the grass beside her under-garments and promptly burst into tears.

Rafe's anger at having harboured a stowaway gave way to a wholly inappropriate desire to laugh, for she looked absurdly like one of those mawkish drawings of an orphaned child. Gathering up the collection of intimate garments, hairbrushes, combs and other rather shabby paraphernalia, he squashed them back into the bandbox and pulled its owner back to her feet. 'Come, stop that noise, else anyone passing will stop and accuse me of God knows what heinous crime.'

He meant it as a jest, but it served only to make his woebegone companion sob harder. Realising that she was genuinely overwrought, Rafe picked up the blanket and led her over to his favourite spot on the riverbank, where he sat her down and handed her a large square of clean linen. 'Dry your eyes and compose yourself, tears will get us nowhere.'

'I know that. There is no need to tell me so, I know it *perfectly* well,' Henrietta wailed. But it took her some moments of sniffing, dabbing and deep breaths to do as he urged, by which time she was certain she must look a very sorry sight indeed, with red cheeks and a redder nose.

Watching her valiant attempts to regain control of herself, Rafe felt his conscience, normally the most complacent of creatures, stir and his anger subside. Obviously Henrietta had been dismissed. Obviously her ridiculous tale of housebreakers was at the root of it. Obviously Helen Ipswich hadn't believed her. He hadn't expected her to, but despite that fact, he had sent her off to face her fate alone. Faced with the sorry and very vulnerable-looking evidence of this act before him, Rafe felt genuine remorse. Those big chocolate-brown eyes of Henrietta Markham's were still drowning in tears. Her full bottom lip was trembling. Not even the ordeal of lying in a ditch overnight had resulted in tears. Something drastic must have occurred. 'Tell me what happened,' he said.

The gentleness in his tone almost overset her again. The change in his manner, too, from that white-lipped fury to—to—almost, she could believe he cared. Almost. 'It's nothing. Nothing to do with you. I am just—it is nothing.' Henrietta swallowed hard and stared resolutely at her hands. His kerchief was of the finest lawn, his initials embroidered in one corner. She could not have achieved such beautiful stitchery. She wondered who had sewn it. She sniffed again. Sneaking a look, she saw that his eyes were blue, not stormy-grey, that his mouth was formed into something that looked very like a sympathetic smile.

'I take it that you have left Lady Ipswich's employ?'

Henrietta clenched her fists. 'She accused me of theft.'

He had not expected that. Unbelievable as her tale was, he had not thought for a moment that she was a thief. 'You're not serious?'

'Yes, I am. She said I was in cahoots with the house-breaker. She said I opened the safe and broke a window to make it look as if he had broken in.'

'A safe? Then whatever was stolen was of some value?'

Henrietta nodded. 'An heirloom. The Ipswich

emeralds. The magistrate has summoned a Bow Street Runner. Lady Ipswich ordered me to stay in my room until he arrives to arrest me.'

Rafe looked at her incredulously. 'The Ipswich emeralds? Rich pickings indeed for a common housebreaker.'

'Exactly. It's a hanging matter. And she—she—by implicating me—she—I had to leave, else I would have been cast into gaol.' Henrietta's voice trembled, but a few more gulps of air stemmed the tears. 'I don't want to go to gaol.'

Rafe tapped his riding crop on his booted foot. 'Tell me exactly what was said when you returned this morning.'

Henrietta did so, haltingly at first in her efforts to recall every detail, then with increasing vehemence as she recounted the astonishing accusations levelled at her. 'I still can't quite believe it. I would never, never do such a thing,' she finished fervently. 'I couldn't just sit there and wait to be dragged off to prison. I couldn't bear for Papa to be told that his only child was being held in gaol.'

'So you stowed away in my carriage.'

Rafe's eyes were hooded by his lids again. She could not read his thoughts. She had never come across such an inscrutable countenance, nor one which could change so completely yet so subtly. 'Yes, I did,' she declared defensively. 'I didn't have any option, I had to get away.'

'Do you realise that by doing so you have embroiled me, against my will, in your little melodrama? Did you think of that?'

'No. I didn't. It didn't occur to me.'

'Of course not, because you act as you speak, don't you, without thinking?'

'That's not fair,' Henrietta said indignantly. She knew it *was* fair, but that fact made her all the more anxious to defend herself. 'It's your fault, you make me nervous; besides, I didn't know it was your carriage.'

'As well for you that it was. Did you think what might have happened if it had belonged to some buck?' Rafe's mouth thinned again. 'But I forgot, it could not be worse, could it, for you are now at the mercy of a notorious rake. Consider that, Miss Markham.'

'I am considering it,' she threw back at him, angry enough now to speak the truth. 'This morning I was even more at your mercy, in your bed in my underclothes, and you pretended to but really, you made no real attempt at all to—to…'

'To what?' He knew he was being unfair, but he could not help it. Something about her exasperated him. She made him want to shake the innocence out of her, yet at the same time he was fighting the quite contrary urge to protect her. He didn't understand it. He didn't try. 'What, could it be that you are insulted by my gentlemanly behaviour? Did you want me to kiss you, Miss Markham?'

Colour flooded her face. 'Of course I did not. I was *pleased* you did not find me attractive.'

'But you are quite mistaken. I do.'

His tone was mocking, his expression almost predatory. His thigh was brushing hers. *How had he come to be so close?* She could feel the warmth of him, even through the heavy folds of her cape and gown. Though he had shaved this morning, she could already see a shadow of stubble on his jaw line. She felt as if she couldn't breathe. Or as if her breath had become sharp. It hurt her throat. Her pulses were pounding. She felt afraid. Not afraid, exactly. Apprehension mixed with excitement. And for some reason, it was a nice feeling.

She didn't know how the conversation had taken this turn. All she could think about was that Rafe St Alban had admitted that he found her, Henrietta Markham, attractive. Even though she knew for a fact that she wasn't beautiful. Mama was beautiful. Mama said that it was as well that Henrietta didn't take after her, because such beauty was dangerous. It attracted the wrong sort of man. It attracted men like Rafe St Alban. Except Henrietta wasn't a dangerous beauty and Rafe St Alban was apparently still attracted to her.

'Lost for words, most verbose Miss Markham?'

He was so close she could feel his breath on her face. She should move, but she couldn't. Didn't want to. 'I don't…'

'Such a notorious rake as you think I am,' Rafe said huskily, 'it seems only fair that I should live up to my reputation. It seems only fair, my delectable stowaway, that you should pay the price for taking advantage of me. Twice, now, you have given me no option but to rescue you. I am entitled to some form of reward.'

He hadn't meant to do it, but he couldn't seem to stop himself. He hadn't realised how much he had been tempted until he gave in and kissed her. He hadn't realised just how much he wanted to, until he kissed the little tilt at the corner or her mouth, which made her look as if she was always on the verge of a smile. He had meant it as only a small rebuke, a mild punishment, but she tasted so sweet, she smelled so fresh, of sunshine and tears, and her mouth was quite the most kissable he had ever seen, that it was he who was punished by the eruption of unwelcome desire. Uncontrollable desire. Her mouth was plump, pink and soft. A veritable cushion for kisses. He allowed his lips to drift over hers and kissed her again, an appetiser of a kiss. And then, when she made no move to pull away, he teased her lips open with his tongue and kissed her again, and for the first time in a very, very long time, Rafe forgot all about where he was and who he was and how things were, and lost himself in the simple pleasure of a pair of soft, welcoming lips and the delight of a soft, welcoming body.

For Henrietta, time stopped, though the birds still sang, the breeze still rustled in the tree above them. Her heart, too, seemed to stop. She was afraid to move, lest the spell be broken. Her first kiss. And such a kiss. His mouth so very different from hers. His touch on her shoulders, her back, moulding her into him. She allowed herself to be moulded. Then she began to relish it. She should be shocked, but she was not shocked. She was entranced.

When he released her she could only stare, clutching at his coat in a most undignified manner, raising a hand to her mouth in wonder. 'I've never been kissed before,' she blurted out, then blushed vividly.

'I could tell,' Rafe said.

'Oh. Was it—was I…?'

'It was very nice.' *Much too nice*—it had provoked a disconcerting reaction in him. He, who prided himself on his self-control, had felt something akin to abandon flare in him. Not lust, something more primal, more sensual. He shifted on the blanket in order to put some distance between them, to disguise the incontrovertible evidence of his own arousal.

'Oh.'

'I, on the other hand, am not nice. You would do well to remember that, Henrietta.'

The warning in his voice was unmistakable. When he laughed, he looked like a different person, but already the shutters were coming back down, his lids shielding his eyes, his mouth straightening. 'I think you would like me to think so,' Henrietta replied daringly.

'I thought you already did?'

An ominous silence followed as Henrietta tried desperately to assemble her thoughts. 'I did,' she admitted finally, 'but now I'm confused.'

He admired her honesty, though he would not dream of emulating it. He was confused himself. He shouldn't have kissed her. He had meant it as a punishment, but it had backfired. She had awoken something long dormant in him. A kiss with feeling. He didn't want to kiss with feeling, any more than he wanted to deal with the problem of what to do with her.

'I stopped here to eat,' he said, getting quickly to his feet. 'You must be hungry, too. Perhaps a full stomach will help us sort out this damned predicament you've placed me in.'

Henrietta watched in something of a daze as Rafe strode over to the phaeton and began to haul out a hamper, which she hadn't previously noticed, from behind his portmanteau. She touched her lips, which still tingled from his caress. He had kissed her! Rafe

St Alban had kissed her, and she had kissed him back. She was a shameless hussy!

Was she? She didn't feel shameless. She felt—she had no idea how she felt. As if she did not know if she was on her head or her heels. As if her brain was cotton wool. As if the world had turned upside down and deposited her in a strange land. She felt as if she had drunk too much of the cherry brandy one of the villagers gave Papa at Christmas, or as if she were dreaming, for nothing that had happened in the last few hours bore any resemblance at all to her usual life. Especially not that kiss.

She touched her lips again, trying to recapture it. Heady, like wine. Sweet, like honey. Melting. No wonder kisses led people astray. Another of Rafe St Alban's kisses and she would willingly have been led astray. Wherever astray was. A place inhabited by rakes. Rakes who preyed upon the innocent. Once again, Henrietta reminded herself to be on her guard. The problem was, there was a rebellious part of her, a part which Rafe's kiss had conjured into life, that wasn't at all interested in being on guard. Mama implied that what maidens suffered at the hands of rakes was unpleasant. What Henrietta had suffered had been quite the contrary. Surely Mama could not be wrong?

Rafe placed the hamper down on the blanket at Henrietta's feet. 'I often stop here on my journey between Woodfield and London, I much prefer it to a posting inn.'

He began to unpack the food. There was a game pie, the pastry golden brown and flaky, a whole chicken roasted and fragrant with sage-and-onion stuffing, quails eggs, cold salmon in aspic jelly, a Derby cheese and a basket of early strawberries.

'Goodness, there's enough here to feed a small army,' Henrietta said, looking at the delightful feast laid out before her with awe.

Rafe was busy with bottles and glasses. 'Is there? We are not obliged to eat it all, you know. Do you wish claret or burgundy? I'd recommend the claret myself, the burgundy is a little too heavy for alfresco eating.'

Henrietta giggled. 'Claret, please.'

'What's so amusing?'

'This. You and me, the earl and the governess, having a meal by the Thames. I've never seen such a delicious picnic in my life.'

'It's plain enough fare.'

'For you, maybe. I am used to much plainer at home.'

Rafe helped them both to a generous wedge of pie. 'Tell me more about your family.'

'There's nothing much to tell.'

'Are you an only child?'

'Yes.'

'And you have no other relatives?'

'I have an aunt, but I've never met her. Mama's family considered Papa beneath them. They did not approve of the match and liked it a lot less when they realised he intended to spend his life helping other people to better themselves, rather than doing the same for his own family.'

'You admire your father?'

Henrietta considered this. 'Yes, in a way. I don't necessarily agree with how he goes about things, nor indeed with his priorities, but he is true to himself. And to Mama.'

Her hand was hovering over a bowl of strawberries. Rafe picked one out and popped it into her mouth. The juice glistened on her lips. He leaned towards her, catching it with his thumb. Her tongue automatically flicked out to lick it clean. Awareness shot like an arrow through his blood, making him instantly hard. He leaned closer, replacing his thumb with his mouth. A brief touch, no more, enough for her eyes to widen, her lips to soften in anticipation, his erection to harden.

Enough and not nearly enough. 'You have the most kissable lips I have ever come across, Henrietta Markham, you should be aware of that, and consider yourself warned. Have you had enough?'

'Enough?' She stared at him in incomprehension. Could he see the way her heart was beating? The way her flesh was covered in goose bumps? Could he sense the way she turned hot, then cold?

'Have you had sufficient to eat? Because if you have, I feel it is time to address the thorny question of what the deuce I'm going to do with you.'

'Do with me? You need do nothing more than deposit me in London, if you please.'

'What do you intend to do there, go into hiding? This will not blow over, you know. The Ipswich emeralds are no fripperies.'

'I know. Do you think me an idiot as well as a thief?'

'I think you any number of things, but I don't think you're capable of stealing. You are far too honest.'

'Oh.'

'You are also far too quick to share your opinions,

even quicker to judge. You make wild assumptions based on nothing but hearsay, you see the world in black and white and refuse to acknowledge any sort of grey, but like your father, I suspect, you are true to yourself. I don't think you are a thief.'

She hadn't realised until this point how much it mattered. To be thought of so ill had cut her to the quick. Even though he was a rake, it mattered. 'So you believe me?'

'Poor Henrietta, you have had a torrid time of it these last few hours.'

'There are always people more unfortunate than oneself,' Henrietta said stoutly. 'That is what Papa says.'

Rafe looked sceptical, wondering what Henrietta's other-worldly father would make of his daughter's current predicament. 'Not so very many. You do realise that by running away you have made a difficult situation much worse?'

'I know, but—'

'Your doing so will be seen to simply confirm your guilt.'

'I *know*, but I could not think of any other—'

'By rights I should hand you over to the authorities, let you take your chances. You are, after all, innocent. The problem is you have, by your actions, behaved guiltily and worse, implicated me.'

'But no one saw me climb into your carriage, and...'

'They do know that I found you. They know that I was involved in sending you back to Helen Ipswich's. When it becomes also known that I left Woodfield at about the same time you disappeared, even a Bow Street Runner will put two and two together. You have placed me in an impossible position. I cannot turn you in without risking being found guilty by association, but neither can I in all conscience simply abandon you.'

Rafe was not a man given to chivalry. He was not a man much given to impulsive action, either, but Henrietta Markham's endearing courage, her genuine horror at the accusations levelled against her and the very real dangers that she faced, roused him now to both. Whether he wanted to be or not, he was involved in this farce. That his involvement would, of necessity, postpone the unpleasant task of putting his grandmother straight was a small bonus. 'I have no choice. I'll help you,' he said, nodding to himself. It was the only way.

'Help me to do what?'

'Find the thief. The emeralds. Whatever it takes to clear your name.'

'I am perfectly capable of doing that myself,' Henrietta said indignantly and quite contrarily, because for a moment there, when he had offered, her heart had leapt in relief.

'How?'

'What do you mean?'

'Have you contacts in the underworld?'

'No, but—'

'Do you have any idea how to go about tracing stolen property?'

'No, but—'

'Admit it, Henrietta, you have no idea at all how to go about anything, have you? No plan.'

'No, none whatsoever.'

Rafe's smile lurked. His pleasure at her admission was quite out of proportion. It was a small enough victory, but it felt significant. He liked that she did not prevaricate even when it cost her dear. 'Then it is very fortunate that I do,' he said. The pleasure he took in her smile was also quite out of proportion.

'You do?'

'Obviously you need someone to assist you,' Rafe said, allowing his own smile to widen. 'A man with contacts in the underworld, who can trace the stolen jewellery, the thief or ideally both.'

'Obviously,' Henrietta replied, feeling slightly dazed by the prospect. 'Next you will tell me how I should go about finding such a man?'

'There is no need. You have already found him. Me.'

Chapter Four

'**Y**ou?' Henrietta said incredulously.

She was staring at him as if he had just escaped from Bedlam. Once more, he had to bite his lip to suppress his smile. 'I have an acquaintance in London who has any number of contacts in such circles,' Rafe explained. 'A prize haul such as the Ipswich emeralds should not be too difficult to trace for someone in the know.'

'You are making a May game of me, you must be. How do you come to know such a person? And even if you did—I mean do—I mean, I don't understand. Why would you?'

'Under the circumstances, you have left me no option but to help you sort out this appalling mess.' The prospect was surprisingly appealing, but Rafe chose not to share this information. Indeed, he barely acknowledged it himself.

But, annoyingly, Henrietta shook her head most decidedly. 'Truly, I am much obliged for your generous offer, but my plight is my responsibility.'

'You would be most unwise to refuse my offer of help.'

She chewed her lip. What other options did she have, really? What was worse, placing herself in the hands of a rake who might or might not have designs on her virtue, but seemed honestly to be intent upon clearing her name, or taking the risk of being imprisoned, perhaps condemned? What use was virtue if she was deported or dead? And for goodness' sake, it wasn't as if she was about to surrender her virtue, anyway. It wasn't as if her virtue was to be payment. *Was it?* Was kissing to be considered payment for his helping her? Was there a higher price to be paid? Would he expect more?

She was being ridiculous. No matter what his expectations, she would not oblige him and one thing of which she was certain was that he would not take what was not given. He could have done *that* this morning. She was perfectly safe from him. Provided she was sure of herself. Which she was. Of course she was.

Henrietta nodded to herself. Rafe St Alban was clearly the lesser of two evils. The only sensible option. She would be a fool not to accept his offer. 'You are right, I don't have any choice,' she said.

'Very sensible, Miss Markham.'

'I like to think I am.'

'So you will trust me?'

She hesitated, alerted by the hint of something in his voice. 'To help me. Yes, I will trust you to do that.'

'Very careful and very wise, Henrietta. An equivocal response.'

'Lord Pentland…'

'Rafe will do. I think we've gone well beyond observing the niceties.'

'Rafe. It suits you.'

'Thank you. Let me return the compliment. I have never before been acquainted with a Henrietta, but the name seems to be made for you.'

'Thank you. I think. I was named for Papa.'

The way he was looking at her was giving her a shivery feeling, as if she were standing on the brink of something. Was she really thinking of throwing her lot in with him, an incredibly, devastatingly handsome stranger who had a reputation? 'Won't people be expecting you in town?'

Rafe considered that. There was his grandmother, with her list of eligible brides waiting for his approval. There were no doubt a new stack of gilt-edged invitations on his desk, for the Season was in full swing. Despite his notorious reclusiveness—exclusiveness, as Lucas liked to refer to it—Lord Pentland's attendance at any party or rout or ball was a feather in the hostess's cap, so he continued to receive them by the hatful.

'Save for Lucas, to be honest, I don't think there's a single person who will really miss me, any more than I can think of a single engagement which I would actually enjoy attending.'

'Who is Lucas?'

'The Right Honourable Lucas Hamilton. One of my oldest friends. We met at the Falls of Tivoli while on our respective Grand Tours. Hadrian's Villa is near there, you know, so it's *de rigueur* to visit, though I have to say I was disappointed by it. We found we were both destined for Greece and met up again there. Lucas's ancient Greek put mine to shame. He's much more of a scholar than I, though he keeps that fact very quiet. Prefers to be known for his prowess in the ring.'

'He fights?'

Rafe laughed. 'Not professionally—though he'd be up for it, most likely, if it were offered. No, whatever you may say of him, Lucas is ever the gentleman. He boxes only with fellow gentlemen at Jackson's. He fences with fellow gentlemen at Angelo's. And he drinks every fellow gentleman who is up for the challenge under the table.'

'He sounds a very colourful character,' Henrietta said doubtfully.

'He does get into some scrapes when I'm not around to keep an eye on him.'

'It sounds as if he's very lucky to have you.'

Rafe's smile faded. 'I'm Lucas's friend, not his keeper. For reasons known only to himself, Lucas seems hellbent on self-destruction. He will do that whether I am there to take care of him or not. You know, I can't think why I'm telling you this. In any event it should only take a few days to clean this emeralds business up. Lucas can look after himself until then.'

'How can you know that it will only take us a few days?'

'Distinctive emeralds and a very distinctive house-breaker must leave a distinctive trail, if one knows where to look. I'm pretty sure we'll be able to track one or both down very quickly. At least, my friend will.'

'I'm very grateful for your help. Truly I am.'

'I am very glad to offer it,' Rafe said, surprising him-self with the truth. She was dressed quite atrociously in badly cut and patchily darned brown. He had never seen quite such a lopsided bow on a bonnet, but she was looking at him as if her life depended upon him and he supposed that at present it did. 'Really and truly.'

Whatever the next few days held in store for him, it was unlikely to be boring. Anxious, now that he had committed himself, to be gone, Rafe set about untethering the horses.

Sitting beside him on the narrow seat of the phaeton, Henrietta was acutely aware of Rafe's presence. Her thigh brushed against his. She nudged his whip hand by mistake. *Was she insane to be setting out with him like this?* She knew almost nothing about him save that he was rich and titled and a rake and a very accomplished kisser. Probably on account of being a rake. And yet here she was, sitting nonchalantly—sort of nonchalantly—beside him. She *must* be mad! She ought to think so, and certainly her inner governess did think so, but Henrietta was finding it increasingly easy to ignore her inner governess.

What an odd picture they must make, she in her ancient cloak and out-of-date bonnet and he the epitome of fashion. She counted at least six capes on his drab driving coat. His gloves were of the softest York tan leather; his buckskins fitted so tightly that they looked as if he had been sewn into them; his black boots had light-brown tops, which she had once heard one of her charges describe as all the crack. It made her horribly conscious of her own shabby attire. She pulled the carriage blanket more tightly around her in an effort to disguise it.

'Are you cold?'

'No. Oh, no. I was just thinking that I wished my clothes were more appropriate for your elegant carriage,' Henrietta replied, 'I'm afraid governesses are not accustomed to dressing in silk and lace.'

'For what it's worth, I think silk and lace would suit you very well,' Rafe said, and then wondered at his saying so. The image was appealing. His thoughts seemed to be increasingly straying to the carnal. Maybe it was time he selected a new mistress from the many willing volunteers available to him. The idea filled him with ennui.

Henrietta, whose imagination ran rather to silk promenade dresses than lace peignoirs, was looking wistful. 'I have never owned a silk gown, or even gone to a ball. Not that I can dance. Anyway, Mama says that clothes do not make a woman.'

'Mama has obviously never visited Almack's on a Wednesday night,' Rafe said drily. 'What about Papa—what has he to say on the subject?'

Henrietta giggled. 'I don't think the topic has ever come up.' A few hours ago, the question would have set her on edge. She was no longer so nervous that she allowed her tongue to run away with her, though it could not by any stretch of the imagination be said that she was relaxed.

'Never?' Rafe said in mock astonishment. 'Has Papa no ambition to find you a husband?'

Annoyed by what she took to be implied criticism, Henrietta bristled. 'Papa would not consider a husband found at a dance to be particularly suitable.'

'How refreshing,' Rafe said ironically, 'and quite

contrary to the opinion of all the other papas of my acquaintance.'

'That does not make him wrong and there is no need to be so rude.'

'I apologise. I did not intend to insult your father.'

'Yes, you did,' Henrietta said forthrightly.

Rafe was not used to people saying what they meant and certainly not women, but Henrietta was not at all like any other woman he had ever met. 'I did,' he admitted, 'but I will endeavour not do so again.'

'Thank you.'

'You are most welcome. At least now I know why you have reached the ripe old age of what—twenty-one?'

'I am three and twenty.'

'Three and twenty, and you are still unattached. Most young ladies would consider themselves practically on the shelf. You must learn to dance, Henrietta, while there is still time.'

She knew he was teasing her because she could see his mouth twitch, as if he were suppressing a smile. 'Oh, you mistake the matter entirely,' she said airily. 'Papa and Mama have already introduced me to several eligible young men of their acquaintance.'

'What happened, did none of them come up to scratch?'

'If you mean did they propose, then, yes. And each one was more worthy and more sincere than the last.'

'And therefore unutterably dull and boring.'

'Yes! Oh, now look what you have made me say.'

'Henrietta Markham, you ought to be ashamed.'

'Oh, I am.' She bit her lip, but it was impossible not

to laugh when he looked at her just so. 'Oh dear. I know I *ought* to be, but...'

'But you are a romantic and you wish to be swept off your feet and cannot be ashamed of being disappointed by the worthy young men your father has presented to you?'

'What is wrong with that? Every woman wants to be swept off her feet. I mean, respect and worthiness are all very well, but...'

'You want to fall in love.'

'Yes, of course. Doesn't everyone?'

'Certainly everyone says so, though they rarely mean it. *I love you* is what people say when they think it will get them what they want.'

His mouth was still smiling, but it seemed to have frozen. 'That's very cynical,' Henrietta said, thinking of the beautiful woman in the portrait. She touched his sleeve sympathetically. 'I know you don't mean it, it is probably that you are still grieving.'

'What are you talking about?'

'Mrs Peters told me about your wife.'

'Told you what, exactly?'

'Only that she died tragically young. She showed me her portrait. She was very beautiful.'

'I don't wish to discuss her,' Rafe snapped. 'I see I shall have to take steps to ensure that my housekeeper is reminded of the value I put upon discretion.'

'Oh, *indeed*, it was not her fault, it was mine. I was surprised you had not mentioned—I said I did not know you were married, and then she said that you were a widower and then—oh dear, I'm so sorry, I didn't mean to get her into trouble. I didn't mean to intrude.'

'And yet you have done so. I will not tolerate people prying behind my back.'

'I was not prying, I was just curious. It's a natural enough thing to ask. After all, you have just asked me the same sort of questions about my family.'

'It is not the same,' Rafe said curtly.

'Very well, then, I shall keep quiet.' Henrietta folded her lips and her arms, and sat back, turning her attention firmly to the passing scenery. 'Very quiet,' she said, a few minutes later. She had said the wrong thing again, clearly, but how was she to know what was the right thing? What was wrong with him, that he couldn't even have a perfectly normal conversation about his dead wife? His dead, beautiful wife with the soulless eyes, who had presumably known him before he acquired the cynicism that he wore like a suit of armour.

Shifting in her seat, she took covert surveillance of the brooding bulk of man at her side. He didn't like to be questioned and didn't like to be contradicted. He most certainly didn't like to explain himself. Could such a man really fall in love? But then, maybe all those years ago he had been a different man. Maybe all those years ago he had been happy. He certainly wasn't happy now. What had happened to make him so? The question, which had hovered upon her lips almost from the moment she had first set eyes on him, refused to go away.

Henrietta continued to study him from the shadow of her poke bonnet. Five years he had been a widower. Five years was a long time. The Earl of Pentland could surely have his pick of marriageable ladies. *Why had he not remarried?*

'I beg your pardon?'

Only when he spoke did Henrietta realise to her utter horror that she had posed the question aloud. She stared at him, too stricken to reply.

'I have no wish to marry again.'

'You mean never?' Henrietta said incredulously.

'Never.' Rafe's tone was positively glacial, but he should have known by now that Henrietta would take no heed.

She did not, too astonished to even notice. 'I would have thought that you would need to remarry, if for no other reason than to produce an heir to pass the title on to. Unless—oh, it didn't occur to me, do you have a child already?'

It seemed a natural enough question given that he *had* been married, but she saw at once that Rafe did not think so. His countenance did an excellent impression of turning to granite.

'Nor did it occur to you that your impertinence knows no bounds,' he said. He cracked the whip to urge the horses into a gallop. An hour passed, with Henrietta increasingly conscious of the strained silence, of the anger simmering in the man sitting rigidly by her side, horribly aware that she had touched some very private and painful wound. He had visibly retreated from her; she could almost see the dark cloud which hovered over him. Miserably aware that she had been the one to summon it, albeit unwittingly, she was also quite unable to summon up the courage to do anything about it, for fear of being further rebuffed.

It was early evening as they neared London. The traffic on the road became noticeably heavier, forcing

Rafe to concentrate on his driving. Carts, drays and gigs jostled for position with lumbering stagecoaches, town coaches and other sporting vehicles. The mail thundered past in a cloud of dust.

Henrietta became more tense with every passing mile. Though the noise and bustle of the city-bound traffic were exciting and it was most certainly busy enough to give her ample opportunity to admire Rafe's consummate driving skills, she was concerned with more mundane matters. For a start she had almost no money. It was one thing to accept Rafe's help, quite another to be beholden to him. She had no idea how much a night at a London hostelry would cost, but suspected her meagre finances would not run to more than one or two.

She cleared her throat. 'I was wondering, shall we meet up with your—your friend tonight?'

He did not take his eyes from the road. 'Hopefully.'

'And when we have spoken with him, shall we—shall you—what do you intend to do then?'

Having negotiated a safe path between a dray heavily laden with beer barrels and a small gig, Rafe risked a glance over at her. 'I have no intention of abandoning you, if that's what you are worried about.'

'It's not that. Only partly. But you will want to go to your London home, will you not?'

'I sent no word ahead. Besides, I can't go there, not yet, just in case the Runner, finding me not at home in Woodfield Manor, decides to come to London to try to obtain an interview with me at my town address in Mount Street. They are dogged fellows once on the scent, apparently. So you see, I have no option but to stay with you and keep you company.'

'I suppose. When you put it like that,' Henrietta said, telling herself firmly that the relief she felt was everything to do with having a familiar face around and nothing at all to do with the excitement of it being that particular face.

As they crossed the river it was dusk, and quite dark by the time they pulled up outside the Mouse and Vole in Whitechapel. The inn was small, but surprisingly well kept, with its bedrooms facing on to a central courtyard and a large, busy taproom from which the hum of male conversation emanated into the cool night air. Rafe drove the carriage directly round to the stables, leapt agilely from the high seat and helped Henrietta down, removing her bandbox and his own portmanteau before handing the reins to a waiting groom, slipping him a coin and leading Henrietta not to the front, but to a small side door of the inn where she followed him through what appeared to be a boot room, and down a dimly lit corridor.

'If you don't mind my saying so, this seems a rather strange place for a man such as yourself to frequent.'

'But surely, Henrietta, a man such as I would be expected to hobnob with low life?'

For once, she failed to rise to the bait, being quite overcome with nerves now that they had actually arrived in London. A burst of song came from the taproom. A servant girl scurried by with a large bucket of coals. Rafe pushed open a small door under the stairs, and, telling her curtly to wait, not to leave the room until he returned, and on no account to speak to anyone, he dumped their luggage at her feet and left without another word.

Compared to the open carriage, it felt warm in the musty little parlour. Pushing back her cloak and stripping off her gloves, Henrietta pressed her forehead to the dusty window pane. Outside, she could hear the clump of horses' hooves in the stable yard. In the corridor, a muffled giggle, a male voice calling for someone called Bessie to fetch a mop. Where was Rafe? She idly drew a question mark on the glass. Why was he so unhappy? She drew another. Why was he so secretive about his wife? One more. And why—?

The door creaked open. Henrietta jumped. Rafe appeared before her, holding aloft a well-trimmed lamp. 'I thought you'd forgotten all about me.' Henrietta scrubbed at her question marks with her glove, flustered by just how quickly her heart began to beat at the mere sight of him.

Rafe closed the door and leant against it. 'There's good news and bad. I'm afraid Benjamin is away tonight, but Meg, his wife, assures me he'll be back tomorrow morning.'

'You mentioned good news?'

'Despite the fact that there is a much-anticipated mill—a fist fight—taking place less than a mile from here in the morning, Meg has managed to secure a room for us.'

'A room. You mean just one?'

Rafe nodded. 'We're lucky to get anything at all. That's the other bit of bad news, I'm afraid. We're going to have to share.'

'Oh. Cannot one of us spend the night here?' She indicated the empty parlour. Save for a rickety table and a narrow settle, there was no furniture. 'I'm sure I could...' she said dubiously.

'No. There is no lock on the door, it would not be safe given some of the clientele this place attracts. Besides,' Rafe said, levering himself away from the door and holding out his hand, 'you are exhausted. It's been a very long day. You need to rest and you shall do so in a bed. If it is your virtue you are worried about, let me assure you that I am far too tired to make any attempt to relieve you of it,' he said, ushering her out of the door. 'Tonight, at least.'

'I assume that is a poor attempt at a jest.'

'I haven't decided yet.'

Giving her no time to reply to this ambiguous comment, he led the way down the hallway and up the stairs. The room was small, but clean, with a wooden chair, a cupboard and a night stand upon which stood a spotted mirror.

And a bed. A solitary bed. And not a particularly wide one at that, Henrietta noted. 'I'll sleep on the chair,' she said, trying to keep the panic from her voice.

'Nonsense.'

'Or the floor. I could be perfectly comfortable on the floor, if you could ask Meg for some more bedclothes.'

'Henrietta, I can only speak for myself, but the events of the last twelve hours, while fascinating, have left me completely drained. Carnal thoughts are the last thing on my mind. Let me assure you that even Helen of Troy would not tempt me tonight. And you must be utterly exhausted yourself, after all you've been through.'

She nodded uncertainly.

'Then it is settled. There is no need for anyone to sleep on the floor. We will share the bed, I will refrain from undressing, and, to satisfy your maidenly modesty, we will place a pillow between us.'

Serious or teasing? On balance, she decided he was being serious. On balance, Henrietta decided, she was relieved because she was exhausted.

A tap on the door heralded a maidservant bearing a jug of hot water. Rafe, who was used to bathing daily and felt sweaty and dusty after the whirlwind carriage journey to London, nevertheless forced himself to do the gentlemanly thing, for he could see that Henrietta was eyeing the jug longingly. Not for the first time that day, he put her needs before his own. It was less difficult than he might have imagined. 'I'll leave you to freshen up,' he said, 'I'll go and organise some dinner for us.'

Alone, Henrietta stripped off her hat and cloak, her shoes and stockings, and made as good a *toilette* as circumstances would allow. Rummaging in her bandbox, she drew out her faded-red flannel nightgown, which, she thought, pulling it over her head, was voluminous enough, and practical enough to deter even the most determined of rakes. Not that she knew what determined rakes like Rafe did, exactly. Nor did she really know what Rafe meant specifically when he referred to carnal desires. It was, she had been led to believe by Mama, an exclusively male province. And yet, when she thought about the way he had kissed her, how it had felt when she had licked the strawberry juice from his finger, the shivery, tingly feeling came back and the goose bumps, too, and another feeling, a sort of indefinable longing—was that carnal desire?

Rafe, returning, bearing a tray upon which was their dinner, interrupted these thoughts. 'It's just the half-crown ordinary, meagre fare, I'm afraid,' he said, looking in vain for a table, eventually placing it carefully on the bed.

'Half a crown for an ordinary! Good heavens, I had no idea things were so expensive. I am afraid I cannot— The thing is, running away as I did, and I do not get paid until the end of the quarter—I'm afraid I don't have enough money,' Henrietta said. 'Actually, I don't suppose I'll get paid at all now.'

'There is no need to worry about money. I have more than sufficient.'

'There is every need. I am already enough in your debt.'

Rafe sighed. 'I might have known you would be contrary in this as in all other matters. Very well, if you insist, you can reimburse me when your parents return, but there is really no need.'

'There is every need,' Henrietta said determinedly. 'It is only right and proper.'

It amused Rafe that it didn't seem to have occurred to her that it was very wrong and even more improper that they should be sharing a room, never mind a bed. It should be refreshing, to encounter a female set on paying her way. It was certainly a novelty, yet Rafe was irked, for rather irrationally, the more she asserted her independence, the more he wanted to take care of her. 'I really have no interest in disputing the repayment of a paltry few shillings at present. Come, our dinner is getting cold.'

They perched on the edge of the bed to eat, Henrietta with her toes curled under her flannel nightgown, terribly aware of Rafe's proximity, trying desperately not to think of what was to happen next, and as a result unable to think of anything else.

Determined to put her at her ease, Rafe kept up a stream of inconsequential conversation. He was rewarded by seeing her making a reasonable meal, relaxing enough at the end of it to yawn. He, on the other hand, was anything but relaxed. In her faded, frumpy nightgown, with her curls corkscrewing wildly down her back, Henrietta aught to be quite unappealing, but he was finding her positively alluring. How came it about that such thick and opaque material somehow served to make him wonder all the more about what delights lay underneath?

When they had finished their repast, Rafe placed the tray outside the door and turned the key in the lock. Then he pulled back the covers of the bed, placing one of the pillows in the middle. 'Try to get some sleep,' he said, carefully averting his gaze as Henrietta clambered into the bed and pulled the covers up to her chin. Exhausted as he was by his sleepless night and the long day that had just passed, Rafe was beginning to wonder if he might be better off sleeping on the settle downstairs, after all.

Lying in bed, Henrietta tried to do as he had bid her, but the sleepiness that had enveloped her had melted away. She tried not to watch as Rafe stripped off his coat and waistcoat, removed his fob and snuff box and carefully wound his watch, before placing them under the pillow. She tried not to look as he splashed water on to his face, fastidiously scrubbed his hands, cleaned his teeth. He seemed indifferent to her presence.

She peeped out from under her lashes as he sat on the edge of the bed to remove his topboots, cursing under his breath as he did so. She supposed he must be accustomed to having a valet do such things for him.

His hose were next. He stood to take them off, then tossed them carelessly on to the floor beside his portmanteau. In which, no doubt, were at least two or three more clean pairs. The simplest of movements, pulling his shirt out of his buckskin breeches, only served to emphasise the muscles and sinews of the masculine body underneath. As he tilted his chin up to remove his neckcloth, which followed his hose on to the floor, the strong line of his jaw was revealed, the hard plane of his cheekbone, the straight nose in profile, without even a tiny bump to mar its perfection. Bending over to wipe the dust from his boots, she saw the long line of his leg, the perfectly muscled rear contoured under the leather of his buckskins.

Then he picked up the oil lamp and padded barefoot over to the bed, and Henrietta screwed her eyes tightly shut. The lamp was turned down. The bed creaked, the lumpy mattress sinking under his solid bulk. She lay rigid, hardly daring to breathe, never mind move. Beside her, Rafe sighed, shifted and sighed again.

He wasn't much closer to her than he'd been when sitting on the seat of the phaeton. He wasn't wearing that much less and she had on her all-encompassing flannel, but still it felt incredibly intimate. Illicit. She could hear him breathing, taking deep regular breaths. She could smell the soap he had used. The scent of his linen. A faint trace of leather from his buckskins. And something else. Something distinctively male, making her sensitive to her own distinctively female smell.

His hard, solid weight made her aware of her own soft curves. She was lying in bed with Rafe St Alban, whom she had met only this morning. Rafe St Alban who, in the space of just over half a day, had rescued her twice. Rafe St Alban, who was the most formidable, attractive, cynical, fascinating and very male man she had ever met. Not that she'd met many. But still, Henrietta thought, clinging to the sheet as Rafe turned away from her, on to his side, no matter how many more she met, she doubted she'd meet another quite like him. Her eyes gradually grew heavy. Rafe's deep rhythmic breathing was hypnotic. Though she could have sworn she would find sleep impossible in such circumstances, Henrietta nonetheless fell fast asleep.

Beside her, Rafe lay awake, wholly conscious of the soft bundle in faded-red flannel lying next to him. He never shared his bed. He visited his mistresses in their rooms, just as he had visited his wife in hers.

Julia. He allowed himself to think about her for the first time in years. It was like conjuring up a ghost. He could hardly even remember what she had been like in life, though he had no trouble at all recognising the customary combination of humiliation and guilt her name conjured up. The familiar litany of *what ifs* paraded through his mind with the order and precision of a well-drilled regiment. If his father had not died so prematurely. If he himself had not been so steeped in duty. If he had not been fresh from the excitement and romance of his Grand Tour. If Julia had been younger. If he had been older. If he had tried harder. If he had not enforced the separation. If he had not taken her back. If he had—or if he had not—it was always the same. The outcome was always the same. The deep wells of guilt were always the same. The heaviest of burdens, but one he carried so habitually as to have become accustomed. It would never go away.

Beside him, breathing softly, smelling sweetly, lay a delectable, yielding bundle. Henrietta had neither Julia's beauty nor her lineage, but she was neither cold nor weak. Her flaws did not stem from vanity or selfishness. She never prevaricated. What Henrietta thought, she said. What she felt, she said, too. And what she lacked in inches, she made up for in pluck. Any other lady would have resigned herself to her fate, would have accepted with alacrity his offer of help, but Henrietta was made of much sterner stuff. She was like a pint-sized crusader.

A *naïf*, Julia would have called her, looking down her straight, little aristocratic nose. But she wasn't naïve, just innocent. There was something about Henrietta's lust for life, her *joie de vivre* and those kissable lips, that hinted at a latent sensuality. Those delightful curves would embrace him. Those sweetly curved lips he had so tantalisingly tasted would succour him.

Rafe turned restlessly on the pillow, which he was now convinced was filled with not-very-fresh straw. If only it were Helen of Troy, and not Henrietta Markham lying beside him, he would find sleep easily. He still didn't understand it. No matter how many times he told himself she was out of bounds and therefore undesirable, his body would not be told. Rafe's erection strained against the soft leather of his breeches. Damned uncomfortable things to sleep in, breeches. It didn't seem to occur to Henrietta that no rake worth his salt would be doing so. Damned uncomfortable bed. Damned uncomfortable pillow. Damned uncomfortable and totally inexplicable desire. He would never sleep. Never…

Henrietta drifted awake. Through sleep-laden lids, she could sense the dawn light filtering in through the thin curtain. Already, the Mouse and Vole was sparking into life. The rumbling of a coach preceded the loud call of the driver for his passengers. A clanging bell and a shout of *dust-ho* announced the arrival of the rubbish cart. Outside in the corridor someone was whistling. She tried to move, but could not. Something lay heavy on her waist. Another noise, a soft thudding in her ear. She opened her eyes, then screwed them tight shut again. An arm it was, anchoring her. A chest it was, cushioning her head. Rafe's arm. Rafe's chest. And not a sign of the pillow that he had promised would separate them.

She was practically sprawled on top of him, like a limpet clinging to a rock. Her left knee was trapped between his legs. Buckskin-clad thighs. Rough hair on his calves. Bare skin. Male skin. *How on earth had this happened?*

Her breasts were crushed against his ribcage. Rafe's right arm pinned her securely to him. Her own left hand seemed to be curled into the opening of his shirt and her right arm was somewhere underneath them both. She tried to shift, but Rafe mumbled and tightened his grip. She wriggled and his arm left her waist, found her bottom and pulled her tighter against him. He felt—he felt—he felt…

Hard. Muscled. Solid. Powerful. Safe.

Not *that* safe. He was a man. She was acutely aware of him as a man. So very, very different from herself. She tried to move, just a little, just enough to detach her body from his, but her wriggling merely made his hold tighten, and when his hold tightened, though she knew she should put up more of a fight, what she really wanted to do was to submit. So she lay there quietly, telling herself that soon, very soon, she would move. Just not quite yet.

He smelled of sleep. She lay there, with her eyes closed, and let her body relax. Except her body didn't want to relax. Her body felt alive. Curiosity, her besetting sin, took hold. Why did he feel different? What did a man feel like? What did *this* man feel like? Questions, questions and more questions.

Idly, telling herself it wasn't really she, keeping her eyes closed tight so that she could maintain the self-deceit, Henrietta embarked on a tentative exploration. Her left hand was already there under his shirt, after all; she just had to let it drift a little. Up to his shoulder, down to the hard wall of his chest. Well-defined contours peaked by nipples that were hard but flat. Down next, along the concave line of his ribcage, into the dip of his stomach. She could feel him breathe under the palm of her hand. Feel the heat of his skin. Firm, taut stomach. The indent of his navel, the roughness of hair below.

She hastily withdrew her hand, shocked by her own boldness. She told herself she'd felt and seen enough. Then she started again. Back to his stomach, where she let her fingers linger, enjoying the contrast between smooth skin and rough hair that feathered a path for her hand to follow, down from his navel, disappearing under the barrier formed by the top of his breeches.

A droplet of sweat trickled down the valley between her breasts. She realised her nipples were as hard as hazelnuts, pressing against the cotton of her flannel nightgown. Not just hard, they were tingling, as if clamouring for some sort of attention. Still without allowing herself to think what she was doing, she pressed herself into his chest. A delightful *frisson* shot through her. Now she was even hotter.

She ran the palm of her hand back over the heat of Rafe's stomach. Shocked, but unable to stop herself, she tried to imagine her breasts, free of their protective flannel, pressed into the skin where her hand was. As she imagined, a ripple, like a tiny jolt of lightning, shivered from her belly down to the source of heat between her legs.

Henrietta, who was well read, both in materials considered suitable for a young lady and those ostensibly forbidden to her, was none the less rather vague about what Rafe had called carnal desires. What Mama had called her definitive experience was never elaborated upon. None of the women at the Poor House who had suffered at the hands of predatory men were inclined to enlighten her, either. The limited experience Henrietta had was thus universally negative. Nothing had prepared her for the fact that she might actually find it a pleasant experience, though now she came to think about it, she supposed it must be, else why would it be so many women's downfall? She had never been quite able to imagine *how*, exactly, physical contact might be pleasurable. Until now.

Now she could quite easily understand and could quite easily comprehend how it might make a person lose their inhibitions, cast caution to the winds and behave most improperly. She could understand that this hot, shivery feeling of anticipation, this tingling in her breasts, could be wholly addictive. She could understand why a person could be easily persuaded into going a bit further, and then a bit further still, until it was far too late for a person to stop.

She was going to stop. *She* was not so easily taken in. Indeed, she was truly about to stop when Rafe moved. The arm on her waist lifted, but only to tilt her chin. The arm on her bottom lifted, but only to allow his thigh to drape over hers. His mouth moved, but only to cover hers. Then he sighed. Then he kissed her.

His mouth was warm. His lips were unexpectedly gentle, the slight grating of his stubble a delightful contrast. His kiss was delicate, the kiss of a man who is all the time telling himself that he will not. The kiss of a man who knows he should not, but cannot resist.

Her touch, her innocent exploration, he had borne stoically. He had resisted encouraging her, though he had not stopped her. He could not have stopped her, any more than he could stop himself now from kissing, tasting, licking into the early morning heat of her. She was every bit as soft and yielding as he remembered. Her lips were even more infinitely kissable. Her body nestled into his perfectly.

Too perfectly.

He stopped. He did not want to, but he stopped. With a gargantuan effort he stopped—and immediately regretted it. But still he let her go and turned away to create a space. A cold space, a yawning chasm between them.

Henrietta opened her eyes. Was he asleep or just pretending? Had he kissed her because he wanted to, or was it some instinctive response to her touching him?

'I warned you about those lips of yours,' Rafe murmured.

So she had her answer and should have been mortified, for he had been awake all the time, and yet she was not. Virtue, Mama had always said, was its own reward. And Henrietta, despite the fact that she had always found it far more difficult than Mama to sacrifice her meagre pin money to good causes, to darn last winter's dress rather than have a new one, to wear woollen stockings instead of silk, had nevertheless believed her. Now she discovered that it was perhaps another subject upon which Mama's opinions were suspect. At this particular moment in time, virtue felt like a vastly overrated concept.

'Rafe, I—'

'Henrietta,' Rafe said over his shoulder, 'there are times when it is best not to attempt to explain—this is one of them. Let it suffice that I am doing the gentlemanly thing—for once in my life, and at great cost. Let me warn you that next time I will not. Now go back to sleep.'

Next time? She opened her mouth to tell him that there would absolutely and unequivocally never be a next time, if she had anything to say in the matter, but the words, for lack of truth, froze on her tongue. Not only did she doubt her ability to resist, she doubted that resisting was what she wanted. She leaned over, saw his eyes firmly closed, his lashes soft and sooty black on his cheek. Perhaps it was best not to deny it. Perhaps he would see a denial as a challenge. She shivered at the very idea, then pretended that she hadn't. Actions speak louder than words, she told herself firmly. There would not be a next time. Henrietta shuffled back to her own side of the lumpy bed and resolutely closed her eyes, trying to focus her mind on the not-inconsiderable issue of the missing Ipswich emeralds.

Chapter Five

Ex-Sergeant Benjamin Forbes, the landlord of the
Mouse and Vole, was a swarthy man with a sabre scar
that ran from the corner of his left eye to his earlobe, the
tip of which had been severed, providing a very visible
memento of the Peninsular campaign. Not tall, he was
nevertheless powerfully built, with burly shoulders and
a barrel chest. Possessing the muscular forearms of an
army infantryman, these were maintained in civilian
life by the regular hauling of ale barrels and the occasional spat with an unruly customer. He kept a clean
house, but located as it was, near the rookeries of Gravel
Lane and Wentworth Street, it was inevitable that things
sometimes became somewhat confrontational. Ex-Sergeant Benjamin Forbes's vicious and efficient left hook
ensured that any discord was quickly quelled.

He was in the taproom when Rafe and Henrietta
came in search of him, sleeves rolled up, a large leather apron wrapped round his person, watching with an
eagle eye the rounding up of the pewter pots by the

porter-house boy. 'Lord Pentland,' he exclaimed, ushering the boy out and closing the taproom door firmly behind him, 'Meg said you was here. Sorry I wasn't around last night. Little bit of business to take care of.'

'Benjamin,' Rafe greeted the man with one of his rare, genuine smiles, shaking his hand warmly. 'You're looking well. This is Henrietta Markham. Sergeant Forbes, Henrietta.'

'Pleased to meet you, miss, and it's just plain Mr Forbes now, if you don't mind, been a good few years now since I left the king's forces,' he said, eyeing Henrietta curiously as he ushered them both into a seat by the newly lit fire.

A pot of fresh coffee and some bread rolls were called for. Rafe was served a tankard of frothing ale. Henrietta, intrigued as to the nature of the relationship between the two men, and self-conscious about what must seem her own rather dubious relationship with Rafe, sipped gratefully on the surprisingly good brew. As usual, curiosity got the better of her. 'Have you known Lord Pentland for long, Mr Forbes?'

'Nigh on six years now, miss. You could say I owe my livelihood to him.'

'Oh?'

'Rubbish, Benjamin,' Rafe said. 'You exaggerate.'

'Don't listen to him, miss. I was in a bad state when his lordship here first encountered me. Been in the army all my life, you see. Had no idea how to look after myself when they pensioned me off.' He laughed grimly. 'Not that there was much of a pension to speak of. His lordship stepped in and helped set me up here.'

'It was nothing, the least I could do. You'd earned it,

as far as I'm concerned, and you paid me back every penny.' Aware of Henrietta's too-interested gaze, Rafe took a long draught of ale.

'He's a good man, that's the truth of it,' Benjamin said, nodding in Rafe's direction. 'Despite the reputation he works so hard to maintain.'

'Enough of this,' Rafe said.

'Aye, and never one to take thanks, either,' Benjamin said with a wry smile. 'Why, even down at Saint—'

'I said enough, Benjamin,' Rafe said, curtly. 'You're not usually one to let your tongue run away with you. Henrietta is not interested in your eulogies.'

Henrietta, who was, in fact, very much interested in the innkeeper's revelations, was inclined to protest, but a warning shake of the head from Benjamin silenced her. 'Beg your pardon,' he said, 'don't know what came over me, only I thought—but there, it's none of my business. Tell me instead now—what it is I can do for you?'

'We're interested in some emeralds. A most distinctive set. Henrietta, here, has been accused of stealing them.'

This information, not surprisingly, made Benjamin's jaw drop, causing him to eye his benefactor's unusual companion with a fresh eye. Quality she was, anyone could see that, even if she was worse dressed than Bessie the parlourmaid on her Sunday off. What she was doing with his lordship, well, he had no idea. My lord's tastes ran to expensive bits of muslin and he'd never brought any of them here before.

But as he listened to Henrietta describing the circumstances of the theft, a tale so unlikely as to test his credulity to the limit, Benjamin began to see just what it was that had attracted his lordship to Miss Markham. It wasn't so much the way she looked, as the way her whole face came alive when she spoke. Those eyes of hers, the way they sparkled with anger as she described the accusations against her. The way she talked with her whole body, her hands, even her curls flouncing with indignation, the softer look on her face when she spoke of the shame it would cause her parents. And the way she looked at my lord, too, with something more than admiration as she described his coming to her rescue, and something much less respectful when she forced him to admit that he hadn't believed her story, either, at first. If my lord was not very careful…

But my lord was always careful, which made it all the more inexplicable. Maybe it really was a case of impulsive chivalry? 'So how can I help?' Ben asked when the interesting Miss Markham had finished her extraordinary tale.

'Come, come, Ben, it is surely obvious. A man such as Henrietta has described must surely be known to one of the cracksmen and receivers who frequent your taproom. And the Ipswich emeralds are themselves not exactly run of the mill.'

Benjamin scratched his head. 'Describe him to me again, miss.'

She did so and Benjamin stroked the line of his scar thoughtfully. 'Well, he certainly shouldn't be too hard to trace, a rum-lookin' cove like that, presumin' you know where to look, that is. And the emeralds?'

Henrietta wrinkled her nose. 'The setting is antique, linked ovals of wrought gold, each with a stone at the centre surrounded by diamond chips. The stone in the necklace is very large, and there are in addition two bracelets and a pair of earrings.'

Benjamin shook his head. 'Such distinctive jewellery is nigh on impossible to sell on without arousing suspicion.'

'So it should be quite an easy thing to track him down, then, shouldn't it?' Henrietta said eagerly. 'You will find him for me, Mr Forbes, won't you? Rafe— Lord Pentland was so sure you would and it would mean the world to me.'

'I'll do my best,' Benjamin said, patting Henrietta's hand reassuringly, 'but we'll need to be discreet. People who stick their noses into other peoples' business in the rookeries tend to get them bitten off, if you take my meaning.'

'I would not wish to put you in any danger.'

Benjamin laughed heartily at this. 'I can take care of myself, don't you worry.'

'Well, if you are sure, then I really am extremely grateful,' Henrietta said fervently.

'It's Lord Pentland you should be thanking, miss. I wouldn't do this for any other man in England. It could take a few days, though.'

'A few days!'

'That is not the end of the world,' Rafe said. 'Provided Ben can continue to put a roof over our heads, you are safe from the Runner here.'

'He's right, miss,' Benjamin said. 'Nobody would think to look for you here. You'd both best stay at the Mouse and Vole until I track down that housebreaker. And now if you'll excuse me, I've things to do.'

'Thank you, Ben,' Rafe said, holding out his hand.

'You save your thanks until you've got something to thank me for,' Ben said gruffly. Shaking his head, wondering what on earth Meg would make of the unlikely couple, he left the taproom in search of her.

Alone, Rafe turned back to Henrietta with a quizzical look. 'So, it appears we are condemned to a few more days of each other's company. Do you find the notion tolerable, Henrietta?' He captured her wrist, forcing her to meet his gaze. 'For my own part, I'm more than happy to act as your chaperon.'

She flushed. She wished she didn't flush quite so easily or so often in his presence.

'Now would be a good time for you to reassure me that you feel the same, Henrietta.'

She risked a quick glance, saw that unsettling look in his eyes, then dropped her gaze again, but already she could feel it, that sparkling feeling. Heat spread from her wrist, where his fingers were wrapped around it. Her skin seemed to tug, as if it wanted her to move closer. The image of him, created by her touch this morning, flashed into her mind. 'What would we do?' she asked, then blushed wildly. 'To pass the time, I mean? We can't stay here all day, can we?'

'Cooped up together, you mean? Don't you trust yourself, Henrietta?'

He knew it was unfair, but he could not resist teasing her. He liked to watch the flush steal up her neck and over her cheeks; it made him wonder where it came from. He liked the way she sucked the corner of her bottom lip, just showing the tip of her pink tongue. He liked the way the little gold flecks in her eyes glimmered, the way she looked shocked and excited and tempted—definitely tempted—at the same time.

He stroked her wrist with his thumb and felt the pulse jump beneath him. He slid his hand a little way under the sleeve of her gown, caressing the fragile skin of her forearm. She closed her eyes. Her lips parted. He stroked the crease of her elbow, wondering that he had never before realised what an erotic crease it was, thinking how delightful it would be to lick it, to find other such creases. 'The thing is, Henrietta, you need to be able to trust yourself, because for certain you cannot trust me,' he said, pulling her towards him over the table and claiming her lips.

Henrietta let out a soft sigh as he took her mouth; she shivered as his tongue slid along her lips and moaned as it touched the tip of hers. Velvet soft, darkly illicit, infinitely tempting, his mouth, his kisses, his taste. He deepened the kiss and she softened under the pressure, then returned it. That feeling again. Longing. Deeper this time, in her belly. She tried to move closer, but the table was in the way; she hit her hand on the half-drunk tankard of ale, which tipped over, making them both leap back.

She was breathing too fast. Looking over at Rafe, she noticed with some surprise that so, too, was he. His chest was rising and falling quite rapidly. There was a flush staining the sharp lines of his cheek bones. His eyes were dark, a night storm, the slant of his brows emphasised by his frown. His sleek cap of hair was ruffled—had she done that? She didn't remember. He looked every bit as darkly enticing as his kiss. Every bit as dangerous as his reputation. Not unleashed, not out of control, but as if he could be, and it was that, the idea of that, that was more exciting than anything.

Her lips were tingling. Her nipples were throbbing. There was a knot pulled tight in her belly. She had never felt like this. She hadn't realised she could feel like this. She'd never imagined this, whatever it was, existed. A clawing desire for something, a burning need for something. For someone.

She put a hand to her throat, feeling the pulse jump and jump. She watched wide-eyed as Rafe pushed the table away, then pulled her to her feet. The door flew open and the startled screech of the maidservant made her pull herself free; he shrugged and straightened his necktie as if nothing had happened, then nodded casually to the astonished maid before taking Henrietta's hand and leading her out of the room.

She followed him automatically back up to their bed-chamber. She assumed he was going to kiss her again, but instead he pulled her cloak from the back of a chair and draped it around her, putting her poke bonnet firmly on her head.

He'd been right about that passionate nature of hers. It would be the easiest, most delectable, most desirable thing in the world to take her now, but he could not. Dammit, he *would* not. 'I think we have just proved that it would be most unwise to stay cooped up together. What we both need is a distraction and some fresh air,' Rafe said firmly, tilting her chin to tie the knot, trying not to look at her lips, focusing on the ugliness of her bonnet in the hope that his persistent erection would subside.

'It was just a kiss, Henrietta,' Rafe said curtly, 'and

one of your first. When you have sampled a few more, you will, I'm sure, like all other young ladies, grow more blasé about such things.' Rafe picked up his hat. 'Now, do you want to see the sights of London or not?'

'Aren't you worried that you'll meet someone you know?' Henrietta asked, as they emerged from the forecourt of the Mouse and Vole on to the main thoroughfare.

Rafe grabbed her cloak to pull her clear, just in time, from the muddy splash made by the cumbersome wheels of a passing milk cart. 'London is a large city, I am sure we can manage to avoid my acquaintances easily; it is not as if we are planning on visiting anywhere particularly fashionable. Don't you wish to see the popular sights?' Even as he asked the question, Rafe wondered if he had gone a little mad, for the sights Henrietta would consider worth seeing would undoubtedly be those he made a point of avoiding, forcing them to mingle with Cits and bumpkins.

'Of course I do, but I doubt you have much interest in them,' Henrietta replied, with her usual frankness.

And as usual, it made him contrarily set upon a path he would never normally have followed. 'It will be enlightening to see the metropolis through your eyes,' Rafe said.

'You mean you will be able to laugh at my expense.'

'No.' He tilted her chin up, the better to see her face, which was in the shadow of that horrible bonnet. 'I may find your views amusing because they are refreshingly different, but I never laugh *at* you or mock you.'

'I know that. At least, most of the time I do.'

Rafe suppressed a smile. 'Good, now we understand one another, are you willing to put yourself in my hands?'

Henrietta nodded. 'Yes, thank you, I'd like that.' Out here, in the bustling street under a grey sky washed with a pall of sea-coal smoke, she realised that Rafe had been right to insist they quit the intimacy of their bedchamber. She *did* need some air, though fresh was not exactly how she'd have described this gritty, tangy London atmosphere.

They took a hackney into the city, down Thread-needle Street and past the colonnaded front of the Bank of England. At Cheapside, they abandoned the hack, for Henrietta complained she could see nothing through its small dusty window, and they walked, something of a novelty for Rafe. Henrietta tripped gaily along at his side, exclaiming at the buildings, the mass of printed bills that covered them, the street hawkers who sold their wares on every corner, oblivious to the dangers of carriage wheels, horses' hooves and pickpockets alike. Several times he was forced to steer her clear of noxious puddles while she gazed up admiringly at the architecture. Eventually, he tucked her arm securely into his and wedged her to his side in order to prevent her straying into the path of a carriage.

He liked having her there, so close. He liked the way she bombarded him with questions, never doubting that he would be able to answer. He also liked the way she trusted implicitly that he would keep her safe, even though she had no apprehension of danger. He liked the way she threw herself with gusto into drinking in the ambiance of the bustling city. She paused at every shop to peer in the windows. Drapers, stationers, con-

fectioners, pastry cooks, silversmiths and seal cutters
alike, she was quite indiscriminate, as enthralled by a
display of pen nibs, ink pots and hot-pressed paper as
she was by an array of ribbons, trimmings and button
hooks.

Outside St Paul's, the beggars, hawkers, petty thieves
and pamphleteers fought for space, pushing their wares
under the noses of the better off, slipping their fingers
into the pockets of the unwary, proclaiming their tales
of woe from upturned crates. Henrietta, spotting a filthy
urchin whose flea-bitten dog was making an extremely
feeble attempt to dance on its hind legs, fumbled in her
dress pocket for her purse.

'For God's sake, put that away,' Rafe said hastily, as
they were immediately surrounded by a small crowd
holding out their hands beseechingly.

'But the child—'

'Is very likely part of an organised gang. There are
hundreds, if not thousands, of urchins like that, and very
few are the genuine article. Here, let me, don't waste
your resources, which you've already told me are pitiful enough.' Expertly flicking a shilling at the urchin
with the dog, Rafe took advantage of the diversion and
ushered Henrietta up the shallow flight of steps into the
relative sanctuary of the cathedral.

'You didn't have to do that,' she said, tucking her
purse out of sight again and shaking out her cloak.

'Well, before you add it to that mental list of debt
you're totting up in your head, let me tell you that it was
a gift. And don't bother trying to deny it, I know that's
exactly what you were doing.'

Henrietta's smile was shaky. 'Oh, very well, and

thank you. I have to confess, I was very glad of your presence out there, it was quite overwhelming. I had not realised there could be so very many very poor people. It was a shock. You know, I could not at first fathom why everyone walks so quickly with their noses either to the ground or in the sky, I thought it was simply to give themselves an air of consequence, but now I suspect it is because they don't want to see what is around them.'

'And as I've also already pointed out,' Rafe said drily, 'most of the beggars, especially the aggressive ones, are on the fiddle, believe me.'

Henrietta looked dubious, for it seemed to her that that was precisely what people said when they wanted to justify their apathy, but though Rafe could certainly be both cold and cynical, he was not callous. 'You seem to be uncommonly well informed about life on the capital's streets.'

Rafe shrugged. 'It is common enough knowledge, God knows, there are enough of them. The younger boys start out stealing pocketbooks and silk kerchiefs, then they graduate to more lucrative work, assisting housebreakers, and pilfering from the docks. Foundlings, many of them, though some are sold into the trade by their families.'

'Sold! Good God, you cannot be serious.' She had thought herself well informed upon the subject of poverty through her parents' association with Poor Houses, but that had been in the rural countryside. Here, in the capital, the sheer scale of the problem was beyond her comprehension, the horrors it led to simply unbelievable.

Rafe's expression was bleak. 'I am deadly serious. I don't doubt that, for some of them, it's a case of too many mouths, but for others, it's just gin money. And though there's always the risk of the gallows, it's not as if life as a Borough Boy or Bermondsey Boy is as bad as life as a climbing boy. The gangs at least look after their own. It's in a sweep's interest to keep his boys thin.'

'You sound so—so resigned! Is there not something that can be done to help such families keep their children rather than *sell* them?'

'What do you suggest, Henrietta, that I adopt them all?' Bitter experience had shown him the futility of finding a solution to society's ills. Even the small private contribution he currently made was a mere drop in the ocean. Often, he felt it was futile.

Henrietta was startled by the acidity in his voice. 'Don't you care? You must care, for if you did not, you wouldn't know so much about it all.' She stared up at him, but his face was shaded by the brim of his hat. 'I don't understand. Why do you pretend not to care, when you so obviously do?'

His instinct was to shrug and turn the subject, but, perhaps because her large, chocolate-brown eyes were filled with compassion, perhaps because she refused to believe the worst of him, he chose that rarest of courses, to explain. 'Because if a child is unwanted, there is little to be done to change that.'

'That's a terrible thing to say.'

'The truth is often terrible to behold, but it must be faced all the same.' As he must face that fact every day, despite the funds and time he poured into his attempt at atonement.

'I had thought, in my own small way, through teaching, that I could make a difference, a contribution,' Henrietta said sadly. 'I see now it could only ever be the merest scratch on the surface of the problem.'

'Forgive me, Henrietta, it was not my intention to disillusion you. Your altruism does you credit. Do not let my cynicism infect you, I would not want that on my conscience.'

'I must admit, it's a little disheartening to hear such a bleak view of the world.'

'Then let us turn our thoughts to more uplifting matters. Come, you must see Wren's dome, it is an extraordinary and quite breathtaking spectacle.'

He was already assuming his usual inscrutable look. Henrietta was, however, becoming more attuned to the nuances of his expression. His mouth was always tighter when he was trying *not* to show emotion, his lids always heavier over his eyes. And his tone, too, was always more austere when he didn't want to talk about something.

She followed him as he led the way swiftly along the chequered floor of the nave, her mind seething with questions, but if her brief acquaintance with Rafe St Alban had taught her anything, it was that the direct approach rarely paid dividends. The subject was closed for now, but she added it to the growing list of things she was determined to discover about him before their time together ended: how he came to know so much about the tragic fate of foundlings, why he had helped Benjamin Forbes set up in business, what it was about

Lady Ipswich that prevented him from calling on her, or what happened during his marriage to the beautiful Lady Julia to make him so adamantly against ever marrying again. Then there were the contradictions. His knight errantry and his compassion did not sit with his reputation, any more than did his refusal this morning to take advantage of her.

With so very many questions requiring answers, it never occurred to Henrietta to ask a few of herself: what, exactly, she would do if Rafe kissed her again, or why, if she really did believe his reputation, she continued to place her trust in him? Instead, at Rafe's bidding, she looked up, and caught her breath at the magnificence of the dome of St Paul's, which seemed to fill the sky, and the questions that flooded her mind were concerned with architecture.

After St Paul's, they took another hackney cab and visited the Tower of London, where Henrietta shivered at the sight of Traitor's Gate and the Bloody Tower. Dutifully inspecting the Crown Jewels, she declared them to be, in her humble opinion, rather vulgar.

Rafe suggested that perhaps she refrain from inspecting them too closely, lest she get felonious ideas, making her laugh, declaring that such ostentatious jewellery should be left to men with a northern accent and an eyepatch, which earned them both a reproving look from the Beefeater.

For the small price of a shilling—which Henrietta added to her mental list of debts—they were shown the Menagerie, but here her more tender feelings were roused by the pitiful condition of the caged beasts. 'The grizzly bear looks as if he wants to cry,' she whispered to Rafe, 'and look at those poor lions, they look positively mournful. It seems a shame to keep such proud creatures so confined, something should be done.'

'Do you wish me to have them released? I don't think the people of London would be too pleased to have these creatures at large. They might look pathetic, but I am pretty sure they could still cause a fair bit of carnage.'

'Of course I didn't mean that!'

'Or perhaps you mean to solve two problems at the same time, release the lions and feed the Bermondsey Boys to them. I can't say that it's a particularly humane notion, but I'm sure there are some politicians who would claim merit for the idea.'

'Stop making fun of me,' Henrietta said, biting her lip to suppress a smile.

'Not of you, with you,' Rafe said, as they retraced their steps out of the Lion Tower, 'there is a difference.'

'I know, but I am so unused to either, I forget. It's different for you, I'm sure, you must have lots of people to laugh with, but I…'

'No, I cannot imagine that Mama and Papa, worthy as they are, are much *fun*,' Rafe said.

She tried to stifle her giggles, but could not. 'That is shocking, but it's also true, alas. I'm very much afraid that worthiness precludes any sense of humour. I fear I must be very, very unworthy.'

'And I am very, very glad that you are,' Rafe said, taking her by surprise and raising her gloved hand to his lips. 'Because despite what you might think, my life is not over-full of people I feel able to laugh with, either.'

'You must have friends.'

He hailed a hackney, instructing the driver to take them back to Whitechapel. 'Lots—at least, lots of acquaintances,' Rafe said, 'but since I have a reputation for being a bit of a cold fish...'

'I can't understand how, for it seems to me that one cannot be a cold fish as well as a rake.' She saw his smile fade and regretted her words immediately. 'I didn't mean...'

'I know exactly what you meant,' Rafe said, in his best cold-fish manner. 'I thought, however, that your experience of me would by now have taught you not to believe all you have heard. Obviously I was wrong.' For a moment, just a moment, he was tempted to put her right, but then he would have to explain why, and he could not bear to open that wound. Instead, he resorted to his old armour of anger. 'If you had my wealth and title, you'd be a cold fish, too. You have no idea what it's like to be the fawning target of every mama with an eligible daughter, and every Johnny Raw who claims to be a cousin of a cousin first removed and thinks the Earl of Pentland is their ticket into society, to say nothing of those who claim friendship only because they've been brought to *point non plus* and want me to tow them out of the River Tick.'

She was cowed by the vitriolic nature of his reply, but refused to be silenced. What he said explained so much...and appalled her so much. 'But, Rafe, not everyone is like that. Most people—'

'Most people are exactly like that. I've rarely met anyone who's not on the take in one way or another, and in my experience, the higher the *ton*, the more they'll try to take you for.'

'That's a horribly cynical way of looking at things.'

'Also horribly true,' Rafe said, with a saturnine look.

'No, it's not,' Henrietta declared roundly. 'I'm not saying there aren't people who are as you say—'

'Well, that's something, at least.'

Henrietta glared at him. 'But there are lots of others who aren't, only you won't give them a chance.'

'For the very excellent reason that the one time I did place my trust in someone they repaid it by deceiving me.'

Furious with himself for this unaccountable admission, Rafe clenched his fists, then he hurriedly unclenched them. *God dammit*, what was it about her that made him say such things? How was it that one minute they were laughing and the next minute she had him completely on edge? 'It was a long time ago and I don't wish to discuss it,' he said tightly.

'Yet another thing you don't wish to discuss,' Henrietta said, now equally furious. 'I would add it to my mental list, only it's becoming too long to remember. Why is it that you are permitted to block every subject of conversation, yet you feel free to interrogate me? Who took advantage of you so badly as to make you so bitter?'

'I don't wish to discuss it, Henrietta, not at any time and particularly not in the back of a hackney cab.'

'The driver can't hear us. Who?' Henrietta demanded, now so beside herself with fury that she did not realise she was treading on exceptionally thin ice.

'My wife,' Rafe snarled.

'Oh.' She felt as if she had been winded, so unexpected was the admission.

'Yes, you may well say *oh!* Julia married me for my money. And for the title, of course—such a very old one, and so vast the lands that came with it. She married me because I was one of the only men able to give her the position she felt her looks entitled her to. Are you happy now?'

'Rafe, I didn't mean…'

But he threw her hand off angrily. 'Yes, you did. I told you to stop prying, but you would not desist.'

Remorse squeezed her anger away. She gazed at him helplessly, aghast at having unwittingly inflicted such raw pain as he had so fleetingly displayed. His face was rigid with his efforts *not* to show it, his lips almost white. Nothing had prepared her for this. Her wretched tongue! 'Rafe, I'm truly sorry,' she said, as the hack pulled up at the Mouse and Vole. Rafe threw some coins at the driver and all but dragged Henrietta out of the cab and through the door of the inn. 'Go to the room. I'll have them send some dinner up for you.'

'But what about you? Won't you be joining me?' Henrietta asked in a small voice. 'Rafe, please…'

But he was already gone.

She spent a dreadful night. Though she should have been ravenous from the day's sightseeing, she could only pick at the pigeon pie steaming on the platter. At every footstep on the boards of the corridor, she held her breath, but none halted, or even hesitated as they passed. Miserably, she prepared for bed. Not even the luxury of an entire jug of hot water to herself, and complete privacy in which to make use of it, made any difference to her sombre mood.

Over and over, she replayed their last conversation in her head, trying to isolate a point where she could have turned the subject, avoided it, said something different or been more tactful, but to no avail. Rafe's shocking admission had come out of the blue. She had had no idea. Could have had no idea. Taking herself to task over the matter was pointless. Feeling guilty—and she did feel guilty, even though she knew it was misguided—was also pointless. How on earth could she have been expected to guess?

But logic was no real balm. Unwitting or no, she had ripped open an old wound and felt absolutely terrible. Pulling her red flannel nightgown over her head, tugging her comb through her tangled curls, cleaning her teeth and climbing into a bed which seemed somehow to have grown much larger and much colder, Henrietta bit back the tears, but as the clock in the church tower across the road struck midnight, she pulled the rough sheet over her head and allowed a single tear to escape from her burning eyes. And then another. And another still. Then she sniffed resolutely, and the next tear was refused permission to escape as she began to feel angry.

Not with Rafe, but with that woman. That woman, that beautiful woman with the cold eyes. How had he found out? When had she shattered his illusions? How much had he loved her? That was the question she found hardest to contemplate. Though it explained everything. No wonder he didn't want to marry again. A few years older than him, Mrs Peters had said Lady Julia was. Had she toyed with him, laughed at him? Henrietta clenched her teeth. It would have been a crushing blow to his pride. No wonder he kept his thoughts opaque.

No wonder he cultivated that forbidding air of his. He had been hurt. Obviously he had no intentions of being hurt again.

Henrietta brooded darkly. Such a marriage must have been very unhappy. Was he glad, when Lady Julia died? Relieved? Or did he feel guilty? People did, sometimes, when they wished for something awful and it came to pass. Maybe that was why Rafe kept the portrait of his dead wife on display, as a painful reminder, as a form of penance.

Maybe that was also why he had such a notorious reputation when it came to women. But she couldn't match that to his behaviour. In fact, the more she thought about it, Rafe's reputation didn't conform at all with her experience of him, the Rafe she knew. He just wasn't the type to exact revenge in such a manner. Much more the type to bury it all deep—which is exactly what he *had* done. Was he not, then, the womaniser gossip would have him? But was there not always fire where there was smoke? She couldn't understand it. She probably never would.

The church bell tolled one. Where was he? Was he going to stay away all night? Perhaps another room had become available. So much for his concern about her being alone here. Although Benjamin Forbes *had* been up to check on her several times, and to remind her to keep the door locked, so maybe he was still a little bit concerned. When she'd asked Benjamin where Rafe was, he'd just shaken his head. Did that mean he knew, or he didn't?

Where was he? His portmanteau was still here, she realised hopefully. Except that to someone as rich as

Rafe, a portmanteau or two was neither here nor there. Probably he had lots more of them in his London house. Which was probably where he was now.

Well, if he had abandoned her—though she couldn't quite bring herself to believe that he had—then she'd just have to set about sorting things out herself. 'It's what I was going to do, anyway, before he came along,' Henrietta said stoutly, plumping the pillow, which refused to be plumped, 'so there's absolutely no cause to be downhearted.' But despite the fact that she knew Benjamin Forbes would do his best, it wasn't quite the same as having Rafe by her side. Although she had known him for only a few days, and although she had thought herself quite inured to coping alone, the prospect of not seeing him again was most melancholy.

A spark of indignation flickered in her breast. How dared he do this to her? How dared he make her feel so—so—whatever it was he made her feel—and then just walk away. *How dared he!*

She plumped the pillow again. Then she buried her head under it, in an effort to stop herself thinking. Then she began to fret about how she would pay her shot. And then, finally, exhausted by all the thinking, Henrietta fell asleep.

Chapter Six

She was woken a few hours later, as dawn was rising, by a rattling at the door of the bedchamber. Startled, she sat up, her heart pounding, thinking she must have been dreaming. But the rattling came again, then a heavy fist pounded on the door.

Shaking, she edged from the bed and picked up the pewter candlestick, before creeping over to the door. The handle shook. 'Go away,' she hissed, so quietly that it was not surprising when the handle shook again. 'Go away,' she said, more loudly this time, 'or I'll scream.'

'Open the door, Henrietta.'

'Rafe?'

'Dammit, open the door before I break it down.'

Relief made her clumsy as she fumbled with the lock. Still holding her candlestick in one hand, she peered out into the corridor. It was him, leaning heavily on the doorframe. 'Where have you been?' He pushed the door open and stumbled over the threshold. Only then did she smell the brandy on his breath. 'You've been drinking!'

'Your powers of observation never fail to amaze me,' Rafe slurred, staggering towards the bed. 'I have indeed been drinking, Henrietta Markham. I have, in point of fact, been drinking copiously.'

'That much is obvious,' she said, pushing the door to and pulling back the curtains in order to let in the grey dawn light.

'An enormous amount,' Rafe agreed, dropping on to the bed and nodding vehemently. 'And you know what? It still wasn't enough.' He tried to rise, but his foot slipped.

Henrietta caught him just before he fell on to the floor. With an immense effort, she managed to push him back on to the bed, which he promptly tried to get back up from. 'More brandy, that's what I need.'

'That's the last thing you need,' Henrietta replied, pushing him with a bit more force.

He fell on to his back with a look of extreme surprise, which made her giggle. 'What are you laughing at?'

'Nothing,' she said, quickly covering her mouth.

'I like the way you laugh, Henrietta Markham,' Rafe said with a lopsided grin.

'I like the way you laugh, Rafe St Alban, though you don't do it nearly enough. You should try to sleep. You'll have a terrible head in the morning.'

'Got a terrible head now,' Rafe muttered, 'far too many unpleasant things whirling around inside it. All your fault.'

Endearing. It was not a word she'd ever have thought to associate with him, but that is how he looked, with his hair standing up on end and his neckcloth rumpled and his waistcoat half-undone. The stubble on his jaw was dark, almost bluish. His cheeks were flushed, his eyes slumberous. He looked younger and somehow vulnerable, the way his arms were spread out as if in surrender, one long leg sprawled across the bed, the other dangling over the edge. Henrietta edged closer. 'Rafe, I was worried about you.'

'Come here.'

She hadn't thought him capable of moving so quickly. Before she could get out of his reach, he had grabbed her by the wrist and pulled her down on to the bed beside him. Her breath left her in a whoosh. She was pretty certain she must look every bit as surprised as he had done only a moment before.

'Ha! That showed you, Henrietta Markham.'

'Let me go, Rafe. And stop calling me that.'

'Henrietta Markham. What else shall I call you? Miss Markham? Think we've gone beyond that one. Hettie? No, you're not a Hettie. Hettie sounds like a great-aunt or a chambermaid. Henry? Nope. Nope. Nope. You feel far too feminine for that.' Once more he took her by surprise, rolling her easily over so that she lay breast to breast, thigh to thigh, on top of him. 'Nice,' he murmured, running his hands over her, 'you have a very, very nice bottom, did you know that?'

'Rafe, stop it, you're drunk.'

'I am a little intoxicated, but that does not, I assure you most fervently, stop me from appreciating quite how delightful your bottom is. And, I may add, that touching it is quite delightfully delightful.'

His hands moulded her curves and settled her more firmly on top of him, and, though she knew he was in his cups, she couldn't help agreeing with him. What he was doing was quite delightfully delightful. His coat buttons were pressing into her side. She could feel his fob chain and his watch on her stomach. His chin was rasping against her cheek. He smelled of smoke and brandy and man. Of Rafe.

There was something else pressing into her thigh. She wriggled, in a half-hearted effort to escape, but his hands remained firmly on her bottom, and the something got harder. She realised what it was then and felt herself get very, very hot. Her breasts were flattened against his chest, but still she could feel her nipples harden. She only hoped that brandy and a shirt and a waistcoat would prevent Rafe from noticing. She wriggled again, telling herself she really was trying to free herself, but succeeded only in making Rafe moan and heard herself moan, too, as his arousal pressed more insistently on her thigh.

Her flannel nightgown was getting caught up around her legs. Perhaps if she waited, he would just fall asleep? Cautiously, she lifted her head, only to be met with the glint of slate-blue eyes revealed by very unsleepy lids. 'What are you going to do now, Henrietta? Wriggle some more? You have my permission to do so.'

'Where were you, Rafe?'

'My mind was clogged with poisonous memories. I thought to wash them away with brandy. It didn't really work.' He shrugged dejectedly. 'Did you think I'd abandoned you?'

'No. Yes, well, for a moment. But—no. You said you'd help me, so I knew you'd be back. Hoped you would be. Not that I couldn't have managed on my own if you didn't.'

'But I said I'd take care of you,' Rafe muttered, 'so I did come back. You have no idea how much—how *very* much—I'd like to take care of you at this moment, Henrietta Markham. I did tell you not to trust me, did I not?'

His meaning was quite unmistakable. His meaning made her stomach clench in anticipation—and a little in trepidation. One hand was trailing up and down her spine. It was warm through her nightgown, yet it was making her shiver. And that feeling was back again, tingling and zinging and filling her with a sense of recklessness. *How did he do that?*

'Do what?' Rafe murmured, and she realised she'd spoken out loud again. 'You mean this?' he said with a wicked smile, and how he did it she had no idea, but his hands were on her spine and her bottom, only this time without any material between them.

'Rafe!' One sweeping stroke, from the base of her spine along her back and back down again, played havoc with her breathing. Another, and she felt she could not breathe at all. 'Rafe,' she said again, only this time it was not a protest, but something more akin to a plea. A plea he seemed to heed, for he rolled her over on to her back and now his hands were on her sides, her flank, her stomach. 'Rafe,' she said, only it was more like a moan. And he moaned, too, cupping the weight of her breasts, his thumbs caressing the hard peaks of her nipples, setting her on fire with his touch, making her writhe and arch her back, and ache for more.

Rafe hitched her nightgown up further. In the pearly grey of the morning light, her skin seemed translucent. She was every bit as luscious, as perfectly curved, as agonisingly desirable, as he had imagined. He dipped his head, eager to take one of those rosy nipples into his mouth. He felt the rasp of his stubble on the tender flesh of the underside of her breast.

An image of himself, dishevelled and smelling of brandy, looking every bit the hardened rake Henrietta thought him, flashed into his mind and he paused. He would not. He could not. She did not deserve this. The demons she had aroused, the demons that sinking his aching shaft into her wet, welcoming flesh would exorcise, they were not her demons. He would not use her thus, no matter how much he yearned to.

Yearning. The word echoed round his mind as he pulled her nightgown back down, as he hoisted himself away from her too-tempting flesh, as he sat up shakily on the edge of the bed. Yearning. Not a word he normally associated with himself, but that's what he felt, looking at her. For the union that would be, he knew, the most sensual of all unions. Yearning for the intimacy it would bring. Yearning to feel something. Anything. To give and to receive in return. Yearning, too, for what he had lost for ever. Innocence. Optimism. Idealism. A belief in love. She had them still. He could not deprive her of them, not like this.

'I can't,' he said aloud.

'Do you feel ill?'

Soft arms round his neck. Warmth against his back. The tickle of curls on his cheek. Rafe closed his eyes and groaned. She had taken him literally. Despite his patently obvious arousal tenting his breeches, she had taken him literally.

Sweet irony. He should be relieved, for it were better

she thought him unable to perform than that he betray himself more completely. For she had been right, after all, Henrietta Markham—he was not the cold fish he thought himself.

'Rafe, do you feel ill?' Henrietta asked, slipping off the bed to kneel before him, testing his forehead with the back of her hand.

'Sick to the very pit of my soul, Henrietta Markham, that is how I feel.'

'Let me take care of you.'

He allowed her to help him with his boots. He allowed her to help him out of his coat and waistcoat, but not his breeches. He allowed her to tuck him into the bed, to bathe his brow and to pull the covers gently over him. He closed his eyes as she lay down beside him, not touching him, but not putting the pillow between them, either. The world swam. He closed his eyes tighter. Blackness, welcome, brandy-induced oblivion awaited him. He succumbed willingly to its siren call.

Rafe woke with a start. His head was pounding, his eyes felt as if they had been filed vigorously with a large rasp and his stomach was most decidedly queasy. He had drunk an immense amount of Benjamin's French cognac, far more than was his wont, for he hated to be foxed. Clutching his head, he rolled out of bed and only then realised he was quite alone in the room. Fumbling for his watch, which was still on its fob in his waistcoat pocket, he saw that it was just a little before noon and cursed quietly, fervently hoping that Henrietta had had the sense not to leave the inn without him.

Henrietta. As he tugged his shirt over his head, he

remembered, and groaned. What had he said? Splashing tepid water over his face, snippets of the conversation—if one could call it a conversation—popped into his head, making him wince. He'd left her alone all night. She'd have been perfectly justified in being angry with him, but she'd refrained from uttering even one harsh word. Casting a quick glance around the room, he was relieved beyond proportion to see her shabby bandbox still sitting in the corner, her cloak still draped over the chair.

He rang for fresh water; when it arrived, satisfactorily hot and plentiful, he stripped off his clothes and scrubbed himself thoroughly before shaving. A fresh shirt and neckcloth, clean hose, and he felt almost human again. Human enough for his body to stir at the recollection of Henrietta's soft and luscious body pressed into his. Human enough to imagine what it might have been like had he not stopped himself. Human enough to be both relieved and rather astonished that he *had* stopped himself.

And then he remembered why he had been so drunk in the first place and groaned again. As he struggled into his boots, the guilt resettled, seeming to weigh even heavier on him than before. No doubt because he had allowed himself to recall the reasons for it. God dammit! The rawness of it all made him acutely aware, now, of how far below the surface he had buried it all. Made him realise, too, that his defences were just that: safeguards, but no solution. That the perpetual ennui he suffered was not boredom, but unhappiness.

Shrugging into his coat and brushing his hair, Rafe considered resorting to the brandy bottle again. Sweet oblivion. Except it hadn't worked. He couldn't understand why so many of his peers chose to dip so deep so often. All it gave you was nausea and a head that felt as if it would crack open like an egg. What it didn't allow you to do was either escape or forget. In fact, he recalled with a shudder, the more he drank the more he remembered, all the tiny details he'd tried so very hard to obliterate.

Henrietta was the unwitting cause of it all, for he could see, even through his pain, that she had not meant to rake over his smouldering ashes. He could picture quite clearly the horror on her face. She had had no idea she was treading on forbidden ground. Why should she?

Ironically she was the balm, too, for she, and not the brandy, had finally given him the sweet oblivion he sought. Henrietta on top of him, under him, laughing with him, kissing him, in her hideous flannel nightgown and *not* in her hideous flannel nightgown. *Then* he had found something much more delightful to occupy his mind. Only then.

Sighing heavily, Rafe made his way downstairs to the coffee room. He needed breakfast. 'And bring me a tankard of porter immediately,' he said to the maid-servant.

It arrived within a few moments and so, too, did Henrietta in her brown dress with her brown eyes—more cinnamon than chocolate today, he thought—fixed upon him sympathetically. 'Have you a very sore head?'

Relieved, but not very surprised to discover that she was not the type of female to raise her grudges when a man was at his lowest, Rafe attempted a smile.

'Extremely,' he said wryly, 'but it serves me right. Have you had breakfast?'

'Ages ago. I've been helping Meg bake bread.'

'Is there no end to your talents?'

'Well, most people consider baking bread a basic skill, not a talent,' Henrietta said, as she seated herself opposite him and poured them both coffee from the steaming pot that Bessie had just served. 'I don't have any real talents. I can't play upon the pianoforte—in fact, Mama says I'm tone deaf—and although I can stitch a straight seam, I can't embroider.'

'And you can't dance, either,' Rafe reminded her.

'Well, I can only assume I cannot,' she pointed out, 'given that I've never had the opportunity to find out.'

'Would you like the opportunity?'

'Would you teach me?' she asked with a twinkle. 'Only I'm not so very sure that you'd be a particularly patient teacher, especially not at this precise moment. Probably, you'd end up furious with me.' Her face fell. 'Actually, that's pretty much guaranteed, because you always end up furious with me. I don't know how it is…'

'Any more than I do,' Rafe said feelingly. 'Perhaps it is your tendency to say the most outrageous things.'

'I don't. I don't mean to. I just—'

'Say what you think. I know.' Rafe took a sip of coffee. It was hot and bitter. 'Contrary to what you are thinking, I like it. Most of the time. I'm getting used to it. It's refreshing in its own way. Like this coffee.' He took another sip. The ache in his head was beginning to subside. He realised that Henrietta had not once, since that fateful morning when he had found her in the ditch, complained about her own headache, which must have been considerably more painful. And he hadn't thought to ask. He took another sip of coffee. 'I'm sorry,' he said.

Her startled look would have made him smile had it not first made him feel guilty. 'Sorry for what?'

'I shouldn't have gone off and left you alone like that last night.'

'You asked Mr Forbes to check up on me. He did. Often.'

'You're very generous. More generous than I deserve.'

'And you must be very hung-over to be so complimentary,' Henrietta said, with a chuckle.

He did not deserve such understanding. For a brief moment, he had the most bizarre wish that he did. 'I don't make a habit of getting so disguised,' he said. 'You have every right to be disappointed in me.'

Henrietta grinned. 'It helped to know that an appropriate punishment surely awaited you in the morning.'

Rafe's real smile made a brief appearance. 'Then you should be more than content, for I am paying a heavy price indeed.'

'Is it very painful? Shall I fetch you a compress?'

'Good God, no. What I need is some breakfast, that should do the trick.' He released her hand and sat back in his seat, his long legs sprawled in front of him.

'I heard Mr Forbes tell Meg to give you three eggs, he said you'd need them,' Henrietta informed him helpfully.

'Benjamin Forbes is a very wise man.'

Henrietta picked up a knife and put it down again. Rafe looked paler than usual. His eyelids were heavier.

He had cut himself shaving. A tiny nick, just below his ear. 'I was angry with you for a while last night,' she confessed. 'I am sorry, Rafe, but you cannot have expected me to know....'

'You're right.'

'I am?'

He could almost have laughed at her astonished expression, were he not aware of the rather miserable picture it painted of him. Unknown. Unknowable. He had prided himself on those qualities. His armour. Now Henrietta had pierced it and he was relieved. Glad, almost. He felt as if she were waking him from a torpor. It wasn't a full awakening—there were some scars that were so much part of his being that no one could heal them—but it was enough to tempt him with possibilities. Not least, the possibility of looking forward to the day, rather than simply enduring it.

'You are. On this occasion, Henrietta, you are quite right,' he said, smiling again. It was coming easier, his smile. Practice. That, too, was down to Henrietta. Henrietta, who was still playing with her knife, which meant she had something else on her mind. He waited.

She could feel his eyes upon her, but was not quite able to meet them, despite his surprising admission. After he'd fallen asleep, she'd lain awake until she heard the clattering of pans in the kitchen, just listening to him breathing, only just restraining herself from snuggling into his side. Though she hadn't really thought he'd abandon her, the relief of having him back again was immense. Despite what she knew of him, or what she'd *thought* she knew, despite all of Mama's warnings and despite her principled objections to his way of life, she was not immune to his charms. Far from it.

From the moment she first set eyes upon Rafe, tall, dark, dishevelled and brooding, she had known he was dangerous. It was not just his reputation, but the man himself. He had warned her several times not to trust him, and several times she had failed to heed him. She had paid no heed, either, to her own cautioning inner voice. She was a mass of contradictions, almost as many as he. Before she met Rafe St Alban, her life had been perfectly straightforward. Now though...

She picked up her knife again and began to trace a pattern in the grain of the wooden table with the blade. Now, nothing was at all clear. The more she knew of Rafe, the more she liked him, the more she was attracted to him, yet she still understood him so little. She knew now for certain he was no callous seducer. Last night had proved that.

Why had he stopped? *Why had not she?* Looking at him over the scrubbed wooden table, she wondered if he even remembered. *She* remembered only too well. Last night, she would have given herself to him willingly. Much, much too willingly. Without even thinking about it, until it was too late. Last night she had discovered a side of herself that she hadn't believed existed. A side that seized control of her principles and her morals and contemptuously discarded them—until morn, at least. Last night she hadn't recognised herself.

And that, Henrietta realised with a horrible sense of foreboding that was at the same time horribly exhilarating, showed how very far she had already come already to making him a present of the heart that was beating, as ever, far too fast in his presence. She must be more careful. She must be *much* more on her guard against her own weakness. She nodded to herself resolutely, then jumped as the knife was removed from her hand.

'It would be far safer for you to simply say what's on your mind, Henrietta,' Rafe said, putting the cutlery out of reach, 'you're in danger of cutting yourself.'

'It's nothing.'

'Which means it's about last night.'

She coloured. 'How did you know?'

'Would you rather pretend it didn't happen?'

'Yes. No.'

'No, you're not one of those young ladies who pretend, are you? It's one of the things I like about you.'

'Is it?'

Rafe laughed. 'Don't look so surprised, it's not the only one. I like the way you suck your bottom lip when you're trying to stop yourself saying something you suspect you shouldn't. You twist your hair around your middle finger when you're thinking and you wrinkle your nose when something unpleasant occurs to you. You never complain and you are always putting others before yourself even when, like me this morning, they don't deserve it. You are in turn infuriating and endearing, but at least you are never predictable. I never know what you're going to say next, any more than you do. Just when I think I want to shake you, you make me want to laugh, or you look at me just so, and I want to kiss that delightfully kissable mouth of yours. In fact, there are aspects of you, Henrietta Markham, that I find quite irresistible.'

'Oh.'

'You always say that when I've said the opposite of what you were expecting. Last night, Henrietta,' Rafe continued in a gentler tone, 'I was drunk, but not incapable. I was unshaven, reeking of brandy and reeling with unpleasant memories. You deserve better, far better, than that.'

'Oh.' His tone, even more than the words he spoke, moved her. A lump rose in her throat. She blinked several times, touched by his care for her, which was more than she had had for herself. 'Thank you,' she said softly.

Rafe squeezed her hand. 'It's the truth. You are a rather extraordinary person, Henrietta Markham, and your being quite oblivious of the fact is perhaps the thing I like about you most.'

The coffee room door swung open and Bessie arrived with Rafe's breakfast, a vast plate of ham and the promised three eggs along with the first of the loaves that Henrietta had helped make. 'Excellent timing,' Rafe said, picking up his knife and fork with relish. 'Kill or cure, I suspect.'

Benjamin sought them out after breakfast with an update. 'No firm word of either the housebreaker or the emeralds as yet,' he said, 'but don't despair, I'm waiting on a couple of fences getting back to me in the next day or so.'

Henrietta looked blank.

'A man who sells on stolen goods,' Rafe informed her, 'and before you ask, not a man with whom you will be pursuing an acquaintance. We'll leave it in Ben's capable hands.'

'What shall we do today, then, if I am not to be allowed to meet shady underworld characters?'

'Oh, I'm sure I can find some alternative form of excitement for your delectation,' Rafe replied with a rare grin. 'Leave it up to me.'

He took her to Astley's Amphitheatre in Lambeth, where the entertainment included bareback horse riding and a staged re-enactment of the Battle of Waterloo. While Rafe would normally scorn such spectacles, as he would disdain to mingle with the great unwashed, even he was forced to admit that the horses were exceptionally well trained, though most of the time his eyes were on Henrietta, rather than the sawdust-strewn floor of the stage. She leaned precariously out of their private box, her eyes huge with excitement, her cheeks flushed. Such a simple treat, yet he might as well have given her the Crown Jewels. Then again, now he came to think about it, perhaps not, because she'd said only yesterday that they were vulgar.

He set himself out to entertain her, by way of an apology. A novel experience, yet infinitely rewarding, for Henrietta found everything fascinating and her enthusiasm was infectious. Her absolute faith in his ability to answer her questions, from the latest fashions—fuller skirts, narrower waists—to the accuracy of Astley's battle charge—almost completely lacking—and the King's current state of health—confined to Windsor with gout—he found touching rather than irksome. What would, had it been suggested by one of his peers, have seemed a day out beyond tedium, turned out to be one of the most entertaining he could remember in recent years.

* * *

Afterwards, they ate in a chop house. With a little prompting, Henrietta was persuaded to confide some of her history. As ever, she was self-deprecating. He surmised she had been happy, but rather neglected, her parents more concerned with good works than the welfare of their only child, but recalling how prickly she had been about her sainted papa, he refrained from criticism. Recalling the yearning look upon her face as she gazed upon the *toilettes* of the Astley's audience, cheap imitations of the walking gowns and carriage gowns, full dress and half-dress worn by the *haut ton*, he wished he could make her a present of just one such, but he knew better now than to offer. Not only would her principles forbid such a thing, he would be drawing attention to her own shabby gown; though he detested the thing, it was such an integral part of her that he had come to feel something like affection for it.

They talked on, long after they had cleared their plates of lamb cutlets and thick gravy, oblivious of the comings and goings of other customers, oblivious of the curious looks cast them, he so well dressed and austerely handsome, she so vivacious and yet so dowdy. They talked and they laughed, and they leaned ever closer as the light fell and the rush lights were lit and the chophouse proprietor finally plucked up the courage to tell them it was well past closing.

'Goodness, where did the time go?' Henrietta said, blinking in the gloaming outside as Rafe hailed a hack. 'I've had such a lovely day, thank you.' Rafe's thigh brushed hers as he took his seat beside her in the hackney cab. She watched the driver's head bobbing in front of her through the small window, vaguely aware that they were crossing the river, for she could see the gas lamps were lit. She should be tired after her restless night, but she had never felt so alive. Rafe's leg lay warm against the folds of her cloak. His shoulder brushed hers. Though they were silent now, it was a comfortable silence for once.

Though it was not precisely comfortable. She was too conscious of the man beside her. Irresistible, Rafe had called her. Henrietta had never thought of herself in that way before. She liked it, though it made her nervous, for it contained all sorts of possibilities she suspected she couldn't ever live up to and knew she should not try to do so.

Today she had seen yet another side of Rafe, one she liked very much. One she could grow to like even more. Another side of him that failed to fit the image his reputation ought to have created. She'd thought it was that simple: Rafe was a rake, therefore he was unprincipled. Yet her experience of him was almost entirely the opposite. She just didn't understand it. She could no longer believe him capable of dishonourable behaviour, yet he had not denied it.

Henrietta chewed her lip. Thinking back, every time the subject came up, it had been she who accused and he who refused to comment. Could she have been a little too presumptuous? It was a fault of hers, she knew that.

As they pulled into the yard of the Mouse and Vole and Rafe took her hand to help her down from the carriage, doubt shook her once more. Why would Mrs

Peters, his own housekeeper, have warned her off if there had been no grounds to do so?

She followed him, through the side door, along the corridor, the draught from the taproom door making the wall sconces flicker. Gazing at his tall figure, his wide shoulders, the neat line of his hair, she felt the now-familiar prickle of awareness. Another contradiction, perhaps the most significant, her body's desire for him. A desire quite independent of her mind. She knew she should not, she knew that it was wrong, but her body insisted it was right.

Right or wrong, that was the key question. She wished she had an answer. She wished things didn't have to be so complicated. Or maybe it was Rafe who was complicated? Or she was simplistic? He said she saw things too much in black and white, and he'd been proved right about that several times now.

'Go on up, I'll go and see if Ben has further news,' Rafe said, interrupting the somewhat tangled strands of Henrietta's reasoning. A roar of anger came from the taproom, quickly followed by a louder roar. 'Sounds like he has his hands full,' he said with a wry smile. 'Perhaps now is not the best time to interrupt him.'

They made their way up the stairs to the sanctuary of their chamber. Placing the oil lamp by the bedside, Rafe drew the curtains together. Henrietta unclasped her cloak and placed it over the chair, cast off her gloves, tugged the ribbons of her bonnet and pulled it from her head. Rafe cast aside his coat and loosened his neckcloth. A cosy domestic scene. The thought struck them both at the same time. They caught one another's expression, smiled, looked away, embarrassed by the intimacy—or perhaps unwilling to acknowledge it.

'I had a lovely day. Thank you,' Henrietta said, picking up her hairbrush.

Rafe smiled. The smile that made her feel as if her heart were being squeezed, so she found she had to concentrate on breathing. 'I enjoyed it, too,' he said.

'Confess, you didn't expect to. I can't imagine that Astley's is the sort of place you visit regularly.'

His smile broadened. 'I confess, but I still enjoyed myself. You have the knack of making even the most tedious occasions refreshing.'

'Because I'm so green.'

'Because you are so Henrietta.'

She put her hairbrush down. 'Is that a compliment?'

'Yes.'

She picked her hairbrush up again, looked at it absently and then put it back down. 'Rafe, I wanted to—at least I don't want to but I feel I must. I don't understand and it's confusing me, and so…' She looked at him helplessly, trying desperately to find the words that would not put him instantly on the defensive.

'You are confusing me, too, for I have no idea what you're talking about.'

She bit her lip. If she hesitated now, then she would simply find herself wrestling with the same questions tomorrow, and before that there was tonight to get through, not that she had any intentions at all—far from it—and, anyway, he would not. Probably. So…

'Rafe, are you really a rake?' She could almost see his hackles rise; his brows were drawn together, winging upwards to give him a satanic look, his eyes stormy.

Oh God, why had she had to blurt it out like that? 'I didn't mean to—forget I said it.'

'But you did, so it is obviously troubling you.'

'Well, it is,' she said resolutely. 'I simply don't understand you.'

'What, precisely, don't you understand?'

If she touched him, he would freeze. Not that he would let her touch him. The barriers were invisible, but she could see them all the same. Touch-me-not. 'You,' she said, refusing to back down. 'I don't understand how someone with your reputation can be so—so—well, you just don't behave like a rake at all.'

'And how does a rake behave, Henrietta?'

'Well, they—well, they—Mama says that they seduce innocents.'

'And Mama would know, would she?'

'Yes, she would,' Henrietta said, her temper rising in response to his heavily sarcastic tone. 'She knows because she was seduced by one. Oh!' She put her hand over her mouth, but it was too late, so she blurted out the rest. 'She was young. He promised her marriage. They eloped together and he jilted her.'

'After he had seduced her, presumably.'

Henrietta's colour rose. 'There is no need to be so callous.'

'Surely, if you are to tar me with the same brush as your mother's seducer, you would expect me to be callous,' Rafe said.

Henrietta folded her arms across her chest. She would have the truth from him this time. 'You're not callous,' she said firmly. 'You're not callous and you're not irresponsible, and you're not shallow and you're not selfish.'

He ignored this. 'What happened to your mother?'

'She was devastated. She is very beautiful, not a bit like me, and she had had excellent prospects, but they were all ruined. She retired to the country; it was there she met Papa and he fell in love with her and she agreed to marry him and there was some sort of quarrel with her family over that because Papa is not rich or titled....'

'Your mother was?'

'I believe her family is a good one, but I have never met any of them. They disowned her—not because she was seduced by a rake—he had the benefit of being a well-born man, too—but because she married my father,' Henrietta said indignantly 'What happened to my mother, it was a terrible thing. Awful. It has shaped her whole life. Even though she is happy with Papa, there are times when she is just so sad. You cannot imagine.'

He could. A fading beauty self-obsessed with something that happened more than twenty years ago, too caught up in her own tragedy to admit to any sort of responsibility. He could imagine it only too well, for he had married one such. Now Henrietta had tarred him with the same brush as her mother's seducer and he wanted nothing more than to shake some sense into her. 'And so Mama has filled your head with tragic tales of seducers, has she?'

'She has taught me to believe that such men are to be avoided. That they have no morals. That—'

'So, I am not only a seducer of innocents, but I have

no morals? I wonder that you trust yourself with me, Miss Markham.'

'That's my point, Lord Pentland. I do trust you. You are patently an honourable man.'

'Oh please, Henrietta, don't colour me whiter than snow.'

'I'm not, but you are content to be coloured black as night, and I don't understand why,' she replied furiously.

'I have no intentions of explaining myself.'

'Why not? I explain myself to you all the time. Why should you not tell me—?'

'Because it is none of your business.'

'But it still matters to me.'

'Why?'

'Because it does.' She waited, glaring at him, but she was no match for Rafe's stony countenance. Henrietta gave an infuriated growl. 'I don't understand you and because of that I don't understand myself,' she said. 'Oh, for goodness' sake, if you must know, I just can't reconcile how I can feel—want—I just—last night! Last night, when you kissed me, I wanted you to—and then when you stopped I wished you hadn't. And yet I know you are a rake, so I ought not to want. But I do and that is what I don't understand,' she said, dashing away a tear with the back of her hand. 'And if you are a rake, why have you not seduced me? I don't understand that, either.'

Her brown eyes were sparkling with tears. Her bosom was heaving. She was flushed with mortification and temper. Rafe saw that revealing her mother's past had cost her dear, but not as dear as the frank and totally unexpected admission of her desire. The righteous fury he had been nursing dissipated like a cloud of steam. He took a step towards her and tried to take her hand, but she pushed him away.

'Your honesty puts me to shame, Henrietta.'

'That was not my intention.'

'Which is why it was so effective,' he said ruefully.

'I hate having to think ill of you,' she confessed in a whisper.

'You want to think me an honourable man, is that it, Henrietta?' Rafe countered harshly. 'You want me to deny my past in order for you to reconcile your conscience? I cannot do that. I am no saint, Henrietta. My reputation as a rake is not unfounded.'

She swallowed hard. She felt as if she were shrinking inside.

Rafe pushed his fingers through his hair, casting his eyes up to the ceiling where a cobweb hung from the corner of the plain cornicing. 'I can tell you the truth, if you like.'

Chapter Seven

Was he really contemplating this? 'I can't refute my actions, but I can explain them.'

It seemed he was. Rafe took a quick turn around the room. It mattered that she understood. Only now did he admit to himself how much her opinion of him counted, how hurtful had been her judgements. How had she come to be so important to him? He didn't know. He just knew she was. Telling her would be a relief, if not a release. He wanted to tell her.

He took another turn about the room. Henrietta was still standing in the middle of it, in her brown gown with her brown eyes, watching him. He owed her the truth. He took her hand and led her back over to the bed, sitting down in the chair opposite once more. She looked so compliant, yet there was a core of steel running through her. It gave her a strength of purpose, a solidly grounded moral certainty at her centre that he envied. He might not agree with all of her opinions, but at least she had them and she meant them. She had integrity. He particularly admired that.

Settling back in the uncomfortable wooden seat, Rafe subdued a craven desire to extinguish the lamp and make his confession in the dark. 'I was only nineteen when I married Julia,' he said, launching into his sorry tale before he could think again. 'Lady Julia Toward. She was twenty-three, the same age as you are now.'

Henrietta listened intently. Rafe's voice was not much above a whisper, but the bitterness was there, like a rusty blade hidden in the petals of a flower.

'She was very beautiful,' he continued, 'very beautiful and, though I did not know it, very unstable. She had been betrothed some two years before, but her fiancé died. I thought her over it when I met her. She said she was. I wanted to believe her. When you want something enough, you can persuade yourself of anything.'

Silence. Henrietta waited, biting back the urge to protest. She hated the implications of what he was saying. Despite the evidence—foolishly, she now realised—she had persuaded herself that he had not loved his wife.

'I was just returned from my Grand Tour and was as green as spring asparagus.' Rafe's voice was stronger now. 'My father had packed me off with dire warnings of the dangers of salacious Continental women, but in truth I was more interested in ancient history. I spent my time seeking out every set of crumbling ruins that Greece and Italy had to offer. Father died quite unexpectedly while I was still abroad. When I returned to England, it was to take up the title. I had always known it would be mine, but I hadn't expected it to happen so soon. I was not close to my father, but I was shocked and saddened by his premature death. There was no one else, you see. I have no siblings and my mother had died years before. There was just my grandmother, as there still is. She urged me to marry, saying I needed help in taking up the reins, and there was Julia, ideally positioned to do so. The perfect doyenne, was Julia, it was what she had been raised to be. And she was beautiful and claimed to love me. And I was ripe and ready to fall in love myself. I couldn't have been more primed. So we married.'

'Were you happy?' Henrietta asked. It was churlish of her, awful of her, but she wanted him to say no.

Rafe shrugged. 'At first. It's hard for me to remember, it's like looking back at a shadow play, but, yes, I suppose we must have been. Or I was. Julia was…' He broke off with a heavy sigh. 'You know, I have no real idea what Julia was. There were days when she seemed content, days when she simply withdrew into silence. She'd lock herself away in her bedchamber for up to a week, then she'd come out smiling and pretending nothing had happened. She would shower affection on me, then she would freeze when I touched her. She would drag me to every party we were invited to, wouldn't let me leave her side, then she would take to ignoring me. If I so much as danced with another women, she would wreak havoc, yet she would not allow me to make comment on her coterie of gallants—and, believe me, it was a large coterie. She was terrified that her looks would fade. Actually, she was obsessed with how she looked. It was the source of her power.'

He ran his fingers through his hair. 'I can see all that now. At the time it was a different matter entirely. At the time, I grew tired of her tantrums and tears. I grew tired, too, of her blowing first hot and then cold upon the physical side of our union. I stopped going to her room. I stopped wanting her. I stopped caring about her moods. I stopped loving her.'

Silence again, a deeply uncomfortable one filled with ghosts and spectres. Rafe gazed blankly into the past, forcing himself to relive those days, slowly easing the tattered bandages from the wounds he had garnered, testing to see how much they had healed. 'It was my fault, most of it,' he said bitterly. 'I didn't care enough and she saw that. She didn't love me, but she was terrified of losing me, and she could see that I was by this time—two years or so into our marriage—she could see that I was quite indifferent in the way that only callous youth can be. So she tried to get my attention in the only way she knew how, by making me jealous.'

He had been stroking the back of Henrietta's hand, a rhythmic caress back and forwards, but now he stopped. 'She took a lover. When I found out, she wept and pleaded, begging forgiveness, but when she saw I would not be moved, things turned vicious. She told me she'd never loved me. She told me she married me only for the title and the money. She told me she'd only ever loved one man and he was dead. She told me I could never satisfy her, that she'd taken countless lovers to our marital bed before this one, that I was not man enough for her. That I was not man enough for anyone.'

Rafe's voice was shaking. He was breathing hard, as if he had been running. A cold sweat prickled the small of his back, but now that he had started, he needed to finish, no matter how much it pained him. A flash of the humiliation that had engulfed him at the time struck him with an immediacy which took him aback. It was quickly followed by shame as he remembered how Julia had made him feel. He had forgotten the vicious sting of her barbs that had so effectively lashed his youthful ego, flaying his more innocent self, for a brief time quite destroying his confidence. It had been so long since he had vowed to prove her wrong, so long since he had stopped believing he had any point at all to prove, yet for a moment he felt again as if he did.

He plunged on, eager to conclude now, his words spilling out, staccato-like. 'I know now that it was mere bravado, designed to wound, but I didn't know then. I hated her for what she said. I ended our marriage then and there. A formal separation, but discreetly done. No notices in the press, nor any to her creditors. Julia was banished to an obscure estate, given an adequate allowance to live on, but it was punishment enough for her. Banishment from society and all the vanities and admirers who fed her ego. I punished her because I believed what she said. Then later, to my eternal shame, I continued to punish her because I felt guilty. I hadn't ever truly loved her. I shouldn't have married her, any more than she should have married me, yet we were stuck with one another, married but not married, in a state of limbo. I kept us there because I felt guilty. Because I had failed. I punished myself as well as Julia. I felt I deserved the misery as much as she.'

'Couldn't you have divorced?'

Rafe shook his head vehemently. 'No. God, no. An Act of Parliament, to say nothing of becoming the latest crim. con. for the gossips. No, that would have been a step too far for both our families.' He sat down heavily on the chair, dropping his head into his hands. 'You have to remember, I was young. I'm not excusing what I did, I'm just doing as you ask, telling you why. I was loaded with guilt at not having made Julia happy and humiliated by her jibes. I couldn't make any woman happy, she said. I was hurt. I vowed I'd never let anyone hurt me again. And I—I set out to prove her wrong.'

He faltered here. Having for so long refused to allow himself to remember, he had never questioned the actions he had taken to remedy his sense of humiliation. Having made the decision, he had acted and continued to act without reflection. But now, in the retelling, under Henrietta's clear-sighted, innocent gaze, he did reflect, and found himself on less solid ground than he ought to be. 'It was not so much revenge as—as—I don't know, I suppose it was shoring up my defences, rebuilding my ego. I swear to you, Henrietta, I have never once hurt anyone in the process. I have never seduced any woman who was not a willing partner and I have taken every precaution to ensure that I would not leave her with child, but I cannot deny that there have been very many such women over the years. I have learned to use sex as an emotional shield. I've learned to use it as a release mechanism, to stop me feeling.'

It hurt, his confession, and it pained her soul to see him so raw, to think of him as once so vulnerable, to see the glimpses of that vulnerability still. She loathed the beautiful woman who had spoken so cruelly, but she was not so blind as to think Julia solely to blame. The most painful part of what Rafe was saying was hearing his judgement—his flawed judgement—upon himself. No one could be more ruthless, more self-condemnatory.

'I have my own rules, my own form of morality, if you will,' Rafe continued harshly. 'I have never had any problem in playing by them. I don't engage with women who expect any more than a physical relationship. I don't sleep with the innocent or the vulnerable. I don't allow any real intimacy. Don't look like that, Henrietta—believe me, it's very possible to share your body with someone and feel nothing. It is possible to give and to receive physical pleasure without feeling real desire. I am a rake, Henrietta, but not the kind of rake you think me.'

'Oh, Rafe, I so much wish you were not *any* kind of rake.' How much she wished *that* she had not acknowledged to herself, until now. She had not appreciated how much she had longed for an explanation that would eradicate his past until Rafe made it crystal clear that he could not.

She was torn, moved to tears by the pain and suffering he had endured. There were angry tears for the wanton destruction of Rafe's innocence by Julia, but also for the route to retribution he had chosen. 'I know it is trite, but it is true, none the less: two wrongs don't make a right. I *wish* you had not behaved so.'

'But you understand, Henrietta, why I do? Did.'

Did she? He had trampled a ragged path through her preconceptions, that much was certain. He was not a rake. Yet he was. He had good reasons to feel as he did, but were they sufficient to justify his actions? 'I'm sorry. I do understand, but I can't condone your behaviour, Rafe. I know it's not for me to judge, I was not the one married to Julia, but still.' She shook her head. 'You've been so honest with me, I can't lie to you. I just— I don't know. Tell me what happened after you separated? To Julia, I mean, what happened to Julia?'

The sorrowful look in Henrietta's eyes made him experience something remarkably like remorse, though he suspected it was more for the pain of disillusioning her than wishing his past undone. Bitter experience had taught him just how pointless that was. 'We lived apart for three years. I gradually eased the terms of our separation. I didn't love her, but I cared enough to wish her happy, so when she suggested a reconciliation, vowing it was what she wanted, I was not entirely against it. My instincts were to refuse, but Julia was persistent and my guilty conscience was persistent and so, too, was my grandmother. There was still the issue of an heir, you see. So we were reconciled and then…'

Once again, Rafe got to his feet. He wrenched his neckcloth from his shirt and tossed it on to the floor. 'It was a mistake from the start. To end a sorry tale, she died tragically. Almost exactly five years ago. And despite my grandmother's renewed and extremely determined campaign for my re-entering the matrimonial stakes, I will never marry again. The whole thing was too painful. I don't want that kind of pain again. I am much happier and better off alone.'

And now she did understand the real punishment he was meting out on himself. Not just cutting himself off from pain, he would not think himself deserving of feeling. She understood that now and so much more of it made sense. 'Are you sure you are happier?' she asked softly, already fairly certain of the answer.

Rafe hesitated. 'I was. At least, I thought I was until you waltzed into my life,' he admitted with a rueful smile. 'I sometimes feel as if you have picked me up and thrown me into the air and I can never be sure if I have yet landed, or where. I hate it and it makes me furious, but it also makes me laugh and it makes me want more. You were honest with me, Henrietta, let me be completely honest with you. I don't know how you've managed it, but you make me want to break my rules. You've made it damned difficult not to, if you must have the God's honest truth. There, now you have it all. I wish I could be the man you want me to be, but I'm not and never can be.'

She put her fingers to his mouth. 'You are always telling me not to think in black and white—you should take a lesson from your own book. You are much more than you think you are, Rafe. I wish that you were not quite so determined to see yourself in the poorest possible light. Whether you will admit it or not, you are my knight errant, and whether you will admit to them or not, you have some extremely chivalrous qualities.'

Kneeling up on the bed, she wrapped her arms around his neck. He was not the man he ought to be, not the man he could be, but he was Rafe, and she would not change him even if she could, any more than she would change this moment. An intense need to provide succour swamped her. She was overwhelmingly relieved to be able to explain her own feelings, to have them almost legitimised. Mentally exhausted by the process, she became intensely physically aware. Rafe's pulse was beating at his throat. The scent of him, so achingly familiar, was in her nose. She wanted the taste of him on her tongue. Rafe was not the only one who was finding it difficult to keep to his own rules. She wanted his kisses. She longed for his touch.

Desire! His word, but it rang true. That is what she was feeling. Unconsciously, she nestled herself closer, feeling the rise and fall of his ribs against her breasts. Desire. Was it really so very wrong? She knew the answer, but chose to ignore it.

'Henrietta, if you keep doing that, I won't be responsible for the consequences.'

She didn't want him to be. She didn't want to think. She wanted to feel. She wanted him to feel. She pressed herself closer and looked up at him.

Eyes slate-blue, piercing, seeing too much, more than she was prepared to look at herself. Henrietta tried to look away, but he tilted up her chin. 'Henrietta, I don't want...'

'You do. You said you do. And I do, too. I know I should not, but I do. I can't help it.'

'Dear God, Henrietta...'

'Rafe, just kiss me.'

He kissed her roughly. His mouth was hard on hers, but her lips were so meltingly soft, it didn't matter. He kissed her and his doubts fled, too. This was right. This. And this. And this. His kiss deepened. He pulled her closer, wrapped his arms around her and found it. Sweet oblivion.

As Rafe kissed her, Henrietta's senses whirled. He had kissed her before, tenderly, teasingly, with a promise of more to come, but this time it was there, right from the start. Passion. She had no time to think, she could only respond, melting into his arms as he enfolded her, his lips hard on hers, his tongue plundering her mouth, thrusting into it in a way that made her body tremble, heat and shiver all at once.

His hands were on the laces of her gown. Knowing, expert hands—she wouldn't think about that. He kissed and he unlaced, and the gown fell open at the back; he pulled it down over her arms and she helped him—she didn't care that it was wanton, she wanted to be free of it as much as he wanted her to be. He discarded his own coat and waistcoat. She was in her cotton chemise and his hands were on the plain material, stroking, caressing, his lips tracing a path from her mouth down her neck to the valley between her breasts as his fingers plucked her nipples into an aching hardness that made her moan.

He said her name, breathed her name, his voice hoarse, his breath coming as fast as hers. He said her name as if she were beautiful; the way he touched her made her feel beautiful. The way he touched her made her feel hot. Made her feel restless. Made her feel as if there was something delightful waiting for her, if only he would kiss her more, touch her more. She ran her hands feverishly up his back, feeling the heat of his skin through his shirt, but it wasn't enough, so she tugged his shirt free from his breeches and felt his skin.

He kissed her again, his mouth drugging hers, hot and dark and full of promise. Forbidding and enticing and dangerous, just as she had known from the beginning he would be. She kissed him back just as deeply, just as passionately; she shivered more violently as he pulled her closer and she felt the thick weight of his arousal press solidly against her thigh.

She was sprawled on the bed now and he was looking down at her, his eyes glittering and stormy. His cheeks were flushed. His shirt was open at the neck. A sprinkling of dark hairs. She couldn't remember when he had lost his neckcloth. Or his boots. He knelt down on the floor and untied her garters, delicately peeling down her coarse woollen stockings as if they were made of the finest silk. He kissed her ankle, the faint pulse at the bone. It was as if he had kissed her innermost self.

She shuddered. Heat pooled in her belly. Her body tightened, as if readying itself. He pulled her towards him and untied her chemise, freeing her breasts. He kissed her mouth again, more urgently now. He tangled his fingers in her wildly curling hair, murmuring her name. Then his mouth fastened on her breast, his tongue flicking her nipple.

First one, then the other, he tended to her breasts, cupping their weight in his hands, his tongue flicking over each nipple in turn, his mouth searingly hot on them. Her body was stretched as taut as the rope the tightrope walker had balanced on at Astley's. She felt the same sense of giddy excitement, of precariousness.

She shivered, hot, then cold, hot, then cold. She arched her back. Her fingers clutched at his skin. His shirt was gone. She nuzzled her face into the rough hair of his chest, her hands roaming feverishly over his contours, the ridged muscles of his back, the line of his ribs, the dip in his abdomen. When he licked, she licked, too, and heard him gasp as she gasped. She pressed herself into him with abandon, relishing the hard length of his arousal, wanting more of him, more from him, more.

He pushed her back on the bed and removed her drawers, then kissed the soft inner flesh of her thighs. *What was he doing?* She didn't care, she just wanted him to keep on doing it. He was nudging her thighs apart. She was taut, expectant. 'Rafe.' She writhed on the bed. She arched up as he kissed her thigh again. 'Rafe,' she said more urgently, a plea. She tugged on his shoulders.

He was so hard it ached. She was so ready, there was no need to wait. He had never seen anyone so aroused. He had never felt so aroused himself. She was perfect, ripe and luscious and waiting for him. His erection throbbed. His stomach clenched. He had never wanted anyone so much. Never. *So why in God's name was he hesitating? Again!*

'Rafe?'

He kissed her mouth, her infinitely kissable mouth, and she wrapped her arms around him and he realised what it was. She trusted him. Completely. Implicitly.

He disentangled himself from her arms, ignoring her soft protest. He kissed her breasts and she stopped protesting. He kissed the soft roundness of her belly and felt her tremble. Then he dipped his fingers into the sweet heaven of her sex and felt her wet, hot, so ready for him that almost his resolution crumbled. He heard her say his name, then he kissed where his fingers had been and he heard her cry out with surprise and pleasure; he forgot all about his own needs and, for the first time in his life, took pleasure in attending only to someone else's.

Henrietta's eyes flew open as he kissed her there. And there. Oh God, and there. *What was he doing?* Should he not—should they not—was this right? Then her eyes fell heavily closed as he kissed her again and she surrendered to the sensations he was arousing.

She'd thought she couldn't experience any more sensation, but her body proved her wrong. Everything focused. There. Where his mouth kissed and his tongue licked and his fingers stroked. There. Where she was getting tighter and hotter and climbing higher. There. She couldn't breathe. She heard herself moaning, saying his name, over and over, saying *Rafe, Rafe, Rafe, please, please, please,* though she didn't know why; then he licked her again and she knew why, because that was exactly, exactly, exactly what she wanted, so that when he stopped she wanted to scream. Then he did it again and she did scream as finally the tension became too much and she broke, shattered, flew apart and apart and apart, and then flew again as he licked her again, holding her against his mouth as he kissed her so unbelievably intimately, kissing her again until she floated, curling her body into his as she descended from whatever plane of ecstasy she had inhabited, kissing her mouth, stroking her hair, saying her name, kissing her as if he really meant it, as if she truly was irresistible.

She opened her eyes to meet his, deep indigo, filled with undisguised passion. She was pressed so close to him she could feel his heart beating, slower than hers, but still fast. She waited, knowing there was more, wanting more. She could feel him hard and solid through his breeches.

He still had his breeches on!

He laughed, and she realised that once again she'd spoken out loud. 'I know,' he said.

'But…'

'It's better this way.'

'But you…'

'I am more than satisfied, if you are,' he said. And he meant it. 'Sleep, Henrietta.' He stroked her hair, her shoulders. He cupped her bottom, nestling her closer, and stroked her back. He kissed her eyelids. The tip of her nose. Though his shaft was still throbbing, he felt almost sated, strangely replete.

Her breathing was already slowing. Her hands were loosing their hold on him. He pulled the rough blanket up over both of them. Another night confined in those damned breeches, yet he didn't care. He wasn't in the least tired, but he had no intentions of moving.

Henrietta snuggled her cheek into the crook of his shoulder. She was floating again, on a cloud of blissful happiness.

She awoke next morning to the reassuring thump of his heart. She was still anchored to his side, one of her legs pressed between his thighs. She lay completely still, relishing the feel of him, the solidity of him, the scent of him, the warmth. One of his hands was wrapped around her waist. The other lay on her bottom. She became dimly aware of another sound. An urgent tapping at the door. It was Benjamin and he clearly had some news.

Shyly clutching the sheet around her, Henrietta sat up in bed. Rafe had already pulled on a clean shirt and she was acutely conscious of her own nakedness.

Sitting on the end of the bed, pulling on his boots,

Rafe tried very hard to ignore the alluring and delightfully naked bundle only a few inches away. Intimacy was something he was accustomed to eschewing, but this kind of intimacy, this waking up together, and getting dressed, and starting a new day together—he was finding that he liked it. At least, he liked it with Henrietta. Her hair was curlier than ever in the morning light. Her skin was creamy, rather than white. He liked the way her lips were smudged with his kisses. He dropped his boot.

'Rafe, we— Benjamin is waiting.'

But he kissed her, anyway, and, when her arms went around his neck and the sheet slipped so that her breasts were pressed against his shirt, he kissed her again.

Henrietta disentangled herself with extreme reluctance. Already her body was tingling with anticipation. It was intoxicating, this passion they shared.

She smiled at him, and he felt as if her smile tugged at something inside him. It was the strangest feeling. She had judged him, but she had not found him wanting. She trusted him. And she cared. Perhaps too much. He hadn't thought of that. He hadn't thought of that at all. *Why the hell had he not?*

Guilt made his own smile fade. Because he had not wanted to. He wished—he wished—but wishes were the stuff of fools and he was a fool no more. He turned back to the shaving mirror. 'I'll only be a moment more. I'll go down and order breakfast, you can make your *toilette* in private.'

The door closed and Henrietta got out of bed. The magic of the night had fled, leaving a grey dawning of reality. These last few days had been a flight of fantasy.

If Benjamin's news was positive, it would precede a return to the real world. So successful had she been in forgetting all about the accusations hanging over her head that she had no idea, in fact, what form, exactly, her return to reality would constitute.

She had no source of income. Even with her name cleared, it was unlikely in the extreme that Lady Ipswich would take her back and, knowing what she knew now about the lady's past, Henrietta was far from sure that she wanted to return in any case. She could go to Ireland if she borrowed the fare from Rafe, she supposed, but the very thought of facing Mama and Papa and the inevitable chaos that would surround them made her heart sink.

As she tied her garters and laced her shoes, a tear plopped down on to her hand. 'The thing is,' she said to her melancholy reflection, as she dried her face on a towel smelling of Rafe's shaving soap, 'the thing is that though, of course, I don't love him, I don't want to leave him just yet. Though I know I must.' She sniffed and picked up her brush, dragging it through her tangled curls roughly enough to explain the fresh batch of tears that collected in her eyes.

She cast down her brush and began to stick pins randomly into her hair. 'It is high time you faced facts, Henrietta Markham. Rafe St Alban will very soon— maybe as early as today—be leaving this inn and returning to his privileged life in London. You would do well to turn your mind to what you are going to do next, even if you don't have to worry about Newgate. Which is not yet a foregone conclusion.'

She pushed a final pin into her hair and surveyed the

dismal result. It would have to do. Taking several deep breaths, reminding herself yet again that there were thousands of people worse off than she was, Henrietta left the bedchamber.

Rafe was waiting for her in the coffee room with a substantial breakfast spread before him. 'Ben won't be a moment,' he said, helping her into a chair and pouring her some coffee.

Henrietta buttered a slice of bread, glancing at Rafe as she did so. His expression was impassive. 'You'll be able to go home, if the news is positive,' she said brightly.

'Home?'

'You must have a dozen things to attend to, lots of parties and such. You'll be pleased to finally have the comfort of your own bed, too.'

He had been about to take a bite of beef, but his fork remained suspended halfway to his mouth. 'You are eager to be rid of me?'

'No, of course not, only I am vastly conscious of the amount of time you have already wasted....'

Rafe put his fork back down on his plate, the beef uneaten. 'I don't consider it wasted time.' He took a sip of coffee. He hadn't thought about returning to his solitary life. He wasn't ready. 'Anyway, things are not that simple. Even if Ben has tracked down the housebreaker, he's hardly likely to readily admit to the theft, especially with the threat of the hangman's noose looming over him if he does.'

'Oh.' Henrietta bit into her bread and butter. 'I hadn't taken that into account.'

'Let us wait until we hear what Ben has to say,' Rafe said, as their host entered the room.

What Benjamin had to say was that he had, through a variety of mysterious contacts, tracked down a man who strongly resembled Henrietta's description of the house-breaker. 'Goes by the name of Scouse Larry. Looks like your man, all right, but he's a sneaking budge—a small-time thief, that is. Clothes, the odd piece of silver, is what Scouse Larry deals in, not gew-gaws and he's certainly not tried to fence anything like those emer-alds you described, miss. If they'd been on the market, I'd have heard.' Benjamin tugged at his battle-scarred earlobe. 'I dunno, it's a rum 'un; something about all of this don't add up.'

'Well, there's only one way to find out, and that's to confront him. Will you bring him here, Ben?' Rafe asked.

But Benjamin shook his head adamantly. 'Wouldn't come. He'd think it was a trap and run, then we'd be back to square one. You'll have to go to him.'

Rafe pushed aside his empty plate and got to his feet. 'Where do I find him?'

Henrietta, too, pushed back her chair. 'Where do *we* find him, you mean. Let me just get my cloak.'

'Lord, miss, you can't go. Best leave it to his lord-ship,' Benjamin said, looking at her aghast. 'Scouse Larry's abode is in the stews of Petticoat Lane. It's a terrible place, full of cut-throats and cutpurses, to say nothing of the doxies and molls. Begging your pardon, miss, but you see, a rookery's no place for a lady.'

'Ben is quite right, Henrietta, you'll have to leave this to me.'

'No.'

'Henrietta…'

'Miss…'

'No. I'm coming with you,' Henrietta said determinedly. 'I'm the only one who's actually seen this Scouse Larry. Without me how will you know it's definitely the same man? And besides,' she continued before Rafe could comment, 'it's my neck that's in the noose, not yours. I want to hear for myself what this man has to say.'

'He is unlikely to say anything unless well recompensed. Something beyond your current means,' Rafe said.

Henrietta's face fell. 'I hadn't thought of that.'

Rafe sighed heavily. 'Have it your way, Henrietta, but if we manage to get out of Petticoat Lane the lighter for a few sovereigns alone, we should consider ourselves fortunate. I shall leave my fob and snuffbox here; you would be well advised to leave anything of value here, too. The cutpurses there will steal the clothes from your back if they are not fastened on tightly.'

Henrietta gave a little squeal. 'You mean you will take me, after all?'

Rafe sighed, but his mouth quivered on the brink of a smile. 'If I don't, you'll only follow me, anyway, and I'd rather have you by my side where I can at least keep an eye on you. Go and get your cloak. Just don't blame me if what you see gives you nightmares.'

The stews of Petticoat Lane were sordid beyond belief, a warren of narrow alleyways and blind cul-de-sacs, where the ramshackle tenements leaned precariously towards one another as if attempting a drunken kiss. What little light penetrated between the steeply shelving roofs was blocked by the lines of ragged washing strung out of windows on poles, and further filtered by the acrid smoke of sea coal belching from the chimney pots. Behind the buildings, a labyrinth of wooden stairs, precarious platforms and rotten ladders allowed the rookery's residents to flit unnoticed between the maze of lodging houses, gin houses and hovels where no Charley would dare give chase. In the lanes, the gutters were awash with the foul-smelling waste cast carelessly from the broken windows patched with brown paper. Flea-bitten dogs scratched themselves vigorously, skeletal cats scrounged waste heaps fruitlessly, for they had already been scavenged several times over by the hordes of barefoot urchins too young to be harnessed into a more formal life of crime.

Clutching her cloak tightly around her, Henrietta picked her way carefully through the detritus, trying hard not to breathe too deeply, for the stench was overpowering. Profoundly glad of Rafe's protective presence, she stayed as close to him as it was possible to be without tripping him up. She was utterly appalled at the destitution and vice on blatant display, horrified by the poverty and filth so close to the affluence of the London Rafe had shown her. Nothing, not even the beggars at St Paul's, had prepared her for this. She had had no idea that such a miserable life—if life it could be called—was being scraped out by so many people in their own capital. It made her feel very small, when she thought back to her own too-easily vaunted opinions. She knew nothing. She resolved to find out more, once this was over. It would give her a purpose, finding a way to really make a difference. And when she did, she told herself stoutly, she would feel a lot better.

Ahead of them, Benjamin strode confidently, looking neither to the right nor left, a stout cane held purposefully in his sabre hand. 'By the way, Meg told me this morning what you did for Mr Forbes,' Henrietta said.

'Meg should keep her mouth shut. It was nothing.'

'Meg doesn't think it nothing, and nor does Mr Forbes. If it hadn't been for you, she said, Mr Forbes would likely have starved.'

'She exaggerates. In any case, if Benjamin hadn't come to my rescue, I would likely have been killed.'

'Five of them, Meg said. Footpads. And in the middle of Piccadilly, too.'

'Yes, but it was nigh on two in the morning.'

'What were you doing out and about at that time?'

'Walking. I was just walking.' It was the night Julia had told him her news. Unable to believe it, completely taken aback by the conflicting emotions that swamped him, he'd gone walking to give his head time to clear. His first, most overpowering, feeling had been shock. He hadn't really believed it would happen. He hadn't actually thought about it becoming real. It was quickly followed by despair, for even so short a time after their grand reunion, he knew it had been a mistake to take Julia back. An even bigger mistake, an earth-shattering mistake, was the one he was going to have to deal with as a result.

A tug on his sleeve made Rafe realise he'd come to a stop in the middle of Petticoat Lane. 'You were miles away,' Henrietta said.

'And if we don't hurry up, so too will Benjamin be,' Rafe replied, drawing a curtain in front of his memories. 'Let us make haste and catch him up, this is not the kind of area to get lost in.'

Though Henrietta was desperate to ask what had brought that haunted look of his back, there were more pressing concerns. Like the straggle of urchins grabbing on to Rafe's coat-tails and her cloak, their saucer-eyed faces full of unspoken pleas. She knew that giving them money would be a huge mistake, they would be besieged, but still, her heart was smitten at the sight. 'There must be something to be done for those poor souls,' she said to Rafe. 'They are so dirty and so hungry.'

'And there are too many of them. I told you.'

'Yes,' she said sadly. 'But—'

'Here we are,' Benjamin said from up ahead, pointing to a dark alley. 'Up that set of stairs there—hold on tight, mind, they're coming away from the wall.'

The three of them made their precarious way to the first floor of the tenement. A sharp rap on the door with Benjamin's stick resulted in a shuffling noise on the other side, but the door remained resolutely closed.

'Larry, Scouse Larry!'

Chapter Eight

The door opened a fraction, sufficient for a face to peer out into the gloom of the stairwell. 'Who are you? What do you want? What's that mort doing here?'

Before anyone could stop her, Henrietta stepped forwards. 'I am the—the mort you hit over the head and left for dead in a ditch,' she said, 'and you are the oaf who did it.' She gave the door a violent push, which took the housebreaker sufficiently by surprise to send him staggering back into the room, allowing Henrietta, quickly followed by Rafe, to enter. Benjamin remained outside and on guard.

It was dark, was the overwhelming impression, and immensely stuffy, with smoke billowing from a fireplace over which was suspended a large iron pot. Smoke was billowing from that, too, and a smell of something rancid which, Henrietta suspected, had formed the basis for Scouse Larry's previous week's suppers.

The man himself was short, wiry of build, with a surprising shock of ginger hair and a pair of exceedingly bushy eyebrows. The patch was on his right eye, made of black leather and tied behind his head. Despite the heat of the room, he wore a greasy black greatcoat in addition to a green corduroy jacket, a navy waistcoat, a shirt that may once have been white, nankeen breeches and a pair of boots through one of which his bare toe protruded.

Having no option but to allow the small and horribly familiar female along with her intimidating companion into his lair, Scouse Larry retreated to his stool by the fire. 'I don't know what you're on about,' he said to Henrietta in a wheedling tone. 'Never seen you before in me life.'

Since she had awoken in Woodfield Manor, Henrietta had been too caught up in the chain of events that had followed to give the man who had assaulted her much thought. Even this morning, on their way through the stews to meet him face to face, she had been much more concerned with what he would tell her about the crime of which she had been accused, and had therefore been completely unprepared for the surge of anger that gripped her when she saw him—and recognised him instantly.

'Liar!' she exclaimed, making her way purposefully across to the stool on which the housebreaker cowered. 'Even without that eyepatch, I would know you instantly. That coat for a start,' she said, wrinkling her nose, 'it smells horribly familiar.'

Scouse Larry looked outraged. 'This here coat was given me by Honest Jack hisself. Look at them pockets, could have been made for a budge, pockets like these. Not much they can't hold.'

'They were certainly commodious enough to conceal whatever you used to beat me around the head,' Henrietta said indignantly. She pushed back her cloak and stood with her hands on her hips, her face flushed from a combination of the oppressive heat of the room and the fire of her temper. Watching her fearlessly confronting the man who, small as he was, had proved himself perfectly capable of overpowering her, Rafe felt a stab of pride, though he was not precisely certain that her tactics would prove helpful.

He hadn't expected her to rush into this as she had done. He hadn't expected to have to work so hard to keep his hands, which had instinctively formed into fists, by his side. It occurred to him for the first time that if he had *not* been out riding so early, if he *had* been able to sleep, then he would not have encountered Henrietta. She might well have died. That this pathetic excuse of a man, whose very existence he had sorely doubted, had been responsible for that made Rafe's blood boil. He could think of nothing more satisfying than beating the cur to a pulp.

His fists clenched tighter, but he restrained himself with some difficulty. Violence would not provide the answers they sought. Answers that would take them to the root of the conundrum, for now that he had set eyes upon Scouse Larry, Rafe knew for certain that he was no criminal mastermind. A dupe, at the tail end of things most likely. What they needed was to track down the dog that had wagged this particular tail. Ben was right. There was something rum about this whole affair. 'Who put you up to this? I refuse to believe you have either the brains, the skill or even the guts necessary to carry out such an audacious crime. Come on, man, out with it.'

The housebreaker reeled back in astonishment. 'Audacious crime? What audacious crime? What the hell you talking about?'

Henrietta cast him a contemptuous look. 'You know perfectly well what we're talking about. The emeralds.'

'You what?'

'The Ipswich emeralds. The heirlooms that you stole.'

'Ipswich emeralds!' Scouse Larry fell back on to his stool. 'I didn't. I did no such thing! I don't know— What do you mean?'

'Enough of this,' Rafe said sharply. 'The game is up. Miss Markham here remembers you perfectly. We want the truth. You can tell it to us or you can tell it to the authorities at Bow Street. There is a Runner there who will be more than happy to lend you an ear.'

'A Runner?' Scouse Larry's eyes darted from Henrietta to Rafe, his countenance ashen beneath the grime. 'Are you on the level?'

'I assure you. Lady Ipswich called in the Runners the morning after the crime.'

'The morning after you hit me over the head and left me for dead,' Henrietta said indignantly.

'I didn't mean— You got in the way. I panicked. I didn't mean— I didn't steal no emeralds, I swear. She promised. She promised it was a lark. I never thought— Bloody Norah! The double-crossing bitch!'

'Who?'

'What the devil are you talking about?'

'Her!' Scouse Larry growled. 'It was her.'

'Henrietta?' Rafe said incredulously.

'Who? No, bloody Lady La-di-da Ipswich. It was her that hired me.'

'Lady Ipswich! That is nonsense—why on earth would she want to steal her own jewellery?' Henrietta looked at Rafe in confusion. 'And why would she then accuse me when she must have known perfectly well— I don't understand.'

'Describe her to me and how you met,' Rafe said to Scouse Larry. 'I need proof that you are not spinning tales to save your neck.'

'I never spoke to her but twice,' Scouse Larry said sullenly. 'At the Assizes it was, she said she was looking for someone to do her a bit of an unconventional service, no questions asked. Offered to find me a witness to get me off—which she did—and a goodly purse to boot, so—like I said, I only spoke to her the two times, but I asked about later and I know it was her. Lady Helen Ipswich. My orders was to fake a break-in at her country estate and disappear. Which is what I would've done if Missy here hadn't 'ave stuck her oar in, opening her mouth as if she was about to scream fit to bust. I had to hit her.'

'You could have killed her.'

'I told you,' Scouse Larry said, turning to Henrietta, 'I panicked, no offence intended, miss.'

'And you did not steal anything?'

'I didn't even go into the bloody house. I told you, on me mother's life, I never stole no emeralds.'

'Though I doubt very much that your mother's life holds any value for you,' Rafe said, 'I believe you.'

'She sold them herself, I reckon.'

'I suspect you are right. Rundell & Bridge, on

Ludgate Hill most likely,' Rafe said. 'They have back rooms for such business, I've heard.'

'I still don't understand,' Henrietta said plaintively. 'Why, then, did Lady Ipswich accuse me of being an accomplice?'

Scouse Larry looked startled. 'Did she now?'

'Obviously your being able to identify the house-breaker queered her pitch, as they say,' Rafe said drily. 'And unfortunately this particular housebreaker is rather a distinctive one. Rather than take the risk of him being traced and blowing the whistle on her scheme, she decided to have you locked up where you could do no harm.'

'Let's face it, missy,' Scouse Larry said, nodding furiously, 'she done us both up like a pair of kippers.'

'Yes, she did,' Henrietta said, her voice faltering.

Rafe put a reassuring arm around her shoulders. She was piteously pale and shaking, obviously shocked to the core at the extent of Helen Ipswich's perfidy. 'What is this, my bold Henrietta?' he said breezily. 'Come, don't faint on me now, the floorboards here are quite unsavoury.'

'I won't. I don't faint,' Henrietta said with a wan smile.

'Of course you don't.' Anxious now to be gone, Rafe turned his attention back to Scouse Larry. 'We may need to call on you further if Helen Ipswich requires persuading to do the decent thing, but I sincerely hope not, for brief though this acquaintance has been, it is sufficient to make me quite certain I have no wish to extend it. Much as I'm sure you wish to disappear with-out trace, you will oblige me by remaining on hand until we have this matter cleared up. Present yourself at the Mouse and Vole tomorrow, by which time I will know whether or not Helen Ipswich requires convincing. You will, of course, be remunerated for your trouble, but in turn I require you to keep that mouth of yours firmly closed as to this day's events. Mr Forbes will inform me if you do not and I assure you,' Rafe said, his words all the more menacing for being so quietly spoken, 'that you will not be able to avoid the consequences.' As the housebreaker made to duck, Rafe grabbed him by the throat. His strong fingers tightened on the man's neck, making him gurgle. 'Are we clear?'

Scouse Larry gurgled again, his arms flailing helplessly.

'Excellent,' Rafe said, letting go and allowing him to crumple to the floor. 'I'll take that as a yes. Come, Henrietta, I think our work here is done.'

Rafe took her arm. He left the room without a backwards glance, giving her no option but to follow him. He strode so purposefully when they re-entered Petticoat Lane that both Henrietta and Benjamin struggled to keep pace with him, and though the questions buzzed around like a swarm of flies in Henrietta's mind, she had no breath to ask them. Once back out on Whitechapel Road, Rafe hailed a hack and helped Henrietta in. She was surprised, for it was but a short step to the inn, but also relieved, as her legs were really quite shaky.

'Benjamin will see you back,' Rafe said, nodding to the innkeeper to join her and closing the door behind him.

'But where— What are you going to do?' Henrietta asked, hurriedly lowering the window.

'Confront Helen Ipswich, assuming she has returned to town.'

'Then I'm coming with you.'

'No. Not this time. You are much shaken and most naturally upset by all of this. Besides, it is not beyond the realm of possibility that Helen Ipswich would have you arrested if you just turn up on her doorstep.'

'But what are you going to say to her? How will you make her— What will you do? Rafe, I don't want—'

'Henrietta, look at you, you are in no fit state for confrontations. Just for once, trust me to deal with the matter alone.'

'I do trust you,' she said, 'but—'

'Then act as if you do,' he replied tersely, signalling to the cabbie to go.

The horses pulled away. Leaning out of the window, she saw Rafe hail another hack, heading in the opposite direction.

'Do you think he'll be long?' she asked Benjamin forlornly.

The innkeeper patted her hand. 'No longer than he has to be, don't you worry.'

Which was much easier said than done, Henrietta thought.

As things turned out, Rafe took rather longer than he had anticipated. Lady Ipswich's town house was situated in Upper Brook Street, just on the other side of Grosvenor Square from his own mansion in Mount Street. Though it was too early to worry about the carriages making their way to Hyde Park for the afternoon promenade, the brief hackney trip through Mayfair was fraught, for it seemed to Rafe that almost every house they passed belonged to an acquaintance he wished to avoid.

At the junction of Mount Street and Park Street, the hack was caught up in the chaos caused by a high-perch phaeton whose horses were rearing in the traces. The impatient driver, more flash than substance, was ignoring his groom's attempts to rein them in and lashing them into a frenzy with his inept handling of the whip. A town coach and barouche were attempting to pass, one either side of the phaeton, and the carriers of a sedan chair were shouting contrary directions in a misguided attempt to assist. It took almost fifteen minutes for the road to clear, for most of which Rafe had an almost unobstructed view of the porticos of his own house. Strange to say, he dwelt not on the ample supplies of clean clothes, the starched sheets and feather mattress of his own bed, nor even the prospect of a copper bath filled with copious amounts of steaming hot water. The bare, unheated chamber he shared with Henrietta at the Mouse and Vole seemed more like home. His own mansion, richly furnished and sumptuously carpeted, held no appeal at all, for it did not contain Henrietta.

Depending upon the success of his visit to Helen Ipswich, Henrietta could be freed from danger as early as this evening. Free to leave his protection. Free to carry on with her life. Without him.

He would miss her terribly. The realisation took him aback. He couldn't decide whether to be more astonished at the simple fact itself, or at the fact that it was Henrietta, of all people, who had invoked such alien feelings in him.

He would miss her. *How the hell had that happened?* He had no idea, but somehow, in the space of a few short days, being with Henrietta Markham had become an addiction. She made him laugh. She looked out at the world from behind those big brown eyes of hers in a refreshingly different way. He liked the way she looked at him, too. He more than liked the way she made him feel. Those infinitely kissable lips of hers—no, he had certainly not drunk enough of those. Just remembering her delectable body spread beneath him made him hard.

He wasn't ready to let her go. He *would not* let her go. Surely, dammit all, he could find a way of keeping her with him for a little longer? As the hack pulled up outside the late Lord Ipswich's town house, Rafe racked his brain for a solution. Obviously he could not set her up as his mistress. Appealing as the idea was of swathing her in the silks and laces she admired, of granting her some of the luxuries she had always been deprived of, he knew her better than to suggest such an arrangement. Unwilling to even let him pay for her shot at the inn without keeping a tally, she was hardly likely to allow him to pay the rent on a house for her. In any case, it felt wrong. He couldn't say why it felt wrong, but it did. No, he could not offer to make her his mistress. There must be another way. 'God dammit to hell, there must be!'

It was the fop, stopping in mid-mince to stare, that made him realise he'd caught Henrietta's habit of speaking aloud. It was the same fop, eyeing him through a jewelled quizzing glass, which made Rafe aware of his somewhat dishevelled appearance. In Whitechapel, he had been, compared to the local denizens, the picture of elegance. Here on his home turf in the smart environs of Mayfair, his creased coat and dull boots made him look decidedly shabby. He cast an anxious look around, then ascended the front steps to the town house two at a time. At least the knocker was on the door, which meant his quarry had, as he had hoped, returned to town.

Rafe was solemnly informed by her butler that, most unfortunately, Lady Ipswich was not at home at present. That same butler, knowing Lord Pentland by reputation, couldn't help wondering what on earth had happened to make the famously modish and austere Earl appear so rumpled. 'Madam is at Somerset House for the annual exhibition, my lord,' he said. 'Perhaps if you would care to call round later, or leave your card?'

'I'll wait,' Rafe said firmly, handing over his hat and gloves, giving the astonished retainer no option but to show him into the first-floor drawing room and offer him refreshments.

Rafe had refused tea, Madeira, claret and brandy, and had spent the next hour pacing up and down the room, careful to keep away from the long windows that looked out on to the street lest anyone passing glance up and recognise him. As his wait grew longer and his patience wore thin, the state of cold fury that had enveloped him at Scouse Larry's abode returned with a vengeance.

Denied the cathartic effects of planting a facer on the housebreaker, he was determined to exact revenge on Henrietta's behalf and his thoughts had taken a vicious turn. Though he could not forgive Scouse Larry for his callous treatment of Henrietta, Rafe could at least appreciate that the man had only taken on the job in order to save his neck. Helen Ipswich was a different matter. Her flamboyant lifestyle was obviously outrunning her widow's portion, and he suspected her favours were not so much in demand as they once had been. No doubt she was deep in dun territory, too deep to rely on the pluckings of a few pigeons to pull her out, else she would not be resorting to selling off the family heirlooms.

It wasn't surprising. Selling off heirlooms would mean little to a woman forced to sell her body. He didn't blame her, in a way. He'd seen it himself too often, urchins born into penury biting the hand that fed them, robbing food from their adoptive families. Force of habit, born of necessity. He could see why Helen Ipswich wouldn't place too high a value on a set of emeralds, even if they had been in her husband's family for hundreds of years. Even if they weren't hers to dispose of, but rightly belonged to her eldest son.

Though he would refuse to recognise her socially, Rafe had no personal gripe against women of her ilk. Helen Ipswich had done well for herself, some would say. That she'd done it on her back made her bad *ton* in the eyes of most. True, she'd lied, cheated and cuckolded her husband, which made her contemptible and self-seeking and selfish, but Rafe was in no position to judge anyone harshly. What she had done to Henrietta, on the other hand, was far beyond contempt. For that, she would be made to pay.

Rafe paced the length of the salon for the hundredth time. Picking up a brass toasting fork from the hearth, he swished it to and fro in time to his steps. 'Heartless bitch!' he exclaimed, remembering Henrietta's white-faced shock as she realised the infamous way she had been used, her sheer disbelief that another human being could treat her so cruelly. Henrietta, who was more concerned about what agonies her parents would suffer if they ever found out, than she was by the possibility of rotting in Newgate. Henrietta, the most honest, brave, truly good person he had ever met. What might have happened to her had she not stowed away on his phaeton he couldn't bear to imagine.

The salon door opened. Dropping the toasting fork, Rafe saw that it was bent over upon itself, mangled beyond repair.

'Well! This is indeed a fine way to treat my hospitality,' Helen Ipswich said, eyeing the ruined article with astonishment. 'I assume this is not a social call, my lord?'

When informed by her butler that the Earl of Pentland had called unannounced and was awaiting her inside, Helen Ipswich had been at first extremely pleased. After all these years, her standoffish country neighbour was calling on her. Perhaps she was finally going to be accepted by the *haut ton*. Those prized vouchers for Almack's would be hers this Season. At last!

Her triumph was short-lived, however. As she discarded her bonnet and anxiously checked her reflection in her boudoir mirror, several things colluded to disabuse her of her initial optimism. It was four in the afternoon, well past the time for morning calls. In any case, single gentlemen did not pay morning calls unaccompanied—not unless they had a certain purpose in mind, and she knew for a fact that Rafe St Alban was

not one of those. The man was a rake, but he did not
rake with the likes of her. And come to think of it, the
card of invitation she had sent for her last rout party had
been politely declined and by his secretary at that—she
doubted it had even reached his high-and-mighty lordship's eyes. No, whatever had brought Rafe St Alban
here, it was neither to exchange polite pleasantries nor
offer improper contracts.

In her drawing room, as she looked up into his hard
countenance, at those slate-grey eyes of his that met
hers with cold contempt, Helen Ipswich repressed a
shudder. There were few people capable of intimidating
her, but there was something about this man that warned
her he was not to be trifled with. Wisely, she refrained
from extending her hand and instead took a seat, dis-
posing the full skirts of her salmon-pink walking dress
elegantly around her. 'Well, my lord, I am sorry to have
kept you waiting. If you had perhaps informed me that
you intended calling....'

'I did not know until a short while ago that it would
be necessary.' Rafe remained standing, ignoring her
suggestion that he be seated. 'I have come upon a matter
of some import.'

Now that she had had a chance to recover her nerves,
Helen Ipswich coolly appraised her unexpected guest.
He looked tired and his boots were far from the glossy
perfection for which he was famed. His coat, too, was
somewhat creased, and as for his neckcloth—it looked
as if it had been tied without a mirror. 'We have not
seen you in town this last while,' she said sweetly.

'Since we have very few acquaintance in common,
that is hardly surprising,' Rafe replied curtly.

'I believe you were in the country until recently, like myself. A shame you did not see fit to call on me then,' Helen Ipswich continued, through gritted teeth.

'With luck, this will be my first and last visit.'

'Sir, you are impertinent.'

'And you, my lady, are a fraud.'

Lady Ipswich gasped. 'How dare you!' Beneath her delicately applied rouge, her cheeks flushed. 'I will not stand to be insulted in my own home.' Frantically trawling through her memory for a clue as to what on earth Rafe St Alban could possibly hold against her, Helen Ipswich found herself at a temporary loss. Then a truly horrible thought occurred to her, but it was instantly dismissed. She had covered her tracks too well. She flicked open a fan and applied it vigorously. 'La, my lord, I am sure I have no idea what you are talking about,' she said more confidently.

Rafe forced himself to take a seat opposite her, crossing his legs, taking his time to calm himself, to order his thoughts. Helen Ipswich was definitely rattled. He recrossed his legs. 'Then I shall enlighten you,' he said laconically. 'I require several things, none of them negotiable.'

Helen Ipswich raised a delicately plucked brow. 'Indeed? You will forgive me if I tell you, my lord, that you are impertinent. The days are long gone when I entered into any non-negotiable deal.' She permitted herself a small smile.

Rafe's brows snapped together. 'You will discover to your cost, my lady, that if you do not heed me, then the next deal you will be negotiating will be with the Newgate gatekeeper.' Ignoring her protest, he got to his feet and began to list his demands. 'The first, and most important, thing I want is for the outrageous allegations made by you concerning Henrietta Markham to be withdrawn.'

Lady Ipswich put a hand to her mouth to suppress her gasp of horror. She had no intention of going down without a fight. 'Ah, yes, Miss Markham,' she said with admirable control. 'You have surely not fallen for that cock-and-bull story she told you?'

'You mean the one where she was hit over the head by a housebreaker, then accused by you as an accessory and threatened with incarceration? Not only do I believe her, I have irrefutable proof that she is telling the truth.'

'What proof?'

'Why, the best proof of all, from the horse's mouth,' Rafe said carefully. He watched as the full import of what he had said sank in. Even Helen Ipswich's perfect maquillage could not disguise the grey tinge to her complexion. Her hands were visibly shaking.

'I've met the gentleman you employed to fake the break-in, who goes by the somewhat colourful sobriquet of Scouse Larry, and had a most enlightening conversation with him.'

Helen Ipswich's mouth dropped open most unbecomingly, her fan clattered to the floor, but she made a valiant attempt to pull herself together, sitting up straight in her seat and clasping her fingers tightly together. 'You have quite lost me, I'm afraid.' She sounded as if a sharp stone had caught in her throat. 'I have no idea what you're talking about.'

In contrast, Rafe's tone was smooth. 'He was not over-eager to confess, your stooge, but he was even less eager to go to the gallows for a crime he did not commit. When he found out that you'd duped him, he was most keen to cooperate. The facts are irrefutable. You paid him to fake a break-in in order to cover your own tracks. You'd already sold your emeralds by then. What was it, gambling debts?' He could tell by the way she flinched that he'd hit the mark. 'Don't you know that you shouldn't play if you can't pay, my lady? Very bad *ton*. But then, how would you know?'

'I did not—'

Rafe raised a hand imperiously. 'Do not even attempt to deny it. You will call off that Runner of yours, tell him there was no robbery. Tell him your emeralds were away being cleaned at the jewellers and it slipped your mind. Tell him the housebreaker was a figment of your fevered imagination. Tell him the whole thing was a mean trick being played on you by one of your friends. Tell him anything you like, provided you make it clear there was no crime.'

'But I can't do that. I'll look a complete fool.'

'If you don't, that will be the least of your worries. I'll make you a social outcast, a pariah. To say nothing of ensuring that it is known you are reduced to selling off your children's inheritance.'

Lady Ipswich clutched at her bosom.

Rafe settled back into his chair. Helen Ipswich looked like a whipped cur. 'Let's face facts—were it not for the protection of your dead husband's name, you wouldn't even be tolerated on the fringes of society, as you are now. Your reputation is as flimsy as gossamer; one puff from me and you will be quite gone. Do you really want that?'

'You wouldn't.'

'You know perfectly well that I would and I could.'

She did, perfectly well. It was one thing for the Earl of Pentland to look down his aristocratic nose at her from a distance, but quite another for him to publicly spurn her, and that was all it would take for uncomfortable questions to be raised and all those years of discretion undone. 'How can I tell them it was a mistake? What the devil do you care, anyway, about that damned governess? A mere nobody! Why, she—'

Rafe was towering over her before she could move to avoid him. She shrank back in her chair, her hands instinctively at her throat as if to prevent him throttling her—for that is what he looked as if he would do.

'Unlike you, Henrietta Markham has scruples. Not only is she innocent, the accusations you have levelled upon her weigh extremely heavy. She has been crushed by your maligning her. God dammit, she was in your employ. You were responsible for her. Could not you of all people understand what it is to be alone and helpless? Deception is your stock-in-trade, my lady. I'm sure you will come up with some plausible tale to tell the authorities. I don't give a damn what it is, provided you succeed. Do I make myself perfectly plain?'

Helen Ipswich nodded slowly.

'And I want it done now. Today. At once. Or I fear the rumours will begin to fly, and the paste copies you have no doubt had made of your damned emeralds will be subject to rather closer inspection than they can bear. Are we clear upon that, too?'

Another reluctant nod. Helen Ipswich licked her lips.

They felt dry and thin, despite the carmine she had applied earlier.

'Then I will take my leave, madam. I trust our paths will not have to cross again.'

'I will ensure that they do not,' Helen Ipswich said, through very gritted teeth. 'I will do as you ask.'

'I never doubted it,' Rafe replied contemptuously. 'Self-preservation often walks hand in hand with self-interest. You are endowed with an acute sense of both. I will bid you goodbye.'

The door closed behind him. Helen Ipswich sat for some moments, pleating the elegant fringe that bordered her walking dress, her mind seeking frantically for another way out, darting first one way and another, like a rat in a trap. But there was no other way and she was never a woman to waste energy repining over lost causes.

With a resigned sigh she rose, rang the bell by the fireplace to summon her butler and demanded that her footman be sent immediately to Bow Street and not to return without either the magistrate or a certain Runner, as she had important news for them. Then she set her mind to the tricky task of fabricating a plausible story to tell them.

Henrietta paced up and down the bedchamber at the Mouse and Vole, anxiously checking the time on the clock tower outside. She felt as if she had been whirled too fast in a country jig. Her mind was positively reeling. To have been falsely accused was bad enough, but to discover it had been a quite deliberate act! That someone could be so utterly self-serving, and that someone then turn out to be her employer, was beyond belief. And yet it must be true. Why would Scouse Larry lie?

In the course of these last three days at the Mouse and Vole, while Benjamin had attempted to track down the thief, she had almost forgotten the shame and horror of the accusations levelled against her. Now they returned with full force. When she thought of how close she had come to being arrested, of the real possibility that she would have been found guilty—dear heavens, she felt as if she might faint for the first time in her life. And all because Lady Ipswich needed money. Not that she could really need money, not in the way those people in Petticoat Lane needed it. That was real need! And not even need such as that would justify putting two other innocent lives in danger. A criminal Scouse Larry might be, but he didn't deserve to be hanged. Henrietta's blood positively boiled.

'Let Rafe make her confess,' she said fervently. 'Please, let Rafe make her confess and let her beg for forgiveness on bended knees,' she added, warming to the subject. 'Let her promise to change. Let her see the error of her ways. Oh, and let her call off the Runners. Please let her call off the Runners.'

Where was Rafe? Perhaps Lady Ipswich was not in town, after all. Would he have travelled back to the country in search of her? What if he could not persuade her to drop the charges? What if she simply denied it all? But Rafe would find a way to persuade Lady Ipswich. Most likely he was late because—because…

Where was Rafe?

The clock outside chimed another hour. The time was passing interminably slowly. Pulling a pair of woollen stockings, which were long overdue for darning, from her bandbox, Henrietta threaded a needle and sat down on the bed. He would be back as soon as he could. She had utter faith in him, even if she had no idea where he was and what he was doing.

She set a neat stitch, then paused, her needle in midair. She missed him. She would miss him a lot more in the very near future, when all of this was over. It was a most melancholy fact, and she wished fervently that it had not occurred to her just now, but the thing she had most wanted, to clear her name, was now the thing which would deprive her of her heart's desire.

Her heart's desire.

She loved him.

Oh, dear heavens! She loved him. She was in love with Rafe St Alban. Her needle dropped into her lap. She loved him. It was ridiculous. Impossible. And absolutely, irrefutably true. The Honourable Rafe St Alban, Earl of Pentland, Baron of Gyle and who knows what other titles he possessed—*this* man, *this* one, was the love of her life. Of course he was!

Of course. The smile that was tugging at the corners of her mouth faded. She could not be in love with him. But why else did she feel as she did whenever he was near her? That tingling, bubbling, breathless feeling—what else could that be but love? Why else did she desire him and only him, save that she loved him? Why else had she never felt any of this before? Because she hadn't met him. Because she was still waiting to meet him. Because she would only ever feel any of this for him. Only him.

She loved him. Surely love conquered all? Surely

love could redeem and reform? Surely if he knew—if he could see—if he could…

'Could what, Henrietta?' she asked herself. 'Love you?'

She shivered. Rafe said he could never love again. Rafe said he would never marry again. But Rafe had also said that Henrietta made him break his own rules.

'He said I turn his world upside down,' she said, picking up her needle. 'He said I make him feel. Surely one feeling can lead to another, more profound feeling?' In the first flush of optimism that love inspires, she thought it might. The desperate yearning to have it so ensured that any doubts were banished to the cold recesses of her mind, forbidden even the faint tapping on the window of reality. She loved him. She longed for him to love her. It could happen. It would!

The clock chimed another hour. Her needle was making very desultory progress on the threadbare patch of her stocking, so entranced was she by the dreams she was weaving, that she was barely aware of time passing, until the door opened. Needle, stocking and her spare skein of wool went flying as Henrietta launched herself at the tall figure in the doorway.

Chapter Nine

'You're back. You've been an age. I've been so worried.' Her arms were around his neck before she could stop herself, her body pressed safe against his.

Rafe kicked shut the door, but made no attempt to disentangle himself. He closed his eyes and wrapped his arms around her and leant his chin on her curls and breathed in her scent. It felt so good. She felt so good. 'Lady Ipswich was out when I got there. I had to wait,' he said.

'But you saw her?' With her cheek pressed against his chest, her voice was muffled.

'Yes, I saw her. And it took a bit of persuasion, but she admitted to it all in the end. She will call off her Runner.'

'Oh, my God! I can't believe it. Really? Truly?'

Henrietta raised a shining face to his. Her eyes were dark chocolate-coloured tonight, the gold flecks in them more pronounced. She looked as if he had just given her something priceless. Perhaps he had. 'Really,' Rafe said, planting a kiss on her upturned nose. 'Truly.'

'And I will be cleared of all her accusations?'

'All of them.'

'Oh, Rafe! You're wonderful. I never doubted— But I didn't know how and— But you are simply marvellous.' She pressed a fervent kiss on his gloved hand. 'Sit down and tell me *everything*.'

Rafe laughed. Tossing his hat and gloves on to the table, he pulled her down on the bed beside him and gave her an account of his interview. He could not have asked for a more enthusiastic or grateful audience. Henrietta clapped her hands, praised his ingenuity and positively hissed at Helen Ipswich's perfidy, as if she were the audience at a melodrama. He had thought he understood how much of a burden the crime had weighed upon her, but he realised, seeing her unalloyed delight at it being removed, how much he had underestimated it. He felt good. He felt he had done something good for the first time in ages. 'So, you can now stop fretting about Newgate,' he said, stroking a wayward curl from her cheek.

'And gaol fever,' Henrietta said with a chuckle. The relief was so intense, she felt almost drunk with it. 'I can't tell you how much this means to me,' she said before placing a hand on his shoulder and brushing his cheek with her mouth. A thank-you kiss, no more. But the taste of his skin made her lips linger and he moved his face just a fraction, so that they lingered on his mouth. 'Sorry, I didn't mean— I just wanted to...' She tried to shuffle away from him, but he restrained her. She tried to ignore the sharp stab of awareness that accelerated her breathing. 'Are you hungry?'

'Ravenous,' Rafe murmured, nuzzling his cheek against hers.

'Shall I— Would you like me to ask Meg to send up some food?'

'I'm not that kind of hungry,' Rafe said, kissing her. Then he kissed her again, pulling her closer, absorbing the feel of her, the softness, the curves, the sweetness, the delicious taste of her, with every part of him. He kissed her and she wrapped her arms around him and pulled his head down and kissed him back just exactly as if she felt the same.

Passion flared and quickly, greedily, consumed them. Their kisses fired it, the memory of their previous pleasures fuelled it, the traumatic events of the day lent it an edge of desperation, stood them high on a precipice from which they yearned to tumble.

Henrietta kissed and clutched and moaned and pressed her lips, her breasts, her thighs, closer and closer to the man she loved so desperately, the man she so desperately wanted to love her back. Clothes ripped and were frantically discarded. Rafe's hands on her face, on her arms, her shoulders, her waist, stoked heat and fire and flame, making her burn, searing her, so that the slow build, the gentle climb, to her first climax seemed tame by comparison. This heat, this wild desire, this not-to-be-denied, aching, pulsing need, was beyond anything she had ever dreamed of. If she did not—if he did not—she would die. She would die, anyway, of this, and she didn't care.

His teeth nipped at her lower lip. His tongue thrust against hers. His hands moulded and melded, making of her whatever he wanted and making her want it, too. Vaguely, she heard her laces rip, felt a flutter of a breeze as her gown fell to the floor, then heat again as he picked her up and threw her on to the bed. His chest was bare. Sweat highlighted the broad sweep of his shoulders, the ripple of his muscles, the flex of his sinews. As he lay down on the bed beside her, she rained kisses over him, panting wildly, careless of the picture she made, caught up in this feral, elemental need to take and be taken, to absorb him, to be absorbed, to climb until she could no longer breathe, to heat until she ignited.

She struggled out of her chemise. Wearing only her stockings and garters she lay back on the bed, watching entranced as he removed the remainder of his clothing. His chest heaved with his efforts to breathe. His manhood stood magnificently erect, curved and proud, making her own muscles clench in anticipation.

He kissed her again, on the mouth. He kissed her nipples, sucking each into an aching sweetness that made her writhe. His hands dipped into the damp folds of her sex, making her writhe all the more. He muttered her name. She clung to him, pressed herself against him, kissed him and writhed again as his fingers stroked her sex, quickly, quickly, not quickly enough. She wanted this, and him, and now. She loved him. She wanted him to love her. She wanted to show him how much she loved him. If he knew—if he could see—if he could feel how much, then surely…

'Now, now, now,' she muttered, clutching at his back, her fingernails scoring down his spine, sinking into the taut curves of his buttocks. He stroked her harder, kissed her harder and she felt herself high on a cusp, and clung to it, waiting, clinging, panting. 'Now, oh please, now,' she panted, clutching at his shoulders as she tipped over and began to fall.

Rafe kissed her deeply. The contractions of her climax were unbelievably exciting. He was throbbing, pulsing in response, his shaft so hard he thought it would explode, yet still he had to ask her.

'Are you sure? Henrietta,' he said, breathing hard, 'are you sure?'

'Rafe, please. I want— I'm sure. I promise. Please.'

He couldn't resist any more. He couldn't wait any more. Right now, it felt as if his whole life had been hurtling towards this moment. Tipping her bottom up, he angled himself carefully and entered her, and had to stop, wait, stop, because the sensation of her pulsing around him was almost too much and he didn't want it to be over, not yet, not ever, not yet.

She was tight and hot and wet. He pushed, past the slight resistance of her maidenhead into the glorious heat of her, and caught his breath on a harsh cry. He had never, never, never… 'Henrietta. Oh God, Henrietta.' He thrust and moaned, and felt her cleave to him and hold him and enfold him, the sweetest, most intoxicating feeling. He thrust again and this time she was there with him, and again, and she was there, too, and again, as if they were made for this, as if this were some secret only they could share.

She had thought herself lost in the heights of ecstasy, but now she knew it was but a false summit. All of him, all of his hard velvet thickness, was inside her and she had never dreamed, never, that it could be so marvellous, this filling and emptying, filling and emptying, and each time he filled her more, finding depths in her that she couldn't believe existed, taking her higher with him with each thrust, spiralling her up and up and up until she really was at the top, giddy with being at the top, burning and freezing with being at the top, and he thrust high inside her and she toppled over the edge of the abyss, feeling as though she would pass out from the intensity of it. Then she felt him swell and withdraw just before his own climax exploded, making him cry out, a low groan dragged from him, which he seemed reluctant to release.

He held her so tightly that she could not breathe. Tears tracked down her cheeks and she made no attempt to stop them. He licked them away, saying he was sorry, and she stroked his silken crop of hair and told him that no, no, no, he hadn't hurt her, not even a little.

He planted a soft kiss on the cushion of her lips. Nestling her close, he couldn't have said how he felt, even if he tried. He felt strange. Utterly sated, utterly empty and yet somehow quite complete.

Henrietta's heart came slowly back down to a level that allowed her to breathe normally. She lay mindless, aware only of Rafe's arms around her, his legs over her, luxuriating in the euphoric aftermath of what had been, for her, a life-changing experience.

She had made love to the man she loved. For those ecstatic, blissful minutes he had been inside her, they had been joined. One. Surely he had felt it, too? He cared. He really cared. He did not love her, but despite all the warnings he had given her, as she lay replete, she allowed herself to hope that he might, one day. He was an honourable man. He would not have made love to her unless he had meant—*meant what?*

How could she be so sure he meant anything at all? This had always been an interlude for Rafe, an escape from whatever it was in his own life that he was trying to avoid. She had always had much more at stake. Her good name. Her freedom. She just hadn't expected to lose her heart as well. But she had, irrevocably.

Propping herself up on her elbow, Henrietta forced a bright smile. 'So, this will be the last night we will be required to stay here,' she said, determined at least to say it before he did. 'You will think me foolish, but I have come to think of this little room as home.'

Rafe twined one of her curls around his finger. 'No, I don't think you are foolish, I myself have become inordinately fond of this pokey little room, if not the unutterably uncomfortable mattress. Henrietta, have you given any thought to what you will do next?'

Her heart began to beat frantically. She tried to quell the panic, tried to cling on to her certainties, but of a sudden they seemed not to be so certain. He would not love. He would not marry. He had said so, but she hadn't listened. Was he about to brush her off politely? The utter contentment of their lovemaking fled like a thief from the scene of a crime. 'I don't know,' Henrietta said. 'However Lady Ipswich clears my name, I doubt she'll give me a reference and, without one, I am not like to find a new position very easily.'

'I have to admit, I have become used to being your protector these last few days.'

'Oh.' Her heart stopped, then started again even more quickly. Now she felt quite sick. She daren't hope, but she hoped all the same. She pushed herself upright, the better to see his face. Eyes indigo blue. A slight smile. Oh God, please. Please. Oh please.

'It is a position I am loath to surrender just yet,' Rafe said.

Just yet! If she had been standing, her knees would have given way, crumpling like her hopes. Whatever he was offering was not of a permanent nature. 'Just yet?' She sounded as if she was being strangled. She felt as if she was. 'What do you mean?'

'You told me you had no wish to go to Ireland to join your parents, I'm assuming that you haven't changed your mind?'

'No, I haven't, but…'

'And from what you've told me, you've no other relatives who would take you in?'

'There is my aunt, Mama's sister, but…'

'No doubt some crotchety old widow who lives in seclusion in the country, surrounded by her cats.'

'Well, actually, she—'

'No, we need to find you somewhere to stay in London, till your parents return. Clearly you cannot stay with me. Tempting though it is to offer, I know that would be wholly inappropriate.'

Rafe frowned, tapping his finger on the sheet. 'I have it!' Why had he not thought of it before? 'I've got the perfect solution.'

'What?' *What?* Hope again, irrational hope, flaring up like a candle caught in a draught. 'What is it, Rafe? What have you not thought of before?'

'My grandmother.'

'Your grandmother?' Henrietta's face fell. 'What has your grandmother got to do with me?'

'She is in her ninth decade and, in my opinion, much in need of a companion.'

'She does not sound to me like someone who needs a companion,' Henrietta said dubiously, having conjured up a fairly accurate picture of the indomitable Dowager Countess. 'And even if she did, I still don't understand what it has to do with me.'

'Don't be obtuse, Henrietta, I mean you would be a perfect companion for her. You are neither of you reticent when it comes to expressing your opinions, nor indeed are either of you short of opinions, come to that. I think you will suit very well. My grandmother lives most of the year in London. I could do with visiting her more often—she is my only close relative, after all,' Rafe said, with growing enthusiasm. 'And though she is elderly, she is fiercely independent and takes great pride in having a full engagement book,' he continued, so taken with his idea that he failed to notice Henrietta's horrified expression as realisation of what he was actually proposing dawned. 'You wouldn't be tied to her apron strings, there would be plenty of time for you and me to continue with our—our—to continue to spend time together. You will want to see more of London,' he concluded ingeniously. 'What could be more natural than that I act as your guide? What do you say?'

She said nothing, unable quite to believe what she was hearing, equally unable to believe that he could so misread her character. What he was proposing sounded remarkably like a proposition. An improper one. What he was proposing sounded—it sounded—it sounded like something a rake would say!

'Henrietta? What do you think?'

'I'm not sure what to think,' she said, praying that he would say something, anything, to contradict her assessment of his motives.

'I don't want to let you go. Not yet. I've come to—you must know that I have come to care for you, Henrietta. I thought you had come to care for me.'

She stared at him, nonplussed. He had no idea how much she cared. No idea at all. Just as she had underestimated how determined he was to limit his own feelings. He had warned her. It was her own fault.

'Henrietta?'

'You're asking me to be your mistress.'

'No! I would not…'

'Then what are you suggesting?'

'I just wanted— I want— I thought you wanted…' Rafe ran his fingers through his hair, frowning heavily. This wasn't going as it should. 'I am simply trying to find a way of not ending this.'

'Ending what?' Henrietta demanded. She hadn't realised how high she had been flying the flag of her hopes. It fluttered down to earth now, in total freefall. 'Did you think that by dressing it up as something else I wouldn't realise what it was you were asking? Do you really think I rate myself so low as to consider such a proposal, let alone what it says of your opinion of your unwitting grandmother, from whose house our *affaire* is to be conducted.'

'Henrietta, you're twisting it all. I just want—'

'To have me available whenever you fancy slaking

your thirst,' she said bitterly, resorting to the language of the Minerva Press, her only reference point for such a conversation. 'I know perfectly well what you want.'

'That is a disgusting way to put it.'

She threw herself out of the bed, snatching her chemise from the floor and pulling it over her head. 'It was a disgusting offer.'

Was it? He hadn't meant it that way. He could see now that he had worded it badly, but dammit, he hadn't had time to think it through. Why could she not be less judgemental? Anger rose, spiced with bitterness and a shard of fear. He could not lose her. Pushing back the sheet, he strode over to her and tried to pull her back into his arms, but she pushed him away.

'God dammit, Henrietta, what is wrong with my simply wanting to find a way for us to spend a little more time together?'

'No! I won't let you—'

'What? Persuade you? Force you?' His anger, fuelled with frustration, boiled over. 'I thought you knew me better by now. I have never—'

'No, you have not. Never. You are quite right,' Henrietta admitted, with a defiant tilt of her head, curls flying wildly round her shoulders. 'All this is my fault. I thought that you—that I— I thought— I thought…' She stopped, her breathing ragged.

'Henrietta, can't you just—?'

'No! Leave me alone. Please, Rafe. I can't. I just can't.' She poured herself a glass of water from the carafe by the bed and took several slow sips, willing herself to calm down. It was not his fault. It was her fault. She hadn't listened. But she hadn't listened because she didn't want to. 'What an idiot I've been,' she muttered.

He had pulled on his breeches. Bare-chested, still glistening with sweat from their lovemaking, his hair standing up in spikes, he looked devastatingly handsome. Her heart ached with love for him. There was confusion and hurt and anger in his stormy eyes. And desire, too. She recognised it, for he had taught her very well.

For a moment, a terrible moment, she considered saying yes. She considered surrendering her principles and her will to his, just so that she would not have to say goodbye. There would be time—days, weeks, maybe even months, before he tired of her—to share more lovemaking, to build more memories. She swayed, but then pulled herself upright. It would be wrong. She could not be happy, knowing that what they were doing was wrong. It was one thing to make love in hope. She could not imagine doing so without it. She loved him. She would not have that love tainted by selling it. She would not allow herself to enter into such a demeaning relationship. Not even with Rafe. Especially not with Rafe.

She had no option but to leave. He had left her nowhere to go. Henrietta's hopes finally crashed to earth and shattered painfully. Like the heroines of the Minerva Press, she felt as if her heart was breaking. She did not want to deny him, but deny him she must, for her own sake. 'Rafe, I can't.'

It was the resolution in her voice that made him realise she meant it. That core of steel at her centre, which he had so admired. 'May I ask why not?'

'It's not enough for me.'

'Henrietta, it's more than I've ever offered anyone else since…'

'I know,' she said. 'I understand that it's more than you've offered since—since Julia, but it's still not enough.'

'Is it my reputation?'

She shook her head. 'No. I would wish—but I cannot undo. If I thought that you—that you cared enough, would come to care enough, it wouldn't matter. But I don't, you see, and I—I do. Care. Too much to put up with anything less. You see, we are from different worlds. We've always known that, Rafe, but we forgot, here. I forgot, anyway.' The tears were burning her eyes, but she wouldn't let them fall. She had only her dignity left. She clutched it around her like a swaddling blanket. 'I'm sorry.'

'I see.' He wanted to protest. To persuade. To show her by kissing her just how much she was throwing away, just how much they would both lose. But the armour he had worn for so long, and his own rakish morality, prevented him. 'I see,' Rafe said again, deliberately turning away from those big brown eyes, lest he see the hurt, lest he allow it to persuade him into something he would regret. As he picked his shirt up off the floor, he felt the dark cloud that had been his faithful companion until Henrietta had banished it, returning like a whipped cur in from the cold. He almost welcomed it. At least it was familiar. At least he knew how to manage it.

He finished dressing, throwing the rest of his possessions carelessly into his portmanteau. 'I think it's best if I sleep elsewhere tonight. In the morning, we can make arrangements for whatever you want to do.' He looked at her now, willing her to change her mind, willing her to tell him not to go.

'I'm sorry. I wish— I'm sorry.'

He shrugged.

'Rafe. Thank you. For everything. Don't go like this.'

'I am only going down the hall. I'll see you in the morning. Goodnight, Henrietta.'

'Goodbye, Rafe.'

He closed the door, subduing a horrible feeling that he was missing something important, suppressing the almost irrepressible desire to go back. Setting off in search of Benjamin, it felt as if he was walking away.

On the other side of the door, Henrietta stood frozen. Her heart seemed to crack in two. But she would not compromise herself, she told herself firmly. She would not, for if she did she was doomed. As she set about packing up her possessions into her shabby bandbox, she told herself so several more times and the tears streamed unnoticed down her face.

Chapter Ten

Two weeks later

'Well, my dear, let me take a good look at you.'
Lady Gwendolyn Lattisbury-Hythe surveyed her niece
through the silver lorgnette she habitually wore on a
ribbon hung around her neck.

The thick glass gave her eyes a fishy look, Henrietta thought, shifting nervously from one foot to the
other. Even after two weeks in her company, during
which time Mama's estranged sister had treated her with
unwavering generosity, refusing to discuss the estrange-
ment which, she said, was ancient history, Henrietta still
found her aunt rather formidable.

Lady Gwendolyn was the relict of an eminent
Whig who had, like his friend Mr Fox, divided his
time between vociferous occupation of the opposition
benches and an equally dedicated occupation of the
faro table at Brooks's. Fortunately for his spouse, Sir
Lattisbury-Hythe's fortune was considerable and his

luck rather more consistent than that of the late Mr Fox's. It had run out somewhat spectacularly one evening three years previously when, with his foot heavily bandaged from the gout, he fell down the main staircase of his country home and cracked his head open on the marble plinth upon which a bust of the Roman Emperor Tiberius was mounted.

Sir Lattisbury-Hythe's son Julius inherited the title, but not his father's temperament, being inclined towards the Tory and disinclined to sharing any more of the family fortune with Brooks's. With his mousey wife and fast-multiplying brood of mousey children, parsimonious and staid Sir Julius was content to occupy the stately pile in Sussex in which his father had met his maker, thus leaving Lady Gwendolyn free rein of the town house from which to enjoy her extremely busy London life and equally free to lament the shortcomings of her anodyne first-born.

She did both with gusto. Her parties and breakfasts were always granted the ultimate epithet of being labelled a sad crush. Despite her Whig alliances, Lady Gwendolyn was a close friend of Lady Cowper, that ardent Canningite and most powerful of Almack's patronesses, whose wit was as dry and as sharp as her ladyship's own. This Season, however, had proved a little flat for Lady Gwendolyn who, having successfully fired off each of her three daughters in consecutive years, had no chicks left to launch and only a granddaughter of some eight summers to plan for. Thus, Henrietta's wholly unexpected arrival upon her doorstep, when she had just returned from a tedious night watching the unfortunate Mr Kean being pelted with rotten fruit at Drury Lane Theatre, provided a most welcome diversion.

Too numb from the shock of her sudden flight from the Mouse and Vole to worry about the reception which might await her at the house in Berkeley Square, Henrietta's only thought had been to seek the sanctuary of a roof over her head and some time to come to terms with things. She scarcely remembered that first night, and indeed had proved incapable of providing any coherent answers to her concerned aunt's many questions. Fortunately, Lady Gwendolyn, an eminently practical woman, had taken one look at her strained, lily-white face and, deciding tomorrow was time enough for explanations, packed Henrietta off to bed with strict orders to sip upon a cup of warm milk and sleep without waking until morn.

Exhaustion had set in, and Henrietta had been only too happy to oblige. When morning had come, though the heavy weight of self-blame still threatened to suffocate her, she was determined not to show it. She had been a fool. She had allowed her desires to cloud her judgement, persuading herself that Rafe would change just because she longed for him to. The scars inflicted by his marriage to Lady Julia would not heal because he would not let them. His care for her was sincere, but shallow, and he would not allow it to deepen. Rafe was not incapable of love, but he had chosen to be.

'And the point is,' Henrietta had told herself stoically that first morning in Berkeley Square, as she woke to find a pot of hot chocolate by her bed, a huge copper bath placed behind a screen by the fireside of her chamber, 'the point is that anything less than love would only ever make me unhappy. I could perhaps sacrifice myself and my principles for someone who loved me, but not for someone who doesn't.'

She had had a very lucky escape, she had told herself firmly as she sank into the luxuriously scented water and soaped her hair. 'At least, in time, I'm sure it will feel so,' she had said mournfully, for the painful ache in her heart could not be ignored. 'In time I am sure I will accept that it could never have been and I will hardly miss him at all—or even think of him. In time.'

She had tipped a kettle of warm water over her hair to rinse out the suds and wash away the flurry of tears that dripped down her cheeks. She would not cry! She would not pity herself! This pain she was feeling was completely self-inflicted. She had fallen in love with a man who had encased his heart in ice, whose solution to pain was to numb himself, lest he feel anything of any sort again. It should be a comfort to know that she had not succumbed to the temptation of his improper offer. She would not allow her love, her precious love, to be contaminated or sullied or defiled. She had done as she ought, in walking away with her self-respect, if not her heart, intact.

'And soon, I am sure that will make me feel a lot better,' she had told her reflection forlornly, for there was no escaping the fact that part of her wished she had never left Rafe in the first place. There was a shameful, most shameful bit of her, that would have accepted his proposition, and no amount of talking to and taking in hand and resolution would make it go away entirely.

'What I need to do now is concentrate on the future,' she had muttered, pulling on her brown robe. And so it was the future that she raised with her aunt on that first morning, but Henrietta's notions did not at all meet with Lady Gwendolyn's approval. 'My niece a lowly governess!' she had exclaimed in horror, upon hearing Henrietta's somewhat truncated explanation of how she had come to arrive in Berkeley Square, following what she described as an unwarranted dismissal from her position, careful to make no mention of either emeralds or earls.

'I can't say I'm surprised that your tenure with Lady Ipswich ended in acrimony,' Lady Gwendolyn said. 'In fact, I'm rather glad of it. I had no idea that your mother had detached herself quite so fully from the world as to think that Helen Ipswich was a suitable person to entrust you to—however, I will say no more on that subject. But as to any notion of you taking up another similar position—absolutely not! And as to the notion you have of becoming a teacher in that school in Ireland!' She patted Henrietta's hand and tutted. 'Well, my dear, let us hope that it is all pie in the sky, like the rest of your mother's notions. No, don't protest, you are a sensible chit and I am sure you know as well as I do that it's true. I am simply glad that you had the good sense to come to me when you did, Henrietta. You must place yourself in my hands. I think I can promise to find you some brighter future than toiling away as a mere governess.'

She smiled benignly and Henrietta had tried very hard to smile back, even though at that moment a brighter future seemed a very long way off. 'It has been a great sadness to me that we have never met,' Lady Gwendolyn continued. 'Though I can quite understand the loyalty you must have to your mother, it does seem a shame that you have never felt yourself able take up any of my invitations to visit.'

Henrietta looked at her aunt in dismay. 'But I never received any invitations.'

'Well! That certainly explains a lot,' Lady Gwendolyn said tartly. 'Your father's doing, no doubt. I have never met him, but—'

'Oh, no, Aunt, Papa would not have…' Henrietta faltered to a halt. 'I think it must have been Mama,' she said, blushing. 'She is very—very— She has very strong views on the evils of society. On account of her—her misfortune.'

Lady Gwendolyn tapped her lorgnette in the palm of her hand. 'Well,' she said eventually, deciding that discretion was the better part of valour, much as she longed to set her niece straight, 'well, we will say no more on that subject, either, but be assured, Henrietta, that I am most pleased to have you here.'

'Oh, Aunt, and I am most pleased to be here,' Henrietta said, giving her a hug.

Lady Gwendolyn felt herself adequately rewarded. Henrietta was really unexpectedly charming, with surprisingly excellent manners, given her rusticated upbringing. The Season was well underway, but that was rather an advantage than not, for people were at that stage where a new face was most welcome. It could not be a formal launching, for apart from the fact that Henrietta seemed strangely and most adamantly opposed to the notion of finding a husband, even Lady Gwendolyn recognised she had not the authority to find her niece a match. No, not a launching, but she would show Henrietta off to the world, get her a bit of town polish and dress her to advantage, all of which would stand her in good stead for the future. It would also be fun. That her sister Guinevere would be appalled by the whole thing went without saying, which made Lady Gwendolyn all the more determined to carry it off.

Henrietta had at first been extremely reluctant, for the very last thing she wished was to bump into Rafe again, to say nothing of the fact that she was struggling not to give in to the urge to hide herself in her bedchamber most days and not come out. She reminded herself resolutely every morning that she had no wish to see him at all. Ever. As the days progressed, she missed him with an increasing intensity that was horribly difficult to hide. Several times she had found herself under her aunt's penetrating gaze and been forced to make up a white lie about missing Mama or Papa or Lady Ipswich's sons.

Soon she had run out of excuses. A few tentative enquiries informed her that Lord Pentland's town house was closed, apparently, the knocker off the door, the shutters fastened. That, coupled with Rafe's self-confessed dislike of the *ton* and its soirées, meant any encounter was highly unlikely. Henrietta began to wonder if perhaps the diversion of a month or so under her aunt's wing would be just what she needed to help her forget all about the reclusive earl, so that when Lady Gwendolyn shrewdly suggested that her niece would, in fact, be doing her a great service by accompanying her to her various engagements, her own daughters all being out of town, Henrietta was finally swayed, and Lady Gwendolyn was able to write a triumphant letter to her sister informing her of her daughter's elevation in the world.

The next two weeks had been a whirl of dress fittings, shopping trips and dancing lessons—an activity at which Henrietta was most adept, which proved to be a decidedly double-edged sword, for she could not help recalling Rafe's offer to teach her, could not help wishing herself in Rafe's arms, could not help resenting the dancing teacher for not being Rafe, then could not help but chide herself for being so very ungrateful.

She was overwhelmed by Aunt Gwendolyn's generosity and the sheer number of day dresses, promenade dresses, evening gowns and ball gowns she seemed to think a bare minimum requirement, to say nothing of the silk stockings, satin slippers, kid boots, shawls, pelisses, hats, bonnets, gloves and reticules with which to accessorise them. For the first time in her life, Henrietta felt silk next to her skin. Her chemises were of the finest lawn, lace trimmed, and there was not a trace of serviceable white cotton in her wardrobe anywhere—nor anything brown; she was determined she would never wear anything brown ever again.

She wished that Rafe could see her in her new clothes. She was terrified that he would. Tying the garters of her silk stockings, or shaking out a lace ruffle on the sleeve of her gown, she would catch herself wondering what he would think, how he would look, what he would do if only—and then the lump would form in her throat, the tears would collect in her eyes and she hated herself for being so weak.

She accompanied her aunt on a round of morning calls. She sat in her box at the opera, took ices at Gunter's and took her place in the barouche as it made its sedate way round Hyde Park at five in the afternoon. She attended several select parties, at one of which she met the rather intimidating Lady Cowper who promised her vouchers for the exclusive Almack's. Occasionally, the novel delights of Aunt Gwendolyn's glittering world stopped her thinking about that little bedchamber in the Mouse and Vole, but more often than not the contrast was too obvious to be ignored.

She felt as if she were living a double life. She felt as if she were wearing a mask. She felt lonely and angry at Rafe for making her so. She felt guilty at the lack of pleasure she took when Aunt Gwendolyn was making such an effort to entertain her. While she ate and talked and went to the play and listened to the latest gossip, she wondered what Rafe was doing and who he was with. She did not think he would miss her, though she missed him desperately. When she slept, which she did not do very well, she dreamed of him. She awoke heated and drenched in perspiration, filled with an aching longing. Time and time and time again, when she was out in the town coach with Aunt Gwendolyn, she thought she saw his elegant figure striding a little distance ahead and her heart leapt into her mouth, but it never was him.

She missed him. More than anything, she missed him. So many things she wanted to tell him, to see his lip curling in disdain at some foible she had witnessed, or the smile that turned his eyes from stormy to indigo. She felt haunted.

'There, I think that will do.'

Aunt Gwendolyn's voice brought Henrietta abruptly

back to the present, making her jump, forcing her to plaster her smile back on to her face. The figure in the mirror, who looked like a very splendid version of Henrietta, jumped and smiled rather wanly, too. 'I beg your pardon, Aunt, what did you say?'

'You were miles away, my dear. Are you nervous about tonight? You need not be, it is a private ball, there will be twenty, thirty couples only, quite a small affair. Now, tell me what you think of the gown. I think Madame LeClerc was quite wise to insist on the colour, though it is most unconventional for a débutante. And before you say it again, I know you're not a débutante in the strict sense, but this is nonetheless your first Season. And you have still not told me what you think.'

'I think I hardly recognise myself,' Henrietta said, surveying her reflection in amazement. Her curls had been pinned high on top of her head and fixed in a knot, with ringlets falling in artfully crafted natural tendrils on either side. Two hours it had taken the coiffeur to achieve the effect; so many pins had he used that Henrietta felt her head must topple over with the weight of them, though the result was undoubtedly extremely pleasing, making her look a little more mature and, if not sophisticated, at least a little less naïve. The dress, her first ever ball gown, was a full robe of burnt-orange silk cut in the French fashion, with a natural waist and a skirt that belled out from a sash, a shape which suited her curves. Indeed, Henrietta was concerned that far too much of her creamy bosom was on display, for the ruched décolleté was so low as to skim her shoulders, forming one line to the intricately puffed sleeves. It was hard to refrain from twitching the sleeves up higher.

She still could not quite believe the modiste's assertion that a combination of *mademoiselle*'s bosom and the excellent cut of the robe would keep it in place. A ruffle, the same rich golden colour as the sash, formed the hem of her gown, weighted with an intricate pattern of beading, the same pattern repeated again in the fringed shawl that Aunt Gwendolyn now draped over her shoulders.

'Mama always says that clothes do not make a woman,' Henrietta said wistfully, remembering Rafe's comment about Almack's when she'd told him the same thing, 'but I am not so sure now that she is quite right.'

'My sister was ever a featherbrain,' Lady Gwendolyn replied tartly. 'Clothes matter, as she knows perfectly well. Your mama was used to have the most exquisite taste, my dear, and you seem to have inherited it. Look at yourself. Really, I suspected you had potential when I first laid eyes on you clad in that dreadful brown gown, but I have to say, Henrietta, you have exceeded my expectations. You really are quite charming.'

Henrietta blushed. 'Am I? Really?'

Lady Gwendolyn clucked. 'You will have to learn to take a compliment in a more elegant manner than that, my dear. A lowering of the lids, a polite thank you, or, you are too kind, not an over-eager request for more.'

'Oh, I did not mean—in any case I am sure that it will not—that I will not— I'm sorry.'

'Silly puss. Come now, or we will be late. There is a fine line to be drawn between being too early and arriving with the bumpkins, and too late and arriving with the jug-bitten.'

* * *

'No! It's my first night back in town, I'll be damned if I'll spend it traipsing round a ballroom with a series of doe-eyed debs whose conversation is as insipid as their dancing is uninspired, just because you've promised your sister you'll drag me along.' Rafe poured himself a small glass of port and pushed the decanter down the table towards his friend. 'I am not a trophy to be paraded. Damn it all to hell, Lucas, I'm not going and there's an end to it.'

'Please, Rafe, do it for me. You know what Minerva's like. She fixes you with that stare of hers and it's like being confronted by a basilisk. I found myself saying yes before I even realised. Just an hour, I promise, then we'll pop down to White's.'

'I'm not in the mood for cards, any more than I'm in the mood for dancing.'

The Right Honourable Lucas Hamilton took a pinch of snuff from an elegant silver box, sneezed, took another pinch and poured himself a generous measure of port. He was a tall man, and an exceptionally thin one, whose gaunt cheeks and slightly sunken eyes had inevitably earned him the unwanted appellation of the Cadaver. His constitution was actually extremely hearty; indeed, some would say almost obscenely robust, given the maltreatment it endured and despite his willowy frame—which, were he a young lady, as Rafe delighted in pointing out, would be most fashionable.

Downing his port in one swallow, Lucas poured himself another. 'You're not much in the mood for anything, my dear chap. Even less so than normal, if I may make so bold an observation. What's got into you and where have you been these last weeks, anyway?' he asked, sliding the decanter back up the table. 'We expected you back in town an age ago.'

Rafe shrugged. 'Rusticating. I find the solitude suits me.'

'If you don't mind my saying so, you look much the worse for it. In fact,' Lucas said, 'you look like the devil.'

'Thank you, Lucas, I can always rely on you for a frank opinion.'

His friend laughed. 'Well, someone has to tell you.' He took another pinch of snuff. Rafe didn't just look like the devil, he looked as if he hadn't slept in days. He was thinner, too, and just a little more touchy than usual. Despite the fact they were dining tête-à-tête, he had remained monosyllabic throughout. 'All joshing aside, Rafe, I'm worried about you. Not woman trouble, is it?'

Rafe started. 'What makes you say that?' he snapped.

Lucas raised his eyebrows. 'Good God! It *is* a woman! Don't tell me…'

'I have no intention of telling you anything. *Not* that there is anything to tell.' Rafe pushed back his chair and got to his feet. 'If you are done drinking my cellar dry, then let us go to this blasted party of your sister's. The sooner we get there, the sooner we can leave.'

'You mean it? You'll need to change, you know, Minerva's a stickler for evening dress, so, if you don't mind, I'll continue helping myself to some more of this excellent vintage while you do so.' Lucas drained his glass, got leisurely to his feet and picked up a full decanter from the side table. If Rafe would rather dance with insipid debs than exchange confidences with his oldest friend, he must be in a really bad way.

Standing in front of the mirror in his dressing room, Rafe was thinking much the same thing. In the two weeks that had passed since he had knocked upon her chamber door to summon her for breakfast and discovered Henrietta gone, he felt as if he had been to hell and back.

Stark disbelief had been his first emotion as he looked round the empty bedchamber, at the chair that no longer had her cloak draped over it, the nightstand bereft of her brushes, a scraping of dust on the floorboards where her bandbox had been, the neatly made bed, even the pillows plumped clean of any sign of their passionate lovemaking. He'd found himself, rather preposterously, looking under that bed, as if she might have been hiding there, but all he'd found was the stocking she had been mending. He had it still, in his own portmanteau.

Neither Benjamin nor Meg had any idea what had happened. No one had seen her leave. Disbelief had given way to fear. She had no money. She had nowhere to go. The thought of her without a roof over her head, perhaps wandering the streets of Whitechapel, was terrifying. He'd combed those streets that night, stopping hackney drivers and night watchmen and anyone who would listen, asking them if they'd seen a young lady in a brown cloak, but no one had.

She'd mentioned an aunt, but he had no idea where that aunt might be. He waited in vain for word from her, a note, a letter, an offer to reimburse him for the expenses he had incurred on her behalf, anything. In Mount Street, with the knocker still removed from the door, fear gave way to anger. Didn't she realise how worried he'd be? Time dragged inexorably. He missed her smile and her laughter and her enthusiasm and her blurting out anything and everything the minute she'd thought it; and he missed her big brown eyes, and the way she looked at him, and kissed him and... He realised, though it cost him dear to admit it, even to himself in the dark of night, that he missed her like a part of him was missing.

Devil take it, how dared she do this to him!

Dammit to hell, where was she? Closeted in his town house, the dark cloud of depression that was his customary companion returned with a vengeance, but now there was no prospect of it lifting. Finally granting his butler permission to have the house opened up, Rafe paid his long-overdue visit to his grandmother, who took the news of his absolutely confirmed bachelorhood better than expected, being rather more concerned by the state of his health than his marital status. The victory that would have granted him a small crumb of comfort before he met Henrietta now meant nothing to him.

Allowing his valet to help him into his black evening coat, standing listless while that man gave a final finicky polish to his shoes and handed him his hat, gloves and cane, Rafe felt as if his life were one long, endless trek through an interminable tunnel without a glimmer of light at the end.

Walking the short distance to Grosvenor Square, he listened with half an ear as Lucas recounted some tedious *on dit* about his sister Minerva's husband's brother's attempt to race one of the new hobby-horses against the real thing in Hyde Park at promenade time, a feat that resulted in the bolting of the latter and the destruction of the former.

At Grosvenor Square, there was the usual crush of coaches and sedan chairs. Flambeaux lit the wide set of steps. A plethora of footmen in scarlet livery relieved the gentlemen of their outerwear, and Rafe and Lucas joined the queue of people waiting to be greeted by their hosts. Automatically returning greetings, nodding curtly, shaking the occasional hand, bowing when necessary, Rafe was already counting down the minutes until he could escape. Two dances at most, he thought. He would leave it up to Minerva to find him appropriate partners. At least he would be spared a waltz, which Lucas's sister thought improper.

The greeting line was long, comprising Minerva, her husband, various relatives and hangers-on. The girl, Lucas's niece, for whom all this rigmarole was in aid, had inherited the Hamilton stature and was, like her mother and uncle, thin and bony and too tall. She appeared to have none of Lucas's wit and unfortunately all of Minerva's basilisk stare, but she'd go off all the same, Rafe thought cynically, as he waited impatiently while she wrote down his name on the card dangling at her wrist, for the first country dance.

The crush was unbearable. It was too hot. Too bright. Too noisy. And the tray of claret was too far away. Pushing his way through an ante-room into the ballroom in search of one of the elusive waiters, Rafe was accosted by a formidable woman, resplendent in lavender, a mauve turban with purple feathers on her head, and a silver lorgnette held to her eyes, giving her a haddock-like appearance.

'Lord Pentland.'

Rafe bowed. One of his grandmother's younger cronies. A Whig. Husband was a friend of Fox. Tedious son. Clutch of daughters. He remembered now that the youngest had been rather amusing. 'Lady Gwendolyn.'

'I thought you were in the country.'

'As you see, I am returned.'

'I didn't expect to see you here. You so rarely bless us with your presence.'

'I came to oblige a friend.'

'Oh, Minerva's brother, of course. Lanky fellow, what's his name?'

'Lucas.'

'That's it. No doubt Minerva will have engaged you to dance with that daughter of hers. Unfortunate gal, favours her mother rather too much and has even less conversation—you'll be bored to tears.' Rafe smiled tightly and made to bow his leave, but Lady Gwendolyn tapped his arm with her closed fan. 'Just a moment, I've got someone I'd like to introduce you to. I think you'll find her a much more amusing dance partner. Has a refreshing habit of speaking her mind, just like you. You'll like her. She's my niece.'

'You are very kind, but I fear...'

'My sister's child, she is come to visit me for a few weeks. Where is— Oh, there you are, my dear, what were you doing lurking behind the pillar like that? Come here and make your curtsy. Lord Pentland, may I introduce my niece, Miss Markham.'

'Henrietta!'

'Rafe!'

Lady Gwendolyn looked from one to the other. Both were white as sheets. 'Surely you two cannot be acquainted?' But she was speaking to thin air.

Rafe pushed his way through the crowd, ignoring the curious eyes that followed them, keeping a firm grip on Henrietta's wrist, which left her no option but to follow him, no time to draw breath nor to protest nor to shake off the rush of blood to her head, which made her so dizzy that she couldn't be sure it was actually him.

But it was unmistakably him, pulling back a heavy curtain to reveal a large window embrasure, dragging her behind him into the space, where she blinked and shivered in the relative dark after the blaze of the brightly lit ballroom, in the relative cool after its oppressive, near-tropical heat. Rafe released his grip and Henrietta sank gratefully on to the padded window seat, staring blankly up at the imposing figure resplendent in full evening dress.

She was shaking. Her brain was refusing to function. Her mouth was opening and closing, but no sound was coming from it. He was here. Standing right in front of her, looking every bit as tall and dark and unfairly handsome as he always did. He was here; her heart was pounding and her breathing wasn't functioning properly and she had been wrong, so wrong to think she could cure herself of him, because here he was and all she wanted to do was hurl herself into his arms.

'Rafe. I didn't expect—I thought…'

'Where the hell have you been?'

For a few brief moments he had been simply, over-whelmingly, relieved. For something less than the minute it took him to drag her into this relative sanc-tuary, Rafe felt a surge of joy that picked him up like a huge wave. Then he tumbled from zenith to nadir as reality broke over him. She was not dead. She was not hurt. She had not been arrested and she had clearly not attempted the journey to Ireland alone. What a complete fool he had been to worry so much about her!

Cold fury rent him, the fury of a man who realises he has behaved completely out of character to no purpose at all. After these two weeks of not knowing, after two weeks of cursing her for making him miss her, and two weeks of nights tortured by dreams so vivid he woke up sweating and hard and aching, what he wanted was to vent his spleen on the person responsible. 'Well? Have you nothing to say to me? I came to your room to find you gone. Not a trace, save a stocking. No one knew what had happened. Not Benjamin, not Meg, no one.'

Henrietta could only stare at him in amazement. His anger was so unexpected. It hadn't occurred to her that she would need to explain. 'It was over between us,' she said faintly. 'I thought my going in such a way was for the best. To say goodbye would be too painful. For me, at least. I thought that was obvious.'

'For God's sake, Henrietta, I'd no idea what fate had befallen you. Did it not occur to you that I would be beside myself with worry? Well?'

His hands were on her arms now, dragging her to her feet, his firm grip bruising the exposed flesh between the tops of her long kid gloves and the delicate puffed sleeves of her gown, but she hardly noticed. Her teeth were chattering so much she could hardly speak. 'I didn't think I'd see you again. I didn't *want* to see you again.' She wriggled free from his grasp and slumped back down on to the window seat. 'Of course it didn't occur to me that you'd look for me, Rafe. Why would you? We had nothing more to say to each other.'

'*You didn't think I'd look for you?* God almighty, Henrietta! I knew you had no money. I thought you had nowhere to go. I know your opinion of me is not high, but surely you do not think me so heartless as not to care what happens to you?'

'I'm sorry. I'm sorry, I was not thinking straight. I should have let you know I was safe and well. I did not mean to cause you any more upset, quite the contrary. For that I beg your pardon.'

Rafe sank down on the window seat beside her. His thigh brushed hers, warm through the silk of her gown. Henrietta tried to move away, but he tilted her chin and scrutinised her blatantly. 'You scrub up very well, Miss Markham. I'm surprised. You led me to believe your aunt was some impoverished spinster who lived in the country.'

'I never said that. I hadn't ever met Lady Gwendolyn; it was you who assumed she lived in the country.'

'And you who made no effort to contradict me. I know what I offered you was not to your taste, but I did not deserve to be treated with such contempt.'

'Rafe, I did not—I would not! If you only knew,' Henrietta said wretchedly. 'It is not the improper nature of the proposal you made, it is what it implies of your feelings for me. Or lack of feelings.'

'You know nothing of my feelings.'

'I know you don't have any.'

'You think I don't care? What possible grounds have you for making an assumption like that?'

'I think you won't allow yourself to care. I think you are afraid to care!'

'You're damned right I am. If you knew—if you had any idea…'

'That's my point entirely, Rafe, I don't. Despite what you told me of your marriage, I still don't. Why are you so determined to deny yourself any chance of happiness?'

'Because I don't deserve it!'

'What on earth do you mean by that?'

'I can't offer you more than I already have Henrietta. You've made it perfectly clear it's not enough and I respect your decision. But I have reasons.'

'What reasons?'

'Good reasons, or rather horrible reasons.'

'Then tell me. Make me understand. At least that would be something. Please, Rafe.'

He stared at her for long moments. Make her understand. It would indeed be something. At least then she might not think so ill of him. He didn't like her thinking ill of him. 'Dammit, why not?' he said abruptly. 'In fact, I'll do better than that, I'll show you.'

'Show me what?'

'Not tonight, tomorrow. I'll call for you at ten.'

'But, Rafe…'

'Tomorrow.' He made a sketchy bow and left, pushing his way through the crowd, oblivious of the resentful looks aimed at him by his hostess and her daughter, who was now bereft of a partner for the next dance, of Lady Gwendolyn's gimlet gaze, or Lucas's infuriated one.

By the time Henrietta had sufficiently recovered from the shock of the encounter, he was gone. The room seemed to be full of tall men in black evening coats. It didn't help that the second dance was already forming. She edged her way forwards, only to have her toes trampled by a young lady in dusky pink, practising an over-energetic change. Desperately, she began to work her way round the perimeter of the floor, certain that if she could just reach the main staircase she would catch him before he left, quite uncertain of what she would say if she did, but there were just too many people in her way. It was impossible.

'My dear.'

'Aunt Gwendolyn!'

A firm hand on her back propelled her into a salon set aside for the rest and recuperation of the ladies. 'Sit here, my dear, while I summon the carriage.' Her aunt pushed her gently into a *chaise-longue*. 'My niece is overcome with the heat,' she said to the other two occupants of the room, one of whom was pinning up the lace ruffle of the other's ball gown.

Henrietta did as she was bid. When the carriage was called, she protested weakly that she was perfectly capable of going back to Berkeley Square alone, but Aunt Gwendolyn, whose nose for scandal was by now positively twitching, and whose genuine concern for her niece's welfare was matched only by her desire to hear her niece's account of her acquaintance with the aloof Lord Pentland, would not hear of it.

* * *

She held her tongue for the duration of the coach journey. Once home, she allowed Henrietta time to go upstairs to dispense with her finery while she herself removed her jewellery and replaced her ball gown with a wrapper. Only then did Lady Gwendolyn tap lightly on the door of her niece's chamber.

Henrietta was sitting at the dressing table, staring sightlessly at the mirror, but upon her ladyship's arrival she jumped to her feet and fixed a smile upon her face. 'Dear Aunt, I have been thinking that perhaps London does not suit me, after all. I have been thinking that—'

'Never mind that, child. How came you to be acquainted with Rafe St Alban?'

'Oh, it is nothing,' Henrietta said airily. 'Merely he was Lady Ipswich's neighbour and we came across one another in—in passing. The acquaintance is not of long-standing. It is—it is nothing.'

'It didn't look like nothing to me. The pair of you were staring at each other as if you'd both just seen a ghost.'

'Rafe was— Lord Pentland was not expecting to see me, being unaware of my relationship to you. I expect that was it.'

'Henrietta, has anyone ever told you that you are the most appalling liar, my dear? Just exactly like your mother. Her face is an open book, too.'

'Oh.'

'Precisely. Now, stop prevaricating and tell me what Rafe St Alban is to you.'

Henrietta opened her mouth to speak, but found she could not utter the polite lies which she knew she ought.

Her mouth trembled. Tears filled her eyes. 'Everything,' she sobbed. 'Rafe St Alban is everything to me and I am absolutely nothing to him and— Oh, Aunt Gwendolyn, I love him so much.'

It was not to be expected that such an admission would fill her ladyship's heart with joy. In fact, Lady Gwendolyn's jaw dropped. She groped in vain for her lorgnette. 'But how came you to be—when—what?'

'Please don't ask me to explain.'

But Lady Gwendolyn, a veteran wife of a veteran politician, was relentless. It was like extracting teeth, requiring skill and determination on her part, and resulting in a great deal of suffering on the part of her niece, but she was soon in command of the entire sorry tale.

'You do realise, my dear, that Rafe St Alban is a hardened womaniser? If any of this got out, you would be ruined, for no one would believe it possible for you to have spent so much time in his company without losing your innocence.'

'He is not a womaniser,' Henrietta protested. 'He does not—he only—he's not that type of man. I know he is a rake, but he's not a rake of the worst kind.'

'Well, I was not aware that there was any such thing as a good rake,' Lady Gwendolyn said with a raised brow, her worst fears confirmed.

'Well, that is what Rafe is. He only—he doesn't—he is not a seducer,' Henrietta declared, oblivious of the fact that her words only served to confirm to her aunt that that was exactly what Rafe St Alban was. 'And, anyway, I don't care about what other people say about him except—oh, I could not bear it to reflect upon you, dear Aunt, when you have been so kind.'

Henrietta threw her arms around her aunt. Lady Gwendolyn, a woman not much given to demonstrative gestures, patted her head awkwardly. 'There now, if you assure me that you are—are—that you have nothing to worry about in that direction,' she said, her customary frankness deserting her.

'There is nothing for *you* to worry about, Aunt,' Henrietta replied, not quite meeting her eyes.

Lady Gwendolyn pursed her lips, vastly relieved that Henrietta was her niece and not her daughter. 'Well, so we must hope,' she said drily, casting up a silent prayer that both their hopes would not be misplaced.

Chapter Eleven

Rafe spent an anxious night, pacing back and forwards in his bedchamber. Casting off his evening clothes, he pulled on a silk dressing gown. It reminded him of the brocade one Henrietta had worn that day at Woodfield Manor. She'd looked lost in it. And endearing. And he'd been unable to take his eyes off those lips of hers. Infinitely kissable, he'd called them.

A familiar clenching in his gut made him pace the room restlessly. Throwing open the casement, he gazed out on to the street. Not a sign of life. Not a light in any other window. Just a few streets away, in Berkeley Square, Henrietta would be tucked up in her bed. He wondered if she was sleeping. He wondered if she was thinking of him. He wondered what she was thinking of him.

Dammit all to hell and back!

It was too late, much too late to fool himself into thinking he didn't care. He did and it frightened him, all the more so because he suspected that *how* he cared, and how much, were quite different from the last time, with Julia. All his experience had taught him just how painful caring could be. He wouldn't go through that again. And, more importantly, he wouldn't let Henrietta go through it. He couldn't offer her happiness, that was not in his grasp, but he could make sure he did not make her more unhappy, even if it meant the ultimate sacrifice of giving her up.

For this really was the end. There was nowhere else to go. She had rejected what he could offer—he was not able to offer what she wanted. This was the end. Better a clean break, with the truth once and for all out in the open. He desperately needed her to understand. If he could not have anything else, at least there would be that.

Could he really bear it? Was he really going to tell her all those shameful, unsayable things, so long pent-up, lurking like rats in the dark corners of his mind, gnawing away at him day in, day out—*could* he? Even thinking about it made his gut wrench. But he had no option. A clean break with nothing left to fester. Perhaps then he could reconcile himself to life without her.

The ladies were breaking their fast next morning when a loud rap on the front door announced that a visitor had called at Berkeley Square. 'Really, who on earth can that be at such an ungodly hour?' Lady Gwendolyn asked, for it was far too early for morning callers.

She did not have to wait long for her curiosity to be satisfied. 'Lord Pentland is here, my lady, and requests an interview with Miss Markham,' her butler informed her.

Henrietta's coffee cup clattered into its delicate saucer, spilling the dregs on to the spotless white-linen cloth.

'We are not at home,' Lady Gwendolyn said firmly. 'Do sit back down, dear, and finish your meal.'

'But, Aunt Gwendolyn, I forgot to tell you.'

'Henrietta. I thought we had agreed last night that the subject was closed,' Lady Gwendolyn said, with a reproving look. 'Tell Lord Pentland we are most definitely not at home,' she said firmly to her waiting butler.

'You may tell me yourself. But then you quite patently *are* at home. Good morning, Lady Lattisbury-Hythe.' Rafe stood in the doorway, his hat in one hand, a riding crop in the other. 'Henrietta.' He bowed.

'Rafe! I mean, Lord Pentland. I mean—'

'What mean you by this unseemly interruption, my lord?' Lady Gwendolyn said in her haughtiest voice, reaching for her lorgnette.

'I have come to take your niece for a drive,' Rafe responded, quite unmoved by the fishy-eyed look he was receiving.

'My niece has no wish to go for a drive with you. In fact, my niece wishes to have nothing more to do with you under any circumstances.'

'I am sure you wish it were so,' Rafe said, pushing his way past the butler and entering the morning room, 'but the fact is that she has already made the engagement and I can assure you both it will prove most educational.'

'What arrangement? Henrietta, you would do well to heed my—'

But Henrietta was already pushing her chair back from the table. 'I am sorry, Aunt, but I must. I cannot—

you heard what Rafe—Lord Pentland said. Just this once…'

'If you are seen in his company in public, just this once may be enough to your sully your reputation for ever, especially after the exhibition you made of yourself at the dance last night,' Lady Gwendolyn said frankly. 'Henrietta! For heaven's sake, girl, if you must talk to the man, do so here in private. At least that way you will be safe from disapproving eyes. But I warn you, my lord,' she said, turning to Rafe, 'that the next time you come here uninvited I shall not hesitate to have you summarily shown off the premises, earl or no.'

'I assure you, my lady,' Rafe replied, 'I shall never again come here uninvited. I thank you for the offer of privacy, but I must decline. Henrietta, fetch your hat.'

He was looking quite distraught. Whatever he wanted to show her, it obviously meant a great deal to him. Henrietta planted a brief kiss on her aunt's cheek and left the room without further ado.

Seated beside Rafe in the phaeton ten minutes later, she was a mass of nerves. Clasping her hands in their pretty gloves, dyed emerald green to match her prom- enade dress and three-quarter pelisse, she was so intent on trying to calm herself after a sleepless night spent in fruitless speculation and woeful resolution that she did not register, until they crossed the river at Westminster Bridge, where they were headed.

Rafe drove in silence, a dark frown wreathing his features, giving him a saturnine look, taking a route that led them east of Lambeth towards the docks. Even when they could not see the river, obscured as it was by the huge warehouses that hugged its banks, its presence was mapped by the tall masts of the ships swaying against the gritty skyline. The streets were narrow and jammed full of traffic ferrying goods to and from the warehouses. Stevedores, sailors, draymen and port officials bustled about their business at top speed against a background of constant noise and chatter. The rich tang of spices, cinnamon and pepper, nutmeg and cloves, the ripe sweet smell of hogsheads of tobacco, the scent of perfumed tea from India—all wafted like a top-note on the breeze, overlaying the deeper base notes of muddy river water and dank streets overcrowded with horses and people.

People stared openly at Rafe's stylish equipage. It took Henrietta some time to notice that they were looking not in wonder, but in recognition. Hats were being tipped. Women were bobbing curtsies. A group of small ragged boys had accumulated behind them, running and jostling each other as they kept up. Beside her, Rafe lifted his whip in acknowledgement, occasionally called out a taciturn greeting. He showed a surprising knowledge of the warren of streets he navigated.

Not far from St Saviour's dock, itself not far from the notorious stews of Jacob's Island, which made Petticoat Lane look like Park Lane, he slowed the horses and made a sharp turn through a set of large, wrought-iron gates, the motley crew of urchins close behind them. The place looked like a town house, completely incongruous in its setting and obviously very newly built. With a spacious entrance fronted by four tall pillars, it had two identical wings, each of three stories, each with a set of long windows.

Rafe pulled the horses to a halt in the narrow court-yard and helped Henrietta down. Reaching into his pocket for a handful of pennies, he threw them at their entourage, to loud acclaim. 'Here, Frankie, take the horses round the back,' he said to the tallest of the boys.

'You know him?' Henrietta asked, wide-eyed.

Rafe shrugged.

'And you gave them money. You told me at St Paul's that—'

'These boys are not members of any gang. Yet.'

'How do you know?'

'I know their families.'

He could have laughed at her astonished expression, were he not so tense.

'St Nicholas's Lying-In Hospital,' Henrietta read on the brass plaque. 'Why on earth have you brought me here?'

'I wanted you to see it.'

She frowned, chewing on her lip. 'Are you one of the patrons, is that it? Is that how you came to know so much about those Bermondsey Boys you told me about?'

'I am one of the patrons. I suppose you could call me the founding member.'

'You mean you built it yourself?'

'Not with my own hands,' Rafe said with one of his enigmatic almost-smiles. 'And we do now have a growing number of sponsors these days. Not nearly enough, though. Caring for penniless mothers about to give birth to illegitimate children is not yet an acceptable good cause in polite society, as you know full well from your own charitable work,' he said grimly.

'The Poor House near our village does not allow illegitimate children to stay with their mothers,' Henrietta said sadly. 'They say that the sins of the mother would be visited on the child. It is one of the things that I cannot agree with Mama upon.'

'Well, here they are encouraged to stay together.'

'I can't believe you built this place.' Henrietta shook her head in utter amazement. 'It's so—so beautiful, peaceful, calm, even though it's surrounded by the bedlam out there.'

'It's here because this is where it's needed most. And it looks like this because we want people to come here. And it's left unmolested because the people who use it are also the local people, people with connections. They protect their own. Do you want to go in?'

She nodded. 'If you please.'

Rafe ushered her up to the main door and led her confidently through to a small room. 'This is Mrs Flowers, who is in charge of the nursing staff,' he said, introducing her to a sparrow-like woman dressed in grey kerseymere, who greeted Rafe with a beaming smile. 'You don't mind if I show Miss Markham round, do you?'

'Indeed, no, she is very welcome,' Mrs Flowers said, nodding in a friendly manner to Henrietta. 'We've five or six new arrivals since you were last here, my lord— we've been wondering where you'd got to. The new doctor has started and he's settling in nicely, you'll be pleased to know.'

'You have doctors. Goodness, that is unusual.'

'It is for lying-in, I know,' Mrs Flowers agreed, 'and, of course, if the mother prefers a midwife then that is what she has, but sadly our ladies are often ill as well as pregnant. It was my lord's idea, and a very good one at that. My lord here visits us nigh on every month,' she informed Henrietta, 'and always with some new notion for improving things. You'll see when he shows you round, always asking questions and making suggestions. Off you go, now, and take your time.'

As Henrietta followed Rafe from ward to day room to dining room to nursery, she was astonished by the reception he received. Women—girls, some of them— whether they were in an advanced state of pregnancy or clutching their newborn babes, greeted him not just with deference but with real affection. Rafe seemed quite at ease with them, chatting away about their existing children, enquiring about their husbands—which, to Henrietta's surprise, most of them seemed to have—and admiring the latest editions to their families. There was not a trace of the aloof and formidable earl. He seemed to have shed all reserve at the front door of the hospital. Here was yet another Rafe she did not recognise and Henrietta was enchanted. But it was the way he held the babies that was almost her undoing. Expertly supporting their wobbly little heads, he gazed into the unfocused blue eyes of each new-born with such an expression of tenderness that Henrietta felt the tears well.

'He's got a way with them,' a woman called Rose whispered to her, as she watched Rafe handing the newest of the babies back to its absurdly young mother. 'Don't throw them about like a sack of potatoes, the way my man does. You'll have nothing to worry about with him, love.'

'Oh, he's not my— We are not...' Henrietta protested.

'Get off, you're nuts about him, anyone can see that. Lucky you, he'll make gorgeous little ones. You just wait and see.'

Shaking her head, frantically sniffing back the tears, Henrietta asked for permission to hold Rose's daughter. Burying her nose in the delightful scent of the baby's neck, the notion of a child, her and Rafe's child, filled her for a brief moment with a surge of such yearning, she failed to see him looking at her, regret and sorrow darkening his eyes. By the time she looked up, he was on his feet, making his farewells, waiting patiently for her to rejoin him.

Back in the book room, taking tea with Mrs Flowers while Rafe attended to some business, Henrietta felt dazed. The woman could not enthuse enough about the support Rafe gave the hospital. 'He's a saint, in our eyes,' she said. 'It's not just money he gives, Miss Markham, but his time. He never fails to listen and he never judges. There's some of these lying-in places won't take unmarried women, never mind those who— well, let's say they're not exactly respectable. But here at St Nicholas's they know they won't be turned away. The most important thing is for us to do all we can to keep mother and babe together, no matter what the mother may be. And it works—mostly,' Mrs Flowers said proudly.

'Of course we have our failures,' she continued. 'Some women just can't cope. And some—well, some don't want to, and I don't just mean the people from round here, either. We might be in the heart of Bermondsey, but it's not so very far away from Mayfair. Some of the foundlings we find at the back door come swaddled in the finest linen, wrapped in blankets of the softest lamb's wool. We try to find them proper homes with proper families, our foundlings—his lordship has had several babes adopted by his estate workers. But sometimes we can't and then we have to send them on to the Foundling Hospital in Bloomsbury Fields. We don't like to do that, but—well, there's only so much you can do,' Mrs Flowers said sadly.

Henrietta recalled Rafe's words: *there are too many of them*. She had thought he was being callous, when he had been speaking from experience. Real experience. Far more real than her own pathetic attempts at making a difference. Touched beyond measure by what she had seen at St Nicholas's, she finally realised that what she had taken for Rafe's cynicism that day at St Paul's was actually simple realism. St Nicholas's was a ray of hope, but it was a very small one in the midst of a very dark existence.

What an idiot he must have thought her. When she remembered some of the things she'd said, she felt like a complete fool. Recalling her resolve that day in the stews of Petticoat Lane, to do more in future, she realised she could probably do no better than to consult Rafe on the subject. Then she remembered that, after today, she was not likely to see Rafe again.

'Well, now, I'd best be getting on.' Mrs Flowers bustled to her feet and shook Henrietta's hand. 'It was lovely to meet you, Miss Markham. I hope to see you again. I'll send his lordship up.'

'It's been wonderful. You should be so proud of your

hospital, Mrs Flowers. I've never seen anything quite so— Thank you.'

'Don't thank me. If it wasn't for his lordship there wouldn't be a hospital. He's a fine gentleman. One of the finest in England, if I'm any judge. But then you must already know that. Goodbye, Miss Markham.'

Mrs Flowers left in a swish of starched apron, which she had donned over her kerseymere dress. Alone, Henrietta sat on a straight-backed chair staring into space. Questions, as ever, swirled around her head. Why had he brought her here? How on earth was it related to what they had argued about last night? What did he mean, he did not deserve to be happy?

The door opened and Rafe strode in. 'You had tea?'

'Yes, thank you. Mrs Flowers was most kind. What Papa would call the salt of the earth.'

He was leaning against the small wooden mantel behind the desk. As ever, he was dressed extremely modishly. Dark blue coat with long tails. His neckcloth was intricately tied, a small diamond pin nestling in its snowy folds. His waistcoat was silver-and-dove-grey stripes. The tight-knit pantaloons which encased his legs were also dove grey. His boots were so glossy she could have seen her face in them if she had dared to look. His hair was blue-black, even glossier than his boots. And his face. His face was as it always was. There was a sheen to him of polished perfection. Yet underneath that sheen, so many flaws, so many contradictions and yet so many admirable qualities.

Who was he? Earl, knight errant, rake or philanthropist? The man she loved. Her heart squeezed painfully. She did love him, there was no doubt of that, despite all.

'Rafe, what you have done here, it's—words fail me. I feel so small, thinking of how ineffectual have been my attempts in comparison. You should be proud. I wish I could be part of something so wonderful. Really, truly, it's an admirable place.'

Rafe looked uncomfortable. 'You give me too much credit. I did not start St Nicholas's for philanthropic reasons. I'm not a do-gooder.'

'Like my parents, you mean? No, I know you're not. You're much more practical. Rafe, I wish—'

'Henrietta!'

She jumped.

'Henrietta, you're not listening. I didn't do this for altruistic reasons. At least not at first. I did it to atone.'

His fists were clenched. His shoulders were rigid. He was in the grip of some emotion more fearful than she had yet seen. 'What do you mean, atone?' she asked.

'I thought if I helped those women keep their babies, it would make me feel better. Atone in some small way. For the child I did not keep. Did not want.'

She had the awful sensation of standing on the edge of a steep staircase, knowing she was about to be pushed. She didn't want to know, but she had to ask. 'What child?'

'Mine. Mine and Julia's.'

'What happened to it?'

He couldn't say it, yet he had to say it. A clean break so that he could reconcile himself to their parting, he reminded himself. Last night, alone in his bedchamber, suffering from the after-effects of that ballroom confrontation, it had seemed possible, sensible even. Now, he wasn't so sure. Such a terrible admission—could he really make it? He needed to let her in, in order to let her go, but would the pain of it destroy him?

'Rafe? Rafe, what happened to it? The child.'

He braced himself. It was now or never. He could not face any more regrets. He took a jagged breath. 'I killed it.'

Henrietta's mouth fell open. She must have misheard. Surely she had misheard. 'You killed it?' Her voice was nothing more than a whisper.

'And Julia. I am responsible for her death, also.'

'You can't mean—no, Rafe, you *would* not—I don't believe you. You are not a murderer'

'As good as.'

The floor seemed to be moving. There was a whooshing noise like the sea in her ears. Rafe was still talking, but he sounded as if he was far away, behind a wall of glass. Henrietta could see his mouth moving, but she couldn't make out what he was saying. 'Wait. Stop. I can't—I'm sorry, I didn't…' She clutched her brow and took some deep breaths. This was important. Vitally important. Far too important for her to fall into a faint.

Rafe was looking at her with concern. 'Are you all right? Shall I fetch you some water?'

She waved him away. 'No. I'm all right. Please. Just tell me.'

He sat heavily down on the chair behind the desk upon which was a stack of leather-bound ledgers and picked up a quill. 'You remember—I told you that Julia and I resumed our marriage three years after we had separated?'

Henrietta nodded. 'You said it was for the sake of an heir.'

'It was such a mistake, that reunion, from start to finish. I knew it was wrong. I knew for a fact that I didn't love her, would never love her. But duty was such an ingrained habit, I didn't think through at all what bringing a child into the world would actually mean—any more than Julia did, I believe. When she told me she was pregnant…'

The pen nib bent as he stabbed it on the blotter. 'It was my fault. I shouldn't have taken her back. Julia was—she was—she knew, you see. It was obvious, I suppose, that I went to her bed only out of a sense of duty—no, that's not fair. I made no attempt to pretend and she— It was not her fault, it was just as bad for her, I presume. I'm sorry, I'm not explaining myself very well.'

'Rafe, you are explaining yourself. It's hard because it's a horribly painful thing. If you were more—' she broke off and shrugged '—then you would be feeling less. I know how hard it must be for you. I do know, I promise. I'm listening. Just take your time.'

He grimaced. 'I've never told anyone any of this before, but I needed you to— Anyway, Julia hadn't really forgiven me for our separation and she thought I hadn't forgiven her for being unfaithful. The truth is, I didn't care, which was worse, certainly more hurtful, though I didn't think about that at the time. I was using her to get what I wanted and she was using me. It was a recipe for disaster. We both knew it. I think we were both starting to recognise it, but it was too late by then. Julia was pregnant.'

Rafe drew a shaky breath, forcing himself to go on. Across from him, Henrietta sat perfectly still, her face chalk white. For once, he had no idea what she was thinking. 'The night she told me, I'll never forget it. I realised, you see, that I didn't want a child. Not Julia's child.' He dropped his head into his hands. 'I hadn't realised what it would mean,' he said. 'I was so bloody stupid, I'd thought about an having an heir, but I hadn't thought about having a baby. I hadn't thought about being a father. I had no idea. No bloody clue.'

'But, Rafe, today, with the babies in the nursery, you were so gentle with them—the expression on your face when you held them, you looked so moved. I thought— and Rose thought, too—what a perfect father you would make.'

He shook his head vehemently. 'No, you're wrong. You're quite wrong. I don't deserve such a precious gift. I had my chance and I destroyed it, I don't deserve another. I didn't realise back then how lucky I was. All I could think about was that I'd fail…between us, Julia and I would fail as parents. I was frightened I wouldn't be able to love it because Julia was its mother. I'd realised by then what I hadn't thought of before, that a child would bind us together. I didn't want to be tied to Julia.'

'Oh, Rafe, I wish you could have— Don't you see, what you were feeling is not so very unusual. Of course you were frightened, most new parents are, but once the baby was born…'

'It wasn't born. My baby wasn't born. I told you, I killed it.'

'And I've told you, I can't believe you would do such a thing.'

'But I did, Henrietta. Julia had always been unstable,

but her pregnancy made her mood swings much more marked. She hated what the child was doing to her body. She didn't want it, any more than I did, but she was much more vocal on the subject. I thought it was just the old Julia, trying to manipulate me. I didn't realise she was so close to the edge. I thought her taunts and her petty accusations were just the same old games. I paid her no heed. I didn't want to. I didn't care. I was too racked by my own guilt. Too taken up by my own cares to see that Julia's fears were real. As our child grew inside her, she became more and more hostile. To me. To the baby. She kept threatening to rid herself of it, to take things— I had to have Mrs Peters watch her.'

'My God, Rafe, I can't believe—'

'Don't. Don't say anything. Just let me finish.' Rafe stared sightlessly down at the desk blotter, lost in the nightmare of his past. 'It was at Woodfield Manor. We were alone there but for the servants. Julia didn't want anyone to see her in what she called her bloated state. We were on the second floor, looking at the old nursery. Julia was in one of her moods. I hope it's a girl, she said. More likely it's a monster, sprung from your loins. On and on she went, until she'd worked herself up into such a rage. I've never seen the like, and still I didn't realise…'

He pushed his chair back and went over to the little window. With his back to her, he continued, his speech rushed now, words tumbling from him in his anxiety to have done with them. 'She said she wished she was dead. She said the agony of childbirth was too much for her to bear. She said it would kill her. She said she'd rather kill herself than bear it. She was always threatening to kill herself. I didn't think she meant it. I told her she could do as she wished. She went over to the window. I can still see it now. It seemed to happen so slowly, though it was all over in seconds. She threw the casement open—and then she jumped. She just jumped. So quickly, without a word, not even a sound as she fell—it was as if she had never been in the room. I didn't move. Not until I heard the cry from below. Molly Peters's husband it was who found her.'

He swayed and Henrietta jumped to her feet, staggering with the weight of him as he fell into her arms. 'I couldn't stop her, but I didn't try to,' Rafe said. 'I drove her to it. I didn't love her. I didn't try to make her happy. I didn't want her. I didn't want our baby. I killed her. I killed them both.'

'Rafe, oh God, Rafe. I can't believe—I had no idea you had been through such torments. Must still be going through them. It is awful. Awful. I can't begin to comprehend how awful.'

The scene he had so vividly described replayed over and over in Henrietta's head as she struggled with the enormity of Rafe's totally unexpected confession. She was aghast. Absolutely horrified. 'I just can't believe—God, what you must have gone through.'

'My suffering is deserved.'

'At least Julia's is over,' Henrietta whispered, more to herself than to Rafe, in an effort to make sense of what he had told her. 'Such a very unhappy person she sounds. She must have been a little deranged by her pregnancy. She would not have been responsible for her actions. Poor woman. Poor, poor little baby. Oh, Rafe, if only you'd had the opportunity, you would have loved the child, I know you would have. I could not doubt that, after seeing you today.'

Rafe grasped her by the shoulders, forcing himself to meet her eyes, caring not for the fact that his own were suspiciously bright. 'Henrietta, can't you see? Nothing I can do, no amount of babies and mothers saved, will make up for the child I lost. I thought they would. That's why I built this place. I thought it would help, but it didn't.'

He pushed her away. Henrietta slumped back down on her seat, tugging at the ribbons of her bonnet. Her head was aching. She had no idea what to say. Rafe's face was a blank—his confession had clearly flayed him clean of emotion. She shook her head, as if doing so would clear the fog of confusion that shrouded her mind. She had to try to make sense of things. She needed to, for both their sakes. 'But you have atoned,' she said slowly. 'You continue to atone. St Nicholas's is obviously making an enormous difference. Without it, I don't doubt any number of those babies would not have made it into the world.'

All true, but it wasn't the point. She needed to explain, because he quite obviously didn't understand it all himself. Guilt. That's what he was feeling. That's what drove him. Of course it was. So simple and yet so utterly complex. She felt like sobbing. Instead she forced herself to speak, though she had a horrible suspicion that the end of her speech would signal her own downfall.

'You're tearing yourself apart, Rafe.' Her voice was too much of a whisper. She swallowed. Throat dry. She coughed. 'Guilt. It's guilt. What happened is awful.

Horrible. I simply don't have the words. You are not blameless, but you are nowhere near as much at fault as you believe. Julia and the baby are dead, and nothing you can do will bring them back. Maybe there was nothing you could have done to prevent them suffering in the first place. I don't know, no one knows that, but I do know there is no point at all in continuing to torment yourself. You are allowing what happened to destroy you.'

Rafe made a bitter sound, like a demon laughing. 'I don't deserve anything else, Henrietta. I don't care about myself. What I'm trying to do is stop myself destroying you, too.'

The new twist in his logic threw her. 'Me?'

'I would make you miserable. I have given up the right to be happy. I've given up the right to love. I gave those things away when I killed my wife and child.' His voice cracked. 'I can't offer you those things, even if I wanted to, and you won't accept less—why should you? Now do you understand?'

Henrietta got to her feet, pushing her way past Rafe over to the window, where she pressed her forehead against the glass. Her skin was burning, though she felt freezing. The dread that had been lurking in the shadows of her traumatised mind began to edge its way towards centre stage. She wanted so desperately to help him. She wanted with all her heart to help him, but she could not surrender her soul to him, and that is what she would be doing if she gave in now, if she did not walk away. 'Your giving up the right to happiness is your true penance, isn't it?' Her voice seemed drained of all emotion. Already, she felt defeated, too tired to continue, though she knew she had to, must, or she would be lost. 'Is that what you are saying?'

Rafe nodded.

'Yes. Yes, I see it now.' And how much she wished she were blind, for what she saw was the end, the inevitable, inescapable conclusion she must reach. She spoke with the slow, weary precision of a judge delivering the death sentence. 'I wish with all my heart that I could ease the pain you must feel every day. I cannot imagine what it must be like. I wish you could see, Rafe, I truly wish that you could see that you are not wholly at fault, that there is a time for repenting and a time for taking what you have been given and making the best of it.' She paused for breath. It was painful. 'Do you really think this endless flaying of yourself serves any real purpose? Have you not acknowledged your faults, have you not changed? Is it not time that you forgave yourself?' Her voice was pleading now, though she knew she was advocating the impossible.

'How can I?'

He was too entrenched in his guilt, too far gone for her to reach. She could cast him the rope, but if he would not pull himself to safety, unless she released him, she, too, would drown. 'I can't tell you that,' Henrietta said with infinite sadness. 'I'm sorry. I wish with all my heart that I could but I can't, and so it seems then we must both be condemned to a lifetime of unhappiness.'

'What do you mean?'

'I thought you'd have realised by now,' she said wearily. 'I love you. I'm in love with you.' The words she had so longed to speak fell flat and empty, like her heart. 'I can't ever be happy without you, so you see, by punishing yourself you are punishing me.'

'Henrietta! Don't say that.'

'Don't worry, I won't say it again,' she said, unable to keep the trace of bitter hurt from her voice, 'I know perfectly well my love means nothing to you, but it's precious to me, and I won't let you destroy it.'

'That's not what I said. I meant— Henrietta, I meant— I just—'

'I'm sorry, I just can't take any more. I just can't. I wish I could help you. I wish you would help yourself. I wish that we wanted the same things. Oh God, Rafe, you have no idea how much I wish that, but I can't have what I want, and you can't give me what I want, and I can't live with what you can offer so—can't you see how hopeless it all is?' Her voice broke. She had no hope left. She was too empty even to feel the pain. Her limbs felt heavy, borne down with the dreadful things Rafe had told her. Her heart lay like a leaden weight in her chest. She jammed her bonnet on to her head. Tears burned behind her lids like acid. 'Please, just take me home.'

'Henrietta.' She looked defeated. He had never seen her look defeated before. He didn't want it to end like this. It didn't feel right. It didn't feel like the clean break he had planned. He didn't want—oh God, he didn't know what he wanted. But Henrietta was already opening the door, descending the stairs, clutching at the polished banister for support. Henrietta was walking away and there seemed to be nothing he could do to stop her. He had nothing left to say, after all. But it felt wrong, wrong, wrong.

* * *

The drive back, away from the docks, crossing the river by the new Waterloo Bridge, from a cityscape of oppressive squalor to opulent excess, had been accompanied by silence. At Berkeley Square, Henrietta got out of the phaeton without saying goodbye. She could not bear to look at him, lest she break down. She so desperately didn't want to break down. She made her way quickly to the sanctuary of her bedchamber, relieved to hear that Aunt Gwendolyn had gone out and would go straight on to dinner with Emily Cowper's gathering of Canningites.

She left word with her maid that she did not want to be disturbed until morning. Then she discarded her gown and crawled into bed in her undergarments. Burrowing her head under the pillow, she waited on the tears, but they would not fall. They seared her eyes and lids, but they would not fall. She was icy cold, shivering under the mound of blankets. She was bereft of words and thoughts. Emptied of emotion, she lay, listening to the clock ticking and her heart beating, though it felt like every beat signalled another small, excruciatingly painful, death.

Chapter Twelve

Rafe drove back to Mount Street, barely aware of having made the journey, narrowly avoiding numerous collisions along the way. Handing over the reins of his phaeton, he demanded of his bemused groom that a fresh horse be sent round immediately. Pacing the front steps, clutching his riding crop in one hand and his beaver hat in the other, his frown was forbiddingly deep. An acquaintance, on the brink of doffing his hat and passing the time of day, instead traversed to the other side of the street, averting his gaze. He had seen that look on Rafe St Alban's face once before and did not care to repeat the experience, nor witness the consequences. The crossing boy who habitually earned a sixpence from him chose to hide behind the pillar of the house next door. Careless of the fact that he was quite inappropriately dressed for riding, Rafe mounted, dismissing his groom curtly, urged the chestnut into a canter that would have been dangerous, were he not such an accomplished horseman, and made for Hyde Park.

It was relatively quiet at this time of day. Ignoring the prohibition, Rafe loosed his hold on the frisky horse and gave his mount free rein. The gallop took both their breaths away, as well as that of several outraged onlookers. Finally pulling up, both horse and man panting heavily, Rafe found he felt no better for it.

What the devil was wrong with him? What the devil had gone wrong? He'd wanted her to understand. She'd understood too well. This infuriating thought carried him round another circuit of the park, this time taken at something very slightly less than neck or nothing.

A clean break, he'd thought. But the break felt jagged, as if it would never heal. Not an ending, but something much bleaker. A black mood settled on Rafe, darker than any he had known for a long time. The future looked not grim, but impenetrable. The past equally foggy, clogged as it was now by Henrietta's insights. He felt as if she had taken a well-thumbed book and rewritten it.

Another circuit, at a slow canter this time, was completed before he turned back through the gates. He made his way back to Mount Street, his horse streaming with sweat. The problem with Henrietta—*one* of the problems with Henrietta—was that she never lied. Never.

Doubt, that most stealthy of creatures, had sidled into his mind, sowing the seeds of questions he didn't want to ask, let alone answer. Sitting in his favourite wingback chair in the ground-floor library, surrounded by the ancient tomes his ancestors had acquired with a view to populating the polished walnut shelves rather than their own minds, Rafe fought to reassemble the past in the image he had for so long held deep in his heart, but it was like trying to force the wrong pieces of a dissected puzzle back into place. Distorted. Mangled. A different picture was emerging.

Had he ever loved Julia? He'd thought so at the time, but now—no. Infatuated he might have been, but not in love. How could he be so sure? He didn't know, but he was.

His butler had set out a silver tray of decanters upon the desk. Rafe poured himself a small glass of Madeira, but set it aside after one sip. He needed to think and needed a clear head in order to do so. Guilt. Looking back to those early days of his marriage, he recognised its presence like a shadow. Guilt because he knew he did not love Julia enough. Guilt when he inevitably failed to make her happy.

Guilt, guilt and more guilt for his failure, and then his failing to care enough to try harder. It had not helped, his upbringing with its enormous sense of obligation. He had been raised to be the bearer of burdens. He felt guilty when Julia's unfaithfulness gave him the excuse he was looking for to separate. And he'd felt guilty enough about that to try again. Guilt it was that had driven him to the reconciliation, guilt fed this time by his grandmother, whose ceaseless sponsorship of the claims of the title to an heir he had allowed to sway him. And guilt every time he had forced himself to go to Julia's bed, going through the motions, the pretext of desire, making no attempt to sweeten the pill for her—his own petty punishment. And the ultimate guilt: his rejection of his own child. The two deaths that had resulted from that.

Guilt. Henrietta was right. It was destroying him.

Rafe picked up his Madeira glass, raised it to his mouth, stared at it uncomprehendingly and put it back down again. Henrietta. Such a ridiculous name and yet so very appropriate. She said it was time to forgive himself. Was she right about that, too?

He forced himself for the second time that day to replay the painful facts. Forced himself to ask the painful questions he had asked himself so many times, only this time, he tried to answer without the bias of guilt. He tried to answer them as Henrietta would want him to. As if she had reset his moral compass. *Was he wholly to blame? Could he have done this differently, or that? Had he cared more, or less, would it have changed things?*

He and Julia should never have married, but they had. Duty and circumstances and, yes, in the early days, affection and desire had conspired to join them together. Duty and circumstance had conspired to make them try that second fatal time. They were not faultless, but they were neither of them wholly to blame. Henrietta was right about that, too.

And the child? His child. Their child. Had it been born, would he really have rejected it? He recalled the countless little bundles—other people's bundles—he had held in his arms since founding St Nicholas's. Such helpless, utterly trusting, tiny little beings, smelling of milk and that distinctive baby smell. He allowed himself to remember the yearning, aching longing that enveloped him every time. The fierceness of his desire to keep them safe. The regret each time he handed them back to their mothers. The anxiety each time he watched mother and baby leave.

Relief so immense as to be palpable made him limp. He would not have rejected his own child. He might have wished it born under different circumstances, he might have continued to wish himself free of its mother, but he would not have rejected it. Henrietta was right about that, too. 'God dammit, of course she was!' Rafe exclaimed.

He smiled to himself, for he never used to talk to himself out loud, until he met Henrietta. Henrietta Markham, who had made him face up to some excruciatingly painful truths, who had not flinched from pointing out his wrongs, yet whose sympathy and empathy he never doubted. Henrietta Markham, who said she loved him.

Rafe sat bolt upright. Henrietta loved him. She was in love with him! Bloody hell, she was in love with him. She'd told him so and he'd been so damned caught up in everything else that he'd barely even registered it.

She loved him. Henrietta loved him. What a fool he had been not to see it before. Nothing else would have induced her to give herself to him. No wonder she had been so hurt by his offer. No wonder it was not enough, nor ever could be. Henrietta loved him. Being Henrietta, she would never, ever settle for anything less than everything.

And he? God, what a mull of it he had made. That damned stupid halfway-house proposition of his must have seemed contemptuous, as if he had thrown her love back in her face! 'Dammit, what a bloody, blind, damned fool I've been.' Rafe threw his Madeira glass across the room. It shattered with a satisfying crack on the claw foot of his desk, spraying the rug with wine.

All or nothing. All or nothing. He had chosen nothing and it felt fundamentally wrong. They were meant to be together. He could see that now, so clearly. Unbearably clearly. Just as he could see that he needed to do something about it, and urgently. Because—because…

'Dammit, because I love her!'

He loved her. *That* was why he was now so certain that he had never loved Julia. He loved Henrietta and it felt utterly different from anything he had ever felt before. He loved her. It was true. It must be true, because the bars of the cell in which he had deliberately imprisoned his heart had been suddenly flung open. All he had to do was to step forwards into the light and claim the prize. All he had to do was forgive himself. To stop paying penance, and start the process of redemption. Could he?

Rafe closed his eyes. He took each of his sins and held it up for inspection. Then he laid each down, saying a solemn farewell. The past was not gone, but already the scars were fading. He did not yet feel he deserved to be happy, but he did feel he deserved to try. Love. Love for Henrietta would be his redemption. From their love would grow happiness. A future worth inhabiting.

He wanted to start inhabiting it now. Galvanised by this thought into action, Rafe threw open the door of the library. If happiness really was within his grasp, he would reach out and take it. 'Now, without further ado,' he said to his startled footman.

'My lord?'

'My hat. My gloves,' Rafe said. 'Quickly, man, quickly.'

The items were handed over. Before Edward could pluck up the courage to point out to his master that he was expected to dine with the Dowager Countess in an hour and could not do so in pantaloons and a tailcoat, Rafe was out of the door, down the stairs and heading for Berkeley Square on foot.

It had taken him less than five minutes to reach Lady Gwendolyn's house. He rang the bell impatiently, pushed past her butler impatiently, demanded even more impatiently that Miss Markham be produced at once.

'Miss Markham has retired for the night, my lord,' the butler informed him. 'She gave us most strict instructions that she should not be disturbed. Lady Gwendolyn said—'

'Where is her ladyship?' Rafe demanded, forgetting all about his promise made earlier that day never to cross the threshold of Berkeley Square again uninvited. 'Fetch her, she will rouse Henrietta.'

'Lady Gwendolyn has gone to Lady Cowper's for dinner. I think Miss Markham has the migraine, she did not look at all well when she returned,' the butler said confidentially, though he was beginning to harbour a suspicion that Lord Pentland was the source of Miss Markham's illness.

'Then what I am about to tell her may affect the cure. Fetch her.'

'Lord Pentland…'

'Fetch her now, or I will fetch her myself. In fact, if you tell me where her bedchamber is…'

'My lord! Please, I beg of you, I cannot allow you to do that, her ladyship would have me summarily dismissed— I beseech you, if you will just wait in one of the salons I will endeavour to wake her.'

'Very well, see that you do. Tell her she has five minutes, or I'll come and get her myself.'

Scandalised and fascinated, Lady Gwendolyn's butler scurried up the stairs with Rafe at his heels. Showing his lordship, who had clearly gone quite mad, into a small but elegant withdrawing room, he continued to the second floor, there to tap tentatively on Miss Markham's bedchamber door.

Henrietta was still awake, still in shock, still unable to cry. She ignored the gentle knock on the door, but it came again, louder and more insistent this time. Clutching a wrapper around her, she dragged herself to the door and opened it tentatively.

'Beg pardon, miss,' the butler said, 'I know this is most irregular, but Lord Pentland is downstairs and absolutely insists on seeing you.'

'I can't see him, I won't.'

'Miss, I fear that if you do not—'

'If you do not, I will drag you out of your room myself,' Rafe said, making the butler, who had not heard his footsteps on the stairs, jump clean into the air.

'My lord, you should not—'

'Rafe! What are you doing here?'

'Henrietta, I need to talk to you. It is imperative that I talk to you.'

'No. I can't. There is nothing more left to say.'

'Henrietta…'

'My lord, if you would just…'

'Rafe, just go away.'

'Henrietta! I love you.'

It was hard to say who was more astounded by this declaration. Lady Gwendolyn's stately butler's jaw dropped in a most un-stately manner. Henrietta clutched at the doorknob, letting her hold on her wrapper go and revealing to both Rafe and the butler rather more of the satin and lace she wore next to her skin than either was prepared for.

Rafe himself was so astonished that he could for a moment think of nothing else to say after such momentous words, uttered in such completely mundane circumstances, though he recovered his poise more quickly than his audience.

'Now you know why my business with Miss Markham was so urgent. You can leave us alone and you would be doing me an enormous service if you would ensure our privacy is undisturbed,' he said to the butler. 'As you can imagine, there are a number of delicate matters that require further discussion.' He then prised Henrietta's hand free of the door handle. 'I think it would be safer to talk downstairs rather than in your chamber,' he said, leading her quickly past the gaping butler, back to the room on the first floor to which he had been originally shown.

'Rafe, I—'

'Sit down.'

'Rafe, I—'

'And listen.'

Henrietta sat down. She had no option, for her knees were shaking so much.

Rafe sat by her side and took her hand, rubbing it

between his to heat it. The elation that had carried him from Mount Street to here had deserted him. Now he was so nervous it felt as if a cloud of small butterflies were flapping their wings frantically inside his stomach. 'You were right,' he said finally.

'What about?'

'Everything?' His smile made a brief appearance. He swallowed hard. 'You were right. I've been hiding. I've been afraid.' Now he had started, it was getting easier. 'I've been hiding behind the terrible things that happened, allowing the pain and the guilt to blind me to the truth. I let guilt dictate how I behaved, who I was. I closed myself off lest I expose myself to hurt again. You were right. I've not been living, I've merely been existing, lurking in the shadows of life, holding it cheap. You were right about that, too, Henrietta.' His smile made another brief appearance. 'You see, I meant it. You were right about it all.'

'Oh.'

Rafe laughed. He picked up her hand and rubbed it against his cheek. 'Did you think I wasn't listening to you?'

'I thought you didn't want to,' she said frankly.

'I didn't, but in the end I had no option because there was something I wanted far more and until I faced up to the past I could never hope to have it.'

'What?'

'You.'

'Oh.'

'Henrietta, I know I'm not innocent of blame. I'm not as black as I've painted myself, but I'm no saint. I can't undo the wrongs I've done. I can't escape the fact that

I've done wrong, but I can do as you said. I can forgive myself.'

'Oh, Rafe, do you mean it?'

'Really and truly,' he said, his smile breaking through again. 'You've made me see that I can. Ever since I set eyes on you, you've been like a shaft of sunshine forcing its way through the clouds. Like a blinding ray of pure light coming through a door which is only slightly ajar. I knew what I felt for you was different, right from the start. But the very intensity of it frightened me. I felt exposed. Raw. Vulnerable.'

Her heart was thudding in a peculiar new way. Heavy beats that still left her breathless. She was afraid to hope. Like Rafe, she could see the light shining through the door, but he was still on the other side.

'I love you, Henrietta. I want to spend the rest of my life with you.' Rafe slipped on to the floor and knelt at her feet, clasping her hand between his. 'I love you, and I hope—I hope so very, very much—that you have it in your heart to forgive me for being such an idiot as not to recognise it before. Please, darling Henrietta, say it's not too late.'

'Oh, Rafe, of course it's not too late. I love you. I will always love you. How could you ever have doubted it?'

It was all he needed to hear. He swept her into his arms and kissed her. For the first time in his life, he kissed a lover's kiss, the kiss of a man who loves and is loved in return. Her mouth tasted all the sweeter. Her embrace felt infinitely more delightful. It was a kiss that was a promise of kisses to come, a kiss that lit up the world, forcing the cloud that had hung over him for so long to scud over the horizon and be for ever lost.

He got back down on to one knee. 'Henrietta, I most humbly ask you to do me the honour of becoming my wife. Darling, dearest, most enchanting and true Henrietta, marry me.'

'Oh, Rafe. Oh, Rafe. Do you mean it? Really? Truly?'

He pulled her towards him and kissed her lids. 'I mean it.' Her cheeks. 'Really.' Her upturned little nose. 'Truly.' He feathered kisses into the corners of her smiling mouth. 'I promise.' He rained kisses on to her brow. 'I love you. I love you, Henrietta Markham. I love you really and truly. I promise.'

She had toppled on to the floor beside him now. Their kisses were becoming feverish, their hands, anxious for the reassurance of the other's touch, plucking at clothes to reach skin. Henrietta's wrapper was cast to one side. 'Silk and lace,' Rafe murmured with a wolfish smile, burying his head between her breasts, where the lace edge of her chemise foamed over her flesh. His fingers were already undoing the laces of her stays. He pulled the chemise down to expose her nipples and, with a sigh of satisfaction, took one rosy pink bud into his mouth and sucked.

A jolt, like falling, ran between her nipples and her belly and her sex. Henrietta moaned deeply. Her head fell back to rest on the *chaise* on which she had been sitting only moments before. Rafe's mouth was doing the most delightful things. His fingers rolling her other nipple, tugging the most exquisitely intense shards of pleasure, sending waves of heat rolling and rippling through her. His coat and waistcoat lay discarded beside her wrapper. She slipped her hands under his shirt, tugging it free from his pantaloons. She could see the hard, solid length of his shaft clearly outlined. She stroked it through the tight-knit material, making him shudder, making herself shudder, too, in anticipation.

She wanted him now. She wanted him inside her now. Claiming her. Owning her. Possessing her. She wanted to feel skin on skin. Flesh inside flesh. Deep inside. Hard inside. Hot inside. 'Rafe,' she said urgently, tugging at his shirt. 'Rafe, please.'

He understood. Standing to disrobe quickly, without finesse, clothes landing incongruously on the furnishings of Lady Gwendolyn's salon, his shirt draped over a painted fire screen, his pantaloons wrapped around the delicately scrolled leg of a Hepplewhite pier table, though neither of them noticed. Wriggling out of her stays, her undergarments, Henrietta kept her eyes on Rafe. He was magnificent, naked. Her heart flip-flopped and stepped up to a higher rate as she stared with unashamed relish at the silken length of his manhood, nudging his belly. On her knees before him, she caressed it with her fingertips, then her tongue, the salty heat of him making her belly tighten, swelling and tensing the knot of arousal that burned between her thighs. She cupped him and he moaned again.

'Henrietta, I don't think I can wait much longer.'

'Rafe, I don't want you to.'

He pulled her to him. Kissed her deeply on the mouth. Pressed her hard against him, her breasts crushed to his chest, her thighs enveloping his erection. He kissed her again, then sank down on to the *chaise-longue*, pulling her down with him, on top of him, entering her with one long, swift, hard thrust that made them both gasp.

It was almost too much. Rafe felt himself tighten,

his shaft thicken, the prelude of the pulsing that would be his climax. Clutching on to the delightful curve of Henrietta's bottom, he held her still, breathing deep, resisting the overpowering urge to thrust up, waiting, breathing, holding her still, reaching down, between her dimpled thighs, to stroke the delicious wetness of her.

He stroked and Henrietta shuddered. She clenched her muscles around him, desperate for the thrusting friction that brought such delectable pleasure. Friction that his sliding, gliding fingers were rousing as they coaxed and then commanded the hard nub of her sex towards its climax. She could feel the rippling prelude. She tried to resist it, but it was too strong, a tide of feeling whipping her up, making her moan and arch; just when she thought she could bear it no longer, she climaxed, and into the ebb and flow of her orgasm Rafe gripped her waist and lifted her up, then let her fall, thrusting into her as she did, the force of her climaxing opening her for him.

She panted, picking up the rhythm, gripping his shoulders, lifting herself now, then encasing him, writhing on him as he thrust higher than before, and then again, and again, each lift and sheathing and thrust pulsing the purest of pleasure through her. With a moan that seemed to come from the depths of his being, he came, spurting his hot seed high inside her and telling her over and over that he loved her, loved her, loved her, gazing deep into her eyes, his face raw, ablaze with love, alight with the passion which that love fuelled. He kissed her again. She had never tasted such a kiss. It felt as if she were on the edge of the world. She had never kissed such a kiss, knowing that she loved and was loved. Would always be loved. For ever.

'Always,' Rafe said, reading her thoughts, stroking the wild curls that had become entangled with her lashes clear of her face, so that he could look into her eyes. Chocolate brown, striped with gold, glazed with love. 'I will love you always. I promise.'

'Darling Rafe, I believe you.'

'Darling Henrietta,' he said, looking over her shoulder at the chaos they had caused, 'you realise we are quite naked in your aunt's parlour and you have not yet formally agreed to be my wife. I had not thought you the type to prevaricate.'

Henrietta giggled. 'I think the fact that I am naked with you in my aunt's parlour is answer enough. Goodness, we didn't even lock the door.'

'I don't care about the door. Or the servants. Or even your aunt. Let me pose the question again. Henrietta Markham, will you marry me?'

She caught her breath as he smiled at her. His real smile. Somehow she knew she would be seeing a lot more of it in the future. 'Rafe St Alban, just try to stop me,' Henrietta replied.

Epilogue

It was not to be expected that Henrietta's parents would welcome their daughter's marriage to a notorious rake, no matter how well born or wealthy, without serious reservations. They had arrived in London, in response to the letter sent by Lady Gwendolyn when Henrietta had first arrived on her doorstep, to be greeted by this most unexpected and startling news. The explanation as to how this remarkable turn of events had come to pass, and so swiftly, necessitated their being appraised of the lurid tale of the Ipswich diamonds.

Mr Henry Markham, dressed habitually and entirely in brown clothes, which looked as if they dated, as indeed did their wearer, from some time in the middle of the previous century, was a tall man bent in the middle like a permanent question mark. His hair, a thick grey curtain through which his bald head rose like a brown-speckled egg, tangled with the folding legs of his brass eyeglasses, preventing them, when they slid down his nose—as they did at regular intervals—from actually quitting his face.

His wife was equally slim built, but there the resemblance ended. There was no doubt at all that Guinevere Markham had been, and still was, an extremely beautiful woman, with hair a rich Titian bronze, flawless skin, an equally flawless profile and perfectly arched brows under which eyes the same hue as her daughter's looked out at the world.

Guinevere's gaze was, however, not nearly as clearsighted as her daughter's. Her perceptions for ever coloured by the loss of her innocence at the hands of a rake, she forbade Henrietta's marriage to a man who would, she claimed, weeping copious tears, break her innocent babe's heart.

Neither Henrietta's indignant protests, nor the publication of the forthcoming nuptials in the press, nor even the large emerald-and-diamond encrusted ring, which she wore upon the third finger of her left hand, had any effect on Mrs Markham. Her daughter, whose patience and loyalty was being tested beyond the limits, finally lost her temper and roundly informed Mama that she was three-and-twenty and therefore there was nothing Mama could do about it.

Into this heated exchange walked Lady Gwendolyn and out of this heated exchange emerged the truth of Guinevere's past.

'Which was rather a case of unrequited love than seduction,' Lady Gwendolyn frankly informed her niece, ignoring her sister's flapping denials. Guinevere, it seemed, was the one who did the pursuing. The gentleman in question was not interested in her declarations of love, any more than he was interested in her suggestion that they marry, since he was, in fact, already wed. 'Though to be fair,' Lady Gwendolyn said, 'the poor woman was more or less confined to their country estate by their brood of children.'

'I did not know, Gwen,' Guinevere protested faintly.

'Yes, you did, Gwinnie, for I told you myself,' Lady Gwendolyn said, 'but you were so set upon that blasted man that you weren't interested in listening.'

'He said he loved me.'

'No doubt he did, when you made it perfectly obvious that in return he could have you,' Lady Gwendolyn retorted.

'He said he would marry me.'

Lady Gwendolyn snorted. 'If he did, you knew very well it was a lie.' She eyed her sister through her lorgnette. 'All these years, I've kept my opinions to myself upon the subject, but I won't have you ruining Henrietta's chance of happiness with your foolishness.' She turned her attention back to her niece. 'The round tale is that your mother ran off with him, knowing full well that he had no honourable intentions at all. Our poor father brought her back, two nights after she left. As far as the world was concerned, of course, she was ruined. The fact that she went into a decline confirmed it, but the truth is that her decline was fuelled not by the loss of her innocence, but by the fact that he hadn't seduced her at all!'

With a soft sigh, Guinevere slumped into a faint on the floor. 'Leave her be,' Lady Gwendolyn said when Henrietta made to rush to her mother's aid. 'She always could faint at will. Your mother was not seduced, Henrietta, she was rejected. That is why she went to live in the country—of her own free will, I may add. Why she married your poor father, I don't know. I suspect he fell hook, line and sinker for her tragic tale and played the knight errant. We all have a weakness for that. Whatever the reason, I trust you will not spoil his illusions. The breach between us was Gwinnie's fault, you know. She preferred to fabricate her own version of events and didn't want me putting her straight. It's been so long since anyone forced her to confront the truth, I expect she doesn't know what it is any more.'

The revelations astounded Henrietta, but when she confided them to her future husband, he laughed, and confounded her by admitting that he'd always had his suspicions about the truth of her mother's past. He did not make the connection between Mrs Markham and his dead first wife, but he did not have to. Henrietta made it for herself and, for once, decided to say nothing more upon the subject.

Mrs Markham was forced to resign herself to Henrietta's marriage. Her husband was rather more enthusiastic. Mr Markham, a kindly man with good intentions, even if they were somewhat pedantic, had dedicated his last few years to creating a map of penury. This, he informed Rafe, would ensure that in future philanthropic efforts could be guided to the most appropriate and most deserving of the poor. His future son-in-law was rather impressed by this and saw merit in it, to Henrietta's surprise. Mr Markham, in his turn, unimpressed by the generous settlements and title to which his daughter was about to accede, was so affected by his visit to St Nicholas's that he decided he could overlook Rafe's reputation. A mere five days after his permission for the union was initially sought, it was finally granted.

The wedding took place at the end of June and was hailed as the event of the Season. Everyone who was anyone attended the nuptials. Not to have received one of the gold-edged invitations was to be a social pariah. Lady Helen Ipswich was one such. Though not surprised, it did not make her pain at missing the society event of the year any less acute.

With her niece safely betrothed, Lady Gwendolyn had succumbed to the temptation of letting just the tiniest titbits of the stolen emeralds' story fall upon the ears of a select few. Helen Ipswich was shunned, not only in the best of circles, but in the worst—though to be fair, none of this was Rafe's doing. By the time Rafe was dressing to walk his bride up the aisle of St James's, Helen Ipswich had closed up her London house, packed her sons off to school and retired to the Continent where, as Lady Gwendolyn happily informed her sister, to whom she had been reconciled during the complex and costly process of providing Henrietta with a trousseau, Helen Ipswich would find herself quite at home among the loose morals of the French court.

At the ceremony, the ladies wept, the gentlemen harrumphed into their kerchiefs, Lucas Hamilton, in tribute to the solemnity of the occasion, remained almost sober, and all agreed that the proceedings were most touching, the bridegroom most handsome and the bride herself really rather charming. Though he had insisted on the biggest, most extravagant affair that could be arranged in the shortest amount of time, it could not be said that Rafe noticed, for he had eyes only for Henrietta. As she walked down the short aisle of St James's Church on her father's arm, his heart really did feel as if it were swelling in his chest with love. The sun could not shine brighter than the smile she gave him as he took her hand in his, nor could the stars compete with the look in her eyes when he made his vows and placed the ring upon her finger.

The passionate kiss they exchanged, shocking some of the congregation, filling others with longing and some with unabashed jealousy, sealed their vows. The wedding breakfast, the orange blossom, the champagne and the toasts—all were a blur as they sat together, hands clasped tight under the table, waiting for the time when they could be alone.

Later, the newly-weds made love slowly, disrobing each other item by item, unable to take their eyes from each other, the slow build from overture to crescendo lifting them together to a new plane upon which they began their married life.

They lived for most of the year in Woodfield Manor, their happiness filling the place with noise and joyous laughter, turning the once-sombre house into a home once more. 'It had become a mausoleum this place,' Mrs Peters said, a tear in her eyes, 'and look at it now. Filled with life, just as it should be.'

The cries of their adored first-born had added a new joy, yet another layer to their happiness, which, Rafe declared on the morning of their son's first birthday, could surely not increase further.

Henrietta, lying naked, propped on her side in their huge bed, smiled languorously at her husband. 'You say that at the start of every day,' she said, 'and at the end of every day you change your mind.'

Rafe rolled her on top of him. The crush of her soft curves had an achingly familiar effect. His erection strained between her thighs. 'I know. Isn't it amazing?' he said, kissing the corners of her smiling, infinitely kissable mouth. He could feel her heating, her sex dampening, her nipples hardening. 'Darling Henrietta, there is one way of ensuring that I shall say the same at the end of this day, too.' He wanted to be inside her. He rolled her over, taking one of her rosy nipples into his mouth and sucking hard, at the same time reaching down, between, inside, stroking with unerring precision, making her gasp and arch against the solid heft of his shaft.

'Rafe...'

'Henrietta, I can never get enough of you, you know that.'

'I know,' she said with a deep chuckle. 'And in a month or so, everyone else will know, too.'

'What do you mean?' Her eyes were shining, chocolate and gold. Her mouth was ripe. Like her body. 'Henrietta, do you mean...?'

She nodded. 'Are you pleased?'

'Pleased!' Rafe kissed her tenderly. 'I don't think I could be any happier. I didn't think it was possible to be any happier. I love you so much, my own, lovely, darling wife.' He kissed her softly rounded belly, then he kissed her mouth again.

Henrietta wrapped her arms around her husband. 'Show me how much,' she said, arching up against him.

'With pleasure,' he said. And he did.

* * * * *

MILLS & BOON®

Want to get more from Mills & Boon?

Here's what's available to you if you join the exclusive **Mills & Boon eBook Club** today:

✦ *Convenience – choose your books each month*
✦ *Exclusive – receive your books a month before anywhere else*
✦ *Flexibility – change your subscription at any time*
✦ *Variety – gain access to eBook-only series*
✦ *Value – subscriptions from just £1.99 a month*

So visit **www.millsandboon.co.uk/esubs** today to be a part of this exclusive eBook Club!

MILLS & BOON®

Why shop at millsandboon.co.uk?

Each year, thousands of romance readers find their perfect read at millsandboon.co.uk. That's because we're passionate about bringing you the very best romantic fiction. Here are some of the advantages of shopping at www.millsandboon.co.uk:

* **Get new books first**—you'll be able to buy your favourite books one month before they hit the shops

* **Get exclusive discounts**—you'll also be able to buy our specially created monthly collections, with up to 50% off the RRP

* **Find your favourite authors**—latest news, interviews and new releases for all your favourite authors and series on our website, plus ideas for what to try next

* **Join in**—once you've bought your favourite books, don't forget to register with us to rate, review and join in the discussions

Visit **www.millsandboon.co.uk**
for all this and more today!

MILLS_WEB